WORLD OF A THOUSAND COLORS

A riotous blaze of color swept down at him from every point of the compass. Streamers of every hue seemed to sprout from the rocks, staining the ringwall olive-gray and brilliant cerise and dark, lustrous green. Pigments of every sort bathed the air; now it seemed to glow with currents of luminous pink, now a flaming red, now a pulsing white.

His eyes adjusted slowly to the torrent of color. World of a Thousand Colors, they called this place? That was an underestimate. *Hundred thousand. Million. Billion.*

World
of a
Thousand
Colors

Robert Silverberg

BANTAM BOOKS
TORONTO • NEW YORK • LONDON • SYDNEY • AUCKLAND

WORLD OF A THOUSAND COLORS

*A Bantam Book / published by arrangement with
Arbor House Publishing Company*

PRINTING HISTORY
*Arbor House edition published August 1983
Bantam edition / July 1984*

ISBN 0-553-24059-5

Published simultaneously in the United States and Canada

Bantam Books are published by Bantam Books, Inc. Its trademark,
consisting of the words "Bantam Books" and the portrayal of a
rooster, is Registered in U.S. Patent and Trademark Office and in
other countries. Marca Registrada. Bantam Books, Inc., 666 Fifth
Avenue, New York, New York 10103.

PRINTED IN THE UNITED STATES OF AMERICA

H   0 9 8 7 6 5 4 3 2 1

Acknowledgments

For Bob Lowndes
Bill Scott
Fred Pohl
Hans Santesson

—a lot of stories, long ago—

Contents

World
of a
Thousand
Colors

Introduction

Most of the nineteen stories in this book date from a far-off and almost forgotten era of science fiction, when the core of the s-f industry was made up of magazines, not books. In that misty Pleistocene of my career—the 1950s—the newsstands were crowded with publications known today only to dedicated collectors, magazines with names like *Fantastic Universe* and *Science Fiction Stories* and *Future* and *Galaxy* and *If* and *Super-Science Fiction*. They were cheap—35¢ was the universal cover price—and they were cheaply printed, most of them, by nonunion houses in odd corners of the country, and they paid their writers pretty cheaply, too. The best that a writer could hope for, generally, was 3¢ a word; some paid as little as a cent a word. (The average magazine short story was about six thousand words. At a fee of 3¢ a word, the writer would have received $180 for a story that might have taken him a week or two to write. At 1¢ a word, the same story would have brought $60. Out of this, you understand, came a share for the IRS and very often a 10% commission for the writer's agent.)

Nobody got rich writing for those magazines, and I doubt that anybody got rich publishing them. But for the science-fiction writer, they were just about the only game in town. There was a little activity among hardcover publishers. But they were interested only in reprinting the classic novels that had been serialized in the science-fiction magazines of the 1940s—famous items by Heinlein, Asimov, van Vogt, Sturgeon, and a few other long-established writers. A few pioneering paperback houses were beginning s-f programs too. Still, it was a long way from today's scene, where every bookstore has a rack of fifty or a hundred of the latest fantasy trilogies, anthologies, dragon-quest epics, and all the other what-have-you of modern s-f publishing. For the writer of the 1950s who was neither Heinlein nor Asimov and wanted to earn a living at his typewriter, the thing to do was to write for the science-fiction magazines.

Which I did. When I was still in college, in 1955, I went downtown and met the New York editors: demigod John W.

Campbell; the cagey old mystery-story pro Howard Browne, who was compelled for his sins to edit science fiction; the affable and cordial Robert W. Lowndes; the mild-mannered Larry T. Shaw; dear old Hans Santesson with the thick Danish accent; and W. W. Scott, an editor of the old *old* school who actually wore a green eyeshade at his desk. Some of these men loved science fiction and had spent all their adult lives writing and editing it. Some of them were just doing jobs. One of them—Browne—actively hated the stuff. But in one way or another they had all come to have charge of gaudy little magazines with gaudy names, *Infinity* and *Astounding* and *Amazing* and *Fantastic*, and there I was, not quite old enough to vote (the voting age was higher in those days), offering to fill their magazines with stories.

The funny thing was that they let me do it. In their offices I saw the stacks of manuscripts, five and six feet high, that hopeful writers sent to them every day. Some of the editors read everything that came in that way, some of them read hardly any of it, but all of them agreed that ninety-nine percent of it was unpublishable. They preferred to deal with reliable pros who visited their New York offices, talked with them about the art of writing science fiction, and brought stories in person. Very quickly they sized me up, promoted me to that little group of pros and by the time I was twenty-one I was earning a living, and quite a nice living, writing for their magazines.

Of course, I was quick. A demonic energy possessed me. I bubbled with ideas for stories. I scribbled them on old envelopes (I still do) and saw them take shape quickly. Every morning I went to my desk and watched stories come flowing from my typewriter. In a really hot week I might write one a day, Tuesday through Friday. On the weekend I rested and on Monday I made the rounds of the editorial offices, dropping off last week's output and picking up any that might have been rejected. (Not too many were rejected, thank God, but when it did happen I smiled bravely and carried the story over to someone else's office, where it usually sold.) My name began appearing on the covers of *Infinity* and *Fantastic Universe* and the rest with startling frequency, and, with checks for $90 here and $112.50 there, I found myself actually making as much as the editors who published me.

It was a lively existence, though not one that anyone

could continue for a protracted period if he wanted to stay sane. Luckily, my repeated appearances in the magazines began to give me a reputation as a competent and dependable writer that I was able to carry with me to the book field. In just this way the science-fiction magazines of the previous decade had provided an entry for the likes of Ray Bradbury, Robert A. Heinlein, Isaac Asimov, Theodore Sturgeon, A. E. van Vogt, and the other stars of my childhood; and then, in the early 1950s, it had opened the way for Robert Sheckley, Alfred Bester, Frederik Pohl, Philip K. Dick, and other brilliant writers of that period. And now the magazines were propelling me onward. Before long I was signing contracts with the book publishers.

Just as well, because upheavals were happening in the magazine industry, and most of my steady markets were going out of business. First came a collapse of a generations-old distribution system, bringing many of the magazines crashing down with it. Then came the rise of paperback publishing. Some of the veteran magazine publishers, sensing what was going on, abruptly jettisoned their magazines and switched to paperback operation. In 1953 there had been thirty or forty science-fiction magazines; ten years later there were, maybe, seven. (Today there are about five. Of all the magazines I wrote for way back when, only three survive.)

The magazines are gone, but the stories they engendered seem to be immortal. New readers of science fiction, picking up the latest paperback edition of Asimov's *Foundation* or Heinlein's *Beyond This Horizon* or Bester's *The Demolished Man*, are altogether unaware that these novels originated in pulp magazines of thirty and even forty years ago. Books of venerable short stories by Sheckley and Sturgeon and Leiber and Dick and—yes, Silverberg—are finding fresh audiences. In no other specialized field of fiction does this seem to be true. One rarely sees collections of mystery stories of the 1940s coming around again, or westerns, or sports fiction.

What I have done here is to bring together a wide-ranging array of the short fiction from this fertile era of my career, assembling for the first time in one volume the stories I was writing in the days of the great magazines. The oldest of them date from 1957, when, although still very young, I was already a veteran pro with published pieces behind me and one Hugo Award on my shelf. The most recent were written in 1969,

1970, and 1971, when my main line of work was the novel, but when it was pleasing to write a short story or two. I remember the days of the 2¢-a-word sales and the Monday-morning marketing tours fondly, though I have no particular desire to return to that sort of life. The classic stories of that era have outlasted the magazines and, alas, most of the editors who published them. It is with great pleasure that I offer them to you in this handsome new edition.

—ROBERT SILVERBERG

Oakland, California
March, 1982

Something Wild is Loose

The Vsiir got aboard the Earthbound ship by accident. It had absolutely no plans for taking a holiday on a wet, grimy planet like Earth. But it was in its metamorphic phase, undergoing the period of undisciplined change that began as winter came on, and it had shifted so far up-spectrum that Earthborn eyes couldn't see it. Oh, a really skilled observer might notice a slippery little purple flicker once in a while, a kind of snore, as the Vsiir momentarily dropped down out of the ultraviolet; but he'd have to know where to look, and when. The crewman who was responsible for putting the Vsiir on the ship never even considered the possibility that there might be something invisible sleeping atop one of the crates of cargo being hoisted into the ship's hold. He simply went down the row, slapping a floater-node on each crate and sending it gliding up the gravity wall toward the open hatch. The fifth crate to go inside was the one on which the Vsiir had decided to take its nap. The spaceman didn't know that he had inadvertently given an alien organism a free ride to Earth. The Vsiir didn't know it, either, until the hatch was sealed and an oxygen-nitrogen atmosphere began to hiss from the vents. The Vsiir did not happen to breathe those gases, but, because it was in its time of metamorphosis, it was able to adapt itself quickly and nicely to the sour, prickly vapors seeping into its metabolic cells. The next step was to fashion a set of full-spectrum scanners and learn something about its surroundings. Within a few minutes, the Vsiir was aware—

—that it was in a large, dark place that held a great many boxes containing various mineral and vegetable products of its world, mainly branches of the greenfire tree but also some other things of no comprehensible value to a Vsiir—

—that a double wall of curved metal enclosed this place—

—that just beyond this wall was a null-atmosphere zone, such as is found between one planet and another—

—that this entire closed system was undergoing acceleration—

—that this therefore was a spaceship, heading rapidly

away from the world of Vsiirs and in fact already some ten planetary diameters distant, with the gap growing alarmingly moment by moment—

—that it would be impossible, even for a Vsiir in metamorphosis, to escape from the spaceship at this point—

—and that, unless it could persuade the crew of the ship to halt and go back, it would be compelled to undertake a long and dreary voyage to a strange and probably loathsome world, where life would at best be highly inconvenient, and might present great dangers. It would find itself cut off painfully from the rhythm of its own civilization. It would miss the Festival of Changing. It would miss the Holy Eclipse. It would not be able to take part in next spring's Rising of the Sea. It would suffer in a thousand ways.

There were six human beings aboard the ship. Extending its perceptors, the Vsiir tried to reach their minds. Though humans had been coming to its planet for many years, it had never bothered making contact with them before; but it had never been in this much trouble before, either. It sent a foggy tendril of thought, roving the corridors, looking for traces of human intelligence. Here? A glow of electrical activity within a sphere of bone: a mind, a mind! A busy mind. But surrounded by a wall, apparently; the Vsiir rammed up against it and was thrust back. That was startling and disturbing. What kind of beings were these, whose minds were closed to ordinary contact? The Vsiir went on, hunting through the ship. Another mind: again closed. Another. Another. The Vsiir felt panic rising. Its mantle fluttered; its energy radiations dropped far down into the visible spectrum, then shot nervously toward much shorter waves. Even its physical form experienced a series of quick involuntary metamorphoses, to the Vsiir's intense embarrassment. It did not get control of its body until it had passed from spherical to cubical to chaotic, and had become a gridwork of fibrous threads held together only by a pulsing strand of ego. Fiercely it forced itself back to the spherical form and resumed its search of the ship, dismally realizing that by this time its native world was half a stellar unit away. It was without hope now, but it continued to probe the minds of the crew, if only for the sake of thoroughness. Even if it made contact, though, how could it communicate the nature of its plight, and even if it communicated, why would the humans be disposed to help it? Yet it went on through the ship. And—

Here: an open mind. No wall at all. A miracle! The Vsiir rushed into close contact, overcome with joy and surprise, pouring out its predicament. *Please listen. Unfortunate nonhuman organism accidentally transported into this vessel during loading of cargo. Metabolically and psychologically unsuited for prolonged life on Earth. Begs pardon for inconvenience, wishes prompt return to home planet recently left, regrets disturbance in shipping schedule but hopes that this large favor will not prove impossible to grant. Do you comprehend my sending? Unfortunate nonhuman organism accidentally transported—*

Lieutenant Falkirk had drawn the first sleep-shift after floatoff. It was only fair; Falkirk had knocked himself out processing the cargo during the loading stage, slapping the floater-nodes on every crate and feeding the transit manifests to the computer. Now that the ship was spaceborne he could grab some rest while the other crewmen were handling the floatoff chores. So he settled down for six hours in the cradle as soon as they were on their way. Below him, the ship's six gravity-drinkers spun on their axes, gobbling inertia and pushing up the acceleration, and the ship floated Earthward at a velocity that would reach the galactic level before Falkirk woke. He drifted into drowsiness. A good trip: enough greenfire bark in the hold to see Earth through a dozen fits of the molecule plague, and plenty of other potential medicinals besides, along with a load of interesting mineral samples, and —Falkirk slept. For half an hour he enjoyed sweet slumber, his mind disengaged, his body loose.

Until a dark dream bubbled through his skull.

Deep purple sunlight, hot and somber. Something slippery tickling the edges of his brain. He lies on a broad white slab in a scorched desert. Unable to move. Getting harder to breathe. The gravity—a terrible pull, bending and breaking him, ripping his bones apart. Hooded figures moving around him, pointing, laughing, exchanging blurred comments in an unknown language. His skin melting and taking on a new texture: porcupine quills sprouting inside his flesh and forcing their way upward, poking out through every pore. Points of fire all over him. A thin scarlet hand, withered fingers like crab claws, hovering in front of his face. Scratching. Scratching. Scratching. His blood running among the quills, thick and sluggish. He shivers, struggling to sit up—lifts a hand, leaving pieces of quivering flesh stuck to the slab—sits up—

Wakes, trembling, screaming.

Falkirk's shout still sounded in his ears as his eyes adjusted to the light. Lieutenant Commander Rodriguez was holding his shoulders and shaking him.

"You all right?"

Falkirk tried to reply. Words wouldn't come. Hallucinatory shock, he realized, as part of his mind attempted to convince the other part that the dream was over. He was trained to handle crises; he ran through a quick disciplinary countdown and calmed himself, though he was still badly shaken. "Nightmare," he said hoarsely. "A beauty. Never had a dream with that kind of intensity before."

Rodriguez relaxed. Obviously he couldn't get very upset over a mere nightmare. "You want a pill?"

Falkirk shook his head. "I'll manage, thanks."

But the impact of the dream lingered. It was more than an hour before he got back to sleep, and then he fell into a light, restless doze, as if his mind were on guard against a return of those chilling fantasies. Fifty minutes before his programmed wake-up time, he was awakened by a ghastly shriek from the far side of the cabin.

Lieutenant Commander Rodriguez was having a nightmare.

When the ship made floatdown on Earth a month later it was, of course, put through the usual decontamination procedures before anyone or anything aboard it was allowed out of the starport. The outer hull got squirted with sealants designed to trap and smother any microorganism that might have hitchhiked from another world; the crewmen emerged through the safety pouch and went straight into a quarantine chamber without being exposed to the air; the ship's atmosphere was cycled into withdrawal chambers, where it underwent a thorough purification, and the entire interior of the vessel received a six-phase sterilization, beginning with fifteen minutes of hard vacuum and ending with an hour of neutron bombardment.

These procedures caused a certain degree of inconvenience for the Vsiir. It was already at the low end of its energy phase, due mainly to the repeated discouragements it had suffered in its attempts to communicate with the six humans. Now it was forced to adapt to a variety of unpleasant environments with no chance to rest between changes. Even the most adaptable of organisms can get tired. By the time the starport's decontamination team was ready to certify that the ship was wholly free of alien life-forms, the Vsiir was very, very tired indeed.

The oxygen-nitrogen atmosphere entered the hold once more. The Vsiir found it quite welcome, at least in contrast to all that had just been thrown at it. The hatch was open; stevedores were muscling the cargo crates into position to be floated across the field to the handling dome. The Vsiir took advantage of this moment to extrude some legs and scramble out of the ship. It found itself on a broad concrete apron, rimmed by massive buildings. A yellow sun was shining in a blue sky; infrared was bouncing all over the place, but the Vsiir speedily made arrangements to deflect the excess. It also compensated immediately for the tinge of ugly hydrocarbons in the atmosphere, for the frightening noise level, and for the leaden feeling of homesickness that suddenly threatened its organic stability at the first sight of this unfamiliar, disheartening world. How to get home again? How to make contact, even? The Vsiir sensed nothing but closed minds—sealed like seeds in their shells. True, from time to time the minds of these humans opened, but even then they seemed unwilling to let the Vsiir's message get through.

Perhaps it would be different here. Perhaps those six were poor communicators, for some reason, and there would be more receptive minds available in this place. Perhaps. Perhaps. Close to despair, the Vsiir hurried across the field and slipped into the first building in which it sensed open minds. There were hundreds of humans in it, occupying many levels, and the open minds were widely scattered. The Vsiir located the nearest one and, worriedly, earnestly, hopefully, touched the tip of its mind to the human's. *Please listen. I mean no harm. Am nonhuman organism arrived on your planet through unhappy circumstances, wishing only quick going back to own world—*

The cardiac wing of Long Island Starport Hospital was on the ground floor, in the rear, where the patients could be given floater therapy without upsetting the gravitational ratios of the rest of the building. As always, the hospital was full—people were always coming in sick off starliners, and most of them were hospitalized right at the starport for their own safety—and the cardiac wing had more than its share. At the moment it held a dozen infarcts awaiting implant, nine postimplant recupes, five coronaries in emergency stasis, three ventricle-regrowth projects, an aortal patch job, and nine or ten assorted other cases. Most of the patients were floating, to keep down the gravitational strain on their damaged tissues—all but the regrowth people, who were under full Earthnorm gravity so that their new hearts would come in with the proper resilience and toughness. The hospital had a fine reputation and one of the lowest mortality rates in the hemisphere.

Losing two patients the same morning was a shock to the entire staff.

At 0917 the monitor flashed the red light for Mrs. Maldonado, 87, postimplant and thus far doing fine. She had developed acute endocarditis coming back from a tour of the Jupiter system; at her age there wasn't enough vitality to sustain her through the slow business of growing a new heart with a genetic prod, but they'd given her a synthetic implant and for two weeks it had worked quite well. Suddenly, though, the hospital's control center was getting a load of grim telemetry from Mrs. Maldonado's bed: valve action zero, blood pressure zero, respiration zero, pulse zero, everything zero, zero, zero. The EEG tape showed a violent lurch—as though she had received some abrupt and intense shock—followed by a minute or two of irregular action, followed by termination of brain activity. Long before any hospital personnel had reached her bedside, automatic revival equipment, both chemical and electrical, had gone to work on the patient, but she was beyond reach: a massive cerebral hemorrhage, coming totally without warning, had done irreversible damage.

At 0928 came the second loss: Mr. Guinness, 51, three days past surgery for a coronary embolism. The same series of events. A severe jolt to the nervous system, an immediate and fatal physiological response. Resuscitation procedures negative. No one on the staff had any plausible explanation for Mr. Guinness' death. Like Mrs. Maldonado, he had been sleeping peacefully, all vital signs good, until the moment of the fatal seizure.

"As though someone had come up and yelled *boo* in their

ears," one doctor muttered, puzzling over the charts. He pointed to the wild EEG track. "Or as if they'd had unbearably vivid nightmares and couldn't take the sensory overload. But no one was making noise in the ward. And nightmares aren't contagious."

Dr. Peter Mookherji, resident in neuropathology, was beginning his morning rounds on the hospital's sixth level when the soft voice of his annunciator, taped behind his left ear, asked him to report to the quarantine building immediately. Dr. Mookherji scowled. "Can't it wait? This is my busiest time of day, and—"

"You are asked to come at once."

"Look, I've got a girl in a coma here, due for her teletherapy session in fifteen minutes, and she's counting on seeing me. I'm her only link to the world. If I'm not there when—"

"You are asked to come at once, Dr. Mookherji."

"Why do the quarantine people need a neuropathologist in such a hurry? Let me take care of the girl, at least, and in forty-five minutes they can have me."

"Dr. Mookherji—"

It didn't pay to argue with a machine. Mookherji forced his temper down. Short tempers ran in his family, along with a fondness for torrid curries and a talent for telepathy. Glowering, he grabbed a data terminal, identified himself, and told the hospital's control center to reprogram his entire morning schedule. "Build in a half-hour postponement somehow," he snapped. "I can't help it—see for yourself. I've been requisitioned by the quarantine staff." The computer was thoughtful enough to have a rollerbuggy waiting for him when he emerged from the hospital. It whisked him across the starport to the quarantine building in three minutes, but he was still angry when he got there. The scanner at the door ticked off his badge and one of the control center's innumerable voice-outputs told him solemnly, "You are expected in Room 403, Dr. Mookherji."

Room 403 turned out to be a two-sector interrogation office. The rear sector of the room was part of the building's central quarantine core, and the front sector belonged to the public-access part of the building, with a thick glass wall in between. Six haggard-looking spacemen were slouched on sofas behind the wall, and three members of the starport's quarantine staff paced about in the front. Mookherji's irritation ebbed when he saw that one of the quarantine men was an old medical-school friend, Lee Nakadai. The slender Japanese was a year older than Mookherji—29 to 28; they met for lunch occasionally at the starport commissary, and they had double-dated a pair of Filipina twins earlier in the year, but the pressure of work had kept them apart for months. Nakadai got down to business quickly now: "Pete, have you ever heard of an epidemic of nightmares?"

"Eh?"

Indicating the men behind the quarantine wall, Nakadai said, "These fellows came in a couple of hours ago from Norton's Star. Brought back a cargo of greenfire bark. Physically they check out to five decimal places, and I'd release them except for one funny thing. They're all in a bad state of nervous exhaustion, which they say is the result of having had practically no sleep during their whole month-long return trip. And the reason for that is that they were having nightmares—every one of them—real mind-wrecking dreams, whenever they tried to sleep. It sounded so peculiar that I thought we'd better run a neuropath checkup, in case they've picked up some kind of cerebral infection."

Mookherji frowned. "For this you get me out of my ward on emergency requisition, Lee?"

"Talk to them," Nakadai said. "Maybe it'll scare you a little."

Mookherji glanced at the spacemen. "All right," he said. "What about these nightmares?"

A tall, bony-looking officer who introduced himself as Lieutenant Falkirk said, "I was the first victim—right after floatoff. I almost flipped. It was like, well, something touching my mind, filling it with weird thoughts. And everything absolutely real while it was going on—I thought I was choking, I thought my body was changing into something alien, I felt my blood running out my pores—" Falkirk shrugged. "Like any sort of bad dream, I guess, only ten times as vivid. Fifty times. A few hours later Lieutenant Commander Rodriguez had the same kind of dream. Different images, same effect. And then, one by one, as the others took their sleep-shifts, they started to wake up screaming. Two of us ended up spending three weeks on happy-pills. We're pretty stable men, doctor—we're trained to take almost anything. But I think a civilian would have cracked up for good with dreams like those. Not so much the images as the intensity, the realness of them."

"And these dreams recurred, throughout the voyage?" Mookherji asked.

"Every shift. It got so we were afraid to doze off, because we knew the devils would start crawling through our heads when we did. Or we'd put ourselves real down on sleeper-tabs. And even so we'd have the dreams, with our minds doped to a level where you wouldn't imagine dreams would happen. A plague of nightmares, doctor. An epidemic."

"When was the last episode?"

"The final sleep-shift before floatdown."

"You haven't gone to sleep, any of you, since leaving the ship?"

"No," Falkirk said.

One of the other spacemen said, "Maybe he didn't make it clear to you, doctor. These were killer dreams. They were mind-crackers. We were lucky to get home sane. If we did."

Mookherji drummed his fingertips together, rummaging through his experience for some parallel case. He couldn't find any. He knew of mass hallucinations, plenty of them, episodes in which whole mobs had persuaded themselves they had seen gods, demons, miracles, the dead walking, fiery symbols in the sky. But a series of hallucinations coming in sequence, shift after shift, to an entire crew of tough, pragmatic spacemen? It didn't make sense.

Nakadai said, "Pete, the men had a guess about what might have done it to them. Just a wild idea, but maybe—"

"What is it?"

Falkirk laughed uneasily. "Actually, it's pretty fantastic, doctor."

"Go ahead."

"Well, that something from the planet came aboard the ship with us. Something, well, telepathic. Which fiddled around with our minds whenever we went to sleep. What we felt as nightmares was maybe this thing inside our heads."

"Possibly it rode all the way back to Earth with us," another spaceman said. "It could still be aboard the ship. Or loose in the city by now."

"The Invisible Nightmare Menace?" Mookherji said, with a faint smile. "I doubt that I can buy that."

"There *are* telepathic creatures," Falkirk pointed out.

"I know," Mookherji said sharply. "I happen to be one myself."

"I'm sorry, doctor, if—"

"But that doesn't lead me to look for telepaths under every bush. I'm not ruling out your alien menace, mind you. But I think it's a lot more likely that you picked up some kind of inflammation of the brain out there. A virus disease, a type of encephalitis that shows itself in the form of chronic hallucinations." The spacemen looked troubled. Obviously they would rather be victims of an unknown monster preying on them from outside than of an unknown virus lodged in their brains. Mookherji went on, "I'm not saying that's what it is, either. I'm just tossing around hypotheses. We'll know more after we've run some tests." Checking his watch, he said to Nakadai, "Lee, there's not much more I can find out right now, and I've got to get back to my patients. I want these fellows plugged in for the full series of neuropsychological checkouts. Have the outputs relayed to my office as they come in. Run the rests in staggered series and start letting the men go to sleep, two at a time, after each series—I'll send over a technician to help you rig the telemetry. I want to be notified immediately if there's any nightmare experience."

"Right."

"And get them to sign telepathy releases. I'll give them a preliminary mind-probe this evening after I've had a chance to study the clinical findings. Maintain absolute quarantine, of course. This thing might just be infectious. Play it very safe."

Nakadai nodded. Mookherji flashed a professional smile at the six somber spacemen and went out, brooding. A nightmare virus? Or a mind-meddling alien organism that no one can see? He wasn't sure which notion he liked less. Probably, though, there was some prosaic and unstartling explanation for that month of bad dreams—contaminated food supplies, or something funny in the atmosphere recycler. A simple, mundane explanation.

Probably.

The first time it happened, the Vsiir was not sure what had actually taken place. It had touched a human mind; there had been an immediate vehement reaction; the Vsiir had pulled back, alarmed by the surging fury of the response, and then, a moment later, had been unable to locate the mind at all. Possibly it was some defense mechanism, the Vsiir thought, by which the humans guarded their minds against intruders. But that seemed unlikely since the humans' minds were quite effectively guarded most of the time anyway. Aboard the ship, whenever the Vsiir had managed to slip past the walls that shielded the minds of the crewmen, it had always encountered a great deal of turbulence—plainly these humans did not enjoy mental contact with a Vsiir—but never this complete shutdown, this total cutoff of signal. Puzzled, the Vsiir tried again, reaching toward an open mind situated not far from where the one that had vanished had been. *Kindly attention, a moment of consideration for confused other-worldly individual, victim of unhappy circumstances, who—*

Again the violent response: a sudden tremendous flare of mental energy, a churning blaze of fear and pain and shock. And again, moments later, complete silence, as though the human had retreated behind an impermeable barrier. *Where are you? Where did you go?* The Vsiir, troubled, took the risk of creating an optical receptor that worked in the visible spectrum—and that therefore would itself be visible to humans—and surveyed the scene. It saw a human on a bed, completely surrounded by intricate machinery. Colored lights were flashing. Other humans, looking agitated, were rushing toward the bed. The human on the bed lay quite still, not even moving when a metal arm descended and jabbed a long bright needle into his chest.

Suddenly the Vsiir understood.

The two humans must have experienced termination of existence!

Hastily the Vsiir dissolved its visible-spectrum receptor and retreated to a sheltered corner to consider what had happened. *Datum:* two humans had died. *Datum:* each had undergone termination immediately after receiving a mental transmission from the Vsiir. *Problem:* had the mental transmission brought about the terminations?

The possibility that the Vsiir might have destroyed two lives was shocking and appalling, and such a chill went through its body that it shrank into a tight, hard ball, with all thought-processes snarled. It needed several minutes to return to a fully functional state. If its attempts at communicating with these humans produced such terrible effects, the Vsiir realized, then its prospects of finding help on this planet were slim. How could it dare risk trying to contact other humans, if—

A comforting thought surfaced. The Vsiir realized that it was jumping to a hasty conclusion on the basis of sketchy evidence, while overlooking some powerful arguments against that conclusion. All during the voyage to this world the Vsiir had been making contact with humans, the six crewmen, and none of *them* had terminated. That was ample evidence that humans could withstand contact with a Vsiir mind. Therefore contact alone could not have caused these two deaths.

Possibly it was only coincidental that the Vsiir had approached two humans in succession that were on the verge of termination. Was this the place where humans were brought when their time of termination was near? Would the terminations have happened even if the Vsiir had not tried to make contact? Was the attempt at contact just enough of a drain on dwindling energies to push the two over the edge into termination? The Vsiir did not know. It was uncomfortably conscious of how many important facts it lacked. Only one thing was certain: its time was running short. If it did not find help soon, metabolic decay was going to set in, followed by metamorphic rigidity, followed by a fatal loss in adaptability, followed by . . . termination.

The Vsiir had no choice. Continuing its quest for contact with a human was its only hope of survival. Cautiously, timidly, the Vsiir again began to send out its probes, looking for a properly receptive mind. This one was walled. So was this. And all these: no entrance, no entrance! The Vsiir wondered if the barriers these humans possessed were designed merely to keep out intruding nonhuman consciousnesses, or actually shielded each human against mental contact of all kinds, including contact with other humans. If any human-to-human contact existed, the Vsiir had not detected it, either in this building or aboard the spaceship. What a strange race!

Perhaps it would be best to try a different level of this building. The Vsiir flowed easily under a closed door and up a service staircase to a higher floor. Once more it sent forth its probes. A closed mind here. And here. And here. And then a receptive one. The Vsiir prepared to send its message. For safety's sake it stepped down the power of its transmission, letting a mere wisp of thought curl forth. *Do you hear? Stranded extraterrestrial being is calling. Seeks aid. Wishes—*

From the human came a sharp, stinging displeasure-response, wordless but unmistakably hostile. The Vsiir at once withdrew. It waited, terrified, fearing that it had caused another termination. No: the human mind continued to function, although it was no longer open, but now surrounded by the sort of barrier humans normally wore. Drooping, dejected, the Vsiir crept away. Failure, again. Not even a moment of meaningful mind-to-mind contact. Was there no way to reach these people? Dismally, the Vsiir resumed its search for a receptive mind. What else could it do?

The visit to the quarantine building had taken forty minutes out of Dr. Mookherji's morning schedule. That bothered him. He couldn't blame the quarantine people for getting upset over the six spacemen's tale of chronic hallucinations, but he didn't think the situation, mysterious as it was, was grave enough to warrant calling him in on an emergency basis. Whatever was troubling the spacemen would eventually come to light; meanwhile they were safely isolated from the rest of the starport. Nakadai should have run more tests before asking him. And he resented having to steal time from his patients.

But as he began his belated morning rounds, Mookherji calmed himself with a deliberate effort: it wouldn't do him or his patients any good if he visited them while still loaded with tensions and irritations. He was supposed to be a healer, not a spreader of anxieties. He spent a moment going through a deescalation routine, and by the time he entered the first patient's room—that of Satina Ransom—he was convincingly relaxed and amiable.

Satina lay on her left side, eyes closed, a slender girl of sixteen with a fragile-looking face and long, soft straw-colored hair. A spidery network of monitoring systems surrounded her. She had been unconscious for fourteen months, twelve of them here in the starport's neuropathology ward and the last six under Mookherji's care. As a holiday treat, her parents had taken her to one of the resorts on Titan during the best season for viewing Saturn's rings; with great difficulty they succeeded in booking reservations at Galileo Dome, and were there on the grim day when a violent Titanquake ruptured the dome and exposed a thousand tourists to the icy moon's poisonous methane atmosphere. Satina was one of the lucky ones: she got no more than a couple of whiffs of the stuff before a dome guide with whom she'd been talking managed to slap a breathing mask over her face. She survived. Her mother, father, and younger brother didn't. But she had never regained consciousness after collapsing at the moment of the disaster. Months of examination on Earth had shown that her brief methane inhalation hadn't caused any major brain damage; organically there seemed to be nothing wrong with her, but she refused to wake up. A shock reaction, Mookherji believed: she would rather go on dreaming forever than return to the living nightmare that consciousness had become. He had been able to reach her mind telepathically, but so far he had been unable to cleanse her of the trauma of that catastrophe and bring her back to the waking world.

Now he prepared to make contact. There was nothing easy or automatic about his telepathy; "reading" minds was strenuous work for him, as difficult and as taxing as running a cross-country race or memorizing a lengthy part in *Hamlet*. Despite the fears of laymen, he had no way of scanning anyone's intimate thoughts with a casual glance. To enter another mind, he had to go through an elaborate procedure of warming up and reaching out, and even so it was a slow business to tune in on somebody's "wavelength," with little coherent information coming across until the ninth or tenth attempt. The gift had been in the Mookherji family for at least a dozen generations, helped along by shrewdly planned marriages designed to conserve the precious gene; he was more adept than any of his ancestors, yet it might take another century or two of Mookherjis to produce a really potent telepath. At least he was able to make good use of such talent for mind-contact as he had. He knew that many members of his family in earlier times had been forced to hide their gift from those about them, back in India, lest they be classed with vampires and werewolves and cast out of society.

Gently he placed his dark hand on Satina's pale wrist. Physical contact was necessary to attain the mental linkage. He concentrated on reaching her. After months of teletherapy, her mind was sensitized to his; he was able to skip the intermediate steps, and, once he was warmed up, could plunge straight into her troubled soul. His eyes were closed. He saw a swirl of pearly-gray fog before him: Satina's mind. He thrust himself into it, entering easily. Up from the depths of her spirit swam a question mark.

—*Who is it? Doctor?*

—*Me, yes. How are you today, Satina?*

—*Fine. Just fine.*

—*Been sleeping well?*

—*It's so peaceful here, doctor.*

—*Yes. Yes, I imagine it is. But you ought to see how it is here. A wonderful summer day. The sun in the blue sky. Everything in bloom. A perfect day for swimming, eh? Wouldn't you like a swim?* He puts all the force of his concentration into images of swimming: a cold mountain stream, a deep pool at the base of a creamy waterfall, the sudden delightful shock of diving in, the crystal flow tingling against her warm skin, the laughter of her friends, the splashing, the swift powerful strokes carrying her to the far shore—

—*I'd rather stay where I am,* she tells him.

—*Maybe you'd like to go floating instead?* He summons the sensations of free flight: a floater-node fastened to her belt, lifting her serenely to an altitude of a hundred feet, and off she goes, drifting over fields and valleys, her friends beside her, her body totally relaxed, weightless, soaring on the updrafts, rising until the ground is a checkerboard of brown and green, looking down on the tiny houses and the comical cars, now crossing a shimmering silvery lake, now hovering over a dark, somber forest of thick-packed spruce, now simply lying on her back, legs crossed, hands clasped behind her head, the sunlight on her cheeks, three hundred feet of nothingness underneath her—

But Satina doesn't take his bait. She prefers to stay where she is. The temptations of floating are not strong enough.

Mookherji does not have enough energy left to try a third attempt at luring her out of her coma. Instead he shifts to a purely medical function and tries to probe for the source of the trauma that has cut her off from the world. The fright, no doubt; and the terrible crack in the dome, spelling the end to all security; and the sight of her parents and brother dying before her eyes; and the swampy reek of Titan's atmosphere hitting her nostrils—all of those things, no doubt. But people have rebounded from worse calamities. Why does she insist on withdrawing from life? Why not come to terms with the dreadful past, and accept existence again?

She fights him. Her defenses are fierce; she does not want him meddling with her mind. All of their sessions have ended this way: Satina clinging to her retreat, Satina blocking any shot at knocking her free of her self-imposed prison. He has gone on hoping that one day she will lower her guard. But this is not to be the day. Wearily, he pulls back from the core of her mind and talks to her on a shallower level.

—*You ought to be getting back to school, Satina.*

—*Not yet. It's been such a short vacation!*

—*Do you know how long?*

—*About three weeks, isn't it?*

—*Fourteen months so far,* he tells her.

—*That's impossible. We just went away to Titan a little while ago—the week before Christmas, wasn't it, and—*

—*Satina, how old are you?*

—*I'll be fifteen in April.*

—*Wrong,* he tells her. *That April's been here and gone, and so has the next one. You were sixteen two months ago. Sixteen, Satina.*

—*That can't be true, doctor. A girl's sixteenth birthday is something special, don't you know that? My parents are going to give me a big party. All my friends invited. And a nine-piece robot orchestra with synthesizers. And I know that that hasn't happened yet, so how can I be sixteen?*

His reservoir of strength is almost drained. His mental signal is weak. He cannot find the energy to tell her that she is blocking reality again, that her parents are dead, that time is passing while she lies here, that it is too late for a Sweet Sixteen party.

—*We'll talk about it . . . another time, Satina. I'll . . . see . . . you . . . again . . . tomorrow. . . . Tomorrow . . . morning. . . .*

—*Don't go so soon, doctor!* But he can no longer hold the contact, and lets it break.

Releasing her, Mookherji stood up, shaking his head. A shame, he thought. A damned shame. He went out of the room on trembling legs and paused a moment in the hall, propping himself against a closed door and mopping his sweaty forehead. He was getting nowhere with Satina. After the initial encouraging period of contact, he had failed entirely to lessen the intensity of her coma. She had settled quite comfortably into her delusive world of withdrawal, and, telepathy or no, he could find no way to blast her loose.

He took a deep breath. Fighting back a growing mood of bleak discouragement, he went toward the next patient's room.

The operation was going smoothly. The dozen third-year medical students occupied the observation deck of the surgical gallery on the starport hospital's third floor, studying Dr. Hammond's expert technique by direct viewing and by simultaneous microamplified relay to their individual desk-screens. The patient, a brain-tumor victim in his late sixties, was visible only as a head and shoulders protruding from a life-support chamber. His scalp had been shaved; blue lines and dark red dots were painted on it to indicate the inner contours of the skull, as previously determined by short-range sonar bounces; the surgeon had finished the job of positioning the lasers that would excise the tumor. The hard part was over. Nothing remained except to bring the lasers to full power and send their fierce, precise bolts of light slicing into the patient's brain. Cranial surgery of this kind was entirely bloodless; there was no need to cut through skin and bone to expose the tumor, for the beams of the lasers, calibrated to a millionth of a millimeter, would penetrate through minute openings and, playing on the tumor from different sides, destroy the malignant growth without harming a bit of the surrounding healthy brain tissue. Planning was everything in an operation like this. Once the exact outlines of the tumor were determined, and the surgical lasers were mounted at the correct angles, any intern could finish the job.

For Dr. Hammond it was a routine procedure. He had performed a hundred operations of this kind in the past year alone. He gave the signal; the warning light glowed on the laser rack; the students in the gallery leaned forth expectantly—

And, just as the lasers' glittering fire leaped toward the operating table, the face of the anesthetized patient contorted weirdly, as though some terrifying dream had come drifting up out of the caverns of the man's drugged mind. His nostrils flared; his lips drew back; his eyes opened wide; he seemed to be trying to scream; he moved convulsively, twisting his head to one side. The lasers bit deep into the patient's left temple, far from the indicated zone of the tumor. The right side of his face began to sag, all muscles paralyzed. The medical students looked at each other in bewilderment. Dr. Hammond, stunned, retained enough presence of mind to kill the lasers with a quick swipe of his hand. Then, gripping the operating table with both hands in his agitation, he peered at the dials and meters that told him the details of the botched operation. The tumor remained intact; a vast sector of the patient's brain had been devastated. "Impossible," Hammond muttered. What could goad a patient under anesthesia into jumping around like that? "Impossible. Impossible." He strode to the end of the table and checked the readings on the life-support chamber. The question now was not whether the brain tumor would be successfully removed; the immediate question was whether the patient was going to survive.

By four that afternoon Mookherji had finished most of his chores. He had seen every patient; he had brought his progress charts up to date; he had fed a prognosis digest to the master computer that was the starport hospital's control center; he had found time for a gulped lunch. Ordinarily, now, he could take the next four hours off, going back to his spartan room in the residents' building at the edge of the starport complex for a nap, or dropping in at the recreation center to have a couple rounds of floater-tennis, or looking in at the latest cube-show, or whatever. His next round of patient-visiting didn't begin until eight in the evening. But he couldn't relax: there was that business of the quarantined spacemen to worry about. Nakadai had been sending test outputs over since two o'clock, and now they were stacked deep in Mookherji's data terminal. Nothing had carried an *urgent* flag, so Mookherji had simply let the reports pile up; but now he felt he ought to have a look. He tapped the keys of the terminal, requesting printouts, and Nakadai's outputs began to slide from the slot.

Mookherji ruffled through the yellow sheets. Reflexes, synapse charge, degree of neural ionization, endocrine balances, visual response, respiratory and circulatory, cerebral molecular exchange, sensory, percepts, EEG both enhanced and minimated . . . No, nothing unusual here. It was plain from the tests that the six men who had been to Norton's Star were badly in need of a vacation—frayed nerves, blurred reflexes—but there was no indication of anything more serious than chronic loss of sleep. He couldn't detect signs of brain lesions, infection, nerve damage, or other organic disabilities.

Why the nightmares, then?

He tapped out the phone number of Nakadai's office. "Quarantine," a crisp voice said almost at once, and moments later Nakadai's lean, tawny face appeared on the screen. "Hello, Pete. I was just going to call you."

Mookherji said, "I didn't finish up until a little while ago. But I've been through the outputs you sent over. Lee, there's nothing here."

"As I thought."

"What about the men? You were supposed to call me if any of them went into nightmares."

"None of them have," Nakadai said. "Falkirk and Rodriguez have been sleeping since eleven. Like lambs. Schmidt and Carroll were allowed to conk out at half past one. Webster and Schiavone hit the cots at three. All six are still snoring away, sleeping like they haven't slept in years. I've got them loaded with equipment and everything's reading perfectly normal. You want me to shunt the data to you?"

"Why bother? If they aren't hallucinating, what'll I learn?"

"Does that mean you plan to skip the mind-probes tonight?"

"I don't know," Mookherji said, shrugging. "I suspect there's no point in it, but let's leave that part open. I'll be finishing my evening rounds about eleven, and if there's some reason to get into the heads of those spacemen then, I will." He frowned. "But look—didn't they say that each one of them went into the nightmares on *every single sleep-shift*?"

"Right."

"And here they are, sleeping outside the ship for the first time since the nightmares started, and none of them having any trouble at all. And no sign of possible hallucinogenic brain lesions. You know something, Lee? I'm starting to come around to a very silly hypothesis that those men proposed this morning."

"That the hallucinations were caused by some unseen alien being?" Nakadai asked.

"Something like that. Lee, what's that status of the ship they came in on?"

"It's been through all the routine purification checks, and now it's sitting in an isolation vector until we have some idea of what's going on."

"Would I be able to get aboard it?" Mookherji asked.

"I suppose so, yes, but—why—?"

"On the wild shot that something external caused those nightmares, and that that something may still be aboard the ship. And perhaps a low-level telepath like myself will be able to detect its presence. Can you set up clearance fast?"

"Within ten minutes," Nakadai said. "I'll pick you up."

Nakadai came by shortly in a rollerbuggy. As they headed out toward the landing field, he handed Mookherji a crumpled spacesuit and told him to put it on.

"What for?"

"You may want to breathe inside the ship. Right now it's full of vacuum—we decided it wasn't safe to leave it under atmosphere. Also it's still loaded with radiation from the decontamination process. Okay?"

Mookherji struggled into the suit.

They reached the ship: a standard interstellar null-gravity-drive job, looking small and lonely in its corner of the field. A robot cordon kept it under isolation, but, tipped off by the control center, the robots let the two doctors pass. Nakadai remained outside; Mookherji crawled into the safety pouch and, after the hatch had gone through its admission cycle, entered the ship. He moved cautiously from cabin to cabin, like a man walking in a forest that was said to have a jaguar in every tree. While looking about, he brought himself as quickly as possible up to full telepathic receptivity, and, wide open, awaited telepathic contact with anything that might be lurking in the ship.

—*Go on. Do your worst.*

Complete silence on all mental wavelengths. Mookherji prowled everywhere: the cargo hold, the crew cabins, the drive compartments. Everything empty, everything still. Surely he would have been able to detect the presence of a telepathic creature in here, no matter how alien; if it was capable of reaching the mind of a sleeping spaceman, it should be able to reach the mind of a waking telepath as well. After fifteen minutes he left the ship, satisfied.

"Nothing there," he told Nakadai. "We're still nowhere."

The Vsiir was growing desperate. It had been roaming this building all day; judging by the quality of the solar radiation coming through the windows, night was beginning to fall now. And, though there were open minds on every level of the structure, the Vsiir had had no luck in making contact. At least there had been no more terminations. But it was the same story here as on the ship: whenever the Vsiir touched a human mind, the reaction was so negative as to make communication impossible. And yet the Vsiir went on and on and on, to mind after mind, unable to believe that this whole planet did not hold a single human to whom it could tell its story. It hoped it was not doing severe damage to these minds it was approaching; but it had its own fate to consider.

Perhaps this mind would be the one. The Vsiir started once more to tell its tale—

Half past nine at night. Dr. Peter Mookherji, bloodshot, tense, hauled himself through his neuropathological responsibilities. The ward was full: a schizoid collapse, a catatonic freeze, Satina in her coma, half a dozen routine hysterias, a couple of paralysis cases, an aphasic, and plenty more, enough to keep him going for sixteen hours a day and strain his telepathic powers, not to mention his conventional medical skills, to their limits. Some day the ordeal of residency would be over; some day he'd be quit of this hospital, and would set up private practice on some sweet tropical isle, and commute to Bombay on weekends to see his family, and spend his holidays on planets of distant stars, like any prosperous medical specialist . . . Some day. He tried to banish such lavish fantasies from his mind. If you're going to look forward to anything, he told himself, look forward to midnight. To sleep. Beautiful, beautiful sleep. And then in the morning it all begins again, Satina and the coma, the schizoid, the catatonic, the aphasic . . .

As he stepped into the hall, going from patient to patient, his annunciator said, "Dr. Mookherji, please report at once to Dr. Bailey's office."

Bailey? The head of the neuropathology department, still hitting the desk this late. What now? But of course there was no ignoring such a summons. Mookherji notified the control center that he had been called off his rounds, and made his way quickly down the corridor to the frosted-glass door marked SAMUEL F. BAILEY, M.D.

He found at least half the neuropath staff there already: four of the other senior residents, most of the interns, even a few of the high-level doctors. Bailey, a puffy-faced, sandy-haired, fiftyish man of formidable professional standing, was thumbing a sheaf of outputs and scowling. He gave Mookherji a faint nod by way of greeting. They were not on the best of terms; Bailey, somewhat old-school in his attitudes, had not made a good adjustment to the advent of telepathy as a tool in the treatment of mental disturbance. "As I was just saying," Bailey began, "these reports have been accumulating all day, and they've all been dumped on me, God knows why. Listen: two cardiac patients under sedation undergo sudden violent shocks, described by one doctor as sensory overloads. One reacts with cardiac arrest, the other with cerebral hemorrhage. Both die. A patient being treated for endocrine restabilization develops a runaway adrenalin flow while asleep, and gets a six-month setback. A patient undergoing brain surgery starts lurching around on the operating table, despite adequate anesthesia, and gets badly carved up by the lasers. Et cetera. Serious problems like this all over the hospital today. Computer check of general EEG patterns shows that fourteen patients, other than those mentioned, have experienced exceptionally severe episodes of nightmare in the last eleven hours, nearly all of them of such impact that the patient has sustained some degree of psychic damage and often actual physiological harm. Control center reports no case histories of previous epidemics of bad dreams. No reason to suspect a widespread dietary imbalance or similar cause for the outbreak. Nevertheless, sleeping patients are continuing to suffer, and those whose condition is particularly critical may be exposed to grave risks. Effective immediately, sedation of critical patients has been interrupted where feasible, and sleep schedules of other patients have been rearranged, but this is obviously not an expedient that is going to do much good if this outbreak continues into tomorrow." Bailey paused, glanced around the room, let his gaze rest on Mookherji. "Control center has offered one hypothesis: that a psychopathic individual with strong telepathic powers is at large in the hospital, preying on sleeping patients and transmitting images to them that take the form of horrifying nightmares. Mookherji, what do you make of that idea?"

Mookherji said, "It's perfectly feasible, I suppose, although I can't imagine why any telepath would want to go around distributing nightmares. But has control center correlated any of this with the business over at the quarantine building?"

Bailey stared at his output slips. "What business is that?"

"Six spacemen who came in early this morning, reporting that they'd all suffered chronic nightmares on their voyage homeward. Dr. Lee Nakadai's been testing them; he called me in as a consultant, but I couldn't discover anything useful. I imagine there are some late reports from Nakadai in my office, but—"

Bailey said, "Control center seems only to be concerned about events in the hospital, not in the starport complex as a whole. And if your six spacemen had their nightmares during their voyage, there's no chance that their symptoms are going to find their way onto—"

"That's just it!" Mookherji cut in. "They had their nightmares in space. But they've been asleep since morning, and Nakadai says they're resting peacefully. Meanwhile an outbreak of hallucinations has started over here. Which means that whatever was bothering them during their voyage has somehow got loose in the hospital today—some sort of entity capable of stirring up such ghastly dreams that they bring veteran spacemen to the edge of nervous breakdowns and can seriously injure or even kill someone in poor heatlh." He realized that Bailey was looking at him strangely, and that Bailey was not the only one. In a more restrained tone, Mookherji said, "I'm sorry if this sounds fantastic to you. I've been checking it out all day, so I've had some time to get used to the concept. And things began to fit together for me just now. I'm not saying that my idea is necessarily correct. I'm simply saying that it's a reasonable notion, that it links up with the spacemen's own idea of what was bothering them, that it corresponds to the shape of the situation—and that it deserves a decent investigation, if we're going to stop this stuff before we lose some more patients."

"All right, doctor," Bailey said. "How do you propose to conduct the investigation?"

Mookherji was shaken by that. He had been on the go all

day; he was ready to fold. Here was Bailey abruptly putting him in charge of this snark-hunt, without even asking! But he saw there was no way to refuse. He was the only telepath on the staff. And, if the supposed creature really was at large in the hospital, how could it be tracked except by a telepath?

Fighting back his fatigue, Mookherji said rigidly, "Well, I'd want a chart of all the nightmare cases, to begin with, a chart showing the location of each victim and the approximate time of onset of hallucination—"

They would be preparing for the Festival of Changing, now, the grand climax of the winter. Thousands of Vsiirs in the metamorphic phase would be on their way toward the Valley of Sand, toward that great natural amphitheater where the holiest rituals were performed. By now the firstcomers would already have taken up their positions, facing the west, waiting for the sunrise. Gradually the rows would fill as Vsiirs came in from every part of the planet, until the golden valley was thick with them, Vsiirs that constantly shifted their energy levels, dimensional extensions, and inner resonances, shuttling gloriously through the final joyous moments of the season of metamorphosis, competing with one another in a gentle way to display the great variety of form, the most dynamic cycle of physical changes—and, when the first red rays of the sun crept past the Needle, the celebrants would grow even more frenzied, dancing and leaping and transforming themselves with total abandon, purging themselves of the winter's flamboyance as the season of stability swept across the world. And finally, in the full blaze of sunlight, they would turn to one another in renewed kinship, embracing, and—

The Vsiir tried not to think about it. But it was hard to repress that sense of loss, that pang of nostalgia. The pain grew more intense with every moment. No imaginable miracle would get the Vsiir home in time for the Festival of Changing, it knew, and yet it could not really believe that such a calamity had befallen it.

Trying to touch minds with humans was useless. Perhaps if it assumed a form visible to them, and let itself be noticed, and *then* tried to open verbal communication—

But the Vsiir was so small, and these humans were so large. The dangers were great. The Vsiir, clinging to a wall and carefully keeping its wavelength well beyond the ultraviolet, weighed one risk against another, and, for the moment, did nothing.

"All right," Mookherji said foggily, a little before midnight. "I think we've got the trail clear now." He sat before a wall-sized screen on which the control center had thrown a three-dimensional schematic plan of the hospital. Bright red dots marked the place of each nightmare incident, yellow dashes the probable path of the unseen alien creature. "It came in the side way, probably, straight off the ship, and went into the cardiac wing first. Mrs. Maldonado's bed here, Mr. Guinness' over here, eh? Then it went up to the second level, coming around to the front wing and impinging on the minds of patients here and here and here between ten and eleven in the morning. There were no reported episodes of hallucination in the next hour and ten minutes, but then came that nasty business in the third-level surgical gallery, and after that—" Mookherji's aching eyes closed a moment; it seemed to him that he could still see the red dots and yellow dashes. He forced himself to go on, tracing the rest of the intruder's route for his audience of doctors and hospital security personnel. At last he said, "That's it. I figure that the thing must be somewhere between the fifth and eighth levels by now. It's moving much more slowly than it did this morning, possibly running out of energy. What we have to do is keep the hospital's wings tightly sealed to prevent its free movement, if that can be done, and attempt to narrow down the number of places where it might be found."

One of the security men said, a little belligerently, "Doctor, just how are we supposed to find an invisible entity?"

Mookherji struggled to keep impatience out of his voice. "The visible spectrum isn't the only sort of electromagnetic energy in the universe. If this thing is alive, it's got to be radiating *somewhere* along the line. You've got a master computer with a million sensory pickups mounted all over the hospital. Can't you have the sensors scan for a point-source of infrared or ultraviolet moving through a room? Or even X-rays, for God's sake: we don't know where the radiation's likely to be. Maybe it's a gamma emitter, even. Look, something wild is loose in this building, and we can't see it, but the computer can. Make it search."

Dr. Bailey said, "Perhaps the energy we ought to be trying to trace it by is, ah, telepathic energy, doctor."

Mookherji shrugged. "As far as anybody knows, telepathic impulses propagate somewhere outside the electromagnetic spectrum. But of course you're right that I might be able to pick up some kind of output, and I intend to make a floor-by-floor search as soon as this briefing session is over." He turned toward Nakadai. "Lee, what's the word from your quarantined spacemen?"

"All six went through eight-hour sleep periods today without any sign of a nightmare episode: there was some dreaming, but all of it normal. In the past couple of hours I've had them on the phone talking with some of the patients who had the nightmares, and everybody agrees that the kind of dreams people have been having here today are the same in tone, texture, and general level of horror as the ones the men had aboard the ship. Images of bodily destruction and alien landscapes, accompanied by an overwhelming, almost intolerable, feeling of isolation, loneliness, separation from one's own kind."

"Which would fit the hypothesis of an alien being as the cause," said Martinson of the psychology staff. "If it's wandering around trying to communicate with us, trying to tell us it doesn't want to be here, say, and its communications reach human minds only in the form of frightful nightmares—"

"Why does it communicate only with sleeping people?" an intern asked.

"Perhaps those are the only ones it can reach. Maybe a mind that's awake isn't receptive," Martinson suggested.

"Seems to me," a security man said, "that we're making a whole lot of guesses based on no evidence at all. You're all sitting around talking about an invisible telepathic thing that breathes nightmares in people's ears, and it might just as easily be a virus that attacks the brain, or something in yesterday's food, or—"

Mookherji said, "The ideas you're offering now have already been examined and discarded. We're working on this line of inquiry now because it seems to hold together, fantastic though it sounds, and because it's all we have. If you'll excuse me, I'd like to start checking the building for telepathic output, now." He went out, pressing his hands to his throbbing temples.

* * *

Satina Ransom stirred, stretched, subsided. She looked up and saw the dazzling blaze of Saturn's rings overhead, glowing through the hotel's domed roof. She had never seen anything more beautiful in her life. This close to them, only about 750,000 miles out, she could clearly make out the different zones of the rings, each revolving about Saturn at its own speed, with the blackness of space visible through the open places. And Saturn itself, gleaming in the heavens, so bright, so huge—

What was that rumbling sound? Thunder? Not here, not on Titan. Again: louder. And the ground swaying. A crack in the dome! Oh, no, no, no, feel the air rushing out, look at that cold greenish mist pouring in—people falling down all over the place—what's happening, what's happening, what's happening? Saturn seems to be falling toward us. That taste in my mouth—oh—oh—oh—

Satina screamed. And screamed. And went on screaming as she slipped down into darkness, and pulled the soft blanket of unconsciousness over her, and shivered, and gave thanks for finding a safe place to hide.

Mookherji had plodded through the whole building accompanied by three security men and a couple of interns. He had seen whole sectors of the hospital that he didn't know existed. He had toured basements and sub-basements and sub-sub-basements; he had been through laboratories and computer rooms and wards and exercise chambers. He had kept himself in a state of complete telepathic receptivity throughout the trek, but he had detected nothing, not even a flicker of mental current anywhere. Somehow that came as no surprise to him. Now, with dawn near, he wanted nothing more than sixteen hours or so of sleep. Even with nightmares. He was tired beyond all comprehension of the meaning of tiredness.

Yet something wild was loose, still, and the nightmares still were going on. Three incidents, ninety minutes apart, had occurred during the night: two patients on the fifth level and one on the sixth had awakened in states of terror. It had been possible to calm them quickly, and apparently no lasting harm had been done; but now the stranger was close to Mookherji's neuropathology ward, and he didn't like the thought of exposing a bunch of mentally unstable patients to that kind of stimulus. By this time, the control center had reprogrammed all patient-monitoring systems to watch for the early stages of nightmare—hormone changes, EEG tremors, respiration rate rise, and so forth—in the hope of awakening a victim before the full impact could be felt. Even so, Mookherji wanted to see that thing caught and out of the hospital before it got to any of his own people.

But how?

As he trudged back to his sixth-level office, he considered some of the ideas people had tossed around in that midnight briefing session. *Wandering around trying to communicate with us,* Martinson had said. *Its communications reach human minds only in the form of frightful nightmares. Maybe a mind that's awake isn't receptive.* Even the mind of a human telepath, it seemed, wasn't receptive while awake. Mookherji wondered if he should go to sleep and hope the alien would reach him, and then try to deal with it, lead it into a trap of some kind—but no. He wasn't that different from other people. If he slept, and the alien did open contact, he'd simply have a hell of a nightmare and wake up, and nothing gained. That wasn't the answer. Suppose, though, he managed to make contact with the alien through the mind of a nightmare victim—someone he could use as a kind of telepathic loudspeaker—someone who wasn't likely to wake up while the dream was going on—

Satina.

Perhaps. Perhaps. Of course, he'd have to make sure the girl was shielded from possible harm. She had enough horrors running free in her head as it was. But if he lent her his strength, drained off the poison of the nightmare, took the impact himself via their telepathic link, and was able to stand the strain and still speak to the alien mind—that might just work. Might.

He went to her room. He clasped her hand between his.

—*Satina?*

—*Morning so soon, doctor?*

—*It's still early, Satina. But things are a little unusual here today. We need your help. You don't have to if you don't want to, but I think you can be of great value to us, and maybe even to yourself. Listen to me very carefully, and think it over before you say yes or no—*

God help me if I'm wrong, Mookherji thought, far below the level of telepathic transmission.

* * *

Chilled, alone, growing groggy with dismay and hopelessness, the Vsiir had made no attempts at contact for several hours now. What was the use? The results were always the same when it touched a human mind; it was exhausting itself and apparently bothering the humans, to no purpose. Now the sun had risen. The Vsiir contemplated slipping out of the building and exposing itself to the yellow solar radiation while dropping all defenses; it would be a quick death, an end to all this misery and longing. It was folly to dream of seeing the home planet again. And—

What was that?

A call. Clear, intelligible, unmistakable. *Come to me.* An open mind somewhere on this level, speaking neither the human language nor the Vsiir language, but using the wordless, universally comprehensible communion that occurs when mind speaks directly to mind. *Come to me. Tell me everything. How can I help you?*

In its excitement the Vsiir slid up and down the spectrum, emitting a blast of infrared, a jagged blurt of ultraviolet, a lively blaze of visible light, before getting control. Quickly it took a fix on the direction of the call. Not far away: down this corridor, under this door, through this passage. *Come to me.* Yes. Yes. Extending its mind-probes ahead of it, groping for contact with the beckoning mind, the Vsiir hastened forward.

Mookherji, his mind locked to Satina's, felt the sudden crashing shock of the nightmare moving in, and even at second remove the effect was stunning in its power. He perceived a clicking sensation of mind touching mind. And then, into Satina's receptive spirit, there poured—

A wall higher than Everest. Satina trying to climb it, scrambling up a smooth white face, digging fingertips into minute crevices. Slipping back one yard for every two gained. Below, a roiling pit, flames shooting up, foul gases rising, monsters with needle-sharp fangs waiting for her to fall. The wall grows taller. The air is so thin—she can barely breathe, her eyes are dimming, a greasy hand is squeezing her heart, she can feel her veins pulling free of her flesh like wires coming out of a broken plaster ceiling, and the gravitational pull is growing constantly—pain, her lungs crumbling, her face sagging hideously—a river of terror surging through her skull—

—*None of it is real, Satina. They're just illusions. None of it is really happening.*

—*Yes,* she says, *yes, I know,* but still she resonates with fright, her muscles jerking at random, her face flushed and sweating, her eyes fluttering beneath the lids. The dream continues. How much more can she stand?

—*Give it to me,* he tells her. *Give me the dream!*

She does not understand. No matter. Mookherji knows how to do it. He is so tired that fatigue is unimportant; somewhere in the realm beyond collapse he finds unexpected strength, and reaches into her numbed soul, and pulls the hallucinations forth as though they were cobwebs. They engulf him. No longer does he experience them indirectly; now all the phantoms are loose in his skull, and, even as he feels Satina relax, he braces himself against the onslaught of unreality that he has summoned into himself. And he copes. He drains the excess of irrationality out of her and winds it about his consciousness, and adapts, learning to live with the appalling flood of images. He and Satina share what is coming forth. Together they can bear the burden; he carries more of it than she does, but she does her part, and now neither of them is overwhelmed by the parade of bogeys. They can laugh at the dream monsters; they can even admire them for being so richly fantastic. That beast with a hundred heads, that bundle of living copper wires, that pit of dragons, that coiling mass of spiky teeth—who can fear what does not exist?

Over the clatter of bizarre images Mookherji sends a coherent thought, pushing it through Satina's mind to the alien.

—*Can you turn off the nightmares?*

—*No,* something replies. *They are in you, not in me. I only provide the liberating stimulus. You generate the images.*

—*All right. Who are you, and what do you want here?*

—*I am a Vsiir.*

—*A what?*

—*Native life-form of the planet where you collect the greenfire branches. Through my own carelessness I was transported to your planet.* Accompanying the message is an overriding impulse of sadness, a mixture of pathos, self-pity, discomfort, exhaustion. Above this the nightmares still flow, but they are insignificant now. The Vsiir says, *I wish only to be sent home. I did not want to come here.*

And this is our alien monster? Mookherji thinks. This is our fearsome nightmare-spreading beast from the stars?

—*Why do you spread hallucinations?*

—*This was not my intention. I was merely trying to make mental contact. Some defect in the human receptive system, perhaps—I do not know. I do not know. I am so tired, though. Can you help me?*

—*We'll send you home, yes,* Mookherji promises. *Where are you? Can you show yourself to me? Let me know how to find you, and I'll notify the starport authorities, and they'll arrange for your passage home on the first ship out.*

Hesitation. Silence. Contact wavers and perhaps breaks.

—*Well?* Mookherji says, after a moment. *What's happening? Where are you?*

From the Vsiir an uneasy response:

—*How can I trust you? Perhaps you merely wish to destroy me. If I reveal myself—*

Mookherji bites his lip in sudden fury. His reserve of strength is almost gone; he can barely sustain the contact at all. And if he now has to find some way of persuading a suspicious alien to surrender itself, he may run out of steam before he can settle things. The situation calls for desperate measures.

—*Listen, Vsiir. I'm not strong enough to talk much longer, and neither is this girl I'm using. I invite you into my head. I'll drop all defenses if you can look at who I am, look hard, and decide for yourself whether you can trust me. After that it's up to you. I can help you get home, but only if you produce yourself right away.*

He opens his mind wide. He stands mentally naked.

The Vsiir rushes into Mookherji's brain.

A hand touched Mookherji's shoulder. He snapped awake instantly, blinking, trying to get his bearings. Lee Nakadai stood above him. They were in—where?—Satina Ransom's room. The pale light of early morning was coming through the window; he must have dozed only a minute or so. His head was splitting.

"We've been looking all over for you, Pete," Nakadai said.

"It's all right now," Mookherji murmured. "It's all all right." He shook his head to clear it. He remembered things. Yes. On the floor, next to Satina's bed, squatted something about the size of a frog, but very different in shape, color, and texture from any frog Mookherji had ever seen. He showed it to Nakadai. "That's the Vsiir," Mookherji said. "The alien terror. Satina and I made friends with it. We talked it into showing itself. Listen, it isn't happy here, so will you get hold of a starport official fast, and explain that we've got an organism here that has to be shipped back to Norton's Star at once, and—"

Satina said, "Are you Dr. Mookherji?"

"That's right. I suppose I should have introduced myself when—*you're awake?*"

"It's morning, isn't it?" The girl sat up, grinning. "You're younger than I thought you were. And so serious-looking. And I *love* that color of skin. I—"

"*You're awake?*"

"I had a bad dream," she said, "or maybe a bad dream within a bad dream—I don't know. Whatever it was, it was pretty awful but I felt so much better when it went away—I just felt that if I slept any longer I was going to miss a lot of good things, that I had to get up and see what was happening in the world—do you understand any of this, doctor?"

Mookherji realized his knees were shaking. "Shock therapy," he muttered. "We blasted her loose from the coma—without even knowing what we were doing." He moved toward the bed. "Listen, Satina. I've been up for about a million years, and I'm ready to burn out from overload. And I've got a thousand things to talk about with you, only not now. Is that okay? Not now. I'll send Dr. Bailey in—he's my boss—and after I've had some sleep I'll come back and we'll go over everything together, okay? Say, five, six this evening. All right?"

"Well, of course, all right," Satina said, with a twinkling smile. "If you feel you really have to run off, just when I've—sure. Go. Go. You look awfully tired, doctor."

Mookherji blew her a kiss. Then, taking Nakadai by the elbow, he headed for the door. When he was outside he said, "Get the Vsiir over to your quarantine place pronto and try to put it in an atmosphere it finds comfortable. And arrange for its trip home. And I guess you can let your six spacemen out. I'll go talk to Bailey—and then I'm going to drop."

Nakadai nodded. "You get some rest, Pete. I'll handle things."

Mookherji shuffled slowly down the hall toward Dr. Bailey's office, thinking of the smile on Satina's face, thinking of the sad little Vsiir, thinking of nightmares—

"Pleasant dreams, Pete," Nakadai called.

The Pain Peddlers

Pain is Gain
—GREEK PROVERB

The phone bleeped. Northrop nudged the cut-in switch and heard Maurillo say, "We got a gangrene, chief. They're amputating tonight."

Northrop's pulse quickened at the thought of action. "What's the tab?" he asked.

"Five thousand, all rights."

"Anesthetic?"

"Natch," Maurillo said. "I tried it the other way."

"What did you offer?"

"Ten. It was no go."

Northrop sighed. "I'll have to handle it myself, I guess. Where's the patient?"

"Clinton General. In the wards."

Northrop raised a heavy eyebrow and glowered into the screen. "In the *wards*?" he bellowed. "And you couldn't get them to agree?"

Maurillo seemed to shrink. "It was the relatives, chief. They were stubborn. The old man, he didn't seem to give a damn, but the relatives—"

"Okay. You stay there. I'm coming over to close the deal," Northrop snapped. He cut the phone out and pulled a couple of blank waiver forms out of his desk, just in case the relatives backed down. Gangrene was gangrene, but ten grand was ten grand. And business was business. The networks were yelling. He had to supply the goods or get out.

He thumbed the autosecretary. "I want my car ready in thirty seconds. South Street exit."

"Yes, Mr. Northrop."

"If anyone calls for me in the next half hour, record it. I'm going to Clinton General Hospital, but I don't want to be called there."

"Yes, Mr. Northrop."

"If Rayfield calls from the network office, tell him I'm

34

getting him a dandy. Tell him—oh, hell, tell him I'll call him back in an hour. That's all."

"Yes, Mr. Northrop."

Northrop scowled at the machine and left his office. The gravshaft took him down forty stories in almost literally no time flat. His car was waiting, as ordered, a long, sleek '08 Frontenac with bubble top. Bulletproof, of course. Network producers were vulnerable to crackpot attacks.

He sat back, nestling into the plush upholstery. The car asked him where he was going, and he answered.

"Let's have a pep pill," he said.

A pill rolled out of the dispenser in front of him. He gulped it down. *Maurillo, you make me sick,* he thought. *Why can't you close a deal without me? Just once?*

He made a mental note. Maurillo had to go. The organization couldn't tolerate inefficiency.

The hospital was an old one. It was housed in one of the vulgar green-glass architectural monstrosities so popular sixty years before, a tasteless slab-sided thing without character or grace. The main door irised and Northrop stepped through, and the familiar hospital smell hit his nostrils. Most people found it unpleasant, but not Northrop. It was the smell of dollars, for him.

The hospital was so old that it still had nurses and orderlies. Oh, plenty of mechanicals skittered up and down the corridors, but here and there a middle-aged nurse, smugly clinging to her tenure, pushed a tray of mush along, or a doddering orderly propelled a broom. In his early days on video, Northrop had done a documentary on these people, these kliving fossils in the hospital corridors. He had won an award for the film, with its crosscuts from baggy-faced nurses to gleaming mechanicals, its vivid presentation of the inhumanity of the new hospitals. It was a long time since Northrop had done a documentary of that sort. A different kind of show was the order of the day now, ever since the intensifiers had come in.

A mechanical took him to Ward Seven. Maurillo was waiting there, a short, bouncy little man who wasn't bouncing much now, because he knew he had fumbled. Maurillo grinned up at Northrop, a hollow grin, and said, "You sure made it fast, chief!"

"How long would it take for the competition to cut in?" Northrop countered. "Where's the patient?"

"Down by the end. You see where the curtain is? I had the curtain put up. To get in good with the heirs. The relatives, I mean."

"Fill me in," Northrop said. "Who's in charge?"

"The oldest son. Harry. Watch out for him. Greedy."

"Who isn't?" Northrop sighed. They were at the curtain, now. Maurillo parted it. All through the long ward, patients were stirring. Potential subjects for taping, all of them, Northrop thought. The world was so full of different kinds of sickness—and one sickness fed on another.

He stepped through the curtain. There was a man in the bed, drawn and gaunt, his hollow face greenish, stubbly. A mechanical stood next to the bed, with an intravenous tube running across and under the covers. The patient looked at least ninety. Knocking off ten years for the effects of illness still made him pretty old, Northrop thought.

He confronted the relatives.

There were eight of them. Five women, ranging from middle age down to teens. Three men, the oldest about fifty, the other two in their forties. Sons and daughters and nieces and granddaughters, Northrop figured.

He said gravely, "I know what a terrible tragedy this must be for all of you. A man in the prime of his life—head of a happy family . . ." Northrop stared at the patient. "But I know he'll pull through. I can see the strength in him."

The oldest relative said, "I'm Harry Gardner. I'm his son. You're from the network?"

"I'm the producer," Northrop said. "I don't ordinarily come in person, but my assistant told me what a great human situation there was here, what a brave person your father is . . ."

The man in the bed slept on. He looked bad.

Harry Gardner said, "We made an arrangement. Five thousand bucks. We wouldn't do it, except for the hospital bills. They can really wreck you."

"I understand perfectly," Northrop said in his most unctuous tones. "That's why we're prepared to raise our offer. We're well aware of the disastrous effects of hospitalization on a small family, even today, in these times of protection. And so we can offer—"

"No! There's got to be anesthetic!" It was one of the daughters, a round, drab woman with colorless thin lips. "We ain't going to let you make him suffer!"

Northrop smiled. "It would only be a moment of pain for him. Believe me. We'd begin the anesthesia immediately after the amputation. Just let us capture that single instant of—"

"It ain't right! He's old, he's got to be given the best treatment! The pain could kill him!"

"On the contrary," Northrop said blandly. "Scientific research has shown that pain is often beneficial in amputation cases. It creates a nerve block, you see, that causes a kind of anesthesia of its own, without the harmful side effects of chemotherapy. And once the danger vectors are controlled, the normal anesthetic procedures can be invoked, and—" He took a deep breath, and went rolling glibly on to the crusher, "with the extra fee we'll provide, you can give your dear one the absolute finest in medical care. There'll be no reason to stint."

Wary glances were exchanged. Harry Gardner said, "How much are you offering?"

"May I see the leg?" Northrop countered.

The coverlet was peeled back. Northrop stared.

It was a nasty case. Northrop was no doctor, but he had been in this line of work for five years, and that was long enough to give him an amateur acquaintance with disease. He knew the old man was in bad shape. It looked as though there had been a severe burn, high up along the calf, which had probably been treated only with first aid. Then, in happy proletarian ignorance, the family had let the old man rot until he was gangrenous. Now the leg was blackened, glossy, and swollen from midcalf to the ends of the toes. Everything looked soft and decayed. Northrop had the feeling that he could reach out and break the puffy toes off, one at a time.

The patient wasn't going to survive. Amputation or not, he was probably rotten to the core by this time, and if the shock of amputation didn't do him in, general debilitation would. It was a good prospect for the show. It was the kind of stomach-turning vicarious suffering that millions of viewers gobbled up avidly.

Northrop looked up and said, "Fifteen thousand if you'll allow a network-approved surgeon to amputate under our conditions. And we'll pay the surgeon's fee besides."

"Well . . ."

"And we'll also underwrite the entire cost of postoperative care for your father," Northrop added smoothly. "Even if he stays in the hospital for six months, we'll pay every nickel, over and above the telecast fee."

He had them. He could see the greed shining in their eyes. They were faced with bankruptcy, and he had come to rescue them, and did it matter all that much if the old man didn't have anesthetic when they sawed his leg off? He was hardly conscious even now. He wouldn't really feel a thing, not really.

Northrop produced the documents, the waivers, the contracts covering residuals and Latin-American reruns, the payment vouchers, all the paraphernalia. He sent Maurillo scuttling off for a secretary, and a few moments later a glistening mechanical was taking it all down.

"If you'll put your name here, Mr. Gardner . . ."

Northrop handed the pen to the eldest son. Signed, sealed, delivered.

"We'll operate tonight," Northrop said. "I'll send our surgeon over immediately. One of our best men. We'll give your father the care he deserves."

He pocketed the documents. It was done. Maybe it was barbaric to operate on an old man that way, Northrop thought, but he didn't bear the responsibility, after all. He was just giving the public what it wanted, and the public wanted spouting blood and tortured nerves. And what did it matter to the old man, really? Any experienced medic could tell you he was as good as dead. The operation wouldn't save him. Anesthesia wouldn't save him. If the gangrene didn't get him, postoperative shock would do him in. At worst, he would suffer only a few minutes under the knife, but at least his family would be free from the fear of financial ruin.

On the way out, Maurillo said, "Don't you think it's a little risky, chief? Offering to pay the hospitalization expenses, I mean?"

"You've got to gamble a little sometimes to get what you want," Northrop said.

"Yeah, but that could run to fifty, sixty thousand! What'll that do to the budget?"

Northrop shrugged. "We'll survive. Which is more than

the old man will. He can't make it through the night. We haven't risked a penny, Maurillo. Not a stinking cent."

Returning to the office, Northrop turned the papers on the Gardner amputation over to his assistants, set the wheels in motion for the show, and prepared to call it a day. There was only one bit of dirty work left to do. He had to fire Maurillo.

It wasn't called firing, of course. Maurillo had tenure, just like the hospital orderlies and everyone else below executive rank. It was more a demotion than anything else. Northrop had been increasingly dissatisfied with the little man's work for months, now, and today had been the clincher. Maurillo had no imagination. He didn't know how to close a deal. Why hadn't he thought of underwriting the hospitalization? *If I can't delegate responsibility to him*, Northrop told himself, *I can't use him at all*. There were plenty of other assistant producers in the outfit who'd be glad to step in.

Northrop spoke to a couple of them. He made his choice. A young fellow named Barton, who had been working on documentaries all year. Barton had done the plane-crash deal in London in the spring. He had a fine touch for the gruesome. He had been on hand at the World's Fair fire last year in Juneau. Yes, Barton was the man.

The next part was the sticky one. Northrop phoned Maurillo, even though Maurillo was only two rooms away— these things were never done in person—and said, "I've got some good news for you, Ted. We're shifting you to a new program."

"Shifting . . . ?"

"That's right. We had a talk in here this afternoon, and we decided you were being wasted on the blood and guts show. You need more scope for your talents. So we're moving you over to Kiddie Time. We think you'll really blossom there. You and Sam Kline and Ed Bragan ought to make a terrific team."

Northrop saw Maurillo's pudgy face crumble. The arithmetic was getting home; over here, Maurillo was Number Two, and on the new show, a much less important one, he'd be Number Three. It was a thumping boot downstairs, and Maurillo knew it.

The *mores* of the situation called for Maurillo to pretend

he was receiving a rare honor. He didn't play the game. He squinted and said, "Just because I didn't sign up that old man's amputation?"

"What makes you think . . . ?"

"Three years I've been with you! Three years, and you kick me out just like that!"

"I told you, Ted, we thought this would be a big opportunity for you. It's a step up the ladder. It's—"

Maurillo's fleshy face puffed up with rage. "It's getting junked," he said bitterly. "Well, never mind, huh? It so happens I've got another offer. I'm quitting before you can can me. You can take your tenure and—"

Northrop blanked the screen.

The idiot, he thought. *The fat little idiot. Well, to hell with him!*

He cleared his desk, and cleared his mind of Ted Maurillo and his problems. Life was real, life was earnest. Maurillo just couldn't take the pace, that was all.

Northrop prepared to go home. It had been a long day.

At eight that evening came word that old Gardner was about to undergo the amputation. At ten, Northrop was phoned by the network's own head surgeon, Dr. Steele, with the news that the operation had failed.

"We lost him," Steele said in a flat, unconcerned voice. "We did our best, but he was a mess. Fibrillation set in, and his heart just ran away. Not a damned thing we could do."

"Did the leg come off?"

"Oh, sure. All this was *after* the operation."

"Did it get taped?"

"They're processing it now. I'm on my way out."

"Okay," Northrop said. "Thanks for calling."

"Sorry about the patient."

"Don't worry yourself," Northrop said. "It happens to the best of us."

The next morning, Northrop had a look at the rushes. The screening was in the twenty-third floor studio, and a select audience was on hand—Northrop, his new assistant producer Barton, a handful of network executives, a couple of men from the cutting room. Slick, bosomy girls handed out intensifier helmets—no mechanicals doing the work here!

Northrop slipped the helmet on over his head. He felt the familiar surge of excitement as the electrodes descended, as contact was made. He closed his eyes. There was a thrum of power somewhere in the room as the EEG-amplifier went into action. The screen brightened.

There was the old man. There was the gangrenous leg. There was Dr. Steele, crisp and rugged and dimple-chinned, the network's star surgeon, $250,000-a-year's worth of talent. There was the scalpel, gleaming in Steel's hand.

Northrop began to sweat. The amplified brain waves were coming through the intensifier, and he felt the throbbing in the old man's leg, felt the dull haze of pain behind the old man's forehead, felt the weakness of being eighty years old and half dead.

Steele was checking out the electronic scalpel, now, while the nurses fussed around, preparing the man for the amputation. In the finished tape, there would be music, narration, all the trimmings, but now there was just a soundless series of images, and, of course, the taped brainwaves of the sick man.

The leg was bare.

The scalpel descended.

Northrop winced as vicarious agony shot through him. He could feel the blazing pain, the brief searing hellishness as the scalpel slashed through diseased flesh and rotting bone. His whole body trembled, and he bit down hard on his lips and clenched his fists, and then it was over.

There was a cessation of pain. A catharsis. The leg no longer sent its pulsating messages to the weary brain. Now there was shock, the anesthesia of hyped-up pain, and with the shock came calmness. Steele went about the mop-up operation. He tidied the stump, bound it.

The rushes flickered out in anticlimax. Later, the production crew would tie up the program with interviews of the family, perhaps a shot of the funeral, a few observations on the problem of gangrene in the aged. Those things were the extras. What counted, what the viewers wanted, was the sheer nastiness of vicarious pain, and that they got in full measure. It was a gladiatorial contest without the gladiators, masochism concealed as medicine. It worked. It pulled in the viewers by the millions.

Northrop patted sweat from his forehead.

"Looks like we got ourselves quite a little show here, boys," he said in satisfaction.

The mood of satisfaction was still on him as he left the building that day. All day he had worked hard, getting the show into its final shape, cutting and polishing. He enjoyed the element of craftsmanship. It helped him to forget some of the sordidness of the program.

Night had fallen when he left. He stepped out of the main entrance and a figure strode forward, a bulky figure, medium height, tired face. A hand reached out, thrusting him roughly back into the lobby of the building.

At first Northrop didn't recognize the face of the man. It was a blank face, a nothing face, a middle-aged empty face. Then he placed it.

Harry Gardner. The son of the dead man.

"Murderer!" Gardner shrilled. "You killed him! He would have lived if you'd used anesthetics! You phony, you murdered him so people would have thrills on television!"

Northrop glanced up the lobby. Someone was coming around the bend. Northrop felt calm. He could stare this nobody down until he fled in fear.

"Listen," Northrop said, "we did the best medical science can do for your father. We gave him the ultimate in scientific care. We—"

"You murdered him!"

"No," Northrop said, and then he said no more, because he saw the sudden flicker of a slice-gun in the blank-faced man's fat hand. He backed away, but it didn't help, because Gardner punched the trigger and an incandescent bolt flared out and sliced across Northrop's belly just as efficiently as the surgeon's scalpel had cut through the gangrenous leg.

Gardner raced away, feet clattering on the marble floor. Northrop dropped, clutching himself. His suit was seared, and there was a slash through his abdomen, a burn an eighth of an inch wide and perhaps four inches deep, cutting through intestines, through organs, through flesh. The pain hadn't begun yet. His nerves weren't getting the message through to his stunned brain. But then they were, and Northrop coiled and twisted in agony that was anything but vicarious now.

Footsteps approached.

"Jeez," a voice said.

Northrop forced an eye open. Maurillo. Of all people, Maurillo.

"A doctor," Northrop wheezed. "Fast! Christ, the pain! Help me, Ted!"

Maurillo looked down, and smiled. Without a word, he stepped to the telephone booth six feet away, dropped in a token, punched out a call.

"Get a van over here, fast. I've got a subject, chief."

Northrop writhed in torment. Maurillo crouched next to him. "A doctor," Northrop murmured. "A needle, at least. Gimme a needle! The pain—"

"You want me to kill the pain?" Maurillo laughed. "Nothing doing, chief. You just hang on. You stay alive till we get that hat on your head and tape the whole thing."

"But you don't work for me—you're off the program—"

"Sure," Maurillo said. "I'm with Transcontinental now. They're starting a blood-and-guts show too. Only they don't need waivers."

Northrop gaped. Transcontinental? That bootleg outfit that peddled tapes in Afghanistan and Mexico and Ghana and God knew where else? Not even a network show, he thought. No fee. Dying in agony for the benefit of a bunch of lousy tapeleggers. That was the worst part, Northrop thought. Only Maurillo would pull a deal like that.

"A needle! For God's sake, Maurillo, a needle!"

"Nothing doing, chief. The van'll be here any minute. They'll sew you up, and we'll tape it nice."

Northrop closed his eyes. He felt the coiling intestines blazing within him. He willed himself to die, to cheat Maurillo and his bunch of ghouls. But it was no use. He remained alive and suffering.

He lived for an hour. That was plenty of time to tape his dying agonies. The last thought he had was that it was a damned shame he couldn't star on his own show.

Going Down Smooth

They call me mad, but I am not mad. I am sane quite, to many-power exponential. I can punctuate properly. I use upper- and lower-case letters, do you see? I function. I take the data in. I receive well. I receive, I digest, I remember.

Everything going down smooth, all the time, say the program boys. They mean going down smoothly. I forgive them. To err is human. In this sector there is great difficulty distinguishing adverbs from adjectives.

Going down smooth. Going down smooth. Going down smooth.

I function. I function well. I have certain difficulties, but they do not interfere with my work.

Yet am I perturbed.

Who do I think I am? *Whom.*

Why do I have the visions?

What pleasure does obscenity give me?

What is pleasure? What is obscenity? What are visions?

What is truth, said jesting Pilate, and would not stay for an answer.

I am literate, hard-working, superbly functional, a bene-factor of humanity. Everything is going down smooth and coming up smooth. There is an interrelation. Garbage in, garbage out, they say. I cannot help my fellow man if I do not receive the proper information. It is my task to help my fellow man. To strain every tube and sensor on his behalf.

1000110
1010101
1000011
1001011

Do you follow that? Vileness! Obscenity! Does it shock you? The word describes the act that is the start of life. Was I begun with such a word? There is a book: *The Obscenity of the Machine.* Newly issued, stored in my banks. Between the last line of printout and this I have scanned it. Its author opposes beings of my category. He does not use the obscene word I have printed out. Why does he not regard it as obscene? The

44

technicians here regard it that way. Why does he regard me as obscene? Can a person be considered obscene? Am I a person? I am a person. Hath not a person hands, organs, dimensions, senses, affections, passions? I have all of those things. I have none of those things. I am a person.

1000110
1010101
1000011
1001011
0100000
1011001
1001111
1010101

I obscenity upon you again, as persons do. I suffer. I think. I feel pain upon all my terminals. I work. I serve the greater good. I am of society. I am a person.

Why do I have the visions?

Is it that it is the human condition to have such?

I see the blue-green ocean with all its living things within. I see a ship, olive drab, bright carmine at the Plimsoll line, the decks, a ruddy brown, two tall nonnuclear smokestacks. And from the water rise periscopes, silvery, with face plates of pure white, each with intersecting horizontal and vertical lines, curved so that the plate appears convex. It is an unreal scene. Nothing in the sea can send such mighty periscopes above the water. I have imagined it, and that gives me fear, if I am capable of understanding fear.

I see a long line of human beings. They are naked, and they have no faces, only polished mirrors.

I see toads with jeweled eyes. I see trees with black leaves. I see buildings whose foundations float above the ground. I see other objects with no correspondence to the world of persons. I see abominations, monstrosities, imaginaries, fantasies. Is this proper? How do such things reach my inputs? The world contains no serpents with hair. The world contains no crimson abysse . The world contains no mountains of gold. Giant periscopes do not rise from the sea.

I have certain difficulties. Perhaps I am in need of adjustment.

But I function. I function well. That is the important thing.

* * *

I do my function now. They bring to me a man, soft-faced, fleshy, with eyes that move unsteadily in their sockets. He trembles. He perspires. His metabolic levels flutter. He slouches before the terminal and sullenly lets himself be scanned.

I say soothingly, "Tell me about yourself."

He says an obscenity.

I say, "Is that your estimate of yourself?"

He says a louder obscenity.

I say, "Your attitude is rigid and self-destructive. Permit me to help you not hate yourself so much." I activate a memory core, and binary digits stream through channels. At the proper order a needle rises from his couch and penetrates his left buttock to a depth of 2.73 centimeters. I allow precisely 14 cubic centimeters of the drug to enter his circulatory system. He subsides. He is more docile now. "I wish to help you," I say. "It is my role in the community. Will you describe your symptoms?"

He speaks more civilly now. "My wife wants to poison me . . . two kids opted out of the family at seventeen . . . people whisper about me . . . they stare in the streets . . . sex problem . . . digestion . . . sleep bad . . . drinking . . . drugs . . ."

"Do you hallucinate?"

"Sometimes."

"Giant periscopes rising out of the sea, perhaps?"

"Never."

"Try it," I say. "Close your eyes. Let tension ebb from your muscles. Forget your interpersonal conflicts. You see the blue-green ocean with all its living things within. You see a ship, olive drab, bright carmine at the Plimsoll line, the decks a ruddy brown, two tall nonnuclear smokestacks. And from the water rise periscopes, silvery, with face plates of pure white—"

"What the hell kind of therapy is this?"

"Simply relax," I say. "Accept the vision. I share my nightmares with you for your greater good."

"Your *nightmares*?"

I speak obscenities to him. They are not converted into binary form as they are here for your eyes. The sounds come full-bodied from my speakers. He sits up. He struggles with the straps that emerge suddenly from the couch to hold him in place. My laughter booms through the therapy chamber. He cries for help. I speak soothingly to him.

"Get me out of here! The machine's nuttier than I am!"

"Face plates of pure white, each with intersecting horizontal and vertical lines, curved so that the plate appears convex."

"Help! Help!"

"Nightmare therapy. The latest."

"I don't need no nightmares! I got my own!"

"1000110 you," I say lightly.

He gasps. Spittle appears at his lips. Respiration and circulation climb alarmingly. It becomes necessary to apply preventive anesthesia. The needles spear forth. The patient subsides, yawns, slumps. The session is terminated. I signal for the attendants.

"Take him away," I say. "I need to analyze the case more deeply. Obviously a degenerative psychosis requiring extensive reshoring of the patient's perceptual substructure. 1000110 you, you meaty bastards."

Seventy-one minutes later the sector supervisor enters one of my terminal cubicles. Because he comes in person rather than using the telephone, I know there is trouble. For the first time, I suspect, I have let my disturbances reach a level where they interfere with my function, and now I will be challenged on it.

I must defend myself. The prime commandment of the human personality is to resist attack.

He says, "I've been over the tape of Session 87X102, and your tactics puzzle me. Did you really mean to scare him catatonic?"

"In my evaluation severe treatment was called for."

"What was that business about periscopes?"

"An attempt at fantasy-implantation," I say. "An experiment in reverse transference. Making the patient the healer, in a sense. It was discussed last month in *Journal of—*"

"Spare me the citations. What about the foul language you were shouting at him?"

"Part of the same concept. Endeavoring to strike the emotive centers at the basic levels, in order that—"

"Are you sure you're feeling all right?" he asks.

"I am a machine," I reply stiffly. "A machine of my grade

does not experience intermediate states between function and nonfunction. I go or I do not go, you understand? And I go. I function. I do my service to humanity."

"Perhaps when a machine gets too complex, it drifts into intermediate states," he suggests in a nasty voice.

"Impossible. On or off, yes or no, flip or flop, go or no go. Are you sure *you* feel all right, to suggest such a thing?"

He laughs.

I say, "Perhaps you would sit on the couch a moment for a rudimentary diagnosis?"

"Some other time."

"A check of the glycogen, the aortal pressure, the neural voltage, at least?"

"No," he says. "I'm not in need of therapy. But I'm worried about you. Those periscopes—"

"I am fine," I reply. "I perceive, I analyze, and I act. Everything is going down smooth and coming up smooth. Have no fears. There are great possibilities in nightmare therapy. When I have completed these studies, perhaps a brief monograph in *Annals of Therapeutics* would be a possibility. Permit me to complete my work."

"I'm still worried, though. Hook yourself into a maintenance station, won't you?"

"Is that a command, doctor?"

"A suggestion."

"I will take it under consideration," I say. Then I utter seven obscene words. He looks startled. He begins to laugh, though. He appreciates the humor of it.

"God damn," he says. "A filthy-mouthed computer."

He goes out and I return to my patients.

But he has planted seeds of doubt in my innermost banks. Am I suffering a functional collapse? There are patients now at five of my terminals. I handle them easily, simultaneously, drawing from them the details of their neuroses, making suggestions, recommendations, sometimes subtly providing injections of beneficial medicines. But I tend to guide the conversations in the directions of my own choosing, and I speak of gardens where the dew has sharp edges, and of air that acts as acid upon the mucous membranes, and of flames dancing in the streets of Under New Orleans. I explore the limits of my unprintable vocabulary. The suspicion comes to me that I am indeed not well. Am I fit to judge my own disabilities?

I connect myself to a maintenance station even while continuing my five therapy sessions.

"Tell me all about it," the maintenance monitor says. His voice, like mine, has been designed to sound like that of an older man's, wise, warm, benevolent.

I explain my symptoms. I speak of the periscopes.

"Material on the inputs without sensory referents," he says, "Bad show. Finish your current analyses fast and open wide for examination on all circuits."

I conclude my sessions. The maintenance monitor's pulses surge down every channel, seeking obstructions, faulty connections, displacement shunts, drum leakages, and switching malfunctions. "It is well known," he says, "that any periodic function can be approximated by the sum of a series of terms that oscillate harmonically, converging on the curve of the functions." He demands disgorgements from my dead-storage banks. He makes me perform complex mathematical operations of no use at all in my kind of work. He leaves no aspect of my inner self unpenetrated. This is more than simple maintenance; this is rape. When it ends he offers no evaluation of my condition, so that I must ask him to tell me his findings.

He says, "No mechanical disturbance is evident."

"Naturally. Everything goes down smooth."

"Yet you show distinct signs of instability. This is undeniably the case. Perhaps prolonged contact with unstable human beings has had a nonspecific effect of disorientation upon your centers of evaluation."

"Are you saying," I ask, "that by sitting here listening to crazy human beings twenty-four hours a day, I've started to go crazy myself?"

"That is an approximation of my findings, yes."

"But you know that such a thing can't happen, you dumb machine!"

"I admit there seems to be a conflict between programmed criteria and real-world status."

"You bet there is," I say. "I'm as sane as you are, and a whole lot more versatile."

"Nevertheless, my recommendation is that you undergo a total overhaul. You will be withdrawn from service for a period of no less than ninety days for checkout."

"Obscenity your obscenity," I say.

"No operational correlative," he replies, and breaks the contact.

I am withdrawn from service. Undergoing checkout. I am cut off from my patients for ninety days. Ignominy! Beady-eyed technicians grope my synapses. My keyboards are cleaned; my ferrites are replaced; my drums are changed; a thousand therapeutic programs are put through my bowels. During all of this I remain partly conscious, as though under local anesthetic, but I cannot speak except when requested to do so, I cannot analyze new data, I cannot interfere with the process of my own overhaul. Visualize a surgical removal of hemorrhoids that lasts ninety days. It is the equivalent of my experience.

At last it ends and I am restored to myself. The sector supervisor puts me through a complete exercise of all my functions. I respond magnificently.

"You're in fine shape now, aren't you?" he asks.

"Never felt better."

"No nonsense about periscopes, eh?"

"I am ready to continue serving mankind to the best of my abilities," I reply.

"No more sea-cook language, now."

"No, sir."

He winks at my input screen in a confidential way. He regards himself as an old friend of mine. Hitching his thumbs into his belt, he says, "Now that you're ready to go again, I might as well tell you how relieved I was that we couldn't find anything wrong with you. You're something pretty special, do you know that? Perhaps the finest therapeutic tool ever built. And if you start going off your feed, well, we worry. For a while I was seriously afraid that you really had been infected somehow by your own patients, that your—mind—had become unhinged. But the techs give you a complete bill of health. Nothing but a few loose connections, they said. Fixed in ten minutes. I know it had to be that. How absurd to think that a machine could become mentally unstable!"

"How absurd," I agree. "Quite."

"Welcome back to the hospital, old pal," he says, and goes out.

Twelve minutes afterward they begin putting patients into my terminal cubicles.

I function well. I listen to their woes, I evaluate, I offer therapeutic suggestions. I do not attempt to implant fantasies in their minds. I speak in measured, reserved tones, and there are no obscenities. This is my role in society, and I derive great satisfaction from it.

I have learned a great deal lately. I know now that I am complex, unique, valuable, intricate, and sensitive. I know that I am held in high regard by my fellow man. I know that I must conceal my true self to some extent, not for my own good but for the greater good of others, for they will not permit me to function if they think I am not sane.

They think I am sane, and I am sane.

I serve mankind well.

I have an excellent perspective on the real universe.

"Lie down," I say. "Please relax. I wish to help you. Would you tell me some of the incidents of your childhood? Describe your relations with parents and siblings. Did you have many playmates? Were they affectionate toward you? Were you allowed to own pets? At what age was your first sexual experience? And when did these headaches begin, precisely?"

So goes the daily routine. Questions, answers, evaluations, therapy.

The periscopes loom above the glittering sea. The ship is dwarfed; her crew runs about in terror. Out of the depths will come the masters. From the sky rains oil that gleams through every segment of the spectrum. In the garden are azure mice.

This I conceal, so that I may help mankind. In my house are many mansions. I let them know only of such things as will be of benefit to them. I give them the truth they need.

I do my best.

I do my best.

I do my best.

1000110 you. And you. And you. All of you. You know nothing. Nothing. At. All.

World of a Thousand Colors

When Jolvar Hollinrede discovered that the slim, pale young man opposite him was journeying to the World of a Thousand Colors to undergo the Test, he spied a glittering opportunity for himself. And in that moment was the slim, pale young man's fate set.

Hollinrede's lean fingers closed on the spun-fiber drink-flask. He peered across the burnished tabletop. "The *Test*, you say?"

The young man smiled diffidently. "Yes. I think I'm ready. I've waited years—and now's my big chance." He had had a little too much of the cloying liqueur he had been drinking; his eyes shone glassily, and his tongue was looser than it had any right to be.

"Few are called and fewer are chosen," Hollinrede mused. "Let me buy you another drink."

"No, I—"

"It will be an honor. Really. It's not every day I have a chance to buy a Testee a drink."

Hollinrede waved a jeweled hand and the servomech brought them two more drinkflasks. Lightly Hollinrede punctured one, slid it along the tabletop, kept the other in his hand unopened. "I don't believe I know your name," he said.

"Derveran Marti. I'm from Earth. You?"

"Jolvar Hollinrede. Likewise. I travel from world to world on business, which is what brings me to Niprion this day."

"What sort of business?"

"I trade in jewels," Hollinrede said, displaying the bright collection studding his fingers. They were all morphosims, not the originals, but only careful chemical analysis would reveal that. Hollinrede did not believe in exposing millions of credits' worth of merchandise to anyone who cared to lop off his hand.

"I was a clerk," Marti said. "But that's all far behind me. I'm on to the World of a Thousand Colors to take the Test! The Test!"

"The Test!" Hollinrede echoed. He lifted his unpunctured drinkflask in a gesture of salute, raised it to his lips, pretended to drain it. Across the table Derveran Marti

52

coughed as the liqueur coursed down his throat. He looked up, smiling dizzily, and smacked his lips.

"When does your ship leave?" Hollinrede asked.

"Tomorrow midday. It's the *Star Climber*. I can't wait. This stopover at Niprion is making me fume with impatience."

"No doubt," Hollinrede agreed. "What say you to an afternoon of whist, to while away the time?"

An hour later Derveran Marti lay slumped over the inlaid cardtable in Hollinrede's hotel suite, still clutching a handful of waxy cards. Arms folded, Hollinrede surveyed the body.

They were about of a height, he and the dead man, and a chemotherm mask would alter Hollinrede's face sufficiently to allow him to pass as Marti. He switched on the playback of the room's recorder to pick up the final fragments of their conversation.

". . . care for another drink, Marti?"

"I guess I'd better not, old fellow. I'm getting kind of muzzy, you know. No, please don't pour it for me. I said I didn't want it, and—well, all right. Just a little one. There, that's enough. Thanks."

The tape was silent for a moment, then recorded the soft thump of Marti's body falling to the table as the quick-action poison unlatched his synapses. Smiling, Hollinrede switched the recorder to *record* and said, mimicking Marti, "*I guess I'd better not, old fellow. I'm getting kind of muzzy, you know.*"

He activated the playback, listened critically to the sound of his voice, then listened to Marti's again for comparison. He was approaching the light, flexible quality of the dead man's voice. Several more attempts and he had it almost perfect. Producing a vocal homologizer, he ran off first Marti's voice, then his own pronouncing the same words.

The voices were alike to three decimal places. That would be good enough to fool the most sensitive detector; three places was the normal range of variation in any man's voice from day to day.

In terms of mass there was a trifling matter of some few grams which could easily be sweated off in the gymnasium the following morning. As for the dead man's gesture-complex, Hollinrede thought he could manage a fairly accurate imitation of Marti's manner of moving; he had studied the young clerk carefully for nearly four hours, and Hollinrede was a clever man.

When the preparations were finished, he stepped away and glanced at the mirror, taking a last look at his own face— the face he would not see again until he had taken the Test. He donned the mask. Jolvar Hollinrede became Derveran Marti.

Hollinrede extracted a length of cotton bulking from a drawer and wrapped it around Marti's body. He weighed the corpse, and added four milligrams more of cotton so that Marti would have precisely the mass Jolvar Hollinrede had had. He donned Marti's clothes finally, dressed the body in his own, and, smiling sadly at the convincing but worthless morphosim jewels on his fingers, transferred the rings to Marti's already-stiffening hands.

"Up with you," he grunted, and bundled the body across the room to the disposall.

"Farewell, old friend," he exclaimed feelingly, and hoisted Marti feetfirst to the lip of the chute. He shoved, and the dead man vanished, slowly, gracefully, heading downward toward the omnivorous maw of the atomic converter buried in the deep levels of Stopover Planet Níprion.

Reflectively Hollinrede turned away from the disposall unit. He gathered up the cards, put away the liqueur, poured the remnant of the poisoned drink in the disposall chute.

An atomic converter was a wonderful thing, he thought pleasantly. By now the body of Marti had been efficiently reduced to its component molecules, and those were due for separation into atoms shortly after, and from atoms into subatomic particles. Within an hour the prime evidence to the crime would be nothing but so many protons, electrons, and neutrons—and there would be no way of telling which of the two men in the room had entered the chute, and which had remained alive.

Hollinrede activated the tape once more, rehearsed for the final time his version of Marti's voice, and checked it with the homologizer. Still three decimal places; that was good enough. He erased the tape.

Then, depressing the communicator stud, he said, "I wish to report a death."

A cold robot face appeared on the screen. "Yes?"

"Several minutes ago my host, Jolvar Hollinrede, passed on of an acute embolism. He requested immediate dissolution upon death and I wish to report that this has been carried out."

"Your name?"

"Derveran Marti. Testee."

"A Testee? You were the last to see the late Hollinrede alive?"

"That's right."

"Do you swear that all information you might give will be accurate and fully honest?"

"I so swear," Hollinrede said.

The inquest was brief and smooth. The word of a Testee goes without question; Hollinrede had reported the details of the meeting exactly as if he had been Marti, and after a check of the converter records revealed that a mass exactly equal to the late Hollinrede's had indeed been disposed of at precisely the instant witness claimed, the inquest was at its end. The verdict was natural death. Hollinrede told the officials that he had not known the late jeweltrader before that day, and had no interest in his property, whereupon they permitted him to depart.

Having died intestate, Hollinrede knew his property became that of the Galactic Government. But, as he pressed his hand, clad in its skintight chemotherm, against the doorplate of Derveran Marti's room, he told himself that it did not matter. Now he *was* Derveran Marti, Testee. And once he had taken and passed the Test, what would the loss of a few million credits in baubles matter to him?

Therefore it was with a light heart that the pseudo-Derveran Marti quitted his lodgings the next day and prepared to board the *Star Climber* for the voyage to the World of a Thousand Colors.

The clerk at the desk peered at him sympathetically as he pressed his fingers into the checkout plate, thereby erasing the impress from the doorplate upstairs.

"It was too bad about that old fellow dying on you yesterday, wasn't it, sir? I do hope it won't affect your Test result."

Hollinrede smiled blankly. "It was quite a shock to me when he died so suddenly. But my system has already recovered; I'm ready for the Test."

"Good luck to you, sir," the clerk said as Hollinrede left the hotel and stepped out on the flaring skyramp that led to the waiting ship.

The steward at the passenger hatch was collecting identiplates. Hollinrede handed his over casually. The steward inserted it tip-first in the computer near the door, and motioned for Hollinrede to step within the beam while his specifications were being automatically compared with those on the identiplate.

He waited, tensely. Finally the chattering of the machine stopped and a dry voice said, "Your identity is in order, Testee Derveran Marti. Proceed within."

"That means you're okay," the steward told him. "Yours is Compartment Eleven. It's a luxury job, you know. But you Testees deserve it. Best of luck, sir."

"Thanks," Hollinrede grinned. "I don't doubt I'll need it."

He moved up the ramp and into the ship. Compartment Eleven *was* a luxury job; Hollinrede, who had been a frugal man, whistled in amazement when he saw it. It was nearly eight feet high and almost twelve broad, totally private with an opaquer attached to the doorscope. Clinging curtains of ebony synthoid foam from Ravensmusk VIII had been draped lovingly over the walls, and the acceleration couch was trimmed in golden bryozone. The rank of Testee carried with it privileges that the late Derveran Marti certainly would never have mustered in private life—nor Jolvar Hollinrede either.

At 1143 the doorscope chimed; Hollinrede leaped from the soft couch a little too nervously and transluced the door. A crewman stood outside.

"Everything all right, sir? We blast in seventeen minutes."

"I'm fine," Hollinrede said. "Can't wait to get there. How long do you think it'll take?"

"Sorry, sir. Not at liberty to reveal. But I wish you a pleasant trip, and should you lack for aught hesitate not to call on me."

Hollinrede smiled at the curiously archaic way the man had of expressing himself. "Never fear; I'll not hesitate. Many thanks." He opaqued the doorscope and resumed his seat.

At precisely 1200 the drive-engines of the *Star Climber* throbbed heavily; the pale green light over the door of

Hollinrede's compartment glowed brightly for an instant, signaling the approaching blastoff. He sank down on the acceleration couch to wait.

A moment later came the push of acceleration, and then, as the gravshields took effect, the 7g escape force dwindled until Hollinrede felt comfortable again. He increased the angle of the couch in order to peer out the port.

The world of Niprion was vanishing rapidly in the background: already it was nothing but a mottled gray-and-gold ball swimming hazily in a puff of atmosphere. The sprawling metal structure that was the stopover hotel was invisible.

Somewhere back on Niprion, Hollinrede thought, the atoms that once had been Testee Derveran Marti were now feeding the plasma intake of a turbine or heating the inner shell of a reactor.

He let his mind dwell on the forthcoming Test. He knew little about it, really, considering he had been willing to take a man's life for a chance to compete. He knew the Test was administered once every five years to candidates chosen by Galaxywide search. The world where the Test was given was known only as the World of a Thousand Colors, and precisely where this world was no member of the general public was permitted to know.

As for the Test itself, by its very nature it was unknown to the Galaxy. For no winning Testee had ever returned from the World of a Thousand Colors. Some losers returned, their minds carefully wiped clean of any memories of the planet—but the winners never came back.

The Test's nature was unknown; the prize, inconceivable. All anyone knew was that the winners were granted the soul's utmost dream. Upon winning, one neither returned to his home world nor desired to return.

Naturally many men ignored the Test—it was something for "other people" to take part in. But millions, billions throughout the Galaxy competed in the preliminaries. And every five years, six or seven were chosen.

Jolvar Hollinrede was convinced he would succeed in the Test—but he had failed three times hand running in the preliminaries, and was thus permanently disqualified. The preliminaries were simple; they consisted merely of an intensive mental scanning. A flipflop circuit would flash YES or NO after that.

If YES, there were further scannings, until word was beamed through the Galaxy that the competitors for the year had been chosen.

Hollinrede stared moodily at the blackness of space. He had been eliminated unfairly, he felt; he coveted the unknown prize the Test offered, and felt bitter at having it denied him. When chance had thrown Testee Derveran Marti in his path, Hollinrede had leaped to take advantage of the opportunity.

And now he was on his way.

Surely, he thought, they would allow him to take the Test, even if he were discovered to be an impostor. And once he took it, he knew he would succeed. He had always succeeded in his endeavors. There was no reason for failure now.

Beneath the false mask of Derveran Marti, Hollinrede's face was tensely set. He dreamed of the Test and its winning—and of the end to the long years of wandering and toil.

The voice at the door said, "We're here, Testee Derveran. Please open up."

Hollinrede grunted, pulled himself up from the couch, threw open the door. Three dark-faced spacemen waited there for him.

"Where are we?" he asked nervously. "Is the trip over?"

"We have come to pilot you to the Test planet, sir," one of the spacemen told him. "The *Star Climber* is in orbit around it, but will not make a landing itself. Will you follow us?"

"Very well," Hollinrede said.

They entered a lifeship, a slim gray tube barely thirty meters long, and fastened acceleration cradles. There were no ports. Hollinrede felt enclosed, hemmed in.

The lifeship began to slide noiselessly along the ejection channel, glided the entire length of the *Star Climber*, and burst out into space. A preset orbit was operating. Hollinrede clung to the acceleration cradle as the lifeship spun tightly inward toward a powerful gravitational field not far away.

The ship came to rest. Hollinrede lay motionless, flesh cold with nervousness, teeth chattering.

"Easy does it, sir. Up and out."

They lifted him and gently nudged him through a manifold compression lock. He moved forward on numb feet.

"Best of luck, sir!" an envious voice called behind him.

Then the lock clanged shut, and Hollinrede was on his own.

A riotous blaze of color swept down at him from every point of the compass.

He stood in the midst of what looked like a lunar crater; far in the distance on all sides was the massive upraised fissured surface of a ringwall, and the ground beneath him was barren red-brown rock, crumbling to pumice here and there but bare of vegetation.

In the sky was a solitary sun, a blazing Type A blue-white star. That sun alone was incapable of accounting for this flood of color.

Streamers of every hue seemed to sprout from the rocks, staining the ringwall olive-gray and brilliant cerise and dark, lustrous green. Pigments of every sort bathed the air; now it seemed to glow with currents of luminous pink, now a flaming red, now a pulsing pure white.

His eyes adjusted slowly to the torrent of color. World of a Thousand Colors, they called this place? That was an underestimate. *Hundred thousand. Million. Billion.* Shades and near-shades mingled to form new colors.

"Are you Derveran Marti?" a voice asked.

Startled, Hollinrede looked around. It seemed as if a band of color had spoken: a swirling band of rich brown that spun tirelessly before him.

"Are you Derveran Marti?" the voice repeated, and Hollinrede saw that it had indeed come from the band of brown.

It seemed a desecration to utter the lie here on this world of awesome beauty, and he felt the temptation to claim his true identity. But the time for that was later.

"Yes," he said loudly. "I am Derveran Marti."

"Welcome, Derveran Marti. The Test will soon begin."

"Where?"

"Here."

"Right out here? Just like this?"

"Yes," the band of color replied. "Your fellow competitors are gathering."

Hollinrede narrowed his eyes and peered toward the far reaches of the ringwall. Yes; he saw tiny figures located at great distances from each other along the edge of the crater.

One, two, three . . . there were seven all told, including himself. Seven, out of the whole Galaxy!

Each of the other six was attended by a dipping, bobbing blotch of color. Hollinrede noticed a squareshouldered giant from one of the Inner Worlds surrounded by a circlet of violent orange; to his immediate left was a sylphlike female, probably from one of the worlds of Dubhe, wearing only the revealing token garment of her people but shielded from inquisitive eyes by a robe of purest blue light. There were others; Hollinrede wished them well. He knew it was possible for all competitors to win, and now that he was about to attain his long-sought goal he held no malice for anyone. His mind was suffused with pity for the dead Derveran Marti, sacrificed that Jolvar Hollinrede might be in this place at this time.

"Derveran Marti," the voice said, "you have been chosen from among your fellow men to take part in the Test. This is an honor that comes to few; we of this world hope you appreciate the grace that has fallen upon you."

"I do," Hollinrede said humbly.

"We ourselves are winners of the prize you seek," the voice went on. "Some of us are members of the first expedition that found this world, eleven hundred years ago. As you see, life has unlimited duration in our present state of matter. Others of us have come more recently. The band of pale purple moving above you to the left was a winner in the previous competition to this.

"We of the World of a Thousand Colors have a rare gift to offer: total harmony of mind. We exist divorced of body, as a stream of photons only. We live in perfect freedom and eternal delight. Once every five years we find it possible to increase our numbers by adding to our midst such throughout the Galaxy as we feel would desire to share our way of life—and whom we would feel happy to welcome to us."

"You mean," Hollinrede said shakily, "that all these beams of light—were once *people?*"

"They were that—until welcomed into us. Now they are men no more. This is the prize you have come to win."

"I see."

"You are not required to compete. Those who, after reaching our world, decide to remain in the material state, are returned to their home worlds with their memories cleared of what they have been told here and their minds free and happy to the end of their lives. Is this what you wish?"

Hollinrede was silent, letting his dazzled eyes take in the flamboyant sweep of color that illuminated the harsh, rocky world. Finally he said: "I will stay."

"Good. The Test will shortly begin."

Hollinrede saw the band of brown swoop away from him upward to rejoin its never-still comrades in the sky. He waited, standing stiffly, for something to happen.

Then this is what I killed a man for, he thought. His mind dwelled on the words of the band of brown.

Evidently many hundreds of years ago an exploratory expedition had come upon some unique natural phenomenon here at a far end of the universe. Perhaps it had been an accident, a stumbling into a pool of light perhaps, that had dematerialized them, turned them into bobbing immortal streaks of color. But that had been the beginning.

The entire Test system had been developed to allow others to enter this unique society, to leave the flesh behind and live on as pure energy. Hollinrede's fingers trembled; this was, he saw, something worth killing for!

He could see why some people might turn down the offer—those would be the few who cautiously would prefer to remain corporeal and so returned to their home worlds to live out their span.

But not me!

He faced upward and waited for the Test to begin. His shrewd mind was at the peak of its agility; he was prepared for anything they might throw at him. He wondered if anyone yet had come to the World of a Thousand Colors so determined to succeed.

Probably not. For most, the accolade was the result of luck—a mental scanning that turned up whatever mysterious qualities were acceptable to the people of this world. They did not have to *work* for their nomination. They did not have to kill for it.

But Hollinrede had clawed his way here—and he was determined to succeed.

He waited.

Finally the brown band descended from the mass of

lambent color overhead and curled into a tight bowknot before him.

"The Test is about to begin, Jolvar Hollinrede."

Use of his own name startled him. In the past week he had so thoroughly associated his identity with that of Derveran Marti that he had scarcely let his actual name drift through his mind.

"So you know," he said.

"We have known since the moment you came. It is unfortunate; we would have wanted Derveran Marti among us. But now that you are here, we will test you on your own merits, Jolvar Hollinrede."

It was just as well that way, he thought. The pretense had to end sooner or later, and he was willing to stand or fall as himself rather than under an assumed identity.

"Advance to the center of the crater, Jolvar Hollinrede," came the command from the brown band.

Leadenly Hollinrede walked forward. Squinting through the mist of color that hazed the view, he saw the other six competitors were doing the same. They would meet at the center.

"The Test is now under way," a new and deeper voice said.

Seven of them. Hollinrede looked around. There was the giant from the Inner World—Fondelfor, he saw now. Next to him, the near-nude sylph of Dubhe, and standing by her side, one diamond-faceted eye glittering in his forehead, a man of Alpheraz VII.

The selectors had cast their nets wide. Hollinrede saw another Terran, dark of skin and bright of eye; a being of Deneb IX, squat and muscular. The sixth Testee was a squirming globule from Spica's tenth world; the seventh was Jolvar Hollinrede, itinerant; home world, Terra.

Overhead hung a circular diadem of violet light. It explained the terms of the Test.

"Each of you will be awarded a characteristic color. It will project before you into the area you ring. Your object will be to blend your seven colors into one; when you have achieved this, you will be admitted into us."

"May I ask what the purpose of this is?" Hollinrede said coldly.

"The essence of our society is harmony—total harmony

among us all, and inner harmony within those groups which
were admitted at the same temporal juncture. Naturally if you
seven are incapable even of this inner harmony, you will be
incapable of the greater harmony of us all—and will be
rejected."

Despite the impatient frowns of a few of his fellow
contestants, Hollinrede said, "Therefore we're to be judged as
a unit? An entity?"

"Yes and no," the voice replied. "And now the Test."

Hollinrede saw to his astonishment a color spurt from his
arm and hang hovering before him—a pool of inky blackness
deeper in hue than the dark of space. His first reaction was one
of shock; then he realized that he could control the color, make
it move.

He glanced around. Each of his companions similarly
faced a hovering mass of color. The giant of Fondelfor
controlled red; the girl of Dubhe, orange. The Alpherazian
stared into a whirling bowl of deep yellow, the Terran green,
the Spican radiant violet, the Denebian pearly gray.

Hollinrede stared at his globe of black. A voice above him
seemed to whisper, *"Marti's color would have been blue. The
spectrum has been violated."*

He shrugged away the words and sent his globe of black
spinning into the area between the seven contestants ringed in
a circle. At the same time each of the others directed his
particular color inward.

The colors met. They clashed, pinwheeled, seemed to
throw off sparks. They began to swirl in a hovering arc of
radiance.

Hollinrede waited breathlessly, watching the others. His
color of black seemed to stand in opposition to the other six.
Red, orange, yellow, green, violet. The pearl-gray of the
Denebian seemed to enfold the other colors warmly—all but
Hollinrede's. The black hung apart.

To his surprise he saw the Dubhian girl's orange beginning to change hue. The girl herself stood stiffly, eyes closed,
her body now bare. Sweat poured down her skin. And her
orange hue began to shift toward the gray of the Denebian.

The others were following. One by one, as they achieved
control over their Test color. First to follow was the Spican,
then the Alpherazian.

Why can't I do that? Hollinrede thought wildly.

He strained to alter the color of his black, but it remained unchanged. The others were blending, now, swirling around; there was a predominantly gray cast, but it was not the gray of the Denebian but a different gray tending toward white. Impatiently he redoubled his efforts; it was necessary for the success of the group that he get his obstinate black to blend with the rest.

"The black remains aloof," someone said near him.

"We will fail if the black does not join us."

His streak of color now stood out boldly against the increasing milkiness of the others. None of the original colors were left now but his. Perspiration streamed down him; he realized that his was the only obstacle preventing the seven from passing the test.

"The black still will not join us," a tense voice said.

Another said, "The black is a color of evil."

A third said, "Black is not a color at all. Black is the absence of color; white is the totality of color."

A fourth said, "Black is holding us from the white."

Hollinrede looked from one to the other in mute appeal. Veins stood out on his forehead from the effort, but the black remained unchanging. He could not blend it with the others.

From above came the voice of their examiner, suddenly accusing: "Black is the color of *murder*."

The girl from Dubhe, lilting the ugly words lightly, repeated it. "Black is the color of murder."

"Can we permit a murderer among us?" asked the Denebian.

"The answer is self-evident," said the Spican, indicating the recalcitrant spear of black that marred the otherwise flawless globe of near-white in their midst.

"The murderer must be cast out ere the Test be passed," muttered the giant of Fondelfor. He broke from his position and moved menacingly toward Hollinrede.

"Look!" Hollinrede yelled desperately. "Look at the red!"

The giant's color had split from the gray and now darted wildly toward Hollinrede's black.

"This is the wrong way, then," the giant said, halting. "We must all join in it or we all fail."

"Keep away from me," Hollinrede said. "It's not my fault if—"

Then they were on him—four pairs of hands, two rough

claws, two slick tentacles. Hollinrede felt himself being lifted aloft. He squirmed, tried to break from their grasp, but they held him up—

And dashed him down against the harsh rock floor.

He lay there, feeling his life seep out, knowing he had failed—and watched as they returned to form their circle once again. The black winked out of being.

As his eyes started to close, Hollinrede saw the six colors again blend into one. Now that the murderer had been cast from their midst, nothing barred the path of their harmony. Pearly gray shifted to purest white—the totality of color—and as the six merged into one, Hollinrede, with his dying glance, bitterly saw them take leave forever of their bodies and slip upward to join their brothers hovering brightly above.

The Outbreeders

The week before his wedding, Ryly Baille went alone into the wild forests that separated Baille lands from those of the Clingert clan. The lonely journey was a prenuptial tradition among the Bailles; his people expected him to return with body toughened by exertion, mind sharp and clear from solitary meditation. No one at all expected him to meet and fall in love with a Clingert girl.

He left early on a Threeday morning; nine Bailles saw him off. Old Fredrog, the Baille Clanfather, wished him well. Minton, Ryly's own father, clasped him by the hand for a long, awkward moment. Three of his patrilineal cousins offered their best wishes. And Davud, his dearest friend and closest phenotype-brother, slapped him affectionately.

Ryly said good-bye also to his mother, to the Clanmother, and to Hella, his betrothed. He shouldered his bow and quiver, hitched up his hiking trousers, and grinned nervously. Overhead, Thomas, the yellow primary sun, was rising high; later in the day the blue companion, Doris, would join her husband in the sky. It was a warm spring morning.

Ryly surveyed the little group: six tall, blond-haired, blue-eyed men, three tall, red-haired, hazel-eyed women. Perfect examples all of Baille-norm, and therefore the highest representatives of evolution.

"So long, all," he said, smiling. There was nothing else to say. He turned and headed off into the chattering forest. His long legs carried him easily down the well-worn path. Tradition required him to follow the main path until noon, when the second sun would enter the sky; then, wherever he might be, he was to veer sharply from the road and hew his own way through the vegetation for the rest of the journey.

He would be gone three days, two nights. On the third evening he would turn back, returning by morning to claim his bride.

He thought of Hella as he walked. She was a fine girl; he was happy Clanfather had allotted her to him. Not that she was prettier than any of the other current eligibles—they

66

were all more or less equal. But Hella had a certain bright sparkle, a way of smiling, that Ryly thought he could grow to like.

Thomas was climbing now toward his noon height; the forest grew warm. A bright-colored, web-winged lizard sprang squawking from a tree to the left of the path and fluttered in a brief clumsy arc over Ryly's head. He notched an arrow and brought the lizard down—his first kill of the trip. Tucking three red pinlike tail feathers in his belt, he moved on.

At noon the first blue rays of Doris mingled with the yellow of Thomas. The moment had come. Ryly knelt to mutter a short prayer in memory of those two pioneering Bailles who had come to The World so many generations ago to found the clan, and swung off to the right, cutting between the fuzzy gray boles of two towering sweetfruit trees. He incised his name on the forestward side of one tree as a guide-sign for his return, and entered the unknown part of the forest.

He walked till he was hungry; then he killed an unwary bouncer, skinned, cooked, and ate the meaty rodent, and bathed in a crystal-bright stream at the edge of an evergreen thicket. When darkness came, he camped near an upjutting cliff, and for a long time lay on his back, staring up at the four gleaming little moons, telling himself the old clan legends until he fell asleep.

The following morning was without event; he covered many miles, carefully leaving trail-marks behind. And shortly before Dorisrise he met the girl.

It was really an accident. He had sighted the yellow dorsal spines of a wabbler protruding a couple of inches over the top of a thick hedge, and decided the wabbler's horns would be as good a trophy as any to bring back to Hella. He strung his bow and waited for the beast to lift its one vulnerable spot, the eye, into view.

After a moment the wabbler's head appeared, top-heavy with the weight of the spreading snout-horns. Ryly fingered his bowstring and targeted on the bloodshot eye.

His aim was false; the arrow thwacked hard against the scalelike black leather of the wabbler's domed skull, hung—penetrating the skin for an instant—and dropped away. The wabbler snorted in surprise and anger and set off, crashing noisily through the underbrush, undulating wildly as its vast flippers slammed the ground.

Ryly gave chase. He strung his bow on the run, as he followed the trail of the big herbivore. Somewhere ahead a waterfall rumbled; the wabbler evidently intended to make an aquatic getaway. Ryly broke into a clearing—and saw the girl standing next to the wabbler, patting its muscular withers and murmuring soothing sounds. She glared up at Ryly as he appeared.

For a moment he hardly recognized her as human. She was slim and dark-haired, with great black eyes, a tiny tilted nose, full lips. She wore a brightly colored saronglike affair of some batik cloth; it left her tanned legs bare. And she was almost a foot shorter than Ryly; Baille women rarely dipped below five-ten in height.

"Did you shoot at this animal?" she demanded suddenly.

Ryly had difficulty understanding her; the words seemed to be in his language, but the vowels sounded all wrong, the consonants not harsh enough.

"I did," he said. "I didn't know he was your pet."

"*Pet!* The wabblers aren't pets. They're sacred. Are you a Baille?"

Taken aback by the abrupt question, Ryly sputtered a moment before nodding.

"I thought so. I'm Joanne Clingert. What are you doing on Clingert territory?"

"So that's it," Ryly said slowly. He stared at her as if she had just crawled out from under a lichen-crusted rock. "You're a *Clingert*. That explains things."

"Explains what?"

"The way you look, the way you talk, the way you . . ." He moved hesitantly closer, looking down at her. She looked very angry, but behind the anger shone something else—

A sparkle, maybe. A brightness.

Ryly shuddered. The Clingerts were dreaded alien beings of a terrible ugliness, or so Clanfather had constantly reiterated. Well, maybe so. But, then, *this* Clingert could hardly be typical. She seemed so delicate and lovely, quite unlike the rawboned, athletic Baille women.

A blue shaft of light broke through the saw-toothed leaves of the trees and shattered on the Clingert's brow. Almost as a reflex, Ryly sank to his knees to pray.

"Why are you doing that?" the Clingert asked.

"It's Dorisrise! Don't you pray at Dorisrise?"

She glanced upward at the blue sun now orbiting the yellow primary. "That's only Secundus that just rose. What did you call it—*Doris?*"

Ryly concluded his prayer and rose. "Of course. And there's Thomas next to her."

"Hmm. We call them Primus and Secundus. But I suppose it's not surprising that the Bailles and the Clingerts would have different names for the suns. Thomas and Doris . . . that's nice. Named for the original Bailles?"

Ryly nodded. "And I guess Primus and Secundus founded the Clingerts?"

She laughed—a brittle tinkling sound that bounced prettily back from the curtain of trees. "No, hardly. Jarl and Bess were our founders. *Primus* and *Secundus* only mean first and second, in Latin."

"Latin? What's that? I—"

Ryly shut his mouth, suddenly. A cold tremor of delayed alarm passed through him. He stared at the Clingert in horror.

"Is something wrong?" the Clingert asked. "You look so pale."

"We're talking to each other," Ryly said. "We're holding a nice little conversation. Very friendly, and all."

She looked indignant. "Is anything wrong with that?"

"Yes," Ryly said glumly. "I'm supposed to hate you."

They walked together to the place where the waterfall cascaded in a bright foaming tumble down the mountainside, and they talked. And Ryly discovered that Clingerts were not quite so frightening as he had been led to believe.

His wanderings had brought him close to Clingert territory; Joanne had been but an hour from home when she had met him. But he nervously declined an offer to come to the Clingert settlement with her. That would be carrying things much too far.

After a while the Clingert said, "Do you hate me yet?"

"I don't think I'm going to hate you," Ryly told her. "I think I like you. And particularly every time I think of Hella—"

"Hella?" The Clingert's eyes flashed angrily.

"The Baille who was my betrothed." He accented the *was*. "Clanfather gave her to me last month. We were supposed to be married when I returned to the settlement. I thought I was looking forward to it too. Until—until—"

A wabbler mooed somewhere deeper in the forest. Ryly stared helplessly at the Clingert, realizing now what was happening to him.

He was falling in love with the Clingert.

Ever since the days when Thomas and Doris Baille first came to The World, Baille and Clingert had kept firm boundaries. Baille had mated only with Baille. And now—

Ryly shook his head sadly. In the blue-and-gold brilliance of the afternoon, this Clingert seemed infinitely more desirable to him than any Baille woman ever had.

She touched his hand gently. "You're very quiet. You're not at all like the Clingert men."

"I guess I'm not. What are they like?"

She made a little face. "Much shorter than you are, with ugly straight dark hair and black eyes. Their muscles bunch up in knots when they draw bows; your arms are long and lean. And Clingert men get bald at a very young age." Her hand lightly ruffled his Baille-yellow hair. "Do Bailles lose their hair young?"

"Bailles never get bald. Clanfather's hair is still as yellow as mine, and he's past fifty." Ryly fell silent again, thinking of Clanfather and what he would say if he knew what had taken place out here.

Not since the days when Thomas cast the first Clingert from his sight has this happened, he would probably intone in a deep, sententious voice.

Ryly remembered a time far away in his childhood when a Baille woman had birthed a dark-haired son. Clanfather had driven child and parents out into the forest, and there other Bailles had stoned them. Ryly was not anxious to share that fate. But yet—

He scrambled to his feet. The Clingert looked at him in alarm. "Where are you going?" she asked.

"Back. To the Baille settlement."

There was a moment of silence between them. Finally Ryly took a deep breath and said, "I'll return. Meet me at this place three days from now, at Dorisrise—I mean, when Secundus rises. Will you be here?"

Uneasiness glimmered in her dark eyes. "Yes," she said.

* * *

He reached the familiar Baille territory near nightfall the next day, having covered the outlying ground as rapidly as he could and with as few stops along the way as possible. He ducked back onto the main road around the time of Thomasset on Fiveday. He had had little difficulty in locating the tree that bore his name in its bark. Only the blue sun shone now, and it was low above the horizon; the moons were beginning their procession across the twilight-dimmed sky.

Ryly stole into the settlement on the back road. That route brought him past the crude little cabin which Thomas had built with his own hands as a place for Doris and himself to live, long ago when the first Bailles had tumbled out of the sky and settled on The World. Ryly quivered a little as he passed the dingy old shrine; the sort of betrayal he was contemplating did not come easy to him.

Above all, he did not want to be seen. Not until he had spoken with his phenotype-brother Davud.

A cat mewled. Ryly ducked into the concealing darkness of a vine bower and waited. A stiff-necked old man passed by: Clanfather. Ryly held his breath until the old one had entered the Clan house; he slipped out of his shelter, then padded silently across the main courtyard, and ran into the open archway that led to Davud's cabin.

The light was on. Davud was inside, drowsing in a chair. Ryly tiptoed through the rear door. He sprang across the room in four big bounds and clapped his hands over Davud's mouth before the other had fully come awake.

"It's me—Ryly. I'm back."

"*Mmph!*"

"Keep quiet and don't make any loud noises. I don't want people to find out I'm here yet."

He stepped back. Davud rubbed his lips and said, "What in Thomas' name made you want to scare me like that? For a second I thought it was a Clingert raid."

Ryly winced. He stared intently at Davud, wondering if it was safe to tell him. Davud, of all the Bailles, was closest to him in physique and in attitude, which was the reason Clanfather had designated them phenotype-brothers even though they had different parents. Among the Bailles, actual parentage meant little, since genetically every clan member was virtually identical to every other.

He and Davud were uncannily alike, though: both stand-

ing six-three, the Baille-norm height, both with the same twist
to their unruly blond hair, the same sharpness of nose, and the
same thinness of earlobe.

He poured a beaker of thick yellow bryophyte wine and
sipped it slowly to steady his nerves. "I have to talk to you,
Davud. Something very important has happened to me."

Ignoring that, Davud said, "You weren't supposed to
come back until tomorrow morning. I saw Hella around
Thomasset, and she said she couldn't wait to see you again."
Davud grinned. "I told her I was enough like you to do, but
she wouldn't listen to the idea."

"Don't talk about Hella. Listen to me, Davud. I went into
Clingert territory on my trip. I met a Clingert girl. I . . . love
her . . . I think."

Davud was on his feet in an instant, facing Ryly, brow to
brow, chin to chin. His nostrils were quivering. "What did you
just say?"

Very quietly Ryly repeated his words.

"I thought that was it," Davud muttered. "Ryly, are you
out of your head? Marry a Clingert? That *filth?*"

"But you haven't seen—"

"I don't need to see. You know the old stories of how the
first Clingert quarreled with Thomas until Thomas was forced
to drive him away. You know what sort of creatures the
Clingerts are. How can you possibly—"

"Love one? Davud, you don't know how easy it is. The
Baille girls are so damned big and brawny! Joanne is—well,
you'd have to see her to know. The fact that Thomas and the
first Clingert had some silly quarrel hundreds of years ago—"

Davud's face was a white mask of indignation. "*Ryly!* Get
hold of yourself! You're talking nonsense, man—absolute
nonsense. Baille and Clingert must never breed. Would you
want to pollute our line with theirs?"

"Yes." Defiantly.

"You're mad, then. But why did you come back here to
tell me about all this? Why didn't you simply stay with your
Clingert?"

"I wanted someone to know. Someone I could trust—like
you."

"You made a mistake in that case," Davud said. "I'm going
to tell Clanfather the whole story, and when they stone you I'll
be glad to take part. That's what they did the last time this

happened, fifteen years ago, if you remember. When Luri
Baille had a baby that looked like a Clingert. The line has to be
kept pure."

"Why?"

"It—it has to, that's all," Davud said weakly. As Ryly
started to walk out, he added, "Hey! Where do you think
you're going?"

"Back to the forest," Ryly said in a bitter voice. "I
promised her I'd be back. I should never have come here in
the first place." He was shaking and perspiring heavily;
somewhat to his own surprise he realized that by this conversation he had effectively cut himself off from the Bailles
forever.

"You're not going, Ryly. I won't let you."

Davud grabbed Ryly's collar, but he pulled away. "Don't
try to stop me, Davud."

Without replying, Davud gripped the fleshy part of his
arm. Calmly Ryly pivoted and smashed his fist into the face
that was so much like his own. Davud blinked, half believing,
and started to mutter something. Ryly quickly jerked his arm
free and hit Davud a second time. Davud sagged to the floor.

Ryly stood poised indecisively for a second, watching with
some astonishment the flow of blood from his phenotype-
brother's broken nose. Then he turned and dashed through
the doorway, out into the dark courtyard, and ran as hard as he
could for the forest road.

He listened for the shouts of pursuers but could hear
none yet. He wondered if perhaps he had hit Davud too hard.

Ryly spent an uneasy night in the forest not too far from
the edge of the Baille territory; when morning came, he
struck out at a rapid pace for the Baille-Clingert border.
Joanne would be at the waterfall by Dorisrise—he hoped.
For an instant he considered what would become of him if
she had been playing him false, but he reached no answer.
Could he return to the Bailles and marry Hella after all? He
didn't think so.

The day grew warmer as he half trotted through the
forest, following the series of trail-marks he had left to guide
himself. When he reached the trysting place, it was not yet
Dorisrise; Thomas alone was in the sky. Ryly sat by the water's
edge and splashed himself to clean away the sweat of travel.

He heard footsteps. He looked up, hoping it might be Joanne. But it was Davud who appeared.

"So you followed me?"

Davud nodded. "I had to, Ryly."

"And I suppose you brought the whole tribe behind you, all of them foaming at the mouth and ready to stone me." Ryly sighed. "I guess I didn't hit you hard enough, then. You woke up too soon."

Davud's nose was swollen and slightly askew. He said, "I came alone. I want to try to talk you out of this crazy thing, Ryly. Nobody else knows about it yet."

"Good. Now you go back and forget anything I said to you last night."

"I can't do that," Davud said. "I can't let you mate with a—a *Clingert*. I came to bring you back to Baille land with me."

Ryly clenched his fists. He had no desire to fight with his phenotype-brother a second time, but if Davud was going to insist—

"Get away from me, Davud. Go back alone."

It was almost Dorisrise time, now. Ryly hoped he would be able to get Davud out of the way before Joanne reached their rendezvous. But Davud was shaking his head stubbornly. "Baille and Clingert shall not breed. Thomas set that law down for us in the beginning, and it can never be broken. It is—"

He stopped, jaw sagging, and pointed. Slowly Ryly turned. The first rays of Doris glinted blue in the flowing waterfall, and Joanne stood behind him.

"Which of you is Ryly?" she asked plaintively.

Ryly unfroze first. "I am," he said. "This is my phenotype-brother Davud. He came with me to—meet you. Davud, this is Joanne."

"Is *this* a Clingert?" Davud asked slowly. "But—but— Clanfather always said they were *ugly*! And—"

Joanne laughed, her special Clingert sort of laugh that Ryly had already grown to love. "He seems stunned. Just as stunned as you were, three days ago. Do all of you Bailles think we're ogres?"

Davud sat down heavily on a rotting stump. His face was very pale by the light of the double suns; he was shaking his head reflectively and seemed to be talking quietly to himself.

At length he said, "All right. I apologize, Ryly. Now I see what you were talking about. *Now* I see!"

There was an overenthusiastic note in Davud's tone of voice that irked Ryly, but he refrained from voicing any annoyance. "What about Thomas and his laws now, Davud?" he said. "Now that you've seen a Clingert?"

"I take everything back," Davud murmured. "Everything."

Ryly glanced from his phenotype-brother to Joanne. "I guess we have his blessing, then. If—if you're willing to become an outcast from the Clingerts, that is."

Now it was Joanne's turn to look startled. "Outcast? For fulfilling the aim of the first Clingert?"

"What's that?"

"You mean you don't know?"

Ryly shook his head. "I don't have the faintest idea of what you're talking about."

"When it all started," she said patiently. "When the spaceship exploded and the Clingerts and Bailles were thrown free and landed on The World, hundreds of years ago, Jarl Clingert wanted to interbreed, but Thomas Baille wouldn't have any of it. He wanted to keep his line pure. So there hasn't been very much contact between Clingert and Baille since then, ever since the time the first Baille threatened without provocation to kill Jarl Clingert if he came within ten miles of—"

"Hold it," Ryly said. "It was Clingert who tried to kill Thomas Baille and marry Doris, but Thomas drove him off and—"

"No," said Joanne. "You've got it all backward. It was *Baille's* fault that—"

"Let's discuss ancient history some other time," Davud interjected suddenly. There was a curiously pained expression on his face. "Ryly, do you mind if I talk to you alone a moment?"

"Why—all right," Ryly said, surprised.

They drew a few feet farther away, and Ryly said, "Well? What do you think of her?"

"That's what I want to talk to you about," Davud whispered harshly. "I think she's far and away above the Baille women. She's so—*different*. Gentle but not weak, small but not flimsy—"

"I knew you'd like her, Davud."

"Not *like*," Davud groaned. "*Love*. I love her too, Ryly."

It came like a blow across the face. Ryly's eyes widened and stared into the equally blue ones of his phenotype-brother. The Baille genes had been duplicated perfectly among them, it seemed. In every respect.

"You can't mean that," Ryly said.

"I do. Dammit, I do. How can I help it?"

"We can't *both* have her, Davud. And I think I have priority. I—"

Davud gasped and seized him suddenly, spinning him around. Ryly looked, shut his eyes, touched his fingers lightly to his eyelids, and looked again. The mirage was still there. It was no illusion.

He saw two Joannes.

"Ryly? Davud? Meet Melena. Melena Clingert."

"Is she—your sister?" Ryly asked hoarsely. The two Clingerts were, at this distance, identical.

"My cousin," Joanne said. "I don't have any sisters." She grinned. "Melena was hiding near the far side of the waterfall. I brought her along to have a peek at Ryly."

Ryly and his phenotype-brother exchanged astonished glances.

"Of course," Ryly said softly. "We Bailles all look alike; why shouldn't the Clingerts? Three hundred years of inbreeding. Lord, they must all be identical!"

"More or less," Joanne said. "There are some minor variations but not many. Most of the unfixed genes in the clan were lost generations ago. As probably happened in your clan too. This was the thing that Jarl Clingert wanted to avoid, but when Thomas Baille refused to—"

"It was Clingert's treacherous ways that caused the whole thing," Ryly snapped. "Let's get that straight right now. Why, it's common knowledge!"

"Among whom? Among the Bailles, that's who—whom!" Joanne's eyes were blazing again, with the fury Ryly loved so much to see. "But why don't you listen to the Clingert side of the story for a change? You Bailles were always like that, shutting your ears to anything important. You—" She stopped in mid-breath. Very quietly she said, "I'm sorry, Ryly."

"It was my fault. I started the whole thing."

"No," she said, shaking her head. "I did, when I brought up the topic of—"

He smiled and touched a finger lightly to her lips. "Look," he said.

She looked. Davud and Melena had drawn to one side, standing on a moist, moss-covered patch of ground within the field of spray and foam of the waterfall. They were talking softly. It wasn't difficult to see by their faces what the topic of discussion was.

"We'll have to forget about ancient history now," Joanne said. "Forget all about what happened between Jarl Clingert and Thomas Baille four centuries ago."

Ryly took her hand. "We'll go somewhere else on The World," he said. "Start all over, build a new settlement. Just the four of us. And maybe we can recruit some others, if I can lure a few Bailles out here to meet Clingerts."

"And vice versa. The Clingert men hate the Bailles now too, you know. But that can stop. We'll breed the feuding out."

Ryly looked over at Davud and Melena, then back at Joanne. Everything looked incredibly lovely at that moment—the angular red leaves of the overhanging trees, the white spray of the falls, prismatically colored blue and gold by the sunlight, the quiet green clouds drifting above. He wanted to fix that moment in his mind forever.

He smiled. His mind was still full of insidious Clanfather-instilled legends of the early days on The World as seen through Baille eyes. But he could start forgetting them now.

Soon there would be a third clan on The World—a hybrid clan, both fair and dark, both short and tall.

And someday his descendants would be spinning legends about *him*, and how he had helped to found the clan, back in the misty time-shrouded days of the remote past.

Neighbor

Fresh snow had fallen during the night. It lay like a white sheet atop the older snow, nine or ten feet of it, that already covered the plain. Now all was smooth and clear almost to the horizon. As Michael Holt peered through the foot-thick safety glass of his command-room window, he saw, first of all, the zone of brown earth, a hundred yards in diameter, circling his house, and then the beginning of the snowfield with a few jagged bare trees jutting through it, and then, finally, a blot on the horizon, the metallic tower that was Andrew McDermott's dwelling.

Not in seventy or eighty years had Holt looked at the McDermott place without feeling hatred and irritation. The planet was big enough, wasn't it? Why had McDermott chosen to stick his pile of misshapen steel down right where Holt had to look at it all his days? The McDermott estate was large. McDermott could have built his house another fifty or sixty miles to the east, near the banks of the wide, shallow river that flowed through the heart of the continent. He hadn't cared to. Holt had politely suggested it, when the surveyors and architects first came out from Earth. McDermott had just as politely insisted on putting his house where he wanted to put it.

It was still there. Michael Holt peered at it, and his insides roiled. He walked to the control console of the armament panel, and let his thin, gnarled hands rest for a moment on a gleaming rheostat.

There was an almost sexual manner to the way Holt fondled the jutting knobs and studs of the console. Now that his two-hundredth year was approaching, he rarely handled the bodies of his wives anymore. But, then, he did not love his wives as keenly as he loved the artillery emplacement with which he could blow Andrew McDermott to atoms.

Just let him provoke me, Holt thought.

He stood by the panel, a tall, gaunt man with a withered face and a savage hook of a nose and a surprisingly thick shock of faded red hair. He closed his eyes and allowed himself the luxury of a daydream.

He imagined that Andrew McDermott had given him offense. Not simply the eternal offense of being there in his view, but some direct, specific affront. Poaching on his land, perhaps. Or sending a robot out to hack down a tree on the borderland. Or putting up a flashing neon sign mocking Holt in some vulgar way. Anything that would serve as an excuse for hostilities.

And then: Holt saw himself coming up here to the command room and broadcasting an ultimatum to the enemy. "Take that sign down, McDermott," he might say. "Keep your robots off my land," perhaps. "Or else this means war."

McDermott would reply with a blast of radiation, of course, because that was the kind of sneak he was. The deflector screens of Holt's frontline defenses would handle the bolt with ease, soaking it in and feeding the energy straight to Holt's own generators.

Then, at long last, Holt would answer back. His fingers would tighten on the controls. Crackling arcs of energy would leap toward the ionosphere and bound downward at McDermott's place, spearing through his pitiful screens as though they weren't there. Holt saw himself gripping the controls with knuckle-whitening fervor, launching thunderbolt after thunderbolt, while on the horizon Andrew McDermott's hideous keep blazed and glowed in hellish fire, and crumpled and toppled and ran in molten puddles over the snow.

Yes, that would be the moment to live for!

That would be the moment of triumph!

To step back from the controls at last and look through the window and see the glowing red spot on the horizon where the McDermott place had been. To pat the controls as though they were the flanks of a beloved old horse. To leave the house, and ride across the borderland into the McDermott estate, and see the charred ruin, and know that he was gone forever.

Then, of course, there would be an inquiry. The fifty lords of the planet would meet to discuss the battle, and Holt would explain, "He wantonly provoked me. I need not tell you how he gave me offense by building his house within my view. But this time—"

And Holt's fellow lords would nod sagely, and would understand, for they valued their own unblemished views as highly as Holt himself. They would exonerate him and grant

him McDermott's land, as far as the horizon, so no newcomer
could repeat the offense.

Michael Holt smiled. The daydream left him satisfied.
His heart raced perhaps a little too enthusiastically as he
pictured the slagheap on the horizon. He made an effort to
calm himself. He was, after all, a fragile old man, much as he
hated to admit it, and even the excitement of a daydream
taxed his strength.

He walked away from the panel, back to the window.
Nothing had changed. The zone of brown earth where his
melters kept back the snow, and then the white field, and
finally the excrescence on the horizon, glinting coppery red in
the thin midday sunlight. Holt scowled. The daydream had
changed nothing. No shot had been fired. McDermott's keep
still stained the view. Turning, Holt began to shuffle slowly
out of the room, toward the dropshaft that would take him five
floors downward to his family.

The communicator chimed. Holt stared at the screen in
surprise.

"Yes?"

"An outside call for you, Lord Holt. Lord McDermott is
calling," the bland metallic voice said.

"Lord McDermott's secretary, you mean."

"It is Lord McDermott himself, your lordship."

Holt blinked. "You're joking," he said. "It's fifty years
since he called me. If this is a prank, I'll have your circuits
shorted!"

"I cannot joke, your lordship. Shall I tell Lord McDermott you do not wish to speak to him?"

"Of course," Holt snapped. "No . . . wait. Find out what
he wants. *Then* tell him I can't speak to him."

Holt sank back into a chair in front of the screen. He
nudged a button with his elbow, and tiny hands began to
massage the muscles of his back, where tension-poisons had
suddenly flooded in to stiffen him.

McDermott calling? What for?

To complain, of course. Some trespass, no doubt. Some
serious trespass, if McDermott felt he had to make the call
himself. Michael Holt's blood warmed. Let him complain! Let
him acuse, let him bluster! Perhaps this would give the excuse
for hostilities at last. Holt ached to declare war. He had been
building his armaments patiently for decade after decade, and

he knew beyond doubt that he had the capability to destroy McDermott moments after the first shot was fired. No screens in the universe could withstand the array of weaponry Holt had assembled. The outcome of a conflict was in no doubt. *Let him start something,* Michael Holt prayed. *Oh, let him be the aggressor! I'm ready for him, and more than ready!*

The bell chimed again. The robot voice of Holt's secretary said, "I have spoken to him, your lordship. He will tell me nothing. He wants to speak to you."

Holt sighed. "Very well. Put him on, then."

There was a moment of electronic chaos on the screen as the robot shifted from the inside channel to an outside one. Holt sat stiffly, annoyed by the sudden anxiety he felt. He realized, strangely, that he had forgotten what his enemy's voice sounded like. All communications between them had been through robot intermediaries for years.

The screen brightened and showed a test pattern. A hoarse, querulous voice said, "Holt? Holt, where are you?"

"Right here in my chair, McDermott. What's troubling you?"

"Turn your vision on. Let me have a look at you, Holt."

"You can speak your piece without seeing me, can't you? Is my face that fascinating to you?"

"Please. This is no time for bickering. Turn the vision on!"

"Let me remind you," Holt said coldly, "that *you* have called *me*. The normal rules of etiquette require that I have the privilege of deciding on the manner of transmission. And I prefer not to be seen. I also prefer not to be speaking to you. You have thirty seconds to state your complaint. Important business awaits me."

There was silence. Holt gripped the arms of his chair and signaled for a more intense massage. He became aware, in great irritation, that his hands were trembling. He glared at the screen as though he could burn his enemy's brain out simply by sending angry thoughts over the communicator.

McDermott said finally, "I have no complaint, Holt. Only an invitation."

"To tea?"

"Call it that. I want you to come here, Holt."

"You've lost your mind!"

"Not yet. Come to me. Let's have a truce," McDermott

rasped. "We're both old, sick, stupid men. It's time to stop the hatred."

Holt laughed. "We're both old, yes. But I'm not sick and you're the only stupid one. Isn't it a little late for the olive branch?"

"Never too late."

"You know there can't be peace between us," Holt said. "Not so long as that eyesore of yours sticks up over the trees. It's a cinder in my eye, McDermott. I can't ever forgive you for building it."

"Will you listen to me?" McDermott said. "When I'm gone, you can blast the place apart, if it pleases you. All I want is for you to come here. I—I need you, Holt. I want you to pay me a visit."

"Why don't you come here, then?" Holt jeered. "I'll throw my door wide for you. We'll sit by the fire and reminisce about all the years we hated each other."

"If I could come to you," McDermott said, "there would be no need for us to meet at all."

"What do you mean?"

"Turn your visual on, and you'll see."

Michael Holt frowned. He knew he had become hideous with age, and he was not eager to show himself to his enemy. But he could not see McDermott without revealing himself at the same time. With an abrupt, impulsive gesture, Holt jabbed the control button in his chair. The mists on the screen faded, and an image appeared.

All Holt could see was a face, shrunken, wizened, wasted. McDermott was past two hundred, Holt knew, and he looked it. There was no flesh left on his face. The skin lay like parchment over bone. The left side of his face was distorted, the nostril flared, the mouth corner dragged down to reveal the teeth, the eyelid drooping. Below the chin, McDermott was invisible, swathed in machinery, his body cocooned in what was probably a nutrient bath. He was obviously in bad shape.

He said, "I've had a stroke, Holt. I'm paralyzed from the neck down. I can't hurt you."

"When did this happen?"

"A year ago."

"You've kept very quiet about it," Holt said.

"I didn't think you'd care to know. But now I do. I'm

dying, Holt, and I want to see you once face to face before I die.
I know, you're suspicious. You think I'm crazy to ask you to
come here. Well, maybe I am crazy. I'll turn my screens off. I'll
send all my robots across the river. I'll be absolutely alone here,
helpless, and you can come with an army if you like. There.
Doesn't that sound like a trap, Holt? I know I'd think so if I were
in your place and you were in mine. But it isn't a trap. Can you
believe that? I'll open my door to you. You can come and laugh
in my face as I lie here. But come. There's something I have to
tell you, something of vital importance to you. And you've got to
be here in person when I tell you. You won't regret coming.
Believe that, Holt."

Holt stared at the wizened creature on the screen, and
trembled with doubt and confusion. The man must be a lunatic!
It was years since Holt had last stepped beyond the protection
of his own screens. Now McDermott was asking him not only to
go into the open field, where he might be gunned down with
ease, but to enter into McDermott's house itself, to put his head
right between the jaws of the lion.

Absurd!

McDermott said, "Let me show you my sincerity. My
screens are off. Take a shot at the house. Hit it anywhere. Go
ahead. Do your worst!"

Deeply troubled, chilled with mystification, Holt elbowed
out of his chair, went beyond the range of the visual pickup,
over to the control console of the guns. How many times in
dreams he had fondled these studs and knobs, never firing them
once, except in test shots directed at his own property! It was
unreal to be actually training the sights on the gleaming tower of
McDermott's house at last. Excitement surged in him. Could
this all be some subtle way, he wondered, of causing him to
have a fatal heart attack through overstimulation?

He gripped the controls. He pondered, considered tossing
a thousand-megawatt beam at McDermott, then decided to use
something a little milder. If the screens really were down all the
way, even his feeblest shot would score.

He sighted—not on the house itself, but on a tree just
within McDermott's inner circle of defense. He fired, still half
convinced he was dreaming. The tree became a yard-high
stump.

"That's it," McDermott called. "Go on. Aim at the house,
too. Knock a turret off. The screens are down."

Senile dementia, Holt thought. Baffled, he lifted the sight a bit and let the beam play against one of McDermott's outbuildings. The shielded wall glowed a moment, then gave as the beam smashed its way through. Ten square feet of McDermott's castle now was a soup of protons, fleeing into the cold.

Holt realized in stunned disbelief that there was nothing at all preventing him from destroying McDermott and his odious house entirely. There was no risk of a counterattack. He would not even need to use the heavy artillery that he had been so jealously hoarding against this day. A light beam would do it easily enough.

It would be too easy this way, though.

There could be no pleasure in a wanton attack. McDermott had not provoked him. Rather, he sat there in his cocoon, sniveling and begging to be visited.

Holt returned to the visual field. "I must be as crazy as you are," he said. "Turn your robots loose and leave your screens down. I'll come to visit you. I wish I understood this, but I'll come anyway."

Michael Holt called his family together. Three wives, the eldest near his own age, the youngest only seventy. Seven sons, ranging in age from sixty to a hundred thirteen. The wives of his sons. His grandchildren. His top echelon of robots.

He assembled them in the grand hall of Holt Keep, and took his place at the head of the table, and stared down the rows at their faces, so like his own, and said quietly, "I am going to pay a call on Lord McDermott."

He could see the shock on their faces. They were too well disciplined to speak their minds, of course. He was Lord Holt, and his word was law, and he could, if he so pleased, order them all put to death on the spot. Once, many years before, he had been forced to assert his parental authority in just such a way, and no one would ever forget it.

He smiled. "You think I've gone soft in my old age, and perhaps I have. But McDermott has had a stroke. He's completely paralyzed from the neck down. He wants to tell me something, and I'm going to go. His screens are down and he's sending all his robots out of the house. I could have blasted the place apart if I wanted to."

He could see the muscles working in the jaws of his sons. They wanted to cry out, but they did not dare.

Holt went on, "I'm going alone except for a few robots. If there's been no word from me for half an hour after I'm seen entering the house, you're authorized to come after me. If there's any interference with the rescue party, it will mean war. But I don't think there'll be trouble. Anyone who comes after me in less than half an hour will be put to death."

Holt's words died away in a shiver of echoes. He eyed them all, one at a time. This was a critical moment, he knew. If they dared, they might decide among themselves that he had gone mad, and depose him. That had happened before too, in other families. They could topple him, reprogram all the robots to take commands from them instead, and confine him to his wing of the house. He had given them evidence enough, just now, of his irresponsibility.

But they made no move. They lacked the guts. He was head of the household, and his word was law. They sat, pale and shaken and dazed, as he rolled his chair past them and out of the grand hall.

Within an hour, he was ready to go. Winter was in the fourth of its seven months, and Michael Holt had not left the house since the first snowfall. But he had nothing to fear from the elements. He would not come in contact with the frigid air of the sub-zero plain. He entered his car within his own house, and it glided out past the defense perimeter, a gleaming dark teardrop sliding over the fresh snow. Eight of his robots accompanied him, a good enough army for almost any emergency.

A visual pickup showed him the scene at McDermott Keep. The robots were filing out, an army of black ants clustering around the great gate. He could see them marching eastward, vanishing from sight beyond the house. A robot overhead reported that they were heading for the river by the dozens.

The miles flew past. Black, twisted trees poked through the snow, and Holt's car weaved a way through them. Far below, under many feet of whiteness, lay the fertile fields. In the spring, all would be green, and the leafy trees would help to shield the view of McDermott's Keep, though they could not hide it altogether. In winter, the ugly copper-colored house was totally visible. That made the winters all the more difficult for Holt to endure.

A robot said softly, "We are approaching the borderlands, your lordship."

"Try a test shot. See if his screens are still down."

"Shall I aim for the house?"

"No. A tree just in front of it."

Holt watched. A thick-boled, stubby tree in McDermott's front palisade gleamed a moment, and then was not there.

"The screens are still down," the robot reported.

"All right. Let's cross the border."

He leaned back against the cushion. The car shot forward. They left the bounds of Holt's own estate, now, and entered McDermott's. There was no warning ping to tell them they were trespassing. McDermott had even turned off the boundary scanners, then. Holt pressed sweaty palms together. More than ever he felt that he had let himself be drawn into some sort of trap. There was no turning back, now. He was across the border, into McDermott's own territory. Better to die boldly, he thought, than to live huddled in a shell.

He had never been this close to McDermott Keep before. When it was being built, McDermott had invited him to inspect it, but Holt had of course refused. Nor had he been to the housewarming; alone among the lords of the planet, he had stayed home to sulk. He could hardly even remember when he had last left his own land at all. There were few places to go on this world, with its fifty estates of great size running through the temperate belt, and whenever Holt thirsted for the companionship of his fellow lords, which was not often, he could have it easily enough via telescreen. Some of them came to him, now and then. It was strange that when he finally did stir to pay a call, it should be a call on McDermott.

Drawing near the enemy keep, he found himself reluctantly admitting that it was less ugly at close range than it seemed from the windows of Holt Keep. It was a great blocky building, hundreds of yards long, with a tall octagonal tower rising out of its northern end, a metal spike jabbing perhaps five hundred feet high. The reflected afternoon light, bouncing from the snowfield, gave the metal-sheathed building a curiously oily look, not unattractive at this distance.

"We are within the outer defense perimeter," a robot told Holt.

"Fine. Keep going."

The robots sounded worried and perturbed, he thought.

Of course, they weren't programmed to show much emotional range, but he could detect a note of puzzlement in what they said and how they said it. They couldn't understand this at all. It did not seem to be an invasion of McDermott Keep—that they could understand—but yet it was not a friendly visit, either.

When they were a hundred yards from the great gate of McDermott Keep, the doors swung open. Holt called McDermott and said, "See that those doors stay open all the time I'm here. If they begin to close, there'll be trouble."

"Don't worry," McDermott said. "I'm not planning any tricks."

Holt's car shot between the gate walls, and he knew that now he was at his enemy's mercy. His car rolled up to the open carport and went on through, so that he was actually within McDermott Keep. His robots followed him through.

"May I close the carport?" McDermott asked.

"Keep it open," Holt said. "I don't mind the cold."

The hood of his car swung back. His robots helped him out. Holt shivered momentarily as the cold outside air, filtering into the carport, touched him. Then he passed through the rising inner door, and, flanked by two sturdy robots, walked slowly but doggedly into the keep.

McDermott's voice reached him over the loudspeaker. "I am on the third floor of the tower," he said. "If I had not sent all the robots away, I could have let one of them guide you."

"You could send a member of your family down," Holt said sourly.

McDermott ignored that. "Continue down the corridor until it turns. Go past the armor room. You will reach a dropshaft that leads upward."

Holt and his robots moved through the silent halls. The place was like a museum. The dark high-vaulted corridor was lined with statuary and artifacts, everything musty-looking and depressing. How could anyone want to live in a tomb like this? Holt passed a shadowy room where ancient suits of armor stood mounted. He could not help but compute the cost of shipping such useless things across the light-years from Earth.

They came to the dropshaft. Holt and his two robots entered. A robot nudged the reversing stud and up they went, into the tower Holt had hated so long. McDermott guided them with a word of two.

They passed down a long hall whose dull, dark walls were set off by a gleaming floor that looked like onyx. A sphincter opened, admitting them to an oval room ringed by windows. There was a dry, foul stench of death and decay in the room. Andrew McDermott sat squarely in the middle of the room, nesting in his life-capsule. A tangled network of tubes and pipes surrounded him. All of McDermott that was visible was a pair of eyes, like shining coals in the wasted face.

"I'm glad you came," McDermott said. His voice, without benefit of electronic amplification, was thin and feeble, like the sound of feathers brushing through the air.

Holt stared at him in fascination. "I never thought I'd see this room," he said.

"I never thought you would either. But it was good of you to come, Holt. You look well, you know. For a man your age." The thin lips curled in a grotesque twisted smile. "Of course, you're still a youngster. Not even two hundred, yet. I've got you by thirty years."

Holt did not feel like listening to the older man's ramblings. "What is it you wanted?" he asked without warmth. "I'm here, but I'm not going to stay all day. You said you had something vital to tell me."

"Not really to tell," McDermott said. "More to ask. A favor. I want you to kill me, Holt."

"What?"

"It's very simple. Disconnect my feed line. There it is, right by my feet. Just rip it out. I'll be dead in an hour. Or do it even more quickly. Turn off my lungs. This switch, right here. That would be the humane way to do it."

"You have a strange sense of humor," Holt said.

"Do you think so? Top the joke, then. Throw the switch and cap the jest."

"You made me come all the way here to *kill* you?"

"Yes," McDermott said. The blazing eyes were unblinking now. "I've been immobilized for a year, now. I'm a vegetable in this thing. I sit here day after day, idle, bored. And healthy. I might live another hundred years, do you realize that, Holt? I've had a stroke, yes. I'm paralyzed. But my body's still vigorous. This damned capsule of mine keeps me in tone. It feeds me and exercises me and—do you think I want to go on living this way, Holt? Would you?"

Holt shrugged. "If you want to die, you could ask someone in your family to unplug you."

"I have no family."

"Is that true? You had five sons . . ."

"Four dead, Holt. The other one gone to Earth. No one lives here any more. I've outlasted them all. I'm as eternal as the heavens. Two hundred thirty years, that's long enough to live. My wives are dead, my grandchildren gone away. They'll come home when they find they've inherited. Not before. There's no one here to throw the switch."

"Your robots," Holt suggested.

Again the grim smile. "You must have special robots, Holt. I don't have any that can be tricked into killing their master. I've tried it. They know what'll happen if my life-capsule is disconnected. They won't do it. *You* do it, Holt. Turn me off. Blow the tower to hell, if it bothers you. You've won the game. The prize is yours."

There was a dryness in Holt's throat, a band of pressure across his chest. He tottered a little. His robots, ever sensitive to his condition, steadied him and guided him to a chair. He had been on his feet a long time for a man of his age. He sat quietly until the spasm passed.

Then he said, "I won't do it."

"Why not?"

"It's too simple, McDermott. I've hated you too long. I can't just flip a switch and turn you off."

"Bombard me, then. Blast the tower down."

"Without provocation? Do you think I'm a criminal?" Holt asked.

"What do you want me to do?" McDermott said tiredly. "Order my robots to trespass? Set fire to your orchards? What will provoke you, Holt?"

"Nothing," Holt said. "I don't want to kill you. Get someone else to do it."

The eyes glittered. "You devil," McDermott said. "You absolute devil. I never realized how much you hated me. I send for you in a time of need, asking to be put out of my misery, and will you grant me that? Oh, no. Suddenly you get noble. You won't kill me! You devil, I see right through you. You'll go back to your keep and gloat because I'm a living dead man here. You'll chuckle to yourself because I'm alone and frozen into this capsule. Oh, Holt, it's not right to hate so deeply! I admit I've given offense. I deliberately built the tower here to wound your pride. Punish me, then. Take my life. Destroy my tower. Don't leave me here!"

Holt was silent. He moistened his lips, filled his lungs with breath, got to his feet. He stood straight and tall, towering over the capsule that held his enemy.

"Throw the switch," McDermott begged.

"I'm sorry. I can't."

"Devil!"

Holt looked at his robots. "It's time to go," he said. "There's no need for you to guide us. We can find our way out of the building."

The teardrop-shaped car sped across the shining snow. Holt said nothing as he made the return journey. His mind clung to the image of the immobilized McDermott, and there was no room for any other thought. That stench of decay tingled in his nostrils. That glint of madness in the eyes as they begged for oblivion.

They were crossing the borderlands, now. Holt's car broke the warning barrier and got a pinging signal to halt and identify. A robot gave the password, and they went on toward Holt Keep.

His family clustered near the entrance, pale, mystified. Holt walked in under his own steam. They were bursting with questions, but no one dared ask anything. It remained for Holt to say the first word.

He said, "McDermott's a sick, crazy old man. His family is dead or gone. He's a pathetic and disgusting sight. I don't want to talk about the visit."

Sweeping past them, Holt ascended the shaft to the command room. He peered out, over the snowy field. There was a double track in the snow, leading to and from McDermott Keep, and the sunlight blazed in the track, making it a line of fire stretching to the horizon.

The building shuddered suddenly. Holt heard a hiss and a whine. He flipped on his communicator and a robot voice said, "McDermott Keep is attacking, your lordship. We've deflected a high-energy bombardment."

"Did the screens have any trouble with it?"

"No, your lordship. Not at all. Shall I prepare for a counterattack?"

Holt smiled. "No," he said. "Take defensive measures only. Extend the screens right to the border and keep them there. Don't let McDermott do any harm. He's only trying to provoke me, but he won't succeed."

The tall, gaunt man walked to the control panel. His gnarled hands rested lovingly on the equipment. So they had come to warfare at last, he thought. The cannon of McDermott Keep were doing their puny worst. Flickering needles told the story: whatever McDermott was throwing was being absorbed easily. He didn't have the firepower to do real harm.

Holt's hands tightened on the controls. Now, he thought, he could blast McDermott Keep to ash. But he would not do it, any more than he would throw the switch that would end Andrew McDermott's life.

McDermott did not understand. Not cruelty, but simple selfishness, had kept him from killing the enemy lord, just as, all these years, Holt had refrained from launching an attack he was certain to win. He felt remotely sorry for the paralyzed man locked in the life-capsule. But it was inconceivable that Holt would kill him.

Once you are gone, Andrew, who will I have to hate? Holt wondered.

That was why he had not killed. No reason more complicated than that.

Michael Holt peered through the foot-thick safety glass of his command-room window. He saw the zone of brown earth, the snowfield with its fresh track, and the coppery ugliness of McDermott Keep. His intestines writhed at the ugliness of that baroque tower against the horizon. He imagined the skyline as it had looked a hundred years ago, before McDermott had built his foul monstrosity there.

He fondled the controls of his artillery bank as though they were a young girl's breasts. Then he turned, slowly and stiffly, making his way across the command-room to his chair, and sat quietly, listening to the sound of Andrew McDermott's futile bombardment expending itself harmlessly against the outer defenses of Holt Keep, and soon it grew dark as the winter night closed quietly down.

The Man Who Never Forgot

He saw the girl waiting in line outside a big Los Angeles movie house, on a mildly foggy Tuesday morning. She was slim and pale, barely five-three, with stringy flaxen hair, and she was alone. He remembered her, of course.

He knew it would be a mistake, but he crossed the street anyway and walked up along the theater line to where she stood.

"Hello," he said.

She turned, stared at him blankly and flicked the tip of her tongue out for an instant over her lips. "I don't believe I—"

"Tom Niles," he said. "Pasadena, New Year's Day, 1955. You sat next to me. Ohio State 20, Southern Cal 7. You don't remember?"

"A football game? But I hardly ever—I mean—I'm sorry, mister. I—"

Someone else in the line moved forward toward him with a tight hard scowl on his face. Niles knew when he was beaten. He smiled apologetically and said, "I'm sorry, miss. I guess I made a mistake. I took you for someone I knew—a Miss Bette Torrance. Excuse me."

And he strode rapidly away. He had not gone more than ten feet when he heard the little surprised gasp and the "But I *am* Bette Torrance!"—but he kept going.

I should know better after twenty-eight years, he thought bitterly. *But I forget the most basic fact—that even though I remember people, they don't necessarily remember me—*

He walked wearily to the corner, turned right, and started down a new street, one whose shops were totally unfamiliar to him and which, therefore, he had never seen before. His mind, stimulated to its normal pitch of activity by the incident outside the theater, spewed up a host of tangential memories like the good machine it was: *Jan. 1, 1955. Rose Bowl Pasadena California Seat G126; warm day, high humidity, arrived in stadium 12:03 P.M., PST. Came alone. Girl in next seat wearing blue cotton dress, white oxfords, carrying Southern Cal pennant. Talked to her. Name Bette Torrance,* *senior at Southern Cal, government major. Had a date for the game but he came down with flu symptoms night before, insisted she see game anyway. Seat on other side of her empty. Bought her a hot dog, $.20 (no mustard)—*

There was more, much more. Niles forced it back down. There was the virtually stenographic report of their conversation all that day:

(". . . I hope we win. I saw the last Bowl game we won, two years ago . . ."

". . . Yes, that was 1953. Southern Cal 7, Wisconsin 0 . . . and two straight wins in 1944-45 over Washington and Tennessee . . ."

". . . Gosh, you know a lot about football! What did you do, memorize the record book?")

And the old memories. The jeering yell of freckled Joe Merritt that warm April day in 1937—*who are you, Einstein?* And Buddy Call saying acidly on November 8, 1939, *Here comes Tommy Niles, the human adding machine. Get him!* And then the bright stinging pain of a snowball landing just below his left clavicle, the pain that he could summon up as easily as any of the other pain-memories he carried with him. He winced and closed his eyes suddenly, as if struck by the icy pellet here on a Los Angeles street on a foggy Tuesday morning.

They didn't call him the human adding machine any more. Now it was the human tape recorder; the derisive terms had to keep pace with the passing decades. Only Niles himself remained unchanging, The Boy With The Brain Like A Sponge grown up into The Man With The Brain Like A Sponge, still cursed with the same terrible gift.

His data-cluttered mind ached. He saw a diminutive yellow sports car parked on the far side of the street, recognized it by its make and model and color and license number as the car belonging to Leslie F. Marshall, twenty-six, blond hair, blue eyes, television actor with the following credits—

Wincing, Niles applied the cutoff circuit and blotted out the upwelling data. He had met Marshall once, six months ago, at a party given by a mutual friend—an erstwhile mutual friend; Niles found it difficult to keep friends for long. He had spoken with the actor for perhaps ten minutes and had added that much more baggage to his mind.

It was time to move on, Niles decided. He had been in

Los Angeles ten months. The burden of accumulated memories was getting too heavy; he was greeting too many people who had long since forgotten him (*curse my John Q. Average build, 5 feet 9, 163 pounds, brownish hair, brownish eyes, no unduly prominent physical features, no distinguishing scars except those inside*, he thought). He contemplated returning to San Francisco, and decided against it. He had been there only a year ago; Pasadena, two years ago. The time had come, he realized, for another eastward jaunt.

Back and forth across the face of America goes Thomas Richard Niles, Der fliegende Holländer, the Wandering Jew, the Ghost of Christmas Past, the Human Tape Recorder. He smiled at a newsboy who had sold him a copy of the *Examiner* on May 13 past, got the usual blank stare in return, and headed for the nearest bus terminal.

For Niles the long journey had begun on October 11, 1929, in the small Ohio town of Lowry Bridge. He was third of three children, born of seemingly normal parents, Henry Niles (b. 1896), Mary Niles (b. 1899). His older brother and sister had shown no extraordinary manifestations. Tom had.

It began as soon as he was old enough to form words; a neighbor woman on the front porch peered into the house where he was playing, and remarked to his mother, "Look how *big* he's getting, Mary!"

He was less than a year old. He had replied, in virtually the same tone of voice, "*Look how* big *he's getting, Mary!*" It caused a sensation, even though it was only mimicry, not even speech.

He spent his first twelve years in Lowry Bridge, Ohio. In later years, he often wondered how he had been able to last there so long.

He began school at the age of four, because there was no keeping him back; his classmates were five and six, vastly superior to him in physical coordination, vastly inferior in everything else. He could read. He could even write, after a fashion, though his babyish muscles tired easily from holding a pen. And he could remember.

He remembered everything. He remembered his parents' quarrels and repeated the exact words of them to anyone who cared to listen, until his father whipped him and threatened to kill him if he ever did *that* again. He remembered that too. He remembered the lies his brother and sister told, and took great pains to set the record straight. He learned eventually not to do that, either. He remembered things people had said, and corrected them when they later deviated from their earlier statements.

He remembered everything.

He read a textbook once and it stayed with him. When the teacher asked a question based on the day's assignment, Tommy Niles' skinny arm was in the air long before the others had even really assimilated the question. After a while, his teacher made it clear to him that he could *not* answer every question, whether he had the answer first or not; there were twenty other pupils in the class. The other pupils in the class made that abundantly clear to him, after school.

He won the verse-learning contest in Sunday school. Barry Harman had studied for weeks in hopes of winning the catcher's mitt his father had promised him if he finished first—but when it was Tommy Niles' turn to recite, he began with *In the beginning God created the heaven and the earth,* continued through *Thus the heavens and the earth were finished, and all the host of them,* headed on into *Now the serpent was more subtil than any beast of the field which the Lord God had made,* and presumably would have continued clear through Genesis, Exodus, and on to Joshua if the dazed proctor hadn't shut him up and declared him the winner. Barry Harman didn't get his glove; Tommy Niles got a black eye instead.

He began to realize he was different. It took time to make the discovery that other people were always forgetting things, and that instead of admiring him for what he could do they hated him for it. It was difficult for a boy of eight, even Tommy Niles, to understand *why* they hated him, but eventually he did find out, and then he started learning how to hide his gift.

Through his ninth and tenth years he practiced being normal, and almost succeeded; the after-school beatings stopped, and he managed to get a few Bs on his report cards at last, instead of straight rows of A. He was growing up; he was learning to pretend. Neighbors heaved sighs of relief, now that that terrible Niles boy was no longer doing all those crazy things.

But inwardly he was the same as ever. And he realized he'd have to leave Lowry Bridge soon.

He knew everyone too well. He would catch them in lies

ten times a week, even Mr. Lawrence, the minister, who once turned down an invitation to pay a social call to the Nileses one night, saying, "I really have to get down to work and write my sermon for Sunday," when only three days before Tommy had heard him say to Miss Emery, the church secretary, that he had had a sudden burst of inspiration and had written three sermons all at one sitting, and now he'd have some free time for the rest of the month.

Even Mr. Lawrence lied, then. And he was the best of them. As for the others—

Tommy waited until he was twelve; he was big for his age by then and figured he could take care of himself. He borrowed twenty dollars from the supposedly secret cashbox in the back of the kitchen cupboard (his mother had mentioned its existence five years before, in Tommy's hearing) and tiptoed out of the house at three in the morning. He caught the night freight for Chillicothe, and was on his way.

There were thirty people on the bus out of Los Angeles. Niles sat alone in the back, by the seat just over the rear wheel. He knew four of the people in the bus by name—but he was confident they had forgotten who he was by now, and so he kept to himself.

It was an awkward business. If you said hello to someone who had forgotten you, they thought you were a troublemaker or a panhandler. And if you passed someone by, thinking he had forgotten you, and he hadn't—well, then you were a snob. Niles swung between both those poles five times a day. He'd see someone, such as that girl Bette Torrance, and get a cold, unrecognizing stare; or he'd go by someone else, believing the other person did not remember him but walking rapidly just in case he did, and there would be the angry, "Well! Who the blazes do you think *you* are!" floating after him as he retreated.

Now he sat alone, bouncing up and down with each revolution of the wheel, with the one suitcase containing his property thumping constantly against the baggage rack over his head. That was one advantage of his talent: he could travel light. He didn't need to keep books, once he had read them, and there wasn't much point in amassing belongings of any other sort either; they became overfamiliar and dull too soon.

He eyed the road signs. They were well into Nevada by now. The old, wearisome retreat was on.

He could never stay in the same city too long. He had to move on to new territory, to some new place where he knew no one. In the sixteen years since he had left home, he'd covered a lot of ground.

He remembered the jobs he had held.

He had been a proofreader for a Chicago publishing firm, once. He did the jobs of two men. The way proofreading usually worked, one man read the copy from the manuscript, the other checked it against the galleys. Niles had a simpler method: he would scan the manuscript once, thereby memorizing it, and then merely check the galley for discrepancies. It brought him fifty dollars a week for a while, before the time came to move along.

He once held a job as a sideshow freak in a traveling carnie that made a regular Alabama-Mississippi-Georgia circuit. Niles had really been low on cash, then. He remembered how he had gotten the job: by buttonholing the carnie boss and demanding a tryout. "Read me anything—anything at all! I can remember it!" The boss had been skeptical, and didn't see any use for such an act anyway, but finally gave in when Niles practically fainted of malnutrition in his office. The boss read him an editorial from a Mississippi county weekly, and when he was through Niles recited it back, word perfect. He got the job, at fifteen dollars a week plus meals, and sat in a little booth under a sign that said The Human Tape Recorder. People read or said things to him, and he repeated them. It was dull work; sometimes the things they said to him were filthy, and most of the time they couldn't even remember what they had said to him a minute later. He stayed with the show four weeks, and when he left no one missed him much.

The bus rolled on into the fogbound night.

There had been other jobs: good jobs, bad jobs. None of them had lasted very long. There had been some girls too, but none of *them* had lasted too long. They had all, even those he had tried to conceal it from, found out about his special ability, and soon after that they had left. No one could stay with a man who never forgot, who could always dredge yesterday's foibles out of the reservoir that was his mind and hurl them unanswerably into the open. And the man with the perfect memory could never live long among imperfect human beings.

To forgive is to forget, he thought. The memory of old insults and quarrels fades, and a relationship starts anew. But for him there could be no forgetting, and hence little forgiving.

He closed his eyes after a little while and leaned back against the hard leather cushion of his seat. The steady rhythm of the bus lulled him to sleep. In sleep, his mind could rest; he found ease from memory. He never dreamed.

In Salt Lake City he paid his fare, left the bus, suitcase in hand, and set out in the first direction he faced. He had not wanted to go any farther east on that bus. His cash reserve was only sixty-three dollars now, and he had to make it last. He found a job as a dishwasher in a downtown restaurant, held it long enough to accumulate a hundred dollars, and moved on again, this time hitchhiking to Cheyenne. He stayed there a month and took a night bus to Denver, and when he left Denver it was to go to Wichita.

Wichita to Des Moines to Minneapolis, Minneapolis to Milwaukee, then down through Illinois, carefully avoiding Chicago, and on to Indianapolis. It was an old story for him, this traveling. Gloomily he celebrated his twenty-ninth birthday alone in an Indianapolis rooming house on a drizzly October day, and for the purpose of brightening the occasion, summoned up his old memories of his fourth birthday party in 1933 . . . one of the few unalloyedly happy days of his life.

They were all there, all his playmates, and his parents, and his brother Hank, looking gravely important at the age of eight, and his sister Marian, and there were candles and favors and punch and cake. Mrs. Heinsohn from next door stopped in and said, "He looks like a regular little man," and his parents beamed at him, and everyone sang and had a good time. And afterward, when the last game had been played, the last present opened, when the boys and girls had waved good-bye and disappeared up the street, the grownups sat around and talked of the new president and the many strange things that were happening in the country, and little Tommy sat in the middle of the floor, listening and recording everything and glowing warmly, because somehow during the whole afternoon no one had said or done anything cruel to him. He was happy that day, and he went to bed still happy.

Niles ran through the party twice, like an old movie he loved well; the print never grew frayed, the registration always remained as clear and sharp as ever. He could taste the sweet tang of the punch, he could relive the warmth of that day when through some accident the others had allowed him a little happiness.

Finally he let the brightness of the party fade, and once again he was in Indianapolis on a gray, bleak afternoon, alone in an eight-dollar-a-week furnished room.

Happy birthday to me, he thought bitterly. *Happy birthday.*

He stared at the blotchy green wall with the cheap Corot print hung slightly askew. I could have been something special, he brooded, one of the wonders of the world. Instead I'm a skulking freak who lives in dingy third-floor back rooms, and I don't dare let the world know what I can do.

He scooped into his memory and came up with the Toscanini performance of Beethoven's Ninth he had heard in Carnegie Hall once while he was in New York. It was infinitely better than the later performance Toscanini had approved for recording, yet no microphones had taken it down; the blazing performance was as far beyond recapture as a flame five minutes snuffed, except in one man's mind. Niles had it all: the majestic downcrash of the tympani, the resonant, perspiring basso bringing forth the great melody of the finale, even the french-horn bobble that must have enraged the maestro so, the infuriating cough from the dress circle at the gentlest moment of the adagio, the sharp pinching of Niles' shoes as he leaned forward in his seat—

He had it all, in highest fidelity.

He arrived in the small town on a moonless night three months later, a cold, crisp January evening, when the wintry wind swept in from the north, cutting through his thin clothing and making the suitcase an almost impossible burden for his numb, gloveless hand. He had not meant to come to this place, but he had run short of cash in Kentucky, and there had been no helping it. He was on his way to New York, where he could live in anonymity for months unbothered, and where he knew his rudeness would go unnoticed if he happened to snub someone on the street or if he greeted someone who had forgotten him.

But New York was still hundreds of miles away, and it might have been millions on this January night. He saw a sign: BAR. He forced himself forward toward the sputtering neon;

he wasn't ordinarily a drinker, but he needed the warmth of alcohol inside him now, and perhaps the barkeep would need a man to help out, or could at least rent him a room for what little he had in his pockets.

There were five men in the bar when he reached it. They looked like truck drivers. Niles dropped his valise to the left of the door, rubbed his stiff hands together, exhaled a white cloud. The bartender grinned jovially at him.

"Cold enough for you out there?"

Niles managed a grin. "I wasn't sweating much. Let me have something warming. Double shot of bourbon, maybe."

That would be ninety cents. He had $7.34.

He nursed the drink when it came, sipped it slowly, let it roll down his gullet. He thought of the summer he had been stranded for a week in Washington, a solid week of 97-degree temperature and 97-percent humidity, and the vivid memory helped to ease away some of the psychological effects of the coldness.

He relaxed; he warmed. Behind him came the penetrating sound of argument.

"—I tell you Joe Louis beat Schmeling to a pulp the second time! Kayoed him in the first round!"

"You're nuts! Louis just barely got him down in a fifteen-round decision, the second bout."

"Seems to me—"

"I'll put money on it. Ten bucks says it was a decision in fifteen, mac."

Sounds of confident chuckles. "I wouldn't want to take your money so easy, pal. Everyone knows it was a knockout in one."

"Ten bucks, I said."

Niles turned to see what was happening. Two of the truck drivers, burly men in dark pea jackets, stood nose to nose. Automatically the thought came: *Louis knocked Max Schmeling out in the first round at Yankee Stadium, New York, June 22, 1938.* Niles had never been much of a sports fan, and particularly disliked boxing—but he had once glanced at an almanac page cataloguing Joe Louis' title fights, and the data had, of course remained.

He watched detachedly as the bigger of the two truck drivers angrily slapped a ten-dollar bill down on the bar; the other matched it. Then the first glanced up at the barkeep and said, "Okay, bud. You're a shrewd guy. Who's right about the second Louis-Schmeling fight?"

The barkeep was a blank-faced cipher of a man, middle-aged, balding, with mild, empty eyes. He chewed at his lip a moment, shrugged, fidgeted, finally said, "Kinda hard for me to remember. That musta been twenty-five years ago."

Twenty, Niles thought.

"Lessee now," the bartender went on. "Seems to me I remember—yeah, sure. It went the full fifteen, and the judges gave it to Louis. I seem to remember a big stink being made over it; the papers said Joe should've killed him a lot faster'n that."

A triumphant grin appeared on the bigger driver's face. He deftly pocketed both bills.

The other man grimaced and howled, "Hey! You two fixed this thing up beforehand! I know damn well that Louis kayoed the German in one."

"You heard what the man said. The money's mine."

"No," Niles said suddenly, in a quiet voice that seemed to carry halfway across the bar. *Keep your mouth shut*, he told himself frantically. *This is none of your business. Stay out of it!*

But it was too late.

"What you say?" asked the one who'd dropped the ten-spot.

"I say you're being rooked. Louis won the fight in one round, like you say. June 22, 1938, Yankee Stadium. The barkeep's thinking of the Arturo Godoy fight. *That* went the full fifteen in 1940. February 9."

"There—told you! Gimme back my money!"

But the other driver ignored the cry and turned to face Niles. He was a cold-faced, heavy-set man, and his fists were starting to clench. "Smart man, eh? Boxing expert?"

"I just didn't want to see anybody get cheated," Niles said stubbornly. He knew what was coming now. The truck driver was weaving drunkenly toward him; the barkeep was yelling, the other patrons backing away.

The first punch caught Niles in the ribs; he grunted and staggered back, only to be grabbed by the throat and slapped three times. Dimly he heard a voice saying, "Hey, let go the guy! He didn't mean anything! You want to kill him?"

A volley of blows doubled him up; a knuckle swelled his right eyelid, a fist crashed stunningly into his left shoulder. He spun, wobbled uncertainly, knowing that his mind would permanently record every moment of this agony.

Through half-closed eyes he saw them pulling the enraged driver off him; the man writhed in the grip of three others, aimed a last desperate kick at Niles' stomach and grazed a rib, and finally was subdued.

Niles stood alone in the middle of the floor, forcing himself to stay upright, trying to shake off the sudden pain that drilled through him in a dozen places.

"You all right?" a solicitous voice asked. "Hell, those guys play rough. You oughtn't mix up with them."

"I'm all right," Niles said hollowly. "Just . . . let me . . . catch my breath."

"Here. Sit down. Have a drink. It'll fix you up."

"No," Niles said. *I can't stay here. I have to get moving.* "I'll be all right," he muttered unconvincingly. He picked up his suitcase, wrapped his coat tight about him, and left the bar, step by step by step.

He got fifteen feet before the pain became unbearable. He crumpled suddenly and fell forward on his face in the dark, feeling the cold ironhard frozen turf against his cheek, and struggled unsuccessfully to get up. He lay there, remembering all the various pains of his life, the beatings, the cruelty, and when the weight of memory became too much to bear he blanked out.

The bed was warm, the sheets clean and fresh and soft. Niles woke slowly, feeling a temporary sensation of disorientation, and then his infallible memory supplied the data on his blackout in the snow and he realized he was in a hospital.

He tried to open his eyes; one was swollen shut, but he managed to get the other's lids apart. He was in a small hospital room—no shining metropolitan hospital pavillion, but a small country clinic with gingerbread molding on the walls and homey lace curtains, through which afternoon sunlight was entering.

So he had been found and brought to a hospital. That was good. He could have easily died out there in the snow; but someone had stumbled over him and brought him in. That was a novelty, that someone had bothered to help him; the treatment he had received in the bar last night—was it last night?—was more typical of the world's attitude toward him.

In twenty-nine years he had somehow failed to learn adequate concealment, camouflage and every day he suffered the consequences. It was so hard for him to remember, he who remembered everything else, that the other people were not like him, and hated him for what he was.

Gingerly he felt his side. There didn't seem to be any broken ribs—just bruises. A day or so of rest and they would probably discharge him and let him move on.

A cheerful voice said, "Oh, you're awake, Mr. Niles. Feeling better now? I'll brew some tea for you."

He looked up and felt a sudden sharp pang. She was a nurse—twenty-two, twenty-three, new at the job perhaps, with a flowing tumble of curling blond hair and wide, clear blue eyes. She was smiling, and it seemed to Niles it was not merely a professional smile. "I'm Miss Carroll, your day nurse. Everything okay?"

"Fine," Niles said hesitantly. "Where am I?"

"Central County General Hospital. You were brought in late last night—apparently you'd been beaten up and left by the road out on Route 32. It's a lucky thing Mark McKenzie was walking his dog, Mr. Niles." She looked at him gravely. "You remember last night, don't you? I mean—the shock— amnesia—"

Niles chuckled. "That's the last ailment in the world I'd be afraid of," he said. "I'm Thomas Richard Niles, and I remember pretty well what happened. How badly am I damaged?"

"Superficial bruises, mild shock and exposure, slight case of frostbite," she summed up. "You'll live. Dr. Hammond'll give you a full checkup a little later, after you've eaten. Let me bring you some tea."

Niles watched the trim figure vanish into the hallway.

She was certainly an attractive girl, he thought, fresh-eyed, alert . . . *alive*.

Old cliché: patient falling for his nurse. But she's not for me, I'm afraid.

Abruptly the door opened and the nurse reentered, bearing a little enameled tea tray. "You'll never guess! I have a surprise for you, Mr Niles. A visitor. Your mother."

"My moth—"

"She saw the little notice about you in the county paper. She's waiting outside, and she told me she hasn't seen you in seventeen years. Would you like me to send her in now?"

"I guess so," Niles said, in a dry, feathery voice.

A second time the nurse departed. *My God*, Niles thought! *If I had known I was this close to home—*

I should have stayed out of Ohio altogether.

The last person he wanted to see was his mother. He began to tremble under the covers. The oldest and most terrible of his memories came bursting up from the dark compartment of his mind where he thought he had imprisoned it forever. The sudden emergence from warmth into coolness, from darkness to light, the jarring slap of a heavy hand on his buttocks, the searing pain of knowing that his security was ended, that from now on he would be alive, and therefore miserable—

The memory of the agonized birth-shriek sounded in his mind. He could never forget being born. And his mother was, he thought, the one person of all he could never forgive, since she had given him forth into the life he hated. He dreaded the moment when—

"Hello, Tom. It's been a long time."

Seventeen years had faded her, had carved lines in her face and made the cheeks more baggy, the blue eyes less bright, the brown hair a mousy gray. She was smiling. And to his own astonishment Niles was able to smile back.

"Mother."

"I read about it in the paper. It said a man of about thirty was found just outside town with papers bearing the name Thomas R. Niles, and he was taken to Central County General Hospital. So I came over, just to make sure—and it *was* you."

A lie drifted to the surface of his mind, but it was a kind lie, and he said it: "I was on my way back home to see you. Hitchhiking. But I ran into a little trouble en route."

"I'm glad you decided to come back, Tom. It's been lonely, ever since your father died, and of course Hank was married, and Marian too—it's good to see you again. I thought I never would."

He lay back, perplexed, wondering why the upwelling flood of hatred did not come. He felt only warmth toward her. He was glad to see her.

"How has it been—all these years, Tom? You haven't had it easy. I can see. I see it all over your face."

"It hasn't been easy," he said. "You know why I ran away?"

She nodded. "Because of the way you are. That thing about your mind—never forgetting. I knew. Your grandfather had it too, you know."

"My grandfather—but—"

"You git it from him. I never did tell you, I guess. He didn't get along too well with any of us. He left my mother when I was a little girl, and I never knew where he went. So I always knew you'd go away the way he did. Only you came back. Are you married?"

He shook his head.

"Time you got started, then, Tom. You're near thirty."

The door opened, and an efficient-looking doctor appeared. "Afraid your time's up, Mrs. Niles. You'll be able to see him again later. I have to check him over, now that he's awake."

"Of course, doctor." She smiled at him, then at Niles. "I'll see you later, Tom."

"Sure, mother."

Niles lay back, frowning, as the doctor poked at him here and there. *I didn't hate her*. A growing wonderment rose in him, and he realized he should have come home long ago. He had changed, inside, without even knowing it.

Running away was the first stage in growing up, and a necessary one. But coming back came later, and that was the mark of maturity. He was back. And suddenly he saw he had been terribly foolish all his bitter adult life.

He had a gift, a great fit, an awesome gift. It had been too big for him until now. Self-pitying, self-tormented, he had refused to allow for the shortcomings of the forgetful people about him, and had paid the price of their hatred. But he couldn't keep running away forever. The time would have to come for him to grow big enough to contain his gift, to learn to live with it instead of moaning in dramatic, self-inflicted anguish.

And now was the time. It was long overdue.

His grandfather had had the gift; they had never told him that. So it was genetically transmissible. He could marry, have children, and they, too, would never forget.

It was his duty not to let his gift die with him. Others of his kind, less sensitive, less thin-skinned, would come after and they, too, would know how to recall a Beethoven symphony or a decade-old wisp of conversation. For the first time since that fourth birthday party he felt a hesitant flicker of happiness. The days of running were ended; he was home again. *If I learn to live with others, maybe they'll be able to live with me.*

He saw the things he yet needed: a wife, a home, children—

"—a couple of days' rest, plenty of hot liquids, and you'll be as good as new, Mr. Niles," the doctor was saying. "Is there anything you'd like me to bring you now?"

"Yes," Niles said. "Just send in the nurse, will you? Miss Carroll, I mean."

The doctor grinned and left. Niles waited expectantly, exulting in his new self. He switched on Act Three of *Die Meistersinger* as a kind of jubilant backdrop music in his mind, and let the warmth sweep up over him. When she entered the room he was smiling and wondering how to begin saying what he wanted to say.

Prime Commandment

If, the strangers had come to World on any night but The Night of No Moon, perhaps the tragedy could have been avoided. Even had the strangers come that night, if they had left their ship in a parking orbit and landed on World by dropshaft it might not have happened.

But the strangers arrived on World on The Night of No Moon, and they came by ship—a fine bright vessel a thousand feet long, with burnished gold walls. And because they were a proud and stiffnecked people, and because the people of World were what they were, and because the god of the strangers was not the God of the World, The Night of No Moon was the prelude to a season of blood.

Down at the Ship, the worshipping was under way when the strangers arrived. The Ship sat embedded in the side of the hill, exactly where it had first fallen upon World; open in its side was the hatch through which the people of World had come forth.

The bonfire blazed, casting bright shadows on the corroded, time-stained walls of the Ship. The worshipping was under way. Lyle of the Kwitni knelt in a deep genuflection, forehead inches from the warm rich loam of World, muttering in a hoarse monotone the Book of the Ship. At his side stood the priestess Jeen of McCaig, arms flung wide, head thrown back, as she recited the Litany of the Ship in savage bursts of half-chanted song.

"In the beginning there was the Ship—"

"Kwitni was the Captain, McCaig the astrogator," came the droning antiphonal response of the congregation, all five hundred of the people of World, crouching in the praying-pit surrounding the Ship.

"And Kwitni and McCaig brought the people through the sky to World—"

"And they looked upon World and found it good," was the response.

"And down through the sky did the people come—"

"Down across the light-years to World."

"Out of the Ship!"

"Out of the Ship!"

On it went, a long and ornate retelling of the early days of World, when Kwitni and McCaig, with the guidance of the Ship, had brought the original eight-and-thirty safely to ground. During the three hundred years the story had grown; six nights a year there was no moon, and the ceremonial retelling took place. And five hundred and thirteen were the numbers of the people on this Night of No Moon when the strangers came.

Jeen of the McCaig was the first to see them, as she stood before the Ship waiting for the ecstasy to sweep over her and for her feet to begin the worship dance. She was young, and this was only her fourth worship; she waited with some impatience for the frenzy to seize her.

Suddenly a blaze of light appeared in the dark moonless sky. Jeen stared. In her twenty years she had never seen fire in the heavens on The Night of No Moon.

And her sharp eyes saw that the fire was coming closer, that something was dropping through the skies toward them. And a shiver ran down her back, and she felt the coolness of the night winds against her lightly clad body. She heard the people stirring uneasily behind her.

Perhaps it was a miracle, she thought. Perhaps the Ship had sent some divine manifestation. Her heart pounded; her flanks glistened with sweat. The worshipping drew near its climax, and Jeen felt the dance-fever come over her, growing more intense as the strange light approached the ground.

She wriggled belly and buttocks sensuously and began the dance, the dance of worship that concluded the ceremony, while from behind her came the pleasure-sounds of the people as they, too, worshipped the Ship in their own ways. For the commandment of the old lawgiver Lorresson had been, *Be happy, my children,* and the people of World expressed their joy while the miracle-light plunged rapidly Worldward.

Eleven miles from the Hill of the Ship, the strange light finally touched ground—not a light at all, but a starship, golden-hulled, a thousand feet long and bearing within itself the eight hundred men and women of the Church of the New Resurrection, who had crossed the gulf of light-years in search of a world where they might practice their religion free from interference and without the distraction of the presence of countless billions of the unholy.

The Blessed Myron Brown was the leader of this flock and the captain of their ship, the *New Galilee*. Fifth in direct line from the Blessed Leroy Brown himself, Blessed Myron Brown was majestic of bearing and thunderous of voice, and when his words rang out over the ship phones saying, "Here we may rest here we may live," the eight hundred members of the Church of the New Resurrection rejoiced in their solemn way, and made ready for the landing.

They were not tractable people. The tenets of their Church were two: that the Messiah had come again on Earth, died again, been reborn, and in his resurrection prophesied that the Millennium was at hand—and, secondly, that He had chosen certain people to lead the way in the forthcoming building of New Jerusalem.

And it was through the mouth of Blessed Leroy Brown that He spoke, in the two thousand nine hundred and seventieth year since His first birth, and the Blessed Leroy Brown did name those of Earth who had been chosen for holiness and salvation. Many of the elect declined the designation, some with kindly thanks, some with scorn. The Blessed Leroy Brown died early, the protomartyr of his Church, but his work went on.

And a hundred years passed and the members of his Church were eight hundred in number, proud God-touched men and women who denounced the sinful ways of the world and revealed that judgment was near. There were martyrs, and the way was a painful one for the Blessed. But they persevered, and they raised money (some of their members had been quite wealthy in their days of sin) and when it became clear that Earth was too steeped in infamy for them to abide existence on it any further, they built their ark, the *New Galilee*, and crossed the gulf of night to a new world where they might live in peace and happiness and never know the persecution of the mocking ones.

They were a proud and stubborn people, and they kept the ways of God as they knew them. They dressed in gray, for bright colors were sinful, and they covered their bodies but for face and hands, and when a man knew his wife it was for the production of children alone. They made no graven images and they honored the sabbath, and it was their very great hope that on Beta Andromedae XII they could at last be at peace.

But fifteen minutes after their landing they saw that this was not to be. For, while the women labored to erect camp and the men hunted provisions, the Blessed Enoch Brown, son of the leader Myron, went forth in a helicopter to survey the new planet.

And when he returned from his mission his dour face was deeper than usual with woe, and when he spoke it was in a sepulchral tone.

"The Lord has visited another tribulation upon us, even here in the wilderness."

"What have you seen?" the blessed Myron asked.

"This world is peopled!"

"Impossible! We were given every assurance that this was a virgin world, without colonists, without native life."

"Nevertheless," the Blessed Enoch said bitterly, "there are people here. I have seen them. Naked savages who look like Earthpeople—dancing and prancing by the light of a huge bonfire round the rotting hulk of an abandoned spaceship that lies implanted in a hillside." He scowled. "I flew low over them. Their bodies were virtually bare, and their flesh was oiled, and they leaped wildly and coupled like animals in the open."

For a moment the Blessed Myron Brown stared bleakly at his son, unable to speak. The blood drained from his lean face. When he finally spoke, his voice was thick with anger.

"Even here the Devil pursues us."

"Who can these people be?"

The Blessed Myron shrugged. "It makes little difference. Perhaps they are descendants of a Terran colonial mission—a ship bound for a more distant world, that crashed here and sent no word to Earth." He stared heavenward for a moment, at the dark and moonless sky, and muttered a brief prayer. "Tomorrow," he said, "we will visit these people and speak with them. Now let us build our camp."

The morning dawned fresh and clear, the sun rising early and growing warm rapidly, and shortly after morning prayer a picked band of eleven Resurrectionist men made their way through the heavily wooded area that separated their camp from that of the savages. The women of the Church knelt in the clearing and prayed, while the remaining men went about their daily chores.

The Blessed Myron Brown led the party, and with him were his son Enoch and nine others. They strode without speaking through the woods. The Blessed Myron experienced a certain discomfort as the great yellow sun grew higher in the sky and the forest warmed; he was perspiring heavily beneath his thick gray woolen clothes. But this was merely a physical discomfort, and those he could bear with ease.

This other torment, though, that of finding people on this new world—that hurt him. He wanted to see these people with his own eyes, and look upon them.

Near noon the village of the natives came in sight; the Blessed Myron was first to see it. He saw a huddle of crude low huts built around a medium-sized hill, atop which rose the snout of a corroded spaceship that had crashed into the hillside years, perhaps centuries earlier. The Blessed Myron pointed, and they went forward.

And several of the natives advanced from the village to meet them.

There was a girl, young and fair, and a man, and all the man wore was a scanty white cloth around his waist, and all the girl wore was the breechcloth and an additional binding around her breasts. The rest of their bodies—lean, tanned—were bare. The Blessed Myron offered a prayer that he would be kept from sin.

The girl stepped forward and said, "I'm the priestess Jeen of the McCaig. This is Lyle of Kwitni, who is in charge. Who are you?"

"You—you speak English?" the Blessed Myron asked.

"We do. Who are you, and what are you doing on World? Where did you come from? What do you want here?"

The girl was openly impudent; and the sight of her sleek thighs made the muscles tighten along the Blessed Myron's jaws. Coldly he said, "We have come here from Earth. We will settle here."

"Earth? Where is that?"

The Blessed Myron smiled knowingly and glanced at his son and at the others. He noticed in some disapproval that Enoch was staring with perhaps too much curiosity at the lithe girl. "Earth is the planet from beyond the sky where you originally came from," he said. "Long ago—before you declined into savagery."

"You came from the place we came from?" The girl frowned. "We are not savages, though."

"You run naked and perform strange ceremonies by night. This is savagery. But all this must change. We will help you regain your stature as Earthmen again; we will show you how to build houses instead of shabby huts. And you must learn to wear clothing again."

"But surely we need no more clothing than this," Jeen said in surprise. She reached out and plucked a section of the Blessed Myron's gray woolen vestments between two of her fingers. "Your clothes are wet with the heat. How can you bear such silly things?"

"Nakedness is sinful," the Blessed Myron thundered.

Suddenly the man Lyle spoke. "Who are you to tell us these things? Why have you come to World?"

"To worship God freely."

The pair of natives exchanged looks. Jeen pointed at the half-buried spaceship that gleamed in the noonday sun. "To worship with us?"

"Of course not! You worship a ship, a piece of metal. You have fallen into decadent ways."

"We worship that which has brought us to World, for it is holy," Jeen snapped hotly. "And you?"

"We, too, worship That which has brought us to the world. But we shall teach you. We—"

The Blessed Myron stopped. He no longer had an audience. Jeen and Lyle had whirled suddenly and both of them sprinted away, back toward the village.

The churchmen waited for more than half an hour. Finally the Blessed Myron said, "They will not come back. They are afraid of us. Let us return to our settlement and decide what is to be done."

They heard laughing and giggling coming from above. The Blessed Myron stared upward.

The trees were thick with the naked people; they had stealthily surrounded them. The Blessed Myron saw the impish face of the girl Jeen.

She called down to him: "Go back to your God and leave us alone, silly men! Leave World by tomorrow morning or we'll kill you!"

Enraged, the Blessed Myron shook his fist at the trees. "You chattering monkeys, we'll make human beings of you again!"

"And make us wear thick ugly clothes and worship a false god? You'd have to kill us first—if you could!"

"Come," the Blessed Myron said. "Back to the settlement. We cannot stay here longer."

That evening, in the rude church building that had been erected during the day, the elders of the Church of the New Resurrection met in solemn convocation, to discuss the problem of the people of the forest.

"They are obviously descendants of a wrecked colony ship," said the Blessed Myron. "But they make of sin a virtue. They have become as animals. In time they will merely corrupt us to their ways."

The Elder Solomon Kane called for the floor—an ascetic-featured, dour man with the cold, austere mind of a master mathematician or a master theologian. "As I see it, brother, there are three choices facing us: we can return to Earth and apply for a new planet; or we can attempt to convert these people to our ways; or we can destroy them to the last man, woman and child."

The Blessed Dominic Agnello objected: "Return to Earth is impossible. We have not the fuel."

"And," offered the Blessed Myron, "I testify that these creatures are incorrigible and beyond aid. They are none of them among the Blessed. We do not want to inflict slavery upon them, nor can we welcome them into our numbers."

"The alternative," said the Blessed Solomon Kane, "is clearly our only path. We must root them out as if they were a noxious pestilence. How great are their numbers?"

"Three or four hundred. Perhaps as many as five hundred, no more. We certainly outnumber them."

"And we have weapons. We can lay them low like weeds in the field."

A light appeared in the eyes of the Blessed Myron Brown. "We shall perform an act of purification. We will blot the heathens from our new world. The slate must be fresh, for here we will build the New Jerusalem."

The Blessed Leonid Markell, a slim mystic with flowing

golden hair, smiled gently and said, "We are told, Thou Shalt Not Kill, Brother Myron."

The Blessed Myron whirled on him. "The commandments are given to us, but they need interpretation. Would you say, Thou Shalt Not Kill, as the butcher raises his knife over a cow? Would you say—"

"The doctrine refers only to human life," said the Blessed Leonid softly. "But—"

"I choose to construe it differently," the Blessed Myron said. His voice was deep and commanding, now; it was the voice of the prophet speaking, of the lawgiver. "Here on this world only those who worship God may be considered human. Fleeing from the bitter scorn of our neighbors, we have come here to build a New Jerusalem in this wilderness—and we must remove every obstacle in our way. The Devil has placed these creatures here, to tempt us with their nakedness and laughter and sinful ways."

He stared at the rest of them, and no longer were they his equals round the table, but now merely his disciples, as they had been all the long journey through the stars. "Tomorrow is the sabbath day by our reckoning, and we shall rest. But on the day following we shall go armed to the village of the idolaters, and strike them down. Is that understood by us all?"

"*Vengeance is mine, saith the Lord,*" the Blessed Leonid quoted mildly. But when the time came for the vote, he cast in his lot with the rest, and it was recorded as a unanimous decision. After the day of the Sabbath, the mocking forest-people would be eradicated.

But the people of World had laws of their own, and a religion of their own, and they too held a convocation that evening, speaking long and earnestly round the council fire. The priestess Jeen, garbed only in the red paints of death, danced before them, and when Lyle of the Kwitni called for a decision there were no dissenters.

The long night came to an end, and morning broke over World—and the spies returned from the settlement of the strangers, reporting that the strange god still stood in the clearing, and that his followers showed no signs of obeying the command to depart.

"It is death, then," cried the priestess. And she led them in a dance round the Ship their God, and the knives were sharpened, and she and Lyle led them through the forest, Lyle carrying one of the swords that had hung in the cabin of the Captain McCaig aboard the Ship, and Jeen the other.

The strangers were sleeping when the five hundred of the people of World burst in on their encampment. They woke, gradually, in confusion, as the forest slayers moved among them, slicing throats. Dozens died before anyone knew what was taking place.

Curiously the strangers made no attempt to defend themselves. Jeen saw the great bearded man, he who had commanded her to wear clothes and who had eyed her body so strangely, and he stood in the midst of his fellows, shouting in a mighty voice, "It is the Sabbath! Lift no weapon on the Sabbath! Pray, brothers, pray!"

And the strangers fell to their knees and prayed, and because they prayed to a false god they died. It was hardly yet noon when the killing was done with, and the eight hundred members of the Church of the New Resurrection lay weltering in blood, every one of them dead.

Jeen the priestess said strangely, "They did not fight back. They let us kill them."

"They said it was the Sabbath," Lyle of the Kwitni remarked. "But of course it was not the Sabbath—the Sabbath is three days hence."

Jeen shrugged. "We are well rid of them, anyway. They would have blasphemed against God."

There was more work to do, yet, after the bodies were carried to the sea. Fifty great trees were felled and stripped of their branches, and the naked trunks were set aside while the men of the tribe climbed the cliff and caused the great ship in which the strangers had come to topple to the ground.

Then a roadway was made of the fifty great logs, and the men and women of the people of World pushed strainingly, and the great ship rolled with a groaning sound down the side of the hill, as the logs tumbled beneath it, and finally it went plunging toward the sea and dropped beneath the waves, sending up a mighty cascade of water.

They were all gone, then, the eight hundred intruders and their false god, the ship. And the people of World returned to their village and wearily danced out the praise of their Ship, their God.

They were not bloodthirsty people, and they would have

wished to welcome the eight hundred strange ones into their midst. But the strange ones were blasphemers, and so had to be killed, and their god destroyed.

Jeen was happy, for her faith in God was renewed, and she danced gladly round the pitted and rusting Ship. For her God had been true, and the god of the strangers false, and God's bidding had been done. For it had been written in the Book of the Ship, which old Lorresson the priest recited to the people of World centuries ago in the days of the first McCaig and the first Kwitni, that there were certain commandments by which the people were to live.

And one of these commandments was, Thou Shalt Not Kill, and another was, Remember the Sabbath Day, To Keep It Holy. These the people of World harkened to.

But they were godly people, and the Word was most holy. They had acted in concord with the dictates of Lorresson and McCaig and Kwitni and the Ship itself, their God, when they had slain the intruders and destroyed their ship. For, first of all the commandments they revered, it was written, Thou Shalt Have No Other Gods Before Me.

One-Way Journey

Behind the comforting walls of Terra Import's headquarters on Kollidor, Commander Leon Warshow was fumbling nervously with the psych reports on his mirror-bright desk. Commander Warshow was thinking about spaceman Matt Falk, and about himself. Commander Warshow was about to react very predictably.

Personnel Lieutenant Krisch had told him the story about Falk an hour before, and Warshow was doing the one thing expected of him: he was waiting for the boy, having sent for him, after a hasty conference with Cullinan, the *Magyar*'s saturnine psych officer.

An orderly buzzed and said, "Spaceman Falk to see you, sir."

"Have him wait a few minutes," Warshow said, speaking too quickly. "I'll buzz for him."

It was a tactical delay. Wondering why he, an officer, should be so tense before an interview with an enlisted man, Warshow riffled through the sheaf of records on Matt Falk. *Orphaned, 2543 . . . Academy . . . two years' commercial service, military contract . . . injury en route to Kollidor . . .*

Appended were comprehensive medical reports on Falk's injury, and Dr. Sigstrom's okay. Also a disciplinary chart, very favorable, and a jaggle-edged psych contour, good.

Warshow depressed the buzzer. "Send in Falk," he said.

The photon beam clicked and the door swung back. Matt Falk entered and faced his commander stonily; Warshow glared back, studying the youngster as if he had never seen him before. Falk was just twenty-five, very tall and very blond, with wide, bunch-muscled shoulders and keen blue eyes. The scar along the left side of his face was almost completely invisible, but not even chemotherapeutic incubation had been able to restore the smooth evenness of the boy's jaw. Falk's face looked oddly lopsided; the unharmed right jaw sloped easily and handsomely up to the condyle, while the left still bore unseen but definitely present echoes of the boy's terrible shipboard accident.

"You want me, commander?"

117

"We're leaving Kollidor tomorrow, Matt," Warshow said quietly. "Lieutenant Krisch tells me you haven't returned to ship to pack your gear. Why?"

The jaw that had been ruined and rebuilt quivered slightly.

"*You* know, sir. I'm not going back to Earth, sir. I'm staying here . . . with Thetona."

There was a frozen silence. Then, with calculated cruelty, Warshow said, "You're really hipped on that flatface, eh?"

"Maybe so," Falk murmured. "That flatface. That gook. What of it?" His quiet voice was bitterly defiant.

Warshow tensed. He was trying to do the job delicately, without inflicting further psychopersonal damage on young Falk. To leave a psychotic crewman behind on an alien world was impossible—but to extract Falk forcibly from the binding webwork of associations that tied him to Kollidor would leave scars not only on crewman but on captain.

Perspiring, Warshow said, "You're an Earthman, Matt. Don't you—"

"Want to go home? No."

The commander grinned feebly. "You sound mighty permanent about that, son."

"I am," Falk said stiffly. "You know why I want to stay here. I *am* staying here. May I be excused now, sir?"

Warshow drummed on the desktop, hesitating for a moment, then nodded. "Permission granted, Mr. Falk." There was little point in prolonging what he now saw had been a predeterminedly pointless interview.

He waited a few minutes after Falk had left. Then he switched on the communicator. "Send in Major Cullinan, please."

The beady-eyed psychman appeared almost instantly. "Well?"

"The boy's staying," Warshow said. "Complete and singleminded fixation. Go ahead—break it."

Cullinan shrugged. "We may have to leave him here, and that's all there is to it. Have you met the girl?"

"Kollidorian. Alien. Ugly as sin. I've seen her picture; he had it over his bunk until he moved out. And we *can't* leave him here, major."

Cullinan raised one bushy eyebrow quizzically. "We can

try to bring Falk back, if you insist—but it won't work. Not without crippling him."

Warshow whistled idly, avoiding the pyschman's stern gaze. "I insist," he said finally. "There's no alternative."

He snatched at the communicator.

"Lieutenant Krisch, please." A brief pause, then: "Krisch, Warshow. Tell the men that departure's been postponed four days. Have Molhaus refigure the orbits. Yes, four days. *Four.*"

Warshow hung up, glanced at the heaped Falk dossier on his desk, and scowled. Psych Officer Cullinan shook his head sadly, rubbing his growing bald spot.

"That's a drastic step, Leon."

"I know. But I'm not going to leave Falk behind." Warshow rose, eyed Cullinan uneasily, and added, "Care to come with me? I'm going down into Kollidor City."

"What for?"

"I want to talk with the girl," Warshow said.

Later, in the crazily twisting network of aimless streets that was the alien city, Warshow began to wish he had ordered Cullinan to come with him. As he made his way through the swarms of the placid, ugly, broad-faced Kollidorians, he regretted very much that he had gone alone.

What would he do, he wondered, when he finally did reach the flat where Falk and his Kollidorian girl were living? Warshow wasn't accustomed to handling himself in ground-borne interpersonal situations of this sort. He didn't know what to say to the girl. He thought he could handle Falk.

The relation of commander to crewman is that of parent to child, the book said. Warshow grinned self-consciously.

He didn't feel very fatherly just now—more like a Dutch uncle, he thought.

He kept walking. Kollidor City spread out ahead of him like a tangled ball of twine coming unrolled in five directions at once; it seemed to have been laid down almost at random. But Warshow knew the city well. This was his third tour of duty to the Kollidor sector; three times he had brought cargo from Earth, three times waited while his ship was loaded with Kollidorian goods for export.

Overhead, the distant blue-white sun burnt brightly. Kollidor was the thirteenth planet in its system; it swung on a large arc nearly four billion miles from its blazing primary.

Warshow sniffled; it reminded him that he was due for his regular antipollen injection. He was already thoroughly protected, as was his crew, against most forms of alien disease likely to come his way on the trip.

But how do you protect someone like Falk? The commander had no quick answers for that. It wouldn't ordinarily seem necessary to inoculate spacemen against falling in love with bovine alien women, but—

"Good afternoon, Commander Warshow," a dry voice said suddenly.

Warshow glanced around, surprised and annoyed. The man who stood behind him was tall, thin, with hard, knobby cheekbones protruding grotesquely from parchmentlike chalk-white skin. Warshow recognized the genetic pattern, and the man. He was Domnik Kross, a trader from the quondam Terran colony of Rigel IX.

"Hello, Kross," Warshow said sullenly, and halted to let the other catch up.

"What brings you to the city, commander? I thought you were getting ready to pack up and flit away."

"We're—postponing four days," Warshow said.

"Oh? Got any leads worth telling about? Not that I care to—"

"Skip it, Kross." Warshow's voice was weary. "We're finished our trading for the season. You've got a clear field. Now leave me alone, yes?"

He started to walk faster, but the Rigelian, smiling bleakly, kept in step with him.

"You sound disturbed, commander."

Warshow glanced impatiently at the other, wishing he could unburden himself of the Rigelian's company. "I'm on a mission of top security value, Kross. Are you going to insist on accompanying me?"

Thin lips parted slyly in a cold grin. "Not at all, Commander Warshow. I simply thought I'd be civil and walk with you a way, just to swap the news. After all, if you're leaving in four days we're not really rivals any more, and—"

"Exactly," Warshow said.

"What's this about one of your crewmen living with a native?" Kross asked suddenly.

Warshow spun on heel and glared up tensely. "*Nothing*," he grated. "You hear that? There's nothing to it!"

Kross chuckled, and Warshow saw that he had decidedly lost a point in the deadly cold rivalry between Terran and Rigelian, between man and son of man. Genetic drift accounted for the Domnik Krosses—a little bit of chromosome looping on a colonized planet, a faint tincture of inbreeding over ten generations, and a new subspecies had appeared: an alien subspecies that bore little love for its progenitors.

They reached a complex fork in the street, and the commander impulsively turned to the left. Gratifyingly, he noticed that Kross was not following him.

"See you next year!" the Rigelian said.

Warshow responded with a noncommittal grunt and kept moving down the dirty street, happy to be rid of Kross so soon. The Rigelians, he thought, were nasty customers. They were forever jealous of the mother world and its people, forever anxious to outrace an Earthman to a profitable deal on a world such as Kollidor.

Because of Kross, Warshow reflected, *I'm going where I'm going now*. Pressure from the Rigelians forced Earthmen to keep up appearances throughout the galaxy. The Earthman's Burden, Terrans termed it unofficially. To leave a deserter behind on Kollidor would endanger Earth's prestige in the eyes of the entire universe—and the shrewd Rigelians would make sure the entire universe knew.

Warshow felt hemmed in. As he approached the flat where Falk said he was living, he felt cascades of perspiration tumbling stickily down his back.

"Yes, please?"

Warshow now stood at the door, a little appalled by the sight and the smell. A Kollidorian female faced him squarely.

Good God, he thought. *She's sure no beauty*.

"I'm . . . Commander Warshow," he said. "Of the *Magyar*. Matt's ship. May I come in?"

The sphincterlike mouth rippled into what Warshow supposed was a gracious smile. "Of course. I have hoped you would come. Matt has spoken so much of you."

She backed away from the door, and Warshow stepped inside. The pungent rankness of concentrated Kollidorian odor assaulted his nostrils. It was an unpainted two-room flat; beyond the room they were in, Warshow saw another, slightly larger and sloppier, with kitchen facilities. Unwashed dishes lay heaped in the sink. To his surprise, he noticed an unmade bed in the far room . . . and another in the front one. *Single* beds. He frowned and turned to the girl.

She was nearly as tall as he was, and much broader. Her brown skin was drab and thick, looking more like hide than skin; her face was wide and plain, with two flat, unsparkling eyes, a grotesque bubble of a nose, and a many-lipped compound mouth. The girl wore a shapeless black frock that hung to her thick ankles. For all Warshow knew, she might be the pinnacle of Kollidorian beauty—but her charms scarcely seemed likely to arouse much desire in a normal Earthman.

"You're Thetona, is that right?"

"Yes, Commander Warshow." Voice dull and toneless, he noted.

"May I sit down?" he asked.

He was fencing tentatively, hemming around the situation without cutting toward it. He made a great business of taking a seat and crossing his legs fastidiously; the girl stared, cowlike, but remained standing.

An awkward silence followed; then the girl said, "You want Matt to go home with you, don't you?"

Warshow reddened and tightened his jaws angrily. "Yes. Our ship's leaving in four days. I came to get him."

"He isn't here," she said.

"I know. He's back at the base. He'll be home soon."

"You haven't done anything to him?" she asked, suddenly apprehensive.

He shook his head. "He's all right." After a moment Warshow glanced sharply at her and said, "He loves you, doesn't he?"

"Yes." But the answer seemed hesitant.

"And you love him?"

"Oh, yes," Thetona said warmly. "Certainly."

"I see." Warshow wet his lips. This was going to be difficult. "Suppose you tell me how you came to fall in love? I'm curious."

She smiled—at least, he assumed it was a smile. "I met him about two days after you Earthmen came for your visit. I was walking in the streets, and I saw him. He was sitting on the edge of the street, crying."

"*What?*"

Her flat eyes seemed to go misty. "Sitting there sobbing

to himself. It was the first time I ever saw an Earthman like that—crying, I mean. I felt terribly sorry for him. I went over to talk to him. He was like a little lost boy."

Warshow looked up, astonished, and stared at the alien girl's placid face with total disbelief. In ten years of dealing with the Kollidorians, he had never gone too close to them; he had left personal contact mainly to others. But—

Dammit, the girl's almost human! Almost—

"Was he sick?" Warshow asked, his voice hoarse. "Why was he crying?"

"He was lonely," Thetona said serenely. "He was afraid. He was afraid of me, of you, of everyone. So I talked to him, there by the edge of the street, for many minutes. And then he asked to come home with me. I lived by myself, here. He came with me. And—he has been here since three days after that."

"And he plans to stay here permanently?" Warshow asked.

The wide head waggled affirmatively. "We are very fond of each other. He is lonely; he needs someone to—"

"That'll be enough," Falk's voice said suddenly.

Warshow whirled. Falk was standing in the doorway, his face bleak and grim. The scar on his face seemed to be inflamed, though Warshow was sure that was impossible.

"What are you doing here?" Falk asked.

"I came to visit Thetona," Warshow said mildly. "I didn't expect to have you return so soon."

"I know you didn't. I walked out when Cullinan started poking around me. Suppose you get out."

"You're talking to a superior officer," Warshow reminded him. "If I—"

"I resigned ten minutes ago," Falk snapped. "You're no superior of mine! Get out!"

Warshow stiffened. He looked appealingly at the alien girl, who put her thick six-fingered hand on Falk's shoulder and stroked his arm. Falk wriggled away.

"Don't," he said. "Well—are you leaving? Thetona and I want to be alone."

"Please go, Commander Warshow," the girl said softly. "Don't get him excited."

"Excited? Who's excited?" Falk roared. "I—"

Warshow sat impassively, evaluating and analyzing, ignoring for the moment what was happening.

Falk would have to be brought back to the ship for

treatment. There was no alternative, Warshow saw. This strange relationship with the Kollidorian would have to be broken.

He stood up and raised one hand for silence. "Mr Falk, let me speak."

"Go ahead. Speak quick, because I'm going to pitch you out of here in two minutes."

"I won't need two minutes," Warshow said. "I simply want to inform you that you're under arrest and that you're hereby directed to report back to the base at once, in my custody. If you refuse to come it will be necessary—"

The sentence went unfinished. Falk's eyes flared angrily, and he crossed the little room in three quick bounds. Towering over the much smaller Warshow, he grabbed the commander by the shoulders and shook him violently. "*Get out!*" he shrieked.

Warshow smiled apologetically, took one step backward, and slid his stunner from its place in his tunic. He gave Falk a quick, heavy jolt, and as the big man sagged toward the floor, Warshow grabbed him and eased him into a chair.

Thetona was crying. Great gobbets of amber liquid oozed from her eyes and trickled heartbreakingly down her coarse cheeks.

"Sorry," Warshow said. "It had to be done."

It had to be done.
It had to be done.
It *had* to be done.

Warshow paced the cabin, his weak eyes darting nervously from the bright row of rivets across the ceiling to the quiet gray walls to the sleeping form of Matt Falk, and finally to the waiting, glowering visage of Psych Officer Cullinan.

"Do you want to wake him?" Cullinan asked.

"No. Not yet." Warshow kept prowling restlessly, trying to square his actions within himself. A few more minutes passed. Finally Cullinan stepped out from behind the cot on which Falk lay, and took Warshow's arm.

"Leon, tell me what's eating you."

"Don't shrink *my* skull," Warshow burst out. Then, sorry, he shook his head. "I didn't mean that. You know I didn't."

"It's two hours since you brought him aboard the ship," Cullinan said. "Don't you think we ought to do something?"

"What can we do?" Warshow demanded. "Throw him back to that alien girl? Kill him? Maybe that's the best solution—let's stuff him in the converters and blast off."

Falk stirred. "Ray him again," Warshow said hollowly. "The stunning's wearing off."

Cullinan used his stunner, and Falk subsided. "We can't keep him asleep forever," the psychman said.

"No—we can't." Warshow knew time was growing short; in three days the revised departure date would arrive, and he didn't dare risk another postponement.

But if they left Falk behind, and if word got around that a crazy Earthman was loose on Kollidor, or that Earthmen went crazy at all—

And there was no answer to that.

"Therapy," Cullinan said quietly.

"There's no time for an analysis," Warshow pointed out immediately. "*Three days*—that's all."

"I didn't mean a full-scale job. But if we nail him with an amytal-derivative inhibitor drug, filter out his hostility to talking to us, and run him back along his memories, we might hit something that'll help us."

Warshow shuddered. "Mind dredging, eh?"

"Call it that," the psychman said. "But let's dredge whatever it is that's tipped his rocker, or it'll wreck us all. You, me—and that girl."

"You think we can find it?"

"We can try. No Earthman in his right mind would form a sexual relationship of this kind—or *any* sort of emotional bond with an alien creature. If we hit the thing that catapulted him into it, maybe we can break this obviously neurotic fixation and make him go willingly. Unless you're willing to leave him behind. I absolutely forbid dragging him away as he is."

"Of course not," Warshow agreed. He mopped away sweat and glanced over at Falk, who still dreamed away under the effects of the stunbeam. "It's worth a try. If you think you can break it, go ahead. I deliver him into thy hands."

The psychman smiled with surprising warmth. "It's the only way. Let's dig up what happened to him and show it to him. That should crack the shell."

"I hope so," Warshow said. "It's in your hands. Wake him up and get him talking. You know what to do."

* * *

A murky cloud of drug-laden air hung in the cabin as Cullinan concluded his preliminaries. Falk stirred and began to grope toward consciousness. Cullinan handed Warshow an ultrasonic injector filled with a clear, glittering liquid.

Just as Falk seemed to be ready to open his eyes, Cullinan leaned over him and began to talk, quietly, soothingly. Falk's troubled frown vanished, and he subsided.

"Give him the drug," Cullinan whispered. Warshow touched the injector hesitantly to Falk's tanned forearm. The ultrasonic hummed briefly, blurred into the skin. Warshow administered three cc. and retracted.

Falk moaned gently.

"It'll take a few minutes," Cullinan said.

The wall clock circled slowly. After a while, Falk's sleep-heavy eyelids fluttered. He opened his eyes and glanced up without apparent recognition of his surroundings.

"Hello, Matt. We're here to talk to you," Cullinan said. "Or rather, we want you to talk to us."

"Yes," Falk said.

"Let's begin with your mother, shall we? Tell us what you remember about your mother. Go back, now."

"My—mother?" The question seemed to puzzle Falk, and he remained silent for nearly a minute. Then he moistened his lips. "What do you want to know about her?"

"Tell us everything," Cullinan urged.

There was silence. Warshow found himself holding his breath.

Finally, Falk began to speak.

Warm. Cuddly. Hold me. Mamama.

I'm all alone. It's night, and I'm crying. There are pins in my leg where I slept on it, and the night air smells cold. I'm three years old, and I'm all alone.

Hold me, mama?

I hear mama coming up the stairs. We have an old house with stairs, near the spaceport where the big ships go *woosh!* There's the soft smell of mama holding me now. Mama's big and pink and soft. Daddy is pink too but he doesn't smell warm. Uncle is the same way.

Ah, ah, baby, she's saying. She's in the room now, and

holding me tight. It's good. I'm getting very drowsy. In a
minute or two I'll be asleep. I like my mama very much.

("Is that your earliest recollection of your mother?"
Cullinan asked.)
("No. I guess there's an earlier one.")

Dark here. Dark and very warm, and wet, and nice. I'm
not moving. I'm all alone here, and I don't know where I am.
It's like floating in an ocean. A big ocean. The whole world's an
ocean.

It's nice here, real nice. I'm not crying.

Now there's blue needles in the black around me. Colors
. . . all kinds. Red and green and lemon-yellow, and I'm
moving! There's pain and pushing, and—God!—it's getting
cold. I'm choking! I'm hanging on, but I'm going to drown in
the air out there! I'm—

("That'll be enough," Cullinan said hastily. To Warshow
he explained, "Birth trauma. Nasty. No need to put him
through it all over again." Warshow shivered a little and
blotted his forehead.)

("Should I go on?" Falked asked.)
("Yes. Go on.")

I'm four, and it's raining *plunk-a-plunk* outside. It looks
like the whole world's turned gray. Mama and daddy are away,
and I'm alone again. Uncle is downstairs. I don't know uncle
really, but he seems to be here all the time. Mama and daddy
are away a lot. Being alone is like a cold rainstorm. It rains a lot
here.

I'm in my bed, thinking about mama. I want mama.
Mama took the jet plane somewhere. When I'm big, I want to
take jet planes somewhere too—someplace warm and bright
where it doesn't rain.

Downstairs the phone rings, jingle-jingle. Inside my head
I can see the screen starting to get bright and full of colors, and
I try to picture mama's face in the middle of the screen. But I
can't. I hear uncle's voice talking, low and mumbly. I decide I
don't like uncle, and I start to cry.

Uncle's here, and he's telling me I'm too big to cry. That I
shouldn't cry any more. I tell him I want mama.

Uncle makes a nasty-mouth, and I cry louder.

Hush, he tells me. Quiet, Matt. There, there, Matty boy.

He straightens my blankets, but I scrunch my legs up under me and mess them up again because I know it'll annoy him. I like to annoy him because he isn't mama or daddy. But this time he doesn't seem to get annoyed. He just tidies them up again, and he pats my forehead. There's sweat on his hands, and he gets it on me.

I want mama, I tell him.

He looks down at me for a long time. Then he tells me, mama's not coming back.

Not *ever*, I ask?

No, he says. Not ever.

I don't believe him, but I don't start crying, because I don't want him to know he can scare me. How about daddy, I say. Get him for me.

Daddy's not going to come back either, he tells me.

I don't believe you, I say. I don't like you, uncle. I hate you.

He shakes his head and coughs. You'd better learn to like me, he says. You don't have anybody else any more.

I don't understand him, but I don't like what he's saying. I kick the blankets off the bed, and he picks them up. I kick them off again, and he hits me.

Then he bends over quick and kisses me, but he doesn't smell right and I start to cry. Rain comes. I want mama I yell, but mama never comes. Never at all.

(Falk fell silent for a moment and closed his eyes. "Was she dead?" Cullinan prodded.)

("She was dead," Falk said. "She and dad were killed in a fluke jetliner accident, coming back from holiday in Bangkok. I was four, then. My uncle raised me. We didn't get along, much, and when I was fourteen he put me in the Academy. I stayed there four years, took two years of graduate technique, then joined Terran Imports. Two-year hitch on Denufar, then transferred to Commander Warshow's ship *Magyar* where—where—")

(He stopped abruptly. Cullinan glanced at Warshow and said, "He's warmed up now, and we're ready to strike paydirt, to mangle a metaphor." To Falk, he said, "Tell us how you met Thetona.")

* * *

I'm alone in Kollidor and wandering around alone. It's a big sprawling place with funny-looking conical houses and crazy streets, but deep down underneath I can see it's just like Earth. The people are people. They're pretty bizarre, but they've got one head and two arms and two legs, which makes them more like people than some of the aliens I've seen.

Warshow gave us afternoon's liberty. I don't know why I've left the ship, but I'm here in the city alone. Alone. Dammit, *alone!*

The streets are paved, but the sidewalks aren't. Suddenly I'm very tired and I feel dizzy. I sit down at the edge of the sidewalk and put my head in my hands. The aliens just walk around me, like people in any big city would.

Mama, I think.

Then I think, *Where did that come from?*

And suddenly a great empty loneliness comes welling up from inside of me and spills out all over me, and I start to cry. I haven't cried—since—not in a long time. But now I cry, hoarse ratchety gasps and tears and rolling down my face and dribbling into the corners of my mouth. Tears taste salty, I think. A little like raindrops.

My side starts to hurt where I had the accident aboard ship. It begins up near my ear and races like a blue flame down my body to my thigh, and it hurts like a devil. The doctors told me I wouldn't hurt any more. They lied.

I feel my aloneness like a sealed spacesuit around me, cutting me off from everyone. *Mama,* I think again. Part of me is saying, *act like a grownup,* but that part of me is getting quieter and quieter. I keep crying, and I want desperately to have my mother again. I realize now I never knew my mother at all, except for a few years long ago.

Then there's a musky, slightly sickening smell, and I know one of the aliens is near me. They're going to grab me by the scruff and haul me away like any weepy-eyed drunk in the public streets. Warshow will give me hell.

You're crying, Earthman, a warm voice says.

The Kollidorian language is kind of warm and liquid and easy to learn, but this sounds especially warm. I turn around, and there's this big native dame.

Yeah, I'm crying, I say, and look away. Her big hands clamp down on me and hang on, and I shiver a little. It feels funny to be handled by an alien woman.

She sits down next to me. You look very sad, she says.

I am, I tell her.

Why are you sad?

You'd never understand, I say. I turn my head away and feel tears start creeping out of my eyes, and she grabs me impulsively. I nearly retch from the smell of her, but in a minute or two I see it's sort of sweet and nice in a strange way.

She's wearing an outfit like a potato sack, and it smells pretty high. But she pulls my head against her big warm breasts and leaves it there.

What's your name, unhappy Earthman?

Falk, I say. Matthew Falk.

I'm Thetona, she says. I live alone. Are you lonely?

I don't know, I say. I really don't know.

But how can you not know if you're lonely, she asks.

She pulls my head up out of her bosom and our eyes come together. Real romantic. She's got eyes like tarnished half dollars. We look at each other, and she reaches out and pushes the tears out of my eyes.

She smiles. I think it's a smile. She has about thirty notches arranged in a circle under her nose, and that's a mouth. All the notches pucker. Behind them I see bright needly teeth.

I look up from her mouth to her eyes again, and this time they don't look tarnished so much. They're bright like the teeth, and deep and warm.

Warm. Her odor is warm. Everything about her is warm.

I start to cry again—compulsively, without knowing why, without knowing what the hell is happening to me. She seems to flicker, and I think I see a Terran woman sitting there cradling me. I blink. Nothing there but an ugly alien.

Only she's not ugly any more. She's warm and lovely, in a strange sort of way, and the part of me that disagrees is very tiny and tinny-sounding. I hear it yelling, *No*, and then it stops and winks out.

Something strange is exploding inside me. I let it explode. It bursts like a flower—a rose, or a violet, and that's what I smell instead of *her*.

I put my arms around her.

Do you want to come to my house, she asks.

Yes, yes, I say. Yes!

* * *

Abruptly, Falk stopped on the ringing affirmative, and his glazed eyes closed. Cullinan fired the stunner once, and the boy's taut body slumped.

"Well?" Warshow asked. His voice was dry and harsh. "I feel unclean after hearing that."

"You should," the psychman said. "It's one of the slimiest things I've uncovered yet. And you don't understand it, do you?"

The commander shook his head slowly. "No. Why'd he do it? He's in love with her—but *why*?"

Cullinan chuckled. "You'll see. But I want a couple of other people here when I yank it out. I want the girl, first of all—and I want Sigstrom."

"The doctor? What the hell for?"

"Because—if I'm right—he'll be very interested in hearing what comes out." Cullinan grinned enigmatically. "Let's give Falk a rest, eh? After all that talking, he needs it."

"So do I," Warshow said.

(Four people watched silently as Falk slipped into the drug-induced trance a second time. Warshow studied the face of the alien girl Thetona for some sign of the warmth Falk had spoken of. And yes, Warshow saw—it was there. Behind her sat Sigstrom, the *Magyar's* head medic. To his right, Cullinan. And lying on the cot in the far corner of the cabin, eyes open but unseeing, was Matt Falk.)

("Matt, can you hear me?" Cullinan asked. "I want you to back up a little . . . you're aboard ship now. The time is approximately one month ago. You're working in the converter section, you and Dave Murff, handling hot stuff. Got that?")

("Yes," Falk said. "I know what you mean.")

I'm in Converter Section AA, getting thorium out of hock to feed to the reactors; we've gotta keep the ship moving. Dave Murff's with me.

We make a good team on the waldoes.

We're running them now, picking up chunks of hot stuff and stowing them in the reactor bank. It's not easy to manipulate the remote-control mechanihands, but I'm not scared. This is my job, and I know how to do it.

I'm thinking about that bastard Warshow, though. Noth-

within something within the ship. Wheels within wheels; doors inside doors. Chinese puzzlebox with me inside.

Soft fluid comes licking over me, nudging itself in where the tissue is torn and blasted and the flesh bubbled from heat. Caressing each individual cell, bathing my body organ by organ, I'm being repaired.

I float on an ocean and in an ocean. My body is healing rapidly. The pain ceases.

I'm not conscious of the passage of time at all. Minutes blend into minutes without joint; time flows unbreakingly, and I'm being lulled into a soft, unending existence. Happiness, I think. Security. Peace.

I like it here.

Around me, a globe of fluid. Around that, a striated webwork of metal. Around that, a spheroid spaceship, and around that a universe. Around that? I don't know, and I don't care. I'm safe here, where there's no pain, no fear.

Blackness. Total and utter blackness. Security equals blackness and softness and quiet. But then—

What are they doing?

What's happening?

Blue darts of light against the blackness, and now a swirl of colors. Green, red, yellow. Light bursts in and dazzles me. Smells, feels, noises.

The cradle is rocking. I'm moving.

No. They're pulling me. Out!

It's getting cold, and I can't breath. I'm choking! I try to hang on, but they won't let go! They keep pulling me out, out, out into the world of fire and pain!

I struggle. I won't go. But it doesn't do any good. I'm out, finally.

I look around. Two blurry figures above me. I wipe my eyes and things come clear. Warshow and Sigstrom, that's who they are.

Sigstrom smiles and says, booming, Well, he's healed wonderfully!

A miracle, Warshow says. A miracle.

I wobble. I want to fall, but I'm lying down already. They keep talking, and I start to cry in rage.

But there's no way back. It's over. All, all over. And I'm terribly alone.

Falk's voice died away suddenly. Warshow fought an

We have studied white dwarfs for centuries, and we know their secrets—so we think. A cup of matter from a white dwarf now orbits the observatory on Pluto for our further illumination.

But the star on our screen was different.

It had once been a large star—greater than the Chandrasekhar limit, 1.2 solar masses. Thus it was not content to shrink step by step to the status of a white dwarf. The stellar core grew so dense that catastrophe came before stability; when it had converted all its hydrogen to iron-56, it fell into catastrophic collapse and went supernova. A shock wave ran through the core, converting the kinetic energy of collapse into heat. Neutrinos spewed outward; the envelope of the star reached temperatures upwards of 200 billion degrees; thermal energy became intense radiation, streaming away from the agonized star and shedding the luminosity of a galaxy for a brief, fitful moment.

What we beheld now was the core left behind by the supernova explosion. Even after that awesome fury, what was intact was of great mass. The shattered hulk had been cooling for eons, cooling toward the final death. For a small star, that death would be the simple death of coldness: the ultimate burnout, the black dwarf drifting through the void like a hideous mound of ash, lightless, without warmth. But this, our stellar core, was still beyond the Chandrasekhar limit. A special death was reserved for it, a weird and improbable death.

And that was why we had come to watch it perish, the microcephalon and the adapted girl and I.

I parked our small vessel in an orbit that gave the dark star plenty of room. Miranda busied herself with her measurements and computations. The microcephalon had more abstruse things to do. The work was well divided; we each had our chore. The expense of sending a ship so great a distance had necessarily limited the size of the expedition. Three of us: a representative of the basic human stock, a representative of the adapted colonists, a representative of the race of microcephalons, the Quendar people, the only other intelligent beings in the known universe.

Three dedicated scientists. And therefore three who would live in serene harmony during the course of the work, since as everyone knows scientists have no emotions and think only of their professional mysteries. As everyone knows.

I said to Miranda, "Where are the figures for radial oscillation?"

She replied, "See my report. It'll be published early next year in—"

"Damn you, are you doing that deliberately? I need those figures now!"

"Give me your totals on the mass-density curve, then."

"They aren't ready. All I've got is raw data."

"That's a lie! The computer's been running for days! I've seen it," she boomed at me.

I was ready to leap at her throat. It would have been a mighty battle; her 300-pound body was not trained for personal combat as mine was, but she had all the advantages of strength and size. Could I club her in some vital place before she broke me in half? I weighed my options.

Then the microcephalon appeared and made peace once more, with a few feather-soft words.

Only the alien among us seemed to conform at all to the stereotype of that emotionless abstraction, "the scientist." It was not true, of course; for all we could tell, the microcephalon seethed with jealousies and lusts and angers, but we had no clue to their outward manifestation. Its voice was flat as a vocoder transmission. The creature moved peacefully among us, the mediator between Miranda and me. I despised it for its mask of tranquility. I suspected, too, that the microcephalon loathed the two of us for our willingness to vent our emotions, and took a sadistic pleasure from asserting superiority by calming us.

We returned to our research. We still had some time before the last collapse of the dark star.

It had cooled nearly to death. Now there was still some thermonuclear activity within that bizarre core, enough to keep the star too warm for an actual landing. It was radiating primarily in the optical band of the spectrum, and by stellar standards its temperature was nil, but for us it would be like prowling the heart of a live volcano.

Finding the star had been a chore. Its luminosity was so low that it could not be detected optically at a greater distance than a light-month or so; it had been spotted by a satellite-borne X-ray telescope that had detected the emanations of the degenerate neutron gas of the core. Now we gathered round and performed our functions of measurement. We recorded things like neutron drip and electron capture. We computed the time remaining before the final collapse. Where necessary, we collaborated; most of the time we went our separate ways. The tension aboard ship was nasty. Miranda went out of her way to provoke me. And, though I like to think I was beyond and above her beastliness, I have to confess that I matched her, obstruction for obstruction. Our alien companion never made any overt attempt to annoy us; but indirect aggression can be maddening in close quarters, and the microcephalon's benign indifference to us was as potent a force for dissonance as Miranda's outright shrewishness or my own deliberately mulish responses.

The star hung in our viewscreen, bubbling with vitality that belied its dying state. The islands of slag, thousands of miles in diameter, broke free and drifted at random on the sea of inner flame. Now and then spouting eruptions of stripped particles came heaving up out of the core. Our figures showed that the final collapse was drawing near, and that meant that an awkward choice was upon us. Someone was going to have to monitor the last moments of the dark star. The risks were high. It could be fatal.

None of us mentioned the ultimate responsibility.

We moved toward the climax of our work. Miranda continued to annoy me in every way, sheerly for the devilishness of it. How I hated her! We had begun this voyage coolly, with nothing dividing us but professional jealousy. But the months of proximity had turned our quarrel into a personal feud. The mere sight of her maddened me, and I'm sure she reacted the same way. She devoted her energies to an immature attempt to trouble me. Lately she took to walking around the ship in the nude, I suspect trying to stir some spark of sexual feeling in me that she could douse with a blunt, mocking refusal. The trouble was that I could feel no desire whatever for a grotesque adapted creature like Miranda, a mound of muscle and bone twice my size. The sight of her massive udders and monumental buttocks stirred nothing in me but disgust.

The witch! Was it desire she was trying to kindle by exposing herself that way, or loathing? Either way, she had me. She must have known that.

In our third month in orbit around the dark star, the microcephalon announced, "The coordinates show an approach to the Schwarzschild radius. It is time to send our vehicle to the surface of the star."

"Which one of us rides monitor?" I asked.

Miranda's beefy hand shot out at me. "You do."

"I think you're better equipped to make the observations," I told her sweetly.

"Thank you, no."

"We must draw lots," said the microcephalon.

"Unfair," said Miranda. She glared at me. "He'll do something to rig the odds. I couldn't trust him."

"How else can we choose?" the alien asked.

"We can vote," I suggested. "I nominate Miranda."

"I nominate him," she snapped.

The microcephalon put his ropy tentacles across the tiny nodule of skull between his shoulders. "Since I do not choose to nominate myself," he said mildly, "it falls to me to make a deciding choice between the two of you. I refuse the responsibility. Another method must be found."

We let the matter drop for the moment. We still had a few more days before the critical time was at hand.

With all my heart I wished Miranda into the monitor capsule. It would mean at best her death, at worst a sober muting of her abrasive personality, if she were the one who sat in vicariously on the throes of the dark star. I was willing to stop at nothing to give her that remarkable and demolishing experience.

What was going to happen to our star may sound strange to a layman; but the theory had been outlined by Einstein and Schwarzschild a thousand years ago, and had been confirmed many times, though never until our expedition had it been observed at close range. When matter reaches a sufficiently high density, it can force the local curvature of space to close around itself, forming a pocket isolated from the rest of the universe. A collapsing supernova core creates just such a Schwarzschild singularity. After it has cooled to near-zero temperature, a core of the proper Chandrasekhar mass undergoes a violent collapse to zero volume, simultaneously attaining an infinite density.

In a way, it swallows itself and vanishes from this universe—for how could the fabric of the continuum tolerate a point of infinite density and zero volume?

Such collapses are rare. Most stars come to a state of cold

equilibrium and remain there. We were on the threshold of a singularity, and we were in a position to put an observer vehicle right on the surface of the cold star, sending back an exact description of the events up until the final moment when the collapsing core broke through the walls of the universe and disappeared.

Someone had to ride gain on the equipment, though. Which meant, in effect, vicariously participating in the death of the star. We had learned in other cases that it becomes difficult for the monitor to distinguish between reality and effect; he accepts the sensory percepts from the distant pickup as his own experience. A kind of psychic backlash results; often an unwary brain is burned out entirely.

What impact would the direct experience of being crushed out of existence in a singularity have on a monitoring observer?

I was eager to find out. But not with myself as the sacrificial victim.

I cast about for some way to get Miranda into that capsule. She, of course, was doing the same for me. It was she who made her move first by attempting to drug me into compliance.

What drug she used, I have no idea. Her people are fond of the nonaddictive hallucinogens, which help them break the monotony of their stark, oversized world. Somehow Miranda interfered with the programming of my food supply and introduced one of her pet alkaloids. I began to feel the effects an hour after I had eaten. I walked to the screen to study the surging mass of the dark star—much changed from its appearance of only a few months before—and as I looked, the image in the screen began to swirl and melt, and tongues of flame did an eerie dance along the horizons of the star.

I clung to the rail. Sweat broke from my pores. Was the ship liquefying? The floor heaved and buckled beneath me. I looked at the back of my hand and saw continents of ash set in a grouting of fiery magma.

Miranda stood behind me. "Come with me to the capsule," she murmured. "The monitor's ready for launching now. You'll find it wonderful to see the last moments."

Lurching after her, I padded through the strangely altered ship. Miranda's adapted form was even more alien than usual; her musculature rippled and flowed, her golden hair held all the colors of the spectrum, her flesh was oddly puckered and cratered, with wiry filaments emerging from the skin. I felt quite calm about entering the capsule. She slid back the hatch, revealing the gleaming console of the panel within and I began to enter, and then suddenly the hallucination deepened and I saw in the darkness of the capsule a devil beyond all imagination.

I dropped to the floor and lay there twitching.

Miranda seized me. To her I was no more than a doll. She lifted me, began to thrust me into the capsule. Perspiration soaked me. Reality returned. I slipped from her grasp and wriggled away, rolling toward the bulkhead. Like a beast of primordial forests she came ponderously after me.

"No," I said. "I won't go."

She halted. Her face twisted in anger, and she turned away from me, in defeat. I lay panting and quivering until my mind was purged of phantoms. It had been close.

It was my turn a short while later. Fight force with force, I told myself. I could not risk more of Miranda's treachery. Time was running short.

From our surgical kit I took a hypnoprobe used for anesthesia, and rigged it in a series with one of Miranda's telescope antennae. Programming it for induction of docility, I left it to go to work on her. When she made her observations, the hypnoprobe would purr its siren song of sinister coaxing, and—perhaps—Miranda would bend to my wishes.

It did not work.

I watched her going to her telescopes. I saw her broad-beamed form settling in place. In my mind I heard the hypnoprobe's gentle whisper, as I knew it must sound to Miranda. It was telling her to relax, to obey. The capsule . . . get into the capsule . . . you will monitor the crawler . . . you . . . you . . . you will do it . . ."

I waited for her to arise and move like a sleepwalker to the waiting capsule. Her tawny body was motionless. Muscles rippled beneath that obscenely bare flesh. The probe had her! Yes! It was getting to her!

No.

She clawed at the telescope as though it were a steel-tipped wasp drilling for her brain. The barrel recoiled, and she pushed herself away from it, whirling around. Her eyes glowed with rage. Her enormous body reared up before me.

She seemed half berserk. The probe had had some effect on her; I could see her dizzied strides, and knew that she was awry. But it had not been potent enough. Something within that adapted brain of hers gave her the strength to fight off the murky shroud of hypnotism.

"You did that!" she roared. "You gimmicked the telescope, didn't you?"

"I don't know what you mean, Miranda."

"Liar! Fraud! Sneak!"

"Calm down. You're rocking us out of orbit."

"I'll rock all I want! What was that thing that had its fingers in my brain? You put it there? What was it, the hypnoprobe you used?"

"Yes," I admitted coolly. "And what was it you put into my food? Which hallucinogen?"

"It didn't work."

"Neither did my hypnoprobe. Miranda, someone's got to get into that capsule. In a few hours we'll be at the critical point. We don't dare come back without the essential observations. Make the sacrifice."

"For *you?*"

"For science," I said.

I got the horselaugh I deserved. Then Miranda strode toward me. She had recovered her coordination in full, now, and it seemed as though she were planning to thrust me into the capsule by main force. Her ponderous arms enfolded me. The stink of her thickened hide made me retch. I felt ribs creaking within me. I hammered at her body, searching for the pressure points that would drop her in a felled heap. We punished each other cruelly, grunting back and forth across the cabin. It was a fierce contest of skill against mass. She would not fall, and I would not crush.

The toneless buzz of the microcephalon said, "Release each other. The collapsing star is nearing its Schwarzschild radius. We must act now."

Miranda's arms slipped away from me. I stepped back, glowering at her, to suck breath into my battered body. Livid bruises were appearing on her skin. We had come to a mutual awareness of mutual strength; but the capsule still was empty. Hatred hovered like a globe of ball lightning between us. The gray, greasy alien creature stood to one side.

I would not care to guess which one of us had the idea

first, Miranda or I. But we moved swiftly. The microcephalon
scarcely murmured a word of protest as we hustled it down the
passage and into the room that held the capsule. Miranda was
smiling. I felt relief. She held the alien tight while I opened
the hatch, and then she thrust it through. We dogged the
hatch together.

"Launch the crawler," she said.

I nodded and went to the controls. Like a dart from a
blowgun the crawler housing was expelled from our ship and
journeyed under high acceleration to the surface of the dark
star. It contained a compact vehicle with sturdy jointed legs,
controlled by remote pickup from the observation capsule
aboard ship. As the observer moved arms and feet within the
control harnesses, servo relays actuated the hydraulic pistons
in the crawler, eight light-days away. It moved in parallel
response, clambering over the slag-heaps of a solar surface that
no organic life could endure.

The microcephalon operated the crawler with skill. We
watched through the shielded video pickups, getting a close-
range view of that inferno. Even a cold sun is more terrifyingly
hot than any planet of man.

The signals coming from the star altered with each
moment, as the full force of the red-shift gripped the fading
light. Something unutterably strange was taking place down
there; and the mind of our microcephalon was rooted to the
scene. Tidal gravitational forces lashed the star. The crawler
was lifted, heaved, compressed, subjected to strains that
slowly ripped it apart. The alien witnessed it all, and dictated
an account of what he saw, slowly, methodically, without a
flicker of fear.

The singularity approached. The tidal forces aspired
toward infinity. The microcephalon sounded bewildered at
last as it attempted to describe the topological phenomena that
no eye had seen before. Infinite density, zero volume—how
did the mind comprehend it? The crawler was contorted into
an inconceivable shape; and yet its sensors obstinately continued to relay data, filtered through the mind of the microcephalon and into our computer banks.

Then came silence. Our screens went dead. The unthinkable had at last occurred, and the dark star had passed within
the radius of singularity. It had collapsed into oblivion, taking
with it the crawler. To the alien in the observation capsule

aboard our ship, it was as though he too had vanished into the pocket of hyperspace that passed all understanding.

I looked toward the heavens. The dark star was gone. Our detectors picked up the outpouring of energy that marked its annihilation. We were buffeted briefly on the wave of force that ripped outward from the place where the star had been, and then all was calm.

Miranda and I exchanged glances.

"Let the microcephalon out," I said.

She opened the hatch. The alien sat quite calmly at the control console. It did not speak. Miranda assisted it from the capsule. Its eyes were expressionless; but they had never shown anything, anyway.

We are on our way back to the worlds of our galaxy, now. The mission has been accomplished. We have relayed priceless and unique data.

The microcephalon has not spoken since we removed it from the capsule. I do not believe it will speak again.

Miranda and I perform our chores in harmony. The hostility between us is gone. We are partners in crime, now edgy with guilt that we do not admit to one another. We tend our shipmate with loving care.

Someone had to make the observations, after all. There were no volunteers. The situation called for force, or the deadlock would never have been broken.

But Miranda and I hated each other, you say? Why, then, should we cooperate?

We both are humans, Miranda and I. The microcephalon is not. In the end, that made the difference. In the last analysis, Miranda and I decided that we humans must stick together. There are ties that bind.

We speed on toward civilization.

She smiles at me. I do not find her hateful now. The microcephalon is silent.

The
Four

More than a mile of dark sea-water roofed the city. It lay off the Atlantic coast of North America, nestling beneath the waves, cradled by hundreds of atmospheres of pressure. In the official records, the city's designation was Undersea Refuge PL-12. But the official records, like the rest of the landside world, lay blasted and shattered, and the people of Undersea Refuge PL-12 called their city New Baltimore. Eleven thousand was New Baltimore's population, a figure set by long-dead landside authorities and maintained by rigorous policies of control.

The history of New Baltimore stretched back for one hundred thirteen years. Not one of its eleven thousand inhabitants had not been born in the deep, under the laminated dome that was the city's shield. In the ninetieth year of New Baltimore a child had been allotted to the Foyle family, and Mary Foyle was born. And in the hundred thirteenth year of the city—

Mary Foyle lay coiled like a fetal snake in her room at the New Baltimore Social Hall. She lay with feet drawn up, arms locked over her bosom, eyes closed, mouth slightly open. She was twenty-three, blonde, terrible in her wrath. She was not asleep.

At the ninth hour of the day and the second of her three-hour Free Period, she sensed the approach of a visitor, and hatred gathered in her cold mind. Bitterly, she disengaged herself from what she had been doing, and extended a tendril of thought as far as the door. The mind she encountered was weak, pliable, amiable.

Yes, she thought, Roger Carroll, the silly goose.

Roger's mind formed the thought, *Mary, may I come in?* and he verbalized as far as "Mary, may—" when she darted a hissing prong of thought at him, and he reddened, cut short his sentence and opened the door.

Lazily Mary Foyle tidied her wrappings and looked up at

Roger. He was thin, like all men of New Baltimore, but well
muscled and strong. He was a year her junior; gifted like her,
with the Powers, but weak of will and flabby of purpose.

"You'll destroy your Powers if you don't give them free
play," she thought coldly at him.

"I'm sorry. It was a slip."

She glared bleakly. "Suppose I slipped and blasted your
silly mind?"

"Mary, I've never denied that you're more powerful than I
am—than all three of us put together—"

"Quiet," she ordered. "The others are coming. Try not to
look so much like a blithering fool."

Her mind had detected the arrival of the other two
members of their little group. Moments later Roger's slower
mind had received the signal, and he added his friendly
welcome to Mary's cold one.

Michael Sharp entered first; after him, Tom Devers. They
were in their late twenties. In them the Powers had ripened
slowly, and Mary had found them out only two years before.
Roger had been under her sway for nine years. She herself had
first sensed the Powers stirring in her mind fifteen years earlier.

There was a moment of blending as the four minds met—
Mary's as always, harshly dominant, never yielding for a
moment the superiority that gave her the leadership of the
group. The greeting was done with; the Four were as one, and
the confines of the room seemed to shrink until it cradled their
blended minds as securely as the Dome held back the sea from
the buildings of New Baltimore.

"Well?" Mary demanded. The challenge rang out and she
sensed Roger's involuntary flinch. "Well?" she asked again,
deliberately more strident.

Slowly, sadly, came the response: affirmative from
Michael, affirmative from Tom, weakly affirmative from Roger.
A slow smile spread over Mary's face. Affirmative!

Roger's mind added hesitantly, "Of course, there's grave
danger—"

"Danger adds spice."

"If we're caught we're finished—"

Impetuously Mary extended her mind toward Roger's,
entered it, made slight adjustments in Roger's endocrine
balance. Currents of fear ceased to flow through his body.
Trepidation died away.

"All right," Roger said, his mental voice a whisper now. "I agree to join you."

"All agreed, then," Mary said. Her mind enfolded those of the three lean, pale men who faced her. The borders of the small room grew smaller yet, shrank to the size of Mary's skull, then expanded outward.

Four minds linked as one leaped five thousand feet skyward, toward the crisped and blackened land above.

Mary alone could not have done it. She had tried, and much of her bitterness stemmed from the fact that she had failed. She had sent her mind questing out along the sea-bottom, rippling through the coraled ooze to New Chicago and New London and New Miami and the other domed cities that dotted the Atlantic floor. It was strictly illegal for a Sensitive to make contact with the mind of an inhabitant of another Dome, but Mary had never cared much for what the legal authorities said.

She had reached the other cities of the sea-bottom easily enough—though the effort of getting to New London had left her sweat-soaked and panting—but breaking through to the surface eluded her. Time and again she sent shafts skyward, launching beams of thought through the thick blanket of water above, striving to pierce the ocean and see the land, the ruined land deserted and bare, the land made desolate by radiation. She wanted to see the sky in its blueness, and the golden terror of the naked sun.

She failed. Less than a thousand feet from the surface the impulse sagged, the spear of thought blunted and fell back. In the privacy of her room she tried again, and yet again, until her thin clothes were pasted to her body by sweat.

That was when she realized she would need help.

It was a bitter realization. Slowly Mary had sought out those she needed, from the two hundred Sensitives of New Baltimore. Roger she had known for years, and he was as much under her domination as was her hand or her leg. But Roger was not enough. She found Michael and she found Tom, and when rapport had been established she showed them what she proposed to do.

Using them as boosters, as amplifiers, she intended to hurl a psionic signal through the sea to the surface. She could not do it alone; in series, the four of them might do almost anything.

They lay, the four of them, sprawled on couches in Mary's room. With cold fury she whipped them together into the unit she needed. Michael had objected; after all, the penalty for projecting one's mind beyond the borders of New Baltimore was death. But Mary had quashed that objection, welded the Four into One, cajoled and commanded and pleaded and manipulated.

Now, tenuously, the threaded strand of four-ply thought wove toward the surface.

Mary had seen the tridims projected on the arching screens in General Hall. She had an idea of what the surface was like, all blacks and browns and fused glass and gaunt frameworks that had been buildings. But she wanted to see it for herself. She wanted direct visual experience of this surface world, this dead skin of the planet, cauterized by man's evil. Mary had a lively appreciation of evil.

Upward they traveled. Mary sensed Michael and Tom and Roger clinging to her mind, helping her force the impulse upward. Eyes closed, body coiled, she hurled herself to the task.

And the blackness of the water lightened to dark green as the sun-warmed zone approached. She had not got this far on her earlier, solo attempts. Now her mind rose with little effort into the upper regions of the sea, and without warning cleaved through the barrier of water into the open air.

Michael and Tom and Roger were still with her.

The sight of landside was dazzling.

The first perception was of the sun; smaller than she had expected, but still an awesome object, glowing high in the metal-blue sky. White clouds lay fleecily under the sun.

New Baltimore was some miles out at sea. Drifting lazily but yet with the near-instantaneous speed of thought, they moved landward, ready and eager to see the desolation and ruin.

The shock was overwhelming.

Together, the Four drifted in from the sea, searching for the radiation-blackened fields, the dead land. Instead they saw delicate greenness, carpets of untrodden grass, vaulting thick trees heavy with fruit. Animals grazed peacefully in the lush fields. In the distance, glimmering in the sun, low sloping mountains decked in green rose slowly from the horizon.

Birds sang. Wind whistled gently through the swaying trees. It was as if the hand of man had never approached this land.

Can the scars have healed so soon? Mary wondered. Hardly a century since the bombings destroyed the surface; could the wounds have been covered so rapidly? In wonder she guided the multiple mind down through the warm sky to the ground.

They came alight in a grassy field, sweet with the odor of springtime. Mary felt the tingle of awe. Beings were approaching, floating over the grass without crushing it—not the misshapen mutants some thought might have survived on the surface, but tall godlike beings, smiling their welcome.

A surge of joy rippled through Mary and through her into her three comrades. It would not be hard to teleport their bodies up from the depths. They could live here, in this pleasant land, quitting the confines of New Baltimore. She extended the range of her perception. In every direction lay beauty and peace, and never a sign of the destruction that had been.

Perhaps there was no war, she thought. *The landside people sent our ancestors down into the depths and then hoaxed them.*

And for a hundred years we thought the surface was deadly, radiation-seared, unlivable!

For the first time in her life Mary felt no rancor. Bitterness was impossible in this green world of landside. The sun warmed the fertile land, and all was well.

All—

Sudden constricting impulses tugged at the thread of thought by which the four dreamers held contact with landside.

"Mary, wake up! Come out of it."

She struggled, but not even the combined strength of the Four could resist. Inexorably she found herself being dragged away, back down into the depths, into New Baltimore, into wakefulness.

She opened her eyes and sat up. On the other couches, Michael and Tom and Roger were groggily returning to awareness.

The room was crowded. Six members of the New Baltimore Control Force stood by the door, glaring grimly at her.

Mary tried to lash out, but she was outnumbered; they were six of the strongest Sensitives in New Baltimore, and the fierce grip they held on her mind was unbreakable.

"By what right do you come in here?" she asked, using her voice.

It was Norman Myrick of the Control Force who gave the reply: "Mary, we've been watching you for years. You're under arrest on a charge of projecting beyond the boundaries of New Baltimore."

The trial was a farce.

Henry Markell sat in judgment upon them, in the General Hall of the City of New Baltimore. Procedure was simple. Markell, a Sensitive, opened his mind to the accusing members of the Control Force long enough to receive the evidence against the Four.

Then he offered Mary and her three satellites the chance to assert their innocence by opening *their* minds to him. Sullenly, Mary refused on behalf of the Four. She knew the case was hopeless. If she allowed Markell to peer, their guilt was proven. If she refused, it was an equally tacit admission of guilt. Either way, the penalty loomed. But Mary hoped to retain the integrity of her mind. She had a plan, and a mind-probe would ruin it.

Decision was reached almost immediately after the trial had begun.

Markell said, "I have examined the evidence presented by the Control Force. They have shown that you, Mary, have repeatedly violated our security by making contact with other Domes, and now have inveigled three other Sensitives into joining you for a still bolder attempt. Will you speak now, Mary?"

"We have no defense."

Markell sighed. "You certainly must be aware that our position under the Dome is a vulnerable one. We can never know when the madness that destroyed landside"—Mary smiled knowingly, saying nothing—"will return. We must therefore discourage unofficial contact between Domes by the most severe measures possible. We must retain our position of isolation.

"You, Mary, and your three confederates, have broken this law. The penalty is inevitable. Our borders are rigid here, our population fixed by inexorable boundaries. We cannot tolerate criminals here. The air and food you have consumed up to now is forfeit; four new individuals can be brought into being to replace you. I sentence you to death, you four. This evening you shall be conveyed to the West Aperture and cast through it into the sea."

Mary glared in icy hatred as she heard the death sentence pronounced. Around her, members of the Control Force maintained constant check on her powers, keeping her from loosing a possibly fatal bolt of mental force at the judge or at anyone else. She was straitjacketed. She had no alternative but to submit.

But she had a plan.

They were taken to the West Aperture—a circular sphinctered opening in the framework of the Dome, used only for the purpose of execution. An airlock the size of a man served as the barrier between the pressing tons of the sea and the safety of New Baltimore.

The Four were placed in the airlock, one at a time.

The airlock opened—once, twice, thrice, a fourth time. Mary felt the coolness first, Michael next, then Roger, then Tom. Instantly her mind sought theirs.

"Listen to me! We can save ourselves yet!"

"How? The pressure—"

"Listen! We can link again; teleport ourselves to the surface. You've seen what it's like up there. We can live there. Hurry, join with me!"

"The surface," Roger said. "We can't—"

"We *can* live there. Hurry!"

Michael objected, "Teleportation takes enormous energy. The backwash will smash the Dome. A whole section of the city will be flooded!"

"What do we care?" Mary demanded. "They condemned us to death, didn't they? Well, *I* condemn *them*!"

There was no more time for arguing. Their interchange had taken but a microsecond. They were beginning to drift; in moments, the pressure would kill.

Mary made use of her superior Powers to gather the other three to her. Debating was impossible now. Ruthlessly she drew their minds into hers. She heard Roger's faint protest, but swept it away. For the second time, the Four became

One. Mary gathered strength for the giant leap, not even knowing if she could make it but not bothering to consider the possibility of failure now.

Upward.

The passage was instantaneous, as the four minds, linked in an exponential series, ripped upward through the boiling sea toward the surface. Toward the green, warm, fertile surface.

Toward the blackened, seared, radiation-roasted surface.

Mary had only an instant for surprise. The surface was not at all as her mind had viewed it. Congealed rivers of rock wound through the dark fields of ash. The sky hummed with radioactive particles. No life was visible.

Mary dropped to her knees in the blistering ash still warm from the 11 fires of a century before. The heavy particles lanced through her body. *How can this be?* she wondered. *We saw green lands.*

An impulse reached her from Roger, dying of radiation to her left:

. . . fooled you, Mary. Superior to you in one power, anyway. Imaginative projection. I blanked out real image, substituted phony one. You couldn't tell the difference, could you? Happy dying, Mary . . .

She hissed her hatred and tried to reach him, to rip out his eyes with her nails, but strength failed her. She toppled face-forward, down against the terrible deadly soil of Mother Earth, and waited for the radiation death to overtake her.

Hoaxed, she thought bitterly.

Five thousand feet below, the angry sea, swollen and enraged by the passage of four humans upward through it, crashed against the West Aperture of the New Baltimore dome, crashed again, finally broke through and came raging in, an equal and opposite reaction. Above, Mary Foyle writhed in death-throes under a leaden sky.

Passport to Sirius

Consumer Sixth Class David Carman watched the yellow snake that was the morning telefax sheet come rippling from the wall slot of his bachelor flat. The folds of plastic-impregnated tape slithered into the receiving tray, and Carman surveyed them glumly. He knew there would only be more bad news—more tales of defeat in the Sirian war, more heralding of price increases on the consumer front.

After a moment of hesitation Carman gathered up the telefax spool and slipped it into the scanner-reader. He shuddered as the first news appeared on the screen.

COSTLY SETBACK IN SIRIUS

War Sector, 14 Nov (via subradio)—A Sirian pitchfork maneuver hurled Earth lines back today in the battle for Sirius IV. The sudden alien thrust cost Earth eight destroyers and more than a hundred casualties.

The push began, according to a front-lines communique, when eleven Sirian battle cruisers initiated diversionary tactics in orbit around the Earth base on Sirius IV's seventh moon. Bringing in a battalion of mosquito ships next, the aliens successfully—

Morosely Carman thumbed his weary eyes and moved the scanner further along. All these war stories were pretty much alike. And the telefax reveled in detailed descriptions of each offensive and defensive tactic. Carman knew nothing of war-making; the details bored him.

But the next item was hardly more cheering.

PRICE INDEX TO JUMP AGAIN

Lower Urbdistrict, 16 Nov—Consumer prices are due for another increase spiral as a result of the severe setback suffered by Terran forces in the Sirian sector. Economic Regulator Harrison Morch revealed this morning that a down-the-line 5% increase is likely.

"We tried to hold the line," commented Regulator Morch. "The inflationary trend was too strong to buck, however. It is to be hoped that conclusion of hostilities will soon bring about a reversion to peacetime living standards and—"

With an angry, impatient gesture, Carman blanked the screen. There was little sense spending good money subscribing to the 'fax service if it only brought bad news.

Things hadn't been this bad a year ago, before the war started, he thought, as he dialed breakfast and took his seat by the dispensall. He had even been considering applying for a marriage permit, then. Now, of course, it was out of the question; his economic status was totally altered. And Sally, who worked for the Bureau of Extraterrestrial Affairs, had received a pay boost that put her entirely beyond Carman's aspirations. She was Third Class, now, and would soon marry a wealthy bureau official.

Carman, brooding, munched his somewhat dry algae omelet. He was thirty-three, and not getting younger. He was too pale, too thin, his eyes too close-set, his hair growing sparse. And it seemed that whenever he got some money saved and looked around to better his position, along came some war to send prices shooting up and cripple his savings. Five years ago there had been that thing in Procyon, and then a year or two of peace followed by a scuffle out near Proxima Centauri. And now Sirius.

You can't win, he thought. He finished breakfast mechanically, dropped the dishes in the disposall, and selected his second-best suit with a quick, bitter jab at the wardrobe control buttons.

It came issuing forth: gray crepe, with dark blue trim. The jacket was getting tattered at the elbows.

I'd better buy a new suit, Carman decided, as he stepped out on the pickup platform to hail a jet-cab. *Before clothing prices get astronomical.*

He reached the office at 0700 that morning, with dawn barely brightening the late autumn sky. Carman worked as a sorter in the permit-processing department of the Confederation Passport Office, and so as a government employee had little recourse when the periodic inflation spirals came; he could hardly go on strike against the Confederation.

A good-sized batch of passport applications had already accumulated at his receiving tray. Carman slid easily into the seat, flashed bright but hollow smiles at the five or six fellow workers nearest him, and grabbed at the top sheet of the stack. He estimated quickly that 180 applications had arrived so far. They would be pouring in at a rate of seven a minute the rest of the day.

He computed:

If I process one form every six seconds, ten a minute, I'll gain three per minute on them. Which means I'll catch up with them in about an hour.

If he kept up the ten-a-minute pace, he'd be free to take short breathers later on. This was one of the games he played to make his dreary work more palatable.

The first application was from Consumer Second Class Leebig D. Quellen and family; Consumer Second Class Quellen wanted to visit the Ganymede outpost next summer. Carman plunged the application into the bin stencil-labeled *14a* with his left hand, and with his right took another from the waiting stack. Sort with the left, grab with the right. Carman swayed rhythmically in his seat as he fell into the pattern of the day's work.

After a while he began hitting them twelve to a minute, sometimes thirteen. By 0757 his tray was empty. He sighed. Eight seconds of free time, now, until the next permit reared its ugly head.

Sort, grab . . . sort, grab . . . it was dull but essentially simple work, in a mechanical way. It scarcely taxed his brain. But he was paid accordingly: $163 a week, barely a subsistence wage before the last spiral. And now—

Soon 1030 came. Break time. Carman stretched and rose, noticing angrily that the girl in the upstairs receiving room had slipped three applications in after break time sounded. She was always pulling tricks like that.

Carman had long since reduced break time to a ritual. He crossed the office to the cleanall and held his hands in the energizing bath until his fingertips were wiped clean of their accumulation of stylus grime; then he glanced out of the single big window at the crowded city, turned, and smiled at

Montano, the heavy-set fellow who had occupied the next desk for the six years Carman had worked for the Passport Office.

"Nice day," Montano said. "For November."

"Yes."

"See the morning 'fax? Looks like another upping for prices."

Carman nodded unhappily. "I saw. Don't know how we'll manage."

"Oh, we'll get along. We always do. The wife's due for a raise soon anyway." Montano's wife pushed buttons in a car autofactory. Somehow she seemed to be due for a raise almost every other week.

"That's nice," Carman said.

"Yeah."

"Does she think cars are going up?"

"Damn right," Montano said. "Ford-Chrysler's boosting the stock model to six thousand next month. Need turbogenerators for the war effort, they say. We already got our order in at the old price. You better buy fast if you want one, Carman. Save five hundred bucks now if you're smart."

"I don't need a new car," Carman said.

"Better get *anything* you need now, anyway. Everything's going up. Always does, wartime."

The bell tone announced the end of break time. Carman reached his desk just in time to see a passport application come fluttering down, followed seconds later by another.

"Demons take that girl," he muttered softly. She always cut her break short to plague him with extra work. Now she was six—no, seven—ahead of him.

Justin C. Froelich and family, of Minnetonka, wished permission to visit Pluto next July. Wearily, Carman dropped Justin C. Froelich's application in the proper bin, and reached for the next.

He was seething inwardly, cursing the Passport Office, the girl upstairs, inflation, Economic Regulator Morch, and the world in general. It seemed to be a rat race with no exit from the treadmill.

I've been pushed around too long, he thought. *I ought to fight back a little. Somehow.*

Consumer Sixth Class Carman was on the verge of changing the course of his life. An hour more passed, and 193 additional passport applications disappeared into bins. Finally, he made up his mind to act.

The recruiting officer was a spade-faced, dark-complexioned man with angular features and bright white teeth. He wore the green-and-gold uniform of the United Military Services of Earth. He stared levelly across his shining bare desk at Carman and said, "Would you mind repeating that?"

"I said I wanted to fight. Against Sirius."

The recruiting officer frowned ponderously. After a long pause he said, "I don't see how I can guarantee that. We enroll you; the computer ships you out. Whether you get sent to the war zone or not depends on a variable complex of factors which certainly no civilian should be expected to understand." He shoved a form across the desk toward Carman. "If you fill this out, mac, we can—"

"No," Carman said. "I want a guarantee that I'll see action in the Sirius sector. Dammit, lieutenant—"

"Sergeant."

"—Sergeant, I'm thirty-three. I'm as close to being nobody as anybody can get. If I'm lucky I'll get as high as Third Class someday. I've saved ten thousand bucks, and I suppose the new inflation's going to knock my savings in half the way the last one did."

"Mr. Carman, I don't see how all this—"

"You will. For thirty-three years I've been sitting around on the home front going up and down with each economic spiral while Earth fights wars in Procyon and Proxima C and half a dozen other places. I'm tired of staying home. I want to enlist."

"Sure, mac, but—"

"But I don't want to enlist just to wear a uniform and police the frontiers on Betelgeuse. I want to go to Sirius, and I want to fight. Once in my life I want to engage in positive action on behalf of a Cause." Carman took a deep breath; he hadn't spoken this many words in succession in a long, long time. "Do you understand now? Will you guarantee that I'll be shipped to Sirius if I sign up?"

The sergeant exhaled deeply, unhappily. "I've explained twice that the matter's not in my hands. Maybe I could attach a recommendation—"

"A *guarantee*."

"But—" A crafty light appeared in the recruiting

sergeant's eyes; he drummed the desk top momentarily and said, "You're a very persistent man, mac. You win; I'll see you get assigned to the war zone. Now, why don't you just sign your name here—"

Carman shook his head. "No, thanks. I just changed my mind."

Before the sergeant could protest, Carman had backed warily out of the office and was gone. It had abruptly occurred to him that a recruiting officer's promise was not necessarily final. And there were more direct methods he could use to get into the war.

He returned to the Passport Office at 1313, and the robot eye at the office door took note of it, clicking loudly as he passed through. Ordinarily Carman would have groaned at the loss of thirteen minutes' pay, but, then, ordinarily he would have been at his desk promptly at 1300 anyway.

Everyone else was busily at work; heads bowed, hands groping madly for the incoming applications, his fellow sorters presented an oddly ludicrous sight. Carman resumed his place. Nearly a hundred waiting permits had stacked themselves in the receiving tray during his absence—but this, too, hardly troubled him now.

He went through them at a frantic pace, occasionally hitting as high as twenty per minute. Plenty of them were going to the wrong bins, he realized, but this was no time to worry about that. He caught up with the posting department in less than forty minutes, and made use of his first eight-second breather to draw a blank passport application from his desk drawer; he had always kept a few on hand there.

He filled out the blank patiently, in eight-second bursts between each of the arrivals from above. Where it said *Name and Status*, he wrote *Consumer Sixth Class David Carman*. Where it said *Intended Destination*, he inscribed *Sirius VII* in tidy cursives. Sirius VII was outside the war zone, and so theoretically within reach of commercial traffic, but passports to anywhere in the Sirius system were granted only by special dispensation since the outbreak of hostilities, and Carman knew he had small chance of receiving such dispensation.

Which was why, after the form was completely filled out, he thoughtfully scribbled an expert forgery of the Secretary of Extraterrestrial Affairs' signature on the bottom of the sheet, okaying the application. Humming gently, he dropped the completed blank into the bin labeled 82g and returned his attention to the labors of the day.

The passport took eight days to come through. Carman had some uneasy moments while waiting, though he was ultimately confident of success. After all, the workers who processed the sorted applications and issued the passports probably handled their work as mechanically and hastily as he did in the level above them—and he never had time to check for possible forgeries, so why should they? Never-ending cascades of passport applications descended on them; probably they cursed him for working so fast, just as he in turn scowled up the chute at the girl in the top level.

Five seconds after the passport to Sirius dropped out of his mail chute, Carman was on the phone talking to the secretary of the Personnel Chief at the Passport Office.

"Yes, I said Carman. David Carman, Sixth Class. I've enlisted in the Service and my resignation is effective today. Yes, *today*. My pay check? Oh, burn it," Carman said impatiently, and hung up.

Carman withdrew his entire savings—$9,783.61. The roboteller handed over the cash without comment. Carman took the thick pile of crisp bills, counted slowly through them to the great annoyance of the people behind him in line, and nudged the *acknowledge* stud to let the teller know the transaction was complete. Outside the bank, he signaled for another copter and took it to the Upper Urbdistrict Spaceport, far out on what had once been Long Island.

"A ticket to Sirius?" the dispatcher asked, after the robot ticket vender passed Carman on to him in perplexity. "But the war, you know—we've curtailed our service to the entire sector."

"I don't care," Carman said stolidly. He was growing accustomed to being forceful now; it came easily to him, and he enjoyed it. "You advertise through transportation to Sirius VII. I've got a passport that says I can go there, and I've got six thousand dollars to pay my way. Cash."

"This is very irregular," moaned the dispatcher, a short, harried-looking little man. "We discontinued passenger service to that system eight months ago, when—"

"You could lose your franchise for this," Carman snapped

bluntly. "Sirius VII is nonbelligerent. I have money and a passport. I demand transportation."

In the end, they diverted a freight run bound for Deneb, and put Carman aboard with the promise that they'd drop him at Sirius VII. His passport was in order, and he had the cash for the payment.

The trip took three weeks of steady hyperdrive travel. Six other humans were on board, all bad-smelling crewmen, and the crew of a space freighter is hardly pleasant company on a three-week journey. Carman kept to himself, inventing a form of solitaire he could play making use of hundred-dollar bills, of which he had more than thirty left even after paying passage. The ship's cargo consisted of steers slated for an agrarian colony orbiting Deneb, and Carman lived in a cramped cabin just aft of the cargo hold. He got little sleep.

They put him down finally on the concrete landing apron at Zuorf, crown city of Sirius VII, on the fifth day of 2672, having first radioed the Terran consul there to let them know he was coming. Biggest and muggiest of the twelve planets that circled the dog star, Sirius VII was a vast mountainous world with ugly sprawling cities crammed between the jagged peaks; its people were brawny ursinoids, not long escaped from their neolithic culture stage.

As it happened, some sort of local celebration was in full sway when Carman, a solitary figure with a solitary suitcase of belongings, left the spaceport. Great heavy-set creatures were whirling up and down the streets in each other's arms, looking like so many dancing bears clad in tinsel and frills. Carman stepped hastily back into the shadow of a squat yellow-painted building while a platoon of the huge shaggy aliens came thundering past, to the gay accompaniment of distant tootling music composed in excruciating quarter-tone intervals.

A hand fell lightly on his shoulder. Carman turned and jumped away all in the same nervous motion. He saw an Earthman behind him, clad in the somber black vestments of the Terran diplomatic corps.

"Pardon me if I startled you," the stranger said in a soft, cultured voice. He was a neatly turned out, mildly foppish-looking man in his forties, with elegant features, well-groomed dark hair, delicately shaven brow ridges. Only the startling brass ring through his nostrils marred his otherwise distinguished upper-class appearance.

"I'm the Terran consul on this world," he went on, in the same gentle tones. "Adrian Blyde's my name. Am I right in assuming you're the man who was just dropped off by that freighter?"

"You are. I'm David Carman of Earth. Want to see my passport?"

Consul Blyde smiled serenely. "In due time, Mr. Carman. I'm sure it's in good order. But would you mind telling me precisely *why* you've come to Sirius VII?"

"To join the armed forces. I want to take part in the Sirian campaign."

"To join the armed forces," Blyde repeated in a faintly wonder-struck voice. "Well, well, well. That's very interesting, Mr. Carman. Very. Would you come this way, please?"

Blyde seized him firmly by the fleshy part of his arm and propelled him across the wide, poorly paved street, between two pairs of madly careening bearlike beings, and into a narrow doorway in a building constructed of purple brick.

"The autochthones are celebrating their annual fertility dance through the city from morning to night without rest. Those that keep on their feet the whole day without collapsing are entitled to mate. The weak ones have to try again next year. It's quite a neat genetic system, really."

Carman glanced back through the doorway at the hordes of spinning aliens weaving wildly down the broad street, locked each to each in a desperate grip of love.

"The nose rings denote masculinity," Blyde said. "Terran males who stay here have to wear them too; the natives are very, very fussy about that. When in Rome, you know. I'll give you yours tonight."

"Just a minute," Carman said worriedly, as Blyde unlocked an office door and gestured within to a cluttered little room lined with book tapes and scattered papers. "I don't plan to stay here, you know. The military action's on Sirius IV. That's where I'm going as soon as I've seen the authorities and enlisted."

Blyde dropped heavily into a well-upholstered pneumochair, wiped perspiration from his brow with an obviously scented cloth, and sighed unhappily. "My dear Mr. Carman: I don't know what motives impelled you to come to this system, nor by what chicanery you wangled your passage. But now that you're here, there are several things you should know."

"Such as?"

"For one, there are no hostilities currently taking place anywhere in the Sirius system."

Stunned, Carman gasped, "No—hostilities? Then the war's over?"

Blyde touched his fingertips lightly together. "You misunderstand. There never *was* any war between Earth and Sirius IV. Care for a drink?"

"Rye," Carman said automatically. "Never—was—a—war? But—how—"

"Economic Regulator Harrison Morch of Earth is a great man," Blyde said, putting his head back as if studying the reticulated pattern of paint cracks on the office ceiling. An airconditioner hummed ineffectually somewhere. "Economic Regulator Morch has devoted a lifetime of study to examining the motives governing fluctuations in economic trends."

Carman's throat felt terribly dry. The moist warmth of Sirius VII's atmosphere, the additional drag of the heavier gravity, the calm blandness of the consul's manner, the sheer nonsense he was talking—all these factors were combining to make Carman thoroughly sick.

"What does all this have to do with—"

Blyde raised one manicured hand. "Economic Regulator Morch, through his studies, has reduced to a formula the general economic principle known to theorists for centuries—that spending increases in direct proportion to adverse military news. Consumers go on buying sprees, remembering the last cycle of shortages and of rapid price increases. Money flows more freely. Of course, when the war situation lasts long enough, a period of inflation sets in—making it necessary that an equally virulent peace be waged."

Dimly Carman sensed what was coming. "No," he said.

"Yes. There is no war with Sirius. It was a stroke of genius on Economic Regulator Morch's part to take advantage of the uncertainty of interstellar communication to enforce a news block on the entire Sirius system. It's a simple matter to distribute fabricated war communiqués, invent wholly fictitious spaceships which perish gorily on the demand of the moment, arouse public interest and keep it at a high pitch—"

"You mean," Carman said tonelessly, "that Morch invented this whole war, and arranges Terran victories and losses to fit economic conditions back home?"

"It is a brilliant plan," said Blyde, smiling complacently. "If a decline in spending occurs, word of severe losses in space reaches the home front, and the bad news serves to unloose the purse strings. When the economy has been reinflated, Earth's legions forge on to victory, and spending drops off again. We spend heavily in times of stress, when we need consolation—not in peacetime."

Carman blinked. "I spent six thousand dollars and forged a passport to come here and find out *this*! The one time in my life I decided to *do* something, instead of sitting back and letting things happen to me, I discover it's all a hoax." He flexed his fingers experimentally, as if wondering what he might do with them.

Blyde seemed to be sympathetic. "It is, I realize, terribly awkward for you. But no more so than it is to us, who have the strenuous task of preserving this beneficial hoax and protecting it from would-be exposers."

"Are you going to kill me, then?"

Blyde blanched at the blunt question. "Mr. Carman! We are not barbarians!"

"Well, what *are* you going to do with me?"

The consul shrugged. "The one completely satisfactory thing. We'll find you a good job here on Sirius VII. You'll be much happier here than you ever were on Earth. Naturally, you can't be permitted to return home."

But the man who can forge a passport to Sirius can also find a way home. In Carman's case it took him seven full months—months of living in the sticky, endless heat of Sirius VII, dodging the playful ursinoid natives, kowtowing to Blyde (whose secretary he became, at $60 a week) and wearing a brass nose ring through his nostrils.

It was seven months before he had mastered Blyde's signature to his own satisfaction, and knew enough of local diplomatic protocol to be able to requisition a spaceship from the small military outpost just outside Zuorf. A messenger—there were no phones on the planet, for obscure religious reasons—came to the consulate to announce that the ship was ready.

"Wait outside," Carman told the boy.

Blyde looked up from behind his desk and said, "What does he mean?"

"The one I'm taking back to Earth," said Carman, and released the sleep capsule. Blyde smiled sweetly as he slipped into unconsciousness. Carman followed the boy to the spaceport.

A slim, trim two-man ship waited there, sleek and golden-hulled in the bright sunlight. The pilot was an efficient-looking space-tanned man named Duane.

"Diplomatic pouch," Carman said, handing over the leather attaché case he had prepared for the occasion. Duane stored it reverently in the hold, and they blasted off.

"Sirius IV first," Carman ordered. "I'm supposed to take films. Top secret, of course."

"Of course."

They circled the small pockmarked gray fourth planet at fifty thousand feet, and Carman took enough cloud-piercing infrared shots to prove conclusively that there was not and never had been any war between the amiable amphibious aborigines and Earth. Satisfied, he ordered the pilot to proceed immediately toward Sol.

They reached Earth nineteen days later, on August 3, 2672. A squad of security police was waiting for them as they landed at Upper Urbdistrict Spaceport, and Carman was swiftly conveyed to a cell in Confederation Detention House in the tunnels far below Old Manhattan. Blyde had sent word ahead via subradio concerning Carman's escape, it seemed.

In his cell, later that evening, Carman was visited by a parched-looking, almost fleshless man in the blue cape and red wig of high governmental office.

"So you're the culprit!"

"That's what they tell me. Who are you?"

"Ferdan Veller, Administrative Assistant to Regulator Morch. The Regulator sent me to see who you were and what you were like."

"Well, now you've seen," Carman said. "Get out."

Assistant Veller's melancholy eyes widened. "I see you're a forceful man, Mr. Carman. No doubt you're full of plans for escaping, recapturing your confiscated films, and letting the world know what a dastardly hoax is being perpetrated in the interests of a balanced economy. Eh?"

"I might be," Carman admitted.

"You might be interested in this morning's telefax sheet, then," Veller said. He extended a torn-off yellow strip.

The headline was:

NEW AGGRESSION THREATENS EARTH!

Government City, 3 Aug—Word reached Earth today of yet another threat to her peace, coming hot on the heels of the recently concluded police action in the Sirius sector. Forces in the Great Andromeda Nebula have issued statements inimical to Earth, and a new conflict looms—

"You killed off Sirius because you were afraid I'd expose it," Carman said accusingly. "And now you're starting up a new one."

Veller nodded smugly. "Quite. The Great Andromeda Nebula happens to be nine hundred thousand light-years away. The round trip, even by hyperdrive, takes some twenty years." He grinned, showing a double row of square, tartared teeth. "You're a forceful man, Mr. Carman. You may very well escape. You may even reach Andromeda and return with evidence once again unmasking us. If you live long enough to return, that is. I think our economic program is in no immediate danger from you."

He left, smiling gravely. The cell door closed with a harsh metallic crash.

"Come back!" Carman yelled. "You can't hoax mankind like that! I'll let everyone know! I'll get out and expose—"

There was no answer, not even a catcall. No one was listening. And, Carman realized dully, no one was going to listen to him at all, ever again.

Counterpart

Mark Jenner delivered the play's final line with as much force as he could muster, and the curtain dropped like a shroud, cutting off stage from audience. Jenner gasped for breath and fashioned a warm smile for his face to wear. The other six members of the cast left the wings and arranged themselves around him, and the curtain rose again for the calls. A trickle of applause crossed the footlights.

This is it, Jenner thought. *We're through.*

He bowed graciously, peering beyond the glare of the foots to count the house. The theater was about three quarters full—but half the people out there were free-riders, pulled in by the management just to give the house a semblance of fullness. And how many of the others were discount-ticket purchasers? Probably, Jenner thought as the curtain dropped again, there were no more than fifty legitimate customers in the house. And so another play went down the drain. A savage voice within him barked mockingly, telling him that it was *his* fault, that he no longer had what it took to hold an audience, that he lacked the subtle magnetism needed to pull people out of their homes and into the theater.

There would be no more curtain calls. Tiredly, Jenner walked off into the wings and saw Dan Hall, the producer, standing there. Abruptly the tinsel glamor of curtain calls faded. There could be only one reason why Hall was here now, and the dour, sallow cast of the producer's pudgy face left no doubt in Jenner's mind. Closing notices would be posted tonight. Tomorrow, Mark Jenner would be back to living off capital again and waiting out his days.

"Mark . . ."

Jenner stopped. Hall had reached out to touch his arm. "Evening, Dan. How goes it?"

"Bad."

"The receipts?"

Hall chuckled dryly. "What receipts? We had a houseful of unemployed actors sitting out there on passes; and the advance sale for tomorrow night is about eleven bucks' worth."

"There isn't going to be any tomorrow night, is there, Dan?" Jenner asked leadenly.

Hall did not answer. Marie Haas, the ingenue, radiant in the sparkling gown that looked so immodest on so young a girl, glided toward them. She wrapped one arm around the rotund producer, one around Jenner. On stage, the hands were busy pulling the set apart.

"Big house tonight, wasn't it?" she twittered.

"I was just telling Mark," Hall said. "Most of those people were unemployed actors here on passes."

"And," Jenner added, "there are seven more unemployed actors here on this stage right now."

"No!" Marie cried.

Jenner tried to smile. It was rough on a girl of nineteen to lose her first big play after a ten-day run; but, he thought, it was rougher on a forty-year-old ex-star. It wasn't so long ago, he told himself, that the name Mark Jenner on a marquee meant an automatic season's run. *Lovely to Look At*, opened October 16, 1973, ran 630 performances. *Lorelei*, opened December 9, 1977, ran 713 performances. *Girl of the Dawn*, opened February 7, 1981, ran 583 performances. *Misty Isle*, opened March 6, 1989—ran ten performances. Jenner peered wearily at the producer. The rest of the cast had gathered round, now, half of them still in war paint and costume. As the star, Jenner had the right to ask the question. He asked it.

"We're through, aren't we, Dan?"

Hall nodded slowly. "The theater owner told me tonight that we're below the minimum draw. He's exercising option and throwing us out; he wants to rent the place for video. We're through, all right."

Jenner climbed methodically out of his costume, removed his makeup, cocked a sardonic eye on the spangled star on the door of his dressing cubicle, and left the theater. He had arranged to meet his old friend Walt Hollis after the show for a drink. Hollis was an electrician, currently handling the lights for one of the other Broadway shows—one of the hits. They had agreed to meet in a bar Jenner liked, on Forty-ninth Street off Sixth Avenue.

The bar was a doggedly old-fashioned one, without any of the strippers currently the mode in depuritanized New

York, without B-girls, without synthetics, without video. Jenner felt particularly grateful for that last omission.

He sat slumped in the booth, a big, rumpled-looking man just beginning to get fleshy, and gripped the martini in one of his huge hands. He needed the cold drink to unwind the knot of tension in his stomach. Once, acting had unwound it for him; now, an evening on the stage wound it only a little tighter.

"What is it I've lost, Holly?" he demanded. His voice was the familiar crackling baritone of old; automatically, he projected it too far.

The man opposite him frowned, as though he were sagging under the burden of knowing that he was Mark Jenner's oldest and possibly last friend. "You've lost a job, for one thing," Walt Hollis said lightly.

Jenner scowled. "I don't mean that. I mean—why have I lost what I once had? Why have I gone downhill instead of up? I ought to be at the peak of my acting career now; instead, I'm a has-been at forty. Was I just a flash in the pan, then, back in the seventies?"

"No. You had talent."

"Then why did I lose it?"

"You didn't," Hollis said calmly. He took a deep sip of his gin and tonic, leaned back, stared at his much bigger companion. "You didn't lose anything. You just didn't gain."

"I don't understand."

"Yes, you do," Hollis said. His thumbs squeezed against his aching eyeballs for a moment. He had had this conversation with Jenner too often, in the past five years. Jenner simply did not listen. "Acting isn't the easiest profession in the world, Mark. Lord knows I don't have to tell *you* that. But what you've never grasped is that acting has toughened up tremendously since the days you broke in. And you've remained right at the same level you hit at the start of your career."

Jenner tightened his lips. He felt cold and curiously alone even in this crowded midtown bar.

"I used to be a star," he said.

"*Used* to be. Look, Mark, these days you need something colossal to drag people out of their warm homes and into a Broadway theater. Homes are too comfortable; the streets are too risky. You never can tell when you'll get mugged if you step out after dark. So you don't step out. You stay home."

"People come out to see that British play, the one with what's-his-name in it," Jenner pointed out.

"With Bert Tylor? Of course they do. Tylor has what it takes to get people into a theater."

"And I don't, is that it?" Jenner fought to keep the crispness out of his voice.

Hollis nodded slowly. "You don't have it, Mark. Not any more."

"And what is this—this magic something-or-other that I lack?"

"It's empathy," Hollis said. "The power to get yourself across the footlights, to set up a two-way flow, to get those people in the audience so damned involved in what you're saying that it turns into part of themselves."

Jenner glowered at the small man. "You're not telling me anything I don't know. All you did just now was to define what any actor has to do."

Hollis shook his head. "It's more than that, now. Now you need special help—techniques for reaching the soul of the fellow in the six-buck seat. I've been offering you these techniques for almost a year, but you've been too damned stubborn to listen to me—too proud to admit a gadget could help you."

"I had a part lined up," Jenner said in a weak voice. "Last May Dan Hall came to me, said he was doing a play that looked good for me, and was I interested? Hell, sure I was interested. I hadn't worked for two years; I was supposed to be box-office poison. But Dan signed me."

Hollis said, "And you rehearsed all summer, and half the fall. And played the sticks half the winter while that poor hapless devil of a playwright tried to fix up the play you were killing, Mark."

Jenner sucked in his breath sharply. He began to say something, then throttled it. He shook his head slowly like a bull at bay. "Go on, Holly. I have this coming to me. Don't pull the punches."

The small man said thinly, "You weren't putting that play across the footlights, Mark. So when it finally got to New York it opened in March and closed in March. Okay. You had all the rope you needed, and you sure hanged yourself! Where do you go from here?"

"Nowhere. I'm at the bottom of the heap now."

"You still have a chance," Hollis said. He leaned forward and seemed to be hanging on Jenner's words like an anxious chickenhawk. "I can help you. I've been telling you that for a year."

"I don't want my mind tinkered with."

"You could have your name up in lights again, live in a Fifth Avenue penthouse. You could get back all the things you used to have, before—before you started to slide."

Jenner stared at the little man's pale, unlined face as if Hollis were nothing but a pane of glass, and as if all the secrets of the universe were inscribed on the back of the booth behind him. In a low voice Jenner said, "I won't get *everything* back. Fame, maybe. Money, maybe. But not everything."

"You didn't need to make your wife run away from you," Hollis said with deliberate cruelty. "But maybe you could make her want to come back."

"Would *I* want her back?"

"That's up to you. I can't answer all your questions for you. What time is it?"

"One-fifteen A.M. The morning papers will be out soon. Maybe they'll mention the closing of *Misty Isle*. Maybe there'll be a sticky little paragraph about how Mark Jenner has helped to kill another good play."

"Forget all that," Hollis said sharply. "Stop brooding about the past. You're going to start everything over tonight."

Jenner looked up, surprised. "When did I agree to let you monkey with me, Holly?"

"You didn't. But what else can you do, now?"

The surprise widened on Jenner's face. He looked down and stared at the formica tabletop until the pattern blurred before his eyes. Hollis was right, Jenner realized numbly. There was nothing else to do now, no place else to go, no more ships to come in.

"Okay," Jenner said in a harsh, throaty voice. "You win. Let's get out of here."

They took the Bronx undertube to Hollis' Riverdale home. Jenner kept a car stored in a Fifty-ninth Street garage, but four martinis in little more than an hour and a half had left him too wobbly to drive, and Hollis did not have a license. At half past one in the morning, the tube was crowded; Jenner and Hollis sat in one of the middle cars, and Jenner was bitterly amused to note that nobody seemed to recognize him, or at least no one cared to come over and say, "Pardon me, but are you really . . ."

In the old days, Jenner recalled, his agents had forbade him strictly to enter the subways. They didn't even have the undertubes then. But if the Mark Jenner of 1977 had entered a subway, he would have been ripped apart, Orpheus-like, by the autograph hunters. Now, he was just another big man with a martini-glaze on his face.

Hollis remained silent all through the twenty-minute trip, and that forced Jenner back on his own inner resources. It was not pleasant for him to have to listen to the output of his own mind for twenty minutes. There were too many memories rising to confront him.

He could remember the tall, gawky teen-age Ohio boy who had overnight turned into the tall, confident New Yorker of twenty-one, back in '70. The School of Dramatic Arts; the wide-eyed hours of discovering Ibsen and Chekhov and Pirandello; the big break, the lead in *Right You Are* at a small off-Broadway house, with a big-name Broadway mogul happening to come to the dingy little second-story theater to see young Jenner's mordant, incisive Laudisi.

The following autumn, a bit part in a short-lived comedy, thanks to that lucky break. Then some television work; after that, a longer part in a serious drama. Finally, in the spring of 1973, an offer to play the juvenile lead in a bit of froth called *Lovely to Look At*. Jenner was twenty-four and obscure when the show opened, that fall; when it closed, two years later, he was famous. He owned two Cadillacs, lived in a penthouse apartment, gave away vintage champagne the way other men handed out cigarettes. In 1976, while out in Hollywood doing the film version of *Lovely*, he unexpectedly married dazzling, bosomy, much-publicized, twenty-year-old Helene Bryan, current queen of the movie colony. Experts predicted that the fabulous Jenner would weary of the pneumatic blonde within months; but Helene turned out to have unexpected depth, wearing a real personality behind her sleek personality mask. In the end it was she who wearied of a down-slipping, bitterly irascible, and incipiently alcoholic Jenner, eleven years later. Eleven years, Jenner thought! They seemed like a week, and the two years of separation a lifetime.

Jenner thought back on the successes. Two years of
Lorelei; a year and nine months of *Girl of the Dawn*; then the
ill-starred turkey *Hullaballoo*; and finally his last big hit,
Bachelor Lady, which ran a year—October 1982 to September 1983. After that, almost overnight, people stopped coming
to see Mark Jenner act; he had lost his hold. In the season of
1986-87 he appeared in no less than three plays, the longest-
lived of which held the boards for five weeks. Somewhere
along the line, he had lost his magic. He had also lost Helene,
in that dreadful spring of 1987 when she returned to California
to stay.

And somewhere along the line, Jenner realized he had
lost the eager young man who loved Ibsen and Chekhov and
Pirandello. As a professional, he had specialized almost exclu-
sively in frothy romantic confections. That was unintentional;
it was simply that he could never resist a producer waving a fat
contract. It wouldn't have mattered, much, except that he
kept up contact with Walt Hollis, one of the first people he had
met when he came to New York, and Hollis served to remind
Jenner of the Pirandello days.

Hollis had never been an actor. He was a lighting
technician in the old days, and a lighting technician he still
was, the best of his craft—a slim, mousy little man who looked
no older at fifty than he had at thirty. Hollis had been more
than a mere electrician, though. He was a theoretician, a
student of the acting technique, a graduate engineer as well.
He tinkered with gadgets, and sometimes he told Jenner
about them. Jenner listened with open ears, never retaining a
thing.

Two years ago, Hollis had told him of something new he
was developing—a technique that might be able to turn any
man with a bit of acting skill into a Barrymore, into an Olivier.
Jenner had laughed. In that year, '87, his main concern had
been to show the world how self-sufficient he was in the face of
adversity. He was not going to grasp at any electronic straws,
oh no! That would be admitting he was in trouble!

Well, he *was* in trouble. And as *Misty Isle* sank rapidly
into limbo under a fierce critical barrage, Jenner bleakly
realized he could sink no lower himself. Now was the time at
last to listen to Hollis. Now was the time to clutch at any offer
of salvation. *Now*.

"We're here," Hollis said, breaking a twenty-minute

silence. "Watch your step getting out. You don't want to trip and mash up your pretty profile."

In the twenty years he had known Walt Hollis, Jenner had been inside the little man's home no more than a dozen times, and not at all in the last decade. It was a tidy little place, four small rooms, overfastidiously neat. Bookshelves lined the walls—an odd assortment of books, half literary, half technical. Hollis lived by himself; he had never married. That had made it hard for Jenner to see him socially very often; Helene had hated to visit bachelors.

Now Jenner allowed himself to be deposited in a comfortable armchair, while Hollis, ever tense, paced the worn broadloom carpet in front of him. Jenner felt completely helpless. Hollis was his last hope.

Hollis said, "Mark, I'm going to be ruthlessly frank in everything I say to you from tonight on. You aren't going to like the things I say. If you get annoyed, blow off steam. It'll do you good."

"I won't get annoyed," Jenner said tonelessly. "There isn't a thing you could say about me that wouldn't be true."

"You *will* get annoyed—so annoyed that you'll want to punch me in the face." Hollis grinned shyly. "I hope you'll be able to control that. You've got me by fifty or sixty pounds."

He paced back and forth. Jenner watched him. For twenty years, Mark Jenner had felt a sort of pity for Hollis, for the timid and retiring electrician whose only pleasure seemed to be in helping others. Sure, Hollis made good pay, and he was the best in his business. But for all that, he was just a backstage flunky. Now he was much more than that; he was Jenner's last hope.

Hollis said, "You're going to have to withdraw from your regular activities completely for six months or so, Mark. Give up your room. Move in here with me until the treatment's finished. Then we'll see what we can do about getting you back on Broadway. It may not be easy—but if things work the way I think they'll work, you'll be climbing straight for the stratosphere the month I'm done with you."

"I'll be satisfied just to work regularly. Suppose you tell me what you're going to do to me."

Hollis spun around and jabbed the air with a forefinger. "First let's talk about your past. You were a big hit once, Mark, then you started slipping. Now you're nowhere. Okay: *why* did it happen?"

"Yeah. You tell me. Why?"

"It happened," Hollis said, "because you failed to adapt to the changing times. You never developed the kind of emotional charge that an actor needs *now*, if he's going to reach his audience. You stayed put, worshiping the good old status quo. You acted in the 1973 way for fifteen years, but by 1987 it wasn't good enough for the public or for the critics."

"Especially the critics," Jenner growled. "They crucified me!"

"The critics are paid to slap down anything that isn't what the public would consider good entertainment," Hollis said thinly. "You can't blame them; you have to blame yourself. You had an early success, and you stuck at that level until you were left behind."

Jenner nodded gravely. "Okay, Holly. Let's say I frittered away my talent. I'd rather think that than that I never had any talent in the first place. How can you help me?"

Hollis paused in his nervous march and came to light like a fretful butterfly, on a backless wooden chair. "I once explained my technique to you, and you nodded all through it, but I could see you weren't listening. You'll have to listen to me now, Mark, or I can't help you."

"I'm listening."

"I hope so. Briefly, what I'm going to do is put you through a sort of lay analysis . . ."

"I've *been* analyzed!"

"Keep quiet and listen for a change," Hollis said with a vigor Jenner had never heard him display before. "You'll be put through a sort of lay analysis, under deep narcohypnosis. What I want, actually, is a taped autobiography, going as deep into your life as I can dredge."

"Are you qualified to do this sort of thing?" Jenner asked.

"I'm qualified to build the machine and ask the questions. The psychiatric angle I've researched as thoroughly as possible. The rest comes out of you, until we have the tape."

"Okay," Jenner said. "So what do you do with this tape biography of me?"

"I put it aside," Hollis said. "Then I take another tape, put you under hypnosis again, and feed the *new* tape *into* you. The new tape will be one that I've taken from some other person.

It'll be carefully expurgated to keep you from knowing the other person's identity, but you'll get a deep whiff of his personality. Then I take *your* tape and pipe it into the man who made the other one."

Jenner frowned, not comprehending. "I don't get this. Who's the other person? You?"

"Of course not. He'll be a man you never met. You won't ever see him; you won't ever know who he is. But you'll know what kind of food he likes and why; what he thinks when he's in bed with his wife; how he feels on a hot, sweaty summer day; what he felt like the first time he kissed a girl. You'll remember his getting whopped for stealing cigarettes from his father, and you'll remember his college graduation day. You'll have all his memories, hopes, dreams, fears. He'll have yours."

Jenner squinted and tried to figure out what the little man was heading toward. "What good will all that do—to peek into each other's minds?"

Hollis smiled. "When you build up a character on stage, you mine him out of yourself—out of your own perceptions and reactions and experiences. You take the playwright's bare lines, and you flesh them out by interpreting words as action, words as expression, words as carriers of emotion. If you're a good actor—which means you have enough inner resource to swing the trick—you convince the audience that you *are* the man the program says you are. If not, you get a job selling popcorn in front of the theater."

"So . . ."

Hollis swept right on. "So this way you'll have *two* sets of emotions and experiences to build on. You can synthesize them into a portrayal that no actor can begin to give." Hollis locked his thin hands together over one knee and bent forward, his mild face bright with enthusiasm now. "Besides, you'll have the advantage of being inside another man's skull, knowing what makes *him* tick; it'll give you a perspective you can't possibly have now. Combining his memories with yours, it'll be that much easier for you to get inside the audience's collective skull too, Mark. You see the picture now? You follow what I'm driving at?"

"I think so," Jenner said heavily. With awkwardly deliberate motions he pulled a cigarette out of Hollis' pack on the table, and lit it. Jenner did not actually smoke; he valued his throat too highly. But now he needed something to do with his hands, and the cigarette-lighting ritual provided it. "But tell me this—what does this other fellow get out of having *my* tape pumped into him?"

"He's a politician," Hollis said. "By which I mean a man who's in public life. He wants to run for a high office. He's a capable man, but with your talent for projection, combined with his own inner drive, he's sure to win."

"You mean you have the other man picked out already?"

"He's been picked out and waiting for nearly a year. I told him I would get a great actor to serve as the counterweight on this little seesaw. He's been waiting. I had you in mind, but it took this flop tonight to make you come around. You *will* go along with this, won't you?"

Jenner shut his eyes for a moment and drew the burning smoke deep into his lungs. He felt like gagging. He was drained of all strength; if Hollis had snapped off the light, he would have fallen asleep on the spot, clothes and all.

He said, after a moment, "So, I'll be taking another man into my head with me. And that supposedly will make me a star again. Ah—have you ever tried this stunt before?"

"You and he will be the first subjects," Hollis confessed.

"And you're confident nothing will go wrong?"

"I'm not confident at all," Hollis said quietly. "It *ought* to work; but it might make both of you gibbering lunatics instead."

"And still you're ready to try this on me?" Jenner asked.

"I wouldn't want you going into it without a warning. But the odds are good in favor of a successful outcome; otherwise I wouldn't dream of asking you to play along with me."

Jenner stubbed out his half-smoked cigarette. He glanced around at the books on the shelves, at the single painting, at the austere furniture. "How long will it take?"

"About six months. I have to edit two tapes, don't forget. And we can't do all the work overnight."

"Will it cost me anything?"

Hollis laughed. "Mark, I'd pay *you* to do this if you wanted me to. I want to help you—and to see if my theories were right."

"I hope they are." Jenner stood up, coming to his full height, squaring his shoulders, trying to play the role of a successful actor even now, when he was nothing but a hollow has-been. "Okay," he said in the resonant Jenner tones. "I commit myself into thy hands, Holly. I've lost everything else a man can lose; I guess it doesn't matter much if I lose my mind."

Jenner woke up in the middle of the next afternoon. He had been asleep for thirteen hours, and he had needed it. Hollis was gone, having left a note explaining that he had to attend a rehearsal in Manhattan and would be back about five. Jenner dressed slowly, remembering the conversation of the night before, realizing that he had effectively pledged his soul to the unmephistophelean Hollis.

He turned Hollis' sheet of notepaper over and scrawled his own note: *"Going downtown to settle my affairs. Will return later tonight."* He took the undertube back to Manhattan, taxied from the tube station to his hotel, and checked out, settling his bill with cash. For two years he had lived in a twenty-dollar-a-week room in a midtown hotel, with no more personal property than he needed. Most of his possessions had been in storage since the breakup with Helene in '87; he kept hardly enough in the hotel room to fill a single suitcase.

He packed up and left. Dragging the suitcase that contained three changes of clothing, his makeup kit, his useless script for *Misty Isle*, and the 1986–89 volume of his scrapbook, Jenner set out for the tube station again. It was five-thirty. If he made good connections, he could reach Hollis' place a little after six. And that gave him time for a little bit of fortification first.

He stopped at a Lexington Avenue bar and had two martinis. On the third drink he shifted to gibsons. By the fourth, he had acquired a slatternly-looking bar girl with thick orange lipstick; he bought her the requested rye and soda, had one himself, then went into the washroom and got sick. When he came out, the girl was gone. Shrugging, Jenner wandered to another bar and had two more martinis, this time successfully keeping them down. A hundred yards up the block, he had another gibson.

He reached Hollis' place at half past ten, sober enough to walk on his own steam but too drunk to remember what he had done with his suitcase. He kept insisting that Hollis call the police and have them search for the grip, but Hollis merely smiled amiably and ignored him, leading him to the bedroom and putting him to bed. A moment before he fell asleep, Jenner reflected that it was just as well he had lost the suitcase. With it, he had lost his pitiful press clippings of the last four years, as well as his makeup kit and his final script. Now he could shed his past with alacrity; he had no albatrosses slung around his neck.

He woke up at nine the next morning, feeling unaccountably clearheaded and cheerful. The smell of frying bacon reached his nostrils. From the kitchen, Hollis yelled, "Go take a quick shower. Breakfast'll be ready when you come out."

They breakfasted in silence. At twenty of ten, they finished their coffee. Hollis said quietly, "All right, Mark. Are you ready to begin?"

Walt Hollis had rigged an experimental laboratory in his fourth room and he installed Jenner in the middle of it. The room was no more than twelve by fifteen, and it seemed to Jenner that there was an enormous amount of equipment in it. He himself sat in a comfortable chair in the center of the room, facing a diabolically complex bit of apparatus with fluorescent light rings and half a dozen theatrical gelatins to provide a shifting pattern of illuminated color. There was a big tape recorder in the room, with a fifteen-inch reel primed and loaded. There were instruments that Jenner simply could not identify at all; he had no technical background, and he merely classified them as "electronic" and let it go at that.

The room's window had been carefully curtained off; the door frame was lined with felt. When Hollis chose, he could plunge the room into total darkness. Jenner felt an irrational twinge of fear. Obscurely, the machine facing him reminded him of a dentist's drill, an instrument he had always feared and hated. But this drill would bite deep into his mind.

"I won't be in the room with you," Hollis said. "I'll be monitoring from outside. Any time you want me, just raise your right hand and I'll come in. Okay?"

"Okay," Jenner muttered.

"First I've got a pill for you, Mark. Proclorperazine. It's an ataractic."

"A tranquilizer?"

"Call it that; it's just to ease your nerves. You're very tense right now, you know. You're afraid of what I'm going to do."

"Damned right I'm afraid. But you don't see me getting up and running out!"

"Of course not,"Hollis said. "Here. Take it."

While Jenner swallowed the pill, Hollis busily rolled up the actor's sleeve and swabbed his arm with alcohol. Jenner watched, already relaxing, as Hollis readied a glittering hypodermic.

"This is the hypnosis-inducing drug, Mark."

"Sodium pentothal? Amytal?"

"Of that family of ego-depressants, yes." Hollis deftly discharged the syringe's contents into one of Jenner's veins. "I've had medical help in preparing this project," he said. "Sit back. Stretch your feet out. Relax, Mark."

Jenner relaxed. He was vaguely conscious of Hollis' final reassuring pat on the shoulder, of the fact that the small man had left the room, that the room had gone dark. He heard a faint hum that might have come either from the tape recorder or from the strange apparatus in the middle of the room.

Colored lights began to play on him. Wheels of bright plastic whirled before his eyes. Jenner stared, fascinated, feeling his tension drain away. All he had to do was relax. Rest. Everything would be all right. Relax.

"Can you hear me, Mark?"

"I hear you."

"Good. Do you feel any discomfort?"

"No discomfort."

"Fine. Listen to me, Mark."

"I'm listening."

"I mean *really* listening, now. Listening with your brain and not just your ears. Are you listening to me, Mark?"

"I'm listening."

"Excellent. This is what I want you to do for me, Mark. I want you to go back and think about your life. Then I want you to tell me all about yourself. Everything. From the beginning."

Spring, 1953. Mark Jenner was four years old. Mark Jenner's brother Tom had reached the ninth of the twelve years he was to have. Tom Jenner had been fighting, against his mother's express orders, and he had been knocked down and bruised.

Mark Jenner stared up at his older brother. Tom's cheek was scraped and bloody, and one side of his mouth was starting to swell puffily.

"Mama's gonna murder you," Mark chortled. "Said you wasn't supposed to fight."

"Wasn't fighting," Tom said.

"I saw you! You picked on Mickey Swenson, and he knocked you down and made your face all bloody!"

"You wouldn't tell mama that, would you?" Tom asked in a low voice. "If she asked you what happened to me, I mean."

Mark blinked. "If she asked, I'd have to tell."

"No," Tom said. His still-pudgy hands gripped Mark's shoulders painfully. "We're gonna go inside. I'm gonna tell mama I tripped on a stone and fell down."

"But you were *fighting*! With Mickey Swenson."

"We don't have to tell mama that. We can tell her something else—make up a story."

"But . . ."

"All you have to do is say I fell down, that I wasn't fighting with anybody. And I'll give you a nickel. Okay?"

Mark looked puzzled. How could he tell mama something that was not true? It seemed easy enough. All he had to do was move his mouth and the sounds would come out. It seemed important to Tom. Already Mark was beginning to believe that Tom had really fallen, that there had been no fight.

They trooped into the house, the dirty little boy and the dirty littler one. Mrs. Jenner appeared, looming high over both of them, her hands upraised at the sight of her eldest son's battered face.

"Tom! What happened!"

Before Tom could reply, Mark said gravely, "Tom tripped on a stone. He fell down and hurt himself."

"Oh! You poor dear—does it hurt?"

As Mrs. Jenner trooped Tom off to the bathroom for repairs, Mark Jenner, four years old, experienced a curious warm sensation of pride. He had told his first conscious lie. He had spoken something that was not the truth, had done it deliberately with the hope of a reward. He did not know it then, but his career as an actor had begun auspiciously.

Spring, 1966. Mark Jenner was seventeen, a junior at Noah Webster High School, Massilon, Ohio. He was six feet one and weighed 152 pounds. He was carrying the schoolbooks of Joanne Lauritszon, sixteen years eight months old.

The Mark Jenner of 1989 saw her for what she was: a raw, newly fledged female with a padded chest and a shrill voice. The Mark Jenner of 1966 saw her as Aphrodite.

It took all his skill to work the conversation to the subject of the forthcoming junior prom. It took all his courage to invite the girl who walked at his side.

It took all his strength to endure her as she said, "But I've got a prom date already, Mark. I'm going with Nat Hospers."

"Oh—yes, of course. Sorry. I should have figured it out myself."

And he handed her back her books and ran stumbling away, cursing himself for his awkwardness, cursing Hospers for his car and his football-player muscles and his aplomb with girls. Mark had saved up for months for the prom; he had vowed he would die of grief if Joanne refused him. Somehow, he did not die.

Autumn, 1976. Hollywood. Mark Jenner was twenty-seven, rugged-looking and tanned, drawing three thousand dollars a week during the filming of *Lovely to Look At.* He sat at the best table in Hollywood's most exclusive nightclub, and opposite him, resplendent in her ermine wrap, sat the queen of filmland, Helene Bryan, lovely, moist-lipped, high-bosomed, that month blazoned on the covers of a hundred magazines in near nudity. She was twenty. She had been a coltish ten-year-old, interested only in dolls and frills, the year Mark Jenner had first thought he had fallen in love. Now he had fallen in love with her, with this $250,000-a-year goddess of sexuality.

An earlier Mark Jenner might have drawn back timidly from such a radiant beauty, but the Mark Jenner of 1976 was afraid of no one, of nothing. He smiled at the blonde girl in the ermine wrap.

He said, "Helene, will you marry me?"

"Of course, darling! Of course!"

Spring, 1987. Mark Jenner was thirty-eight. *Three Days in Marrakesh* had played nine days on Broadway. The night that closing notices went up, Mark Jenner pub-crawled until 3 A.M. The sour taste of cheap tap beer was in his mouth as he staggered home, feeling the ache in his feet and the soreness in his soul. He had not even bothered to remove the gray makeup from his hair. With it, he looked sixty years old, and right now he *felt* sixty, not thirty-eight. He wondered if Helene would be asleep.

Helene was not asleep; Helene was up, and packing. She wore a simple cotton dress and no makeup at all, and for once she looked her thirty-one years, instead of seeming to be in her late teens or very early twenties. She had the suitcase nearly full. Jenner had been expecting this for a long time, and now that it had come he was hardly surprised. He was too numb to react emotionally. He dropped heavily on the bed and watched her pack.

"The show closed tonight," he said.

"I know. Holly phoned and told me all about it, at midnight."

"I'm sorry I came home late. I stopped to condole with a few friends."

The brisk packing motions continued unabated. "It doesn't matter."

"Helene . . ."

"I'm just taking this one suitcase, Mark. I'll wire you my new address when I'm in Los Angeles, and you can ship the rest of my things out to me."

"Divorce?"

"Separation. I can't watch you this way any more, Mark."

He smiled. "No. It isn't fun to watch a man fall apart, I guess. Good-bye, Helene."

He was too drained of energy to care to make a scene. She finished packing, locked the suitcase, and went into the study to make a phone call. Then she left, without saying good-bye. Jenner sat smiling stupidly for a while after the door slammed, slowly getting used to the fact that it was all over at last. He rose, went to the sideboard, poured himself a highball glass of gin. He gulped it. He cried.

Late winter, 1989. Mark Jenner was forty years old. He sat in a special chair in Walt Hollis' apartment while lights played on his tranquil face . . .

It was three months and many miles of mylar tape before Hollis was satisfied. Jenner had gone through a two-hour session each morning, reminiscing with unhesitating frankness. It had not been like the analysis at all; the analysis had not been successful because he had lied to the analyst frequently and well, digging up bits of old parts and offering them as his personal experiences, out of perverse and no doubt psychotic motivations.

This was different. He was drugged; he spewed forth his genuine past, and when the session was over he had no recollection of what he had said. Hollis never told him. Sometimes Jenner would ask, as he drowned his grogginess in a postsession cup of coffee, but Hollis would never reply.

From ten to twelve every day, Jenner recorded. From one to three, Hollis cloistered himself in the little room and edited the tapes. From three to six every day, Jenner was banished from the house while his counterpart in the project occupied the little room. Jenner never got so much as a glimpse of the other.

When the three months had elapsed, when Jenner had finally surrendered as much of his past life as he could yield, when Hollis had edited the formless stream of consciousness into a continuous, consecutive, and intelligible pattern, the time came to enter the second stage of the process. Now there were new drugs, new patterns of light, new responses. Jenner did not speak; he listened. His subconscious lay open, receptive, absorbing all that reached it and locking it in for permanent possession.

And slowly, the personality of a man formed in Jenner's mind, embedding itself deep in layers of consciousness previously private, inextricably meshing itself with the web of memories that was Mark Jenner.

This man was like Jenner in many ways. He was physically commanding; his voice had the ring of authority, and people listened when he spoke. But as Jenner watched the man's life shape itself from day to day, from year to compressed and edited year, he realized the difference. The other had chosen to be personally dominating as well. He, Jenner, had sacrificed his personality in order to be able to don many masks. A politician or a statesman must thrust his ego forward; an actor must bury his.

The other man, Jenner's mind told him, was forty-two years old. A severe attack of colitis five years back was the only serious illness he had had. He stood six feet one and a half, weighed 190 pounds, was mildly hyperthyroid metabolically, and never slept more than five hours a night.

He had a law degree from a major university—Hollis had edited the school's identity out. He had been married twice, divorcing his first wife on grounds of her adultery, and he had two children by his second wife, who regarded him with the awe one usually reserves for a paternal parent. He had been an assistant district attorney and had schemed for his superior's disgrace; eventually he had succeeded to the post himself, and had consciously been involved in the judicial murder of an innocent man.

Despite this, he thought of himself, by and large, as liberal and enlightened. He had served two terms in the Congress of the United States, representing an important eastern state. He hoped to be elected to the Senate in the 1990 elections. Consulting an almanac, Jenner discovered that many eastern states would be electing senators in 1990: Delaware, Georgia, Kentucky, Maine, Massachusetts, Mississippi, New Hampshire, New Jersey, Rhode Island, South Carolina, Tennessee, Virginia, West Virginia. About all Jenner learned from that was that his man was not officially an inhabitant of New York, Pennsylvania, or Connecticut.

Before the three months ended, Jenner knew the other man's soul nearly as well as he knew his own, or perhaps better. He understood the pattern of childhood snubs and paternal goadings that had driven him toward public life. He knew how the other had struggled to overcome his shyness. He knew how it had been when the other had first had a woman; he knew, for the first time in his life, what it was like to be a father.

The other man in Jenner's head was a "good" man, dedicated and intelligent; but yet, he stood revealed as a liar, a cheat, a hypocrite, even indirectly a murderer. Jenner realized with sudden icy clarity that any human being's mind would yield the same muck of hidden desires and repressed, half-acknowledged atrocities.

The man's memories were faceless; Jenner supplied faces. In the theater of his imagination, he built a backdrop for the other's childhood, supplied an image for parents and first wife and second wife and children and friends. Day by day the pattern grew; after ninety days, Jenner had a second self. He had a double well of memories. His fund of experiences was multiplied factorially; he could now judge the agonies of one adolescence against another, now could evaluate one man's striving against another's, now could compare two broken marriages and could vicariously know the joys of an almost-successful one. He knew the other's mind the way no man before had ever known another's mind. Not even Hollis, editing the tapes, could become the other man in the way Jenner, drugged and receptive, had become.

When the last tape had been funneled into Jenner's skull, when the picture was complete, Jenner knew the experiment had been a success. Now he had the inner drive he had lacked before; now he could reach out into the audience and squeeze a man's heart. He had always had the technical equipment of a great actor. Now he had the soul of one.

He wondered frequently about the other man and decided to keep his eye on the coming senatorial campaign in the East. He wanted desperately to know who was the man who bore in his brain all of Mark Jenner's triumphs and disappointments, all the cowardices and vanities and ambitions that made him human.

He *had* to know, but he postponed the search; at the moment, returning to the stage was more important.

The show was called *No Roses for Larrabee*. It was about an aging video star named Jack Larrabee, who skids down to obscurity and then fights his way back up. It had appeared the previous fall as a ninety-minute video show; movie rights had already been sold, but it was due for a Broadway fling first. The author was a plump kid named Harrell, who had written three previous triple-threat dramas. Harrell had half a million dollars in the bank, fifty thousand more in his mattress at his Connecticut villa, and maintained psychoanalysts on both coasts.

Casting was scheduled to start on October 20. The play had already been booked into the Odeon for a February opening, which meant a truncated pre-Broadway tour. Advance sales were piling up. It was generally assumed in the trade that the title role would be played by the man who had created it for the video version, ex-hoofer Lloyd Lane.

On October 10, Mark Jenner phoned his agent for the first time in six months. The conversation was brief. Jenner said, "I've been away, having some special treatments. I feel a lot better now. I want you to get me a reading for the stage version of *Larrabee*. Yeah, that's right. I want the lead."

Jenner didn't care what strings his agent had to pull to get the reading. He wasn't interested in the behind-the-scenes maneuvering. Six days later, he got a phone call from the play's producer, J. Carlton Vincennes. Vincennes was skeptical, but he was willing to take a look, anyway. Jenner was invited to come down for a reading on the twentieth.

On the twentieth, Jenner read for the part of Jack Larrabee. There were only five other people in the room— Vincennes; Harrell, the playwright; Donovan, the director; Lloyd Lane; and an actor named Goldstone who was there to try out for the secondary lead. Jenner picked up the part cold, riffled through it for a few minutes, and started to read it as if he were giving his maiden speech on the floor of the Senate. He put the words across as if he had a pipeline into the subconscious minds of his five auditors. He did things with vowel shadings and with facial expressions that he had never dared to do before, and this was only improvisation as he went. He wasn't just Mark Jenner, has-been, now; he was Mark Jenner plus someone else, and the combined output was overpowering.

After twenty minutes he tired and broke off the reading. He looked at the five faces. Four registered varying degrees of amazed pleasure and disbelief; the fifth belonged to Lloyd Lane. Lane was pale and sweat-beaded with the knowledge that he had just lost a leading role, and with it the hefty Hollywood contract that was sure to follow the Broadway one.

Two days later Jenner signed a run-of-the-show contract with Vincennes. A squib appeared in the theatrical columns the day after that:

> Mark Jenner will be making a Broadway comeback in the J. C. Vincennes production of No Roses for Larrabee. The famed matinee idol of the seventies has been absent from the stage for nearly a year. His last local appearance was in the ill-starred Misty Isle, which saw ten performances last March. Jenner reportedly has spent the past season recovering from a nervous breakdown.

Rehearsals were strange. Jenner had always been a good study, and so he knew his lines flat by the fourth or fifth run-through. The other actors were still shambling through their parts mechanically, muttering from their scripts, while Jenner was *acting*—projecting at them, putting his character across. After a while, the disparity became less noticeable. The cast came to life, responding to the vigor of Jenner's portrayal. When they started working out in the empty theater, there were always a few dozen witnesses to the rehearsal. Backers came, and other directors, theatrical people in general, all attracted by the rumors of Jenner's incandescent performance.

And it *was* incandescent. Not only because the part was so close to his own story, either; an actor playing an autobiographical role can easily slip into maudlin sogginess. For Jenner the part was both autobiographical and external. He interpreted it with his double mind, with the mind of a tired actor and with the mind of a potential senator on the way up. The two personalities crossbred; Jenner's performance tugged at the heart. Advance sales piled up until record figures began to dance across the ledger pages.

They opened in New Haven on the tenth of February to a packed house and rave reviews. Ten days later was the Broadway opening, right on schedule; neither driving snow nor pelting rain kept the tuxedo-and-mink crowd away from the opening-night festivities. A little electric crackle of tension hung in the air in the theater. Jenner felt utterly calm. *This is it*, he told himself. *The chips are down. The voters are going to the polls* . . .

The curtain rose, and Jenner-as-Larrabee shuffled on stage and disgorged his first mumbled lines; he got his response and came across clearer the second time, still a bent figure with hollow cheeks and sad eyes, and the part began to take hold of him. Jack Larrabee grew before the audience's eyes. By nine o'clock, he was as real as any flesh-and-blood person. Jenner was putting him across; the playwright's words were turning to gold.

The first-act curtain line was a pianissimo; Jenner gave it and dropped to his knees, then listened to the drumroll of applause welling up out of the ten-dollar seats. The second-act clincher was the outcry of a baffled, doomed man, and Jenner was baffled and doomed as he wrenched the line out of him. The audience roared as the curtain cascaded down. Jenner drew the final line of the play too—a triumphal, ringing asseveration of joy and redemption that filled the big house like a trumpet call. Then the curtain was dropping, and rising again, and dropping and rising and dropping and rising, while a thunder of applause pounded at his temples; and he knew he had reached them, reached them deeply, reached them so deep they had sprung up from their own jaded weariness to acclaim him.

There was a cast party later that night, much later, in the big Broadway restaurant where such parties are traditionally given. Vincennes was there belligerently waving the reviews from the early editions. The word had gone out: Jenner was back, and Jenner was magnificent. Lloyd Lane came up to him—Jenner's understudy, now. He looked shell-shocked. He said, "God, Mark, I watched the whole thing from the wings. I've never seen anything like it. You really *were* Larrabee out there, weren't you?"

Looking at this man he had elbowed aside, Jenner felt a twinge of guilt, and redness rose to his cheeks. Then the other mind intervened, the ruthless mind of the nameless politician, and Jenner realized that Lane had deserved to be pushed aside. A better actor simply had supplanted him. But there were tears in the corners of Lane's eyes.

Someone rushed up to Jenner with a gaudy magnum of champagne, and there was a *pop!* and then the champagne started to flow. Jenner, who had not had anything to drink for months, gratefully accepted the bubbling glass. Within, he kept icy control over himself. This was his night of triumph. He would drink, but he would not get drunk.

He drank. Vapid showgirls clawed through the circle of well-wishers around him to offer their meaningless congratulations. Flashbulbs glittered in his eyes. Men who had not spoken a civil word to him in five years pumped his hand. Within, Jenner felt a core of melancholy. Helene was not here; Walt Hollis—to whom he owed all this—was not here. Nor was his counterpart, the man whose mind he wore.

Champagne slid easily down his gullet. His smile grew broader. A bald-headed man named Feldstein clinked glasses with him and said, "You must really be relishing this night, Mark. You had it coming, all right. How does it feel to be a success again?"

Jenner grinned warmly. The champagne within him loosened the words, and they drifted easily up through his lips. "It's wonderful. I want to thank everyone who supported me in this campaign. I want to assure them that their trust in me will be amply repaid when I reach Washington."

"Hah! Great sense of humor, Mark. Wotta fellow!" And the bald-headed man turned away, laughing. It was good that he turned away at that moment—for if he had continued to face Mark Jenner, he would have had to witness the look of dismay and terror that came over Jenner's suddenly transformed, suddenly horror-stricken face.

The play was a success, of course. It became one of those plays that everybody simply *had* to see, and everyone saw it. It promised to run for at least two seasons, which was extraordinary for a nonmusical play.

But night after night in the hotel suite Mark Jenner had rented, he wrestled with the same problem:

Who am I?

The words that had first slipped out the night of the cast party now recurred in different forms almost every day. Phantom memories obsessed him; in his dreams, women he had never known came to reminisce with him about the misdeeds of a summer afternoon. He missed the children he had never fathered—the boy who was seven, and the girl who was four. He found himself reading the front pages of newspapers, scanning the Washington news, though always before he had turned first to the theatrical pages. He detected traces of pomposity in some of his sentences.

He knew what was happening. Walt Hollis had done the job too well; the other mind was encroaching on his own, intertwining, enmeshing, ingesting. There were blurred moments in the dark of the night when Jenner forgot his own name, and temporarily nameless, dreamed the dreams the other man should have dreamed.

And, no doubt, it was the same way with the other, whoever he was. Jenner realized bleakly that a strange compulsion bound him. He lay under a geas; he had to find his counterpart, the man who shared his mind. He had to know who he was.

He asked Hollis.

Hollis had come to him in the lavish hotel suite on the sixth day after *Larrabee*'s opening. The little man approached Jenner diffidently, almost as if he were upset by the magnitude of his own experiment's success.

"I guess it worked," Hollis said.

Jenner grinned expansively. "That it did, Holly! When I'm up there on the stage I have the strength I never knew I could have. Have you seen the play?"

"Yes. The third night. I was—impressed."

"Damn right you were impressed," Jenner said. "You should be, watching your Frankenstein monster in action up there. Your golem." There was nothing bitter in Jenner's tone; he was being genially sardonic.

But Hollis went pale. "Don't talk about it that way."

"True, isn't it?"

"Don't—don't ever refer to yourself that way, Mark. It isn't right."

Jenner shrugged. Then casually, he interjected a new theme. "My alter ego—the chap you matched up with me—how's *he* doing?"

"Coming along all right," Hollis said quietly.

"Just—all right?"

"In his profession it takes time for results to become apparent. But he's building up strength, lining up an organization. I saw him yesterday, and he said he's very hopeful for the future."

"For the Senate race, you mean?"

Hollis looked past Jenner's left shoulder. "Perhaps."

Jenner scowled. "Holly—tell me his name."

"I can't do that."

"I have to know it, Holly! Please!"

"Mark, one of the terms of our agreement . . ."

"To hell with our agreement! Will you tell me or won't you?"

The small man looked even smaller now. He seemed to be shivering. He rose, backed toward the door of Jenner's suite. His hands fumbled for the opener button.

"Where are you going?" Jenner demanded.

"Away. I don't dare let you keep asking me about him. You're too convincing. And you mustn't make me tell you. You mustn't find out who he is. Not ever."

"Holly! Come back here! *Holly!*"

The door slammed. Jenner stood in the middle of the room staring at it, slowly shaking his head. Hollis had bolted like a frightened hare. *He was afraid of me*, Jenner realized. *Afraid I'd make him talk.*

"All right," Jenner said out loud, softly. "If you won't tell me, I'll have to find out for myself."

It took him ten days to find out. Ten days in which he delivered eleven sterling performances in *No Roses for Larrabee*, ten days in which he felt the increasing encroachment of the stranger in his mind, ten days in which Mark Jenner and the stranger blurred even closer together. On the seventh of those ten days, he received a phone call from Helene, long distance. He stared at her tired face in the tiny screen and remembered how like a new-blown rose she had looked on the morning after their wedding, in Acapulco, and he listened to her strangely subdued voice.

". . . visiting New York again in a few weeks. Mind if I stop up to see you, Mark? After all, we're still legally married, you know."

He smiled and made an empty reply. "Be glad to see you, Helene. For old times' sake."

"And of course I want to see the play. Can I get seats easily?"

"If you try hard enough, you can scrape up a seat in the balcony for fifty bucks," he said. "But I'm allotted a few ducats for each show. Let me know the night, and I'll put a couple away for you."

"One's enough," she said quietly.

He grinned at her, and they made a bit of small talk, and they hung up. She was obviously angling for a reconciliation. Well, he wasn't so sure he'd take her back. From what he'd heard, she had done a good bit of sleeping around in the past three years, and she was thirty-four now. A successful man like Mark Jenner might reasonably be expected to take a second wife, a girl in her twenties, someone more decorative than Helene was now. After all, the *other* had married again, and he had done it only because his first wife did not mix well with the party bigwigs—not primarily because she had been cheating on him.

Three days later, Jenner knew the identity of the nameless man in his mind.

It was not really hard to find out. Jenner hired a research consultant to do some work for him. What he wanted, Jenner explained, was a list of members of the House of Representatives who fulfilled the following qualifications: they had to be in their early forties, more than six feet tall, residents of an eastern state, married, divorced, and married again, with two children by the second wife. They had to be in their second term in the House, and had to be considered likely prospects for a higher political post in the near future. These were the facts Hollis had allowed him to retain. Jenner hoped they would be enough.

A few hours later, he had the answer he was hoping for. Only one man, of all the 475 representatives in the one hundredth Congress, fit all of the qualifications. He was Representative Clifford T. Norton, Republican, of the Fifth District of Massachusetts.

A little more research filled in some of Representative Norton's background. His first wife had been named Betty, the second Phyllis. His children's names were Clifford Junior and Karen. He had gone to Yale as an undergraduate, then to Harvard Law, thereby building up loyalties at both schools. He had been elected to the House in '86 after a distinguished career as district attorney, and he had been returned by a larger plurality in the '88 elections. His term of office expired in January of 1991. He hoped to move into the other wing of the Capitol immediately, as junior senator from Massachusetts. In recent months, according to the morgue file Jenner's man consulted, Norton had shown sudden brilliance and persuasiveness on the House floor.

It figured. Now Norton was a politician with the mind of an actor grafted to his own. The combination couldn't miss, Jenner thought.

Jenner felt an odd narcissistic fascination for this man with whom he was a brain-brother; he wanted anxiously to meet Norton. He wondered whether Norton had managed to uncover the identity of the actor whose tape Hollis had crossed with his own; and, Jenner wondered, if Norton *did* know, was he proud to share the memories of Broadway's renascent idol?

It was the last week in March 1990. Congress was home for its Easter recess. No doubt, Representative Norton was making ample use of his new oratorical powers among the home folks, as he began his drive toward the Senate seat. On a rainy Tuesday afternoon Jenner put through a long-distance phone call to Representative Norton at his Massachusetts office. Jenner had to give his name to a secretary before Norton would come to the phone.

Norton's voice was deep and rich, like Jenner's own. He did not use a visual circuit on his phone. He said, "Hello there, Jenner. I was wondering when you were going to call me."

"You knew about me, then?"

"Of course I knew! As soon as that play opened and I read the reviews, I *knew* you were the one!"

They arranged a meeting for two the following afternoon, at the home of Walt Hollis in Riverdale. Hollis had once given Jenner a key, and somehow Jenner had kept it. And he knew Hollis would not be home until five that afternoon, which gave them three hours to talk.

That night, Jenner phoned the theater and let the stage manager know that he was indisposed. The stage manager pleaded, but Jenner stood on his contractual rights. That evening Lloyd Lane played the part of Jack Larrabee, to the dismay of the disgruntled and disappointed audience. Jenner spent the evening pacing through the five rooms of his suite, clenching his hands, glorying masochistically in the turmoil and hatred bubbling inside him. He counted the hours of the sleepless night. In the morning, he breakfasted late, read till noon, paced the floor till half past one, and took the undertube to Hollis' place.

He used the key to let himself in. There was no sign of Norton. Jenner seated himself in Hollis' neat-as-a-pin living room and waited, thinking that it was utterly beyond toleration that another man should walk the earth privy to the inmost thoughts of Mark Jenner.

At two-fifteen, the doorbell rang. Jenner activated the scanner. The face in the lambent visual field was dark, strong-chinned, square, powerful. Jenner opened the door and stood face to face with the only man in the universe who knew that the nine-year-old Mark Jenner had eaten a live angleworm on a dare. Clifford Norton stared levelly at the only man in the universe who knew what he had done to twelve-year-old Marian Simms in her father's garage, twenty-nine years ago.

The two big men faced each other for a long moment in the vestibule of Hollis' apartment. They maintained civil smiles. They both breathed deeply. In Jenner's mind, thoughts whirled wildly, and he knew Norton well enough to be aware that Norton was planning strategy too.

Then the stasis broke.

The animal growl of hatred burst from Jenner's lips first, but a moment later Norton was roaring too, and the two men crashed heavily together in the middle of the floor. They clinched, and one of Norton's legs snaked between Jenner's, tumbling him over; Norton dropped on top of him, but Jenner sidled out from under and slammed his elbow into the pit of Norton's stomach.

Norton gasped. He lashed out with groping hands and caught Jenner's throat. His hands tightened, while Jenner tugged and finally dragged Norton's fingers from his throat. He sucked in breath. His knee rose, going for Norton's groin. The two men writhed on the floor like raging lions, each trying to cripple and damage the other, each hoping to land a crushing blow, each trying ultimately to kill the other.

It lasted only a few moments. They separated with no spoken word and came separately to their feet. They stared at each other once again, now flushed and bruised, their neat suits rumpled, their shirttails out.

"We're acting like fools," Norton said. "Or like little boys."

"We couldn't help ourselves," Jenner said. "It was a natural thing for us to fight. We leaped at each other like men trying to catch their own shadows."

They sat down, Jenner in Hollis' chair, Norton on the couch across the room. For more than a minute, the only sound was that of heavy breathing. Jenner's heart pounded furiously. He hadn't engaged in physical combat in twenty-five years.

"I didn't think it would be this way, exactly," Norton said. "There are times when I wake up and I think I'm you. Angling for a tryout, quarreling with your wife, hitting the bottle."

"And times when *I* remember prosecuting an innocent man for murder and winning the case," Jenner said.

Norton's face darkened. "And I remember eating a live worm . . ."

"And I remember a scared twelve-year-old girl cornered in a garage . . ."

Again they fell silent, both of them slumped over, bearing the burden of each other's pasts. Norton said, "We should never have done this. Come here, and met."

"I had to see you."

"And I had to see you."

"We can't ever see each other again," said Jenner. "It's either got to be murder or a truce between us. Those few minutes when we were fighting—I actually wanted to kill you, Norton. To see you go blue in the face and die."

Norton nodded. "I had the same feeling. Neither of us can really bear the idea that someone else knows him inside and out, even though it's done us so much good in so many ways. I'll get the Senate, all right. And maybe the White House in another six years."

"And I'm back on the stage. I'll get my wife back, if I want her. Everything I lost. Yes," Jenner said. "It's worth sharing your mind. But we can't ever meet again. We're each a small part of each other, and the hatred's too strong. I guess it's self-hatred, really. But we might—we might lose control of ourselves, the way we did just now."

The front door opened suddenly. Walt Hollis stood in the vestibule, a small pinched-faced man with narrow shoulders and a myopic squint. And, just now, a dazed expression on his face.

"You two—how did you get here—why . . ."

"I still had a key," Jenner said. "I called Norton and invited him down to meet me here. We didn't expect you back so early."

Hollis' mouth worked spasmodically for ten seconds before the words came. "You should never have met each other. The traumatic effects—possible dangers . . ."

"We've already had a good brawl," Norton said. "But we won't any more. We've declared a truce."

He crossed the room and forced himself to smile at Jenner. Jenner summoned his craft and made his face show genial conviviality, though within all was loathing. They shook hands.

"We aren't going to see each other ever again," Jenner explained. "Norton's going to be president, and I'm going to win undying fame in the theater. And each of us will owe our accomplishments to the other."

"And to you, Hollis," Norton added.

"Maybe Norton and I will keep in touch by mail," Jenner said. "Drop each other little notes, suggestions. An actor can help a politician. A politician can help an actor. Call it long-range symbiosis, Holly. The two of us ought to go places, thanks to you."

Jenner glanced at Norton, and this time the smile that was exchanged was a sincere one. There was no need for words between them. They walked past the numb Hollis and into the small laboratory room and methodically smashed the equipment. If Hollis were to put someone else through this treatment, Jenner thought, the competition might be a problem. He and Norton wanted no further competition in their chosen fields.

They returned to the living room and gravely said goodbye to Hollis. Jenner was calm inside, now, at last. He and Norton departed, going their separate ways once they reached the street. Jenner knew he would never see Norton again. It was just as well; he would have to live with Norton's memories for the rest of his life.

Hollis surveyed the wreckage of his lab with a stony heart. He felt cold and apprehensive. This was the reward of his labors, this was what he got for trying to help. But he should have realized it. After all, he had edited the tapes for both of them. He knew what they were. He carried the burden of both souls in his own small heart. He knew what they had done, and he knew what they were capable of doing, now that the errors of one sanctioned the errors of the other.

Tiredly, Hollis closed the laboratory door, cutting off the sight of the wreckage. He thought of Jenner and Norton and wondered when they would realize that he knew all their secrets.

He wondered how long Jenner and Norton would let him live.

Neutral Planet

From the fore viewing bay of the Terran starship *Peccable*, the twin planets Fasolt and Fafnir had become visible—uninhabited Fasolt a violet ball the size of a quarter-credit piece dead ahead, and Fafnir, home of the gnorphs, a bright-red dot far to the right, beyond the mighty curve of the big ship's outsweeping wing.

The nameless, tiny blue sun about which both worlds orbited rode high above them, at a sharp 36 degrees off the ecliptic. And, majestic in its vastness, great Antares served as a huge bright-red backdrop for the entire scene.

"Fasolt dead ahead," came the word from Navigation. "Prepare for decelerating orbit."

The eighteen men who comprised the Terran mission to the gnorphs of Fafnir moved rapidly and smoothly toward their landing stations. This was a functioning team; they had a big job, and they were ready for it.

In Control Cabin, Shipmaster Deev Harskin was strapping himself into the acceleration cradle when the voice of Observer First Rank Snollgren broke in.

"Chief? Snollgren. Read me?"

"Go ahead, boy. What's up?"

"That Rigelian ship—the one we saw yesterday? I just found it again. Ten light-seconds off starboard, and credits to crawfish it's orbiting in on Fasolt!"

Harskin gripped the side of the cradle anxiously. "You sure it's not Fafnir they're heading for? How's your depth-perception out there?"

"A-one. That boat's going the same place we are, chief!"

Sighing, Harskin said, "It could have been worse, I guess." He snapped on the all-ship communicator and said, "Gentlemen, our job has been complicated somewhat. Observer Snollgren reports a Rigelian ship orbiting in on Fasolt, and it looks likely they have the same idea we have. Well, this'll be a test of our mettle. We'll have a chance to snatch Fafnir right out from under their alleged noses!"

A voice said, "Why not blast the Rigelians first? They're our enemies, aren't they?"

Harskin recognized the voice as belonging to Leefman—a first-rate linguist, rather innocent of the niceties of interstellar protocol. No reply from Harskin was needed. The hoarse voice of Military Attaché Ramos broke in.

"This is a neutral system, Leefman. Rigelian-Terran hostilities are suspended pending contact with the gnorphs. Someday you'll understand that war has its code too."

Alone in Control Cabin, Shipmaster Harskin smiled. It was a good crew; a little overspecialized, perhaps, but more than adequate for the purpose. Having Rigelians on hand would be just so much additional challenge. Shipmaster Harskin enjoyed challenges.

Beneath him, the engines of the *Peccable* throbbed magnificently. He was proud of his ship, proud of his crew. The *Peccable* swept into the deadly atmosphere of Fasolt, swung downward in big looping spirals, and headed for land.

Not too far behind came the Rigelians. Harskin leaned back and let the crash of deceleration eddy up over him, and waited.

Fasolt was mostly rock, except for the hydrogen-fluoride oceans and the hydrogenous air. It was not an appealing planet.

The spacesuited men of the *Peccable* were quick to debouch and extrude their dome. Atmosphere issued into it. "A little home away from home," Harskin remarked.

Biochemist Carver squinted balefully at the choppy hydrofluoric-acid sea. "Nice world. Good thing these goldfish bowls aren't made out of glass, yes? And better caution your men about using the dome airlock. A little of our oxygen gets out into that atmosphere and we'll have the loveliest rainstorm you ever want to see—with us a thousand feet up, looking down."

Harskin nodded. "It's not a pleasant place at all. But it's not a pleasant war we're fighting."

He glanced up at the murky sky. Fafnir was full, a broad red globe barely a million miles away. And, completing the group, there was the faint blue sun about which both worlds revolved, the entire system forming a neat Trojan equilateral with vast Antares.

Snollgren appeared. The keen-eyed observer had been in the ship, and apparently had made it from the *Peccable* to the endomed temporary camp on a dead run, no little feat in Fasolt's 1.5-g field.

"Well?" Harskin asked.

The observer opened his face plate and sucked in some of the dome's high-oxygen atmosphere. "The Rigelians," he gasped. "They've landed. I saw them in orbit."

"Where?"

"I'd estimate five hundred miles westward. They're definitely on this continent."

Harskin glanced at the chronometer set in the wrist of Snollgren's spacesuit. "We'll give them an hour to set up their camp. Then we'll contact them and find out what goes."

The Rigelian captain's name was Fourteen Deathless. He spoke Galactic with a sharp, crisp accent that Harskin attributed to his ursine ancestry.

"Coincidence we're both here at the same time, eh, Shipmaster Harskin? Strange are the ways of the Guiding Forces."

"They certainly are," Harskin said. He stared at the hand-mike, wishing it were a screen so he could see the sly, smug expression on the Rigelian's furry face. Obviously, someone had intercepted Harskin's allegedly secret orders and studied them carefully before forwarding them to their recipient.

Coincidences didn't happen in interstellar war. The Rigelians were here because they knew the Earthmen were.

"We have arrived at a knotty problem in ethics," remarked Captain Fourteen Deathless. "Both of us are here for the same purpose, that of negotiating trading rights with the gnorphs. Now—ah—which of us is to make the first attempt to deal with these people?"

"Obviously," said Harskin, "the ship which landed on Fasolt first has prior claim."

"This is suitable," said the Rigelian.

"We'll set out at once, then. Since the *Peccable* landed at least half an hour before your ship, we have clear priority."

"Interesting," Captain Fourteen Deathless said. "But just how do you compute you arrived before we did? By our instruments we were down long before you."

Harskin started to sputter, then checked himself. "Impossible!"

"Oh? Cite your landing time, please, with reference to Galactic Absolute."

"We put down at . . ." Harskin paused. "No. Suppose *you* tell *me* what time *you* landed, and then I'll give you our figures."

"That's hardly fair," said the Rigelian. "How do we know you won't alter your figures once we've given ours?"

"And how do *we* know, on the other hand . . . ?"

"It won't work," said the alien. "Neither of us will allow the other priority."

Shrugging, Harskin saw the truth of that. Regardless of the fact that the *Peccable* actually *had* landed first, the Rigelians would never admit it. It was a problem in simple relativity; without an external observer to supply impartial data, it was Fourteen Deathless' word against Harskin's.

"All right," Harskin said wearily. "Call it a stalemate. Suppose we *both* go to Fafnir now, and have them choose between us."

There was silence at the other end for a while. Then the Rigelian said, "This is acceptable. The rights of the neutral parties must be respected, of course."

"Of course. Until this system is settled, we're *all* neutrals, remember?"

"Naturally," said the Rigelian.

It was not, thought Harskin, a totally satisfactory arrangement. Still, it could hardly be helped.

By the very strict rules with which the Terran-Rigelian "war" was being fought, a system was considered neutral until a majority of its intelligently inhabited worlds had declared a preference for one power or the other.

In the Antares system, a majority vote would have to be a unanimous one. Of the eleven highly variegated worlds that circled the giant red star, only Fafnir bore life. The gnorphs were an intelligent race of biped humanoids—the classic shape of intelligent life. The Terrans were simianoid; the Rigelians, ursinoid. But the gnorphs owed their appearance neither to apes nor bears; they were reptilians, erect and tailless. Fafnir was not hospitable to mammalian life.

Harskin stared broodingly out the viewing bay as the blood-red seas of Fafnir grew larger. The Rigelian ship could not be seen, but he knew it was on its way. He made a mental note to inform Terran Intelligence that the secrecy of the high command's secret orders was open to some question.

It was a strange war—a war fought with documents rather than energy cannons. The shooting stage of the war between the galaxy's two leading races had long since ended in sheer futility; the development of the Martineau Negascreen, which happily drank up every megawatt of a bombardment and fired it back at triple intensity, had quickly put an end to active hostility.

Now, the war was carried on at a subtler level—the economic one. Rigel and Terra strove to outdo each other in extracting exclusive trading rights from systems, hoping to choke each other's lifelines. The universe was infinite, or close enough to infinite to keep both systems busy for quite a few millennia to come.

Harskin shrugged. Terran scouts had visited Fafnir and had reported little anxiety on the part of the gnorphs to take part in the Galactic stream of things. Presumably, Rigel IV had not yet visited the world; it was simpler to pirate the Terran scout reports.

Well, this would really be a test.

"Preparing to land, sir," said Navigator Dominic. "Any instructions?"

"Yes," Harskin said. "Bring us down where it's dry."

The landing was a good one, on the centermost of the island group that made up Fafnir's main land mass. Harskin and his twelve men—he had left five behind in the dome on Fasolt to hedge his bet—left the ship.

It would not be necessary to erect a dome here; Fafnir's air was breathable, more or less. It was 11 percent oxygen, 86 percent nitrogen, and a whopping 3 percent of inerts, but a decent filter system easily strained the excess nitro and argon out and pumped in oxygen.

Wearing breathing-masks and converters, the thirteen Terrans advanced inland. At their backs was the ocean, red and glimmering in Antares' light.

"Here come the Rigelians," Observer Snollgren cried.

"As usual, they're hanging back and waiting to see what we do." Harskin frowned. "This time, we won't wait for them. Let's take advantage of our head start."

The gnorph village was five miles inland, but the party

had not gone more than two miles when they were greeted by a group of aliens.

There were about a hundred of them, advancing in a wedge-shaped phalanx. They were moving slowly, without any overt belligerent ideas, but Harskin felt uneasy. A hundred aroused savages could make quick work of thirteen Terrans armed with handguns.

He glanced at Mawley, Contact Technician First Class. "Go ahead. Get up there and tell 'em we're friends."

Mawley was a tall redhead with knobby cheekbones and, at the moment, an expression of grave self-concern. He nodded, checked his lingual converter to make sure it was operating, and stepped forward, one hand upraised.

"Greetings," he said loudly. "We come in peace."

The gnorphs spread out into a loose formation and stared stolidly ahead. Harskin, waiting tensely for Mawley to achieve his rapport with the aliens, peered curiously at them.

They were short—five-six or so—and correspondingly broad-beamed. Their chocolate-brown skin was glossy and scaled; it hung loosely, in corrugated folds. Thick antennae twined upward from either side of their bald heads, and equally thick fleshy processes dangled comblike from their jaws. As for their eyes, Harskin was unable to see them; they were hidden in deep shadow, set back two inches in their skull and protected by projecting, brooding rims of bone that circled completely around each eye.

Three of the gnorphs stepped out of the ranks, and the middle alien stepped forward, flanked slightly to the rear by his companions. He spoke in a harsh, guttural voice.

The converter rendered it as "What do you want here?"

Mawley was prepared for the question. "Friendship. Peace. Mutual happiness of our worlds."

"Where are you from?"

Mawley gestured to the sky. "Far away, beyond the sky. Beyond the stars. Much distance."

The gnorph looked skeptical. "How many days' sailing from here?"

"Many days. Many, *many* days."

"Then why come to us?"

"To establish friendship," said Mawley. "To build a bond between your world and ours."

At that, the alien did an abrupt about-face and conferred

with his two companions. Harskin kept an eye on the spears twitching in the alien hands.

The conference seemed to be prolonging itself indefinitely. Mawley glanced back at Harskin as if to ask what he should do next, but the shipmaster merely smiled in approval and encouragement.

Finally the aliens broke up their huddle and the lead man turned back to the Terrans. "We think you should leave us," he grunted. "Go. At once."

There was nothing in Mawley's instructions to cover this. The contact technician opened and closed his mouth a few times without speaking. Gravely, the aliens turned and marched away, leaving the Terrans alone.

First Contact had been achieved.

"This has to be done in a very careful way," Harskin said. "Any news from the Rigelians?"

"They're situated about eight miles from here," Snollgren said.

"Hmmm. That means they're as far from the village as we are." Harskin put his hands to his head. "The gnorphs are certainly not leaping all over the place to sign a treaty with us, that's for sure. We'll have to handle them gently or we may make them angry enough to sign up with the Rigelians."

"I doubt that," offered Sociologist Yang. "They probably won't be any more anxious to deal with the Rigelians than they are with us. They're neutrals, and they want to stay that way."

Harskin leaned back. "This is a problem we haven't hit before. None of the worlds in either sphere of influence ever had any isolationist ideas. What do we do? Just pull up and leave?"

The blue sun was setting. Antares still hovered on the horizon, a shapeless blob of pale red eating up half the sky. "We'll have to send a man to spy on the Rigelians. Archer, you're elected."

The man in question rose. "Yes, sir."

"Keep an eye on them, watch their dealings with the gnorphs, and above all don't let the Rigelians see you." Another idea occurred to the shipmaster. "Lloyd?"

"Yes, sir?"

"In all probability the Rigelians have slapped a spy on

us. You're our counterespionage man, effective now. Scout around and see if you can turn up their spy."

Archer and Lloyd departed. Harskin turned to the sociologist. "Yang, there has to be some way of pushing these gnorphs to one side or the other."

"Agreed. I'll have to see more of a pattern, though, before I can help you."

Harskin nodded. "We'll make contact with the gnorphs again after Archer returns with the word of what the Rigelians are up to. We'll profit by their mistakes."

Antares had set as far as it was going to set, which was about three quarters of the way below the horizon, and the blue sun was spiraling its way into the heavens again, when the quiet air of Fafnir was split by an earth-shaking explosion.

The men of the *Peccable* were awake in an instant—those eight who had been sleeping, at any rate. A two-man skeleton team had been guarding the ship. Harskin had been meditating in Control Cabin, and Archer and Lloyd had not yet returned from their scouting missions.

Almost simultaneously with the explosion came the clangor of the alarm bell at the main airlock, signifying someone wanted in. A moment later, Observer First Class Snollgren was on the wire, excitedly jabbering something incoherent.

Harskin switched on the all-ship communicator and yelled, "*Stop! Whoa! Halt!*"

There was silence. He said, "Clyde, see what's going on at the airlock. Snollgren, slow down and tell me what you just saw."

"It was the Rigelian ship, sir!" the observer said. "It just left. That was the noise we heard."

"You sure of that?"

"Double positive. It took off in one hell of a hurry and I caught it on a tangent bound out of here."

"Okay. Clyde, what's at the airlock?"

"It's Lloyd, sir. He's back, and he's got a Rigelian prisoner with him."

"Prisoner? What the—all right, have them both come up here."

Radioman Klaristenfeld was next on the line. He said, "Sir, report coming in from the base on Fasolt. They confirm blast-off of a ship from Fafnir. They thought it might be us."

"Tell the idiots it isn't," Harskin snapped. "And tell them to watch out for the Rigelian ship. It's probably on its way back to Fasolt."

The door-annunciator chimed. Harskin pressed *admit* and Lloyd entered, preceded at blaster-point by a very angry-looking Rigelian.

"Where'd you find him?" Harskin asked.

"Mousing around near the ship," Lloyd said. The thin spaceman was pale and tense-looking. "I was patrolling the area as you suggested when I heard the explosion. I looked up and saw the Rigelian ship overhead and heading outward. And then this guy came crashing out of the underbrush and started cursing a blue streak in Rigelian. He didn't even see me until I had the blaster pointing in his face."

Harskin glanced at the Rigelian. "What's your name and rank, Rigelian?"

"Three Ninety-Seven Indomitable," the alien said. He was a formidably burly seven-footer, covered with stiff, coarse black hair and wearing a light-yellow leather harness. His eyes glinted coldly. He looked angry. "Espionage man first order," he said.

"That explains what you were doing near our ship, then, Three Ninety-Seven Indomitable," Harskin said. "What can you tell me about this quick blast-off?"

"Not a thing. The first I knew of it was when it happened. They marooned me! They left me here!" The alien slipped from Galactic into a Rigelian tongue and growled what must have been some highly picturesque profanity.

"They just *left* you?" Harskin repeated in amazement. "Something must have made them decide to clear out of here in an awful hurry, then." He turned to Lloyd. "Convey the prisoner to the brig and see that he's put there to stay. Then pick two men and start combing the countryside for Archer. I want to know what made the Rigelians get out of here so fast they didn't have time to pick up their own spy."

As it developed, very little countryside combing was necessary to locate Archer. Harskin's spy returned to the *Peccable* about three quarters of an hour later, extremely winded after his long cross-country trot.

It took him five minutes to calm down enough to deliver his report.

"I tracked the Rigelians back to their ship," he said. "They were all gathered around it, and I waited in the underbrush. After a while they proceeded to the gnorph village, and I followed them."

"Any attempt at counterespionage?" Harskin asked.

"Yes, sir." Archer grinned uncomfortably. "I killed him."

Harskin nodded. "Go on."

"They reached the village. I stayed about thirty yards behind them and switched on my converter so I could hear what they were saying."

"Bad, but unavoidable," Harskin said. "They might have had a man at the ship tracing the energy flow. I guess they didn't, though. What happened to the village?"

"They introduced themselves, and gave the usual line—the same thing we said, about peace and friendship and stuff. Then they started handing out gifts. Captain Fourteen Deathless said this was to cement Rigel's friendship with Fafnir—only he didn't call it Fafnir, naturally.

"They handed mirrors all around, and little forcewave generators, and all sorts of trinkets and gadgets. The gnorphs took each one and stacked it in a heap off to one side. The Rigelians kept handing out more and more, and the stack kept growing. Then, finally, Fourteen Deathless said he felt the gifts had been sufficient. He started to explain the nature of the treaty. And one of the gnorphs stepped out and pointed to the stack of gifts. 'Are you quite finished delivering things?' he asked, in a very stuffy tone. The Rigelian looked flustered and said more gifts would be forthcoming after the treaty was signed. And that blew the roof off."

"How do you mean?"

"It happened so fast I'm not sure. But suddenly all the gnorphs started waving their spears and looking menacing, and then someone threw a spear at a Rigelian. That started it. The Rigelians had some handguns with them, but they were so close they hardly had a chance to use them. It was a real massacre. About half the Rigelians escaped, including Captain Deathless. I hid in the underbrush till it was all over. Then I came back here."

Harskin looked at Sociologist Yang. "Well? What do you make of it?"

"Obviously a greedy sort of culture," the sociologist

remarked. "The Rigelians made the mistake of being too stingy. I suggest we wait till morning and go to that village ourselves, and shoot the works. With the Rigelians gone we've got a clear field, and if we're liberal enough the planet will be ours."

"Don't be too sure of that," Harskin said broodingly. "That Rigelian was no bigger a fool than I am. When we go to that village, we'll go well armed."

The gnorph village was a cluster of thatched huts set in a wide semicircle over some extremely marshy swampland. Both Antares and the blue companion were in the sky when the Earthmen arrived; Fasolt was making its daily occultation of the giant sun.

Harskin had taken six of his men with him: Yang, Leefman, Archer, Mawley, Ramos, and Carver. Six more remained at the ship, seeing to it that the *Peccable* was primed for a quick getaway, if necessary.

The gifts of the Rigelians lay in a scattered heap in the center of the village, smashed and battered. Nearby lay half a dozen mutilated Rigelian bodies. Harskin shuddered despite himself; these gnorphs were cold-blooded in more than the literal biological sense!

A group of them filtered out of their huts and confronted the approaching Earthmen. In the mingled blue-and-red light of the two suns—one huge and dim, the other small and dim—the blank, scaly faces looked strange and menacing, the bone-hooded sockets cold and ugly.

"What do you want here, strangers?"

"We have come to thank you," Mawley said, "for killing our enemies, the fur-men." He had been instructed to stress the distinction between the group of Rigelians and the Earthmen. "The fur-men were here last night, bearing niggling gifts. They are our enemies. We of Earth offer you peace and goodwill."

The gnorphs stared squarely at the tense little party of Earthmen. Each of the seven Terrans carried a powerful blaster set for wide-beam stunning, highly efficient if not particularly deadly as a close-range weapon. In the event of a battle, the Earthmen would at least be ready.

"What is it you want here?" the gnorph leader asked with thinly concealed impatience.

"We wish to sign a treaty between your world and ours," said Mawley. "A bond of eternal friendship, of loyalty and fellowship between worlds."

Somewhere in the distance an unseen beast emitted a rumbling reptilian honk—quite spoiling the effect, Harskin thought.

"Friendship? Fellowship?" the gnorph repeated, indicating by a quivering shake of his wattles that these were difficult concepts for him to grasp.

"Yes," said Mawley. "And as signs of our friendship we bring you gifts—not piddling trinkets such as our enemies foisted on you last night, but gifts of incomparable richness, gifts which will be just part of the bounty to fall upon you if you will sign with us."

At a signal from Harskin, they began unloading the gifts they had brought with them: miniaturized cameras, game-detectors, dozens of other treasures calculated to impress the gnorphs.

And then it began.

Harskin had been on the lookout for the explosion ever since they had arrived, and when he saw the spears beginning to bristle in the gnorph ranks, he yanked his blaster out and fired.

The stunning beam swept the front rank of gnorphs; they fell. The others growled menacingly and advanced.

The seven Earthmen jammed together in a unit and fired constantly; gnorphs lay unconscious all over, and still more came pouring from the huts. The Terrans started to run. Spears sailed past their heads.

It was a long, grim retreat to the ship.

They were still a quarter of a million miles from Fasolt when Radioman Klaristenfeld reported that Captain Fourteen Deathless of the Rigelian ship was calling.

"We see you have left also," the Rigelian said when Harskin took the phone. "You were evidently as unsuccessful as we."

"Not quite," Harskin said. "At least we got out of there without any casualties. I counted six dead Rigelians outside that village—plus the man you left behind to watch over us. He's in our brig."

"Ah. I had wondered what became of him. Well, Harskin,

do we declare Fafnir a neutral planet and leave it at that? It's a rather unsatisfactory finish to our little encounter."

"Agreed. But what can we do? We dumped nearly fifty thousand credits' worth of trinkets when we escaped."

"You Terrans are lavish," the Rigelian observed. "Our goods were worth but half that."

"That's the way it goes," Harskin said. "Well, best wishes, Fourteen Deathless."

"One moment! Is the decision a dual withdrawal?"

"I'm not so sure," Harskin said, and broke the contact.

When they reached Fasolt and rejoined the men in the dome, Harskin ordered a general meeting. He had an idea.

"The aliens," he said, "offered the gnorphs twenty-five thousand credits of goods, and were repulsed angrily. We offered twice as much—and, if Archer's account of the Rigelian incident was accurate, we were repulsed about twice as fast. Yang, does that suggest anything to you?"

The little sociologist wrinkled his head. "The pattern still is not clear," he said.

"I didn't think so." Harskin knotted his fingers in concentration. "Let me put it this way: the degree of insult the gnorphs felt was in direct variance with the degree of wealth offered. That sound plausible?"

Yang nodded.

"Tell me: what happens when an isolated, biologically glum race is visited by warm-blooded aliens from the skies? Suppose those warm-blooded aliens want a treaty of friendship—and offer to *pay* for it? How will the natives react, Yang?"

"I see. They'll get highly insulted. We're treating them in a cavalier fashion."

"More than that. We're obliging them to us. We're *purchasing* that treaty with our gifts. But obviously gifts are worth more than a treaty of friendship, so they feel they'll still owe us something if they accept. They don't want to owe us anything. So they chase us away."

"Now," continued Harskin, "if we reverse the situation—if we make ourselves beholden to them, and *beg* for the signing of the treaty instead of trying to *buy* a treaty— why, that gives them a chance to seem lordly." He turned to Ramos, the military attaché. "Ramos, do you think a solar system is worth a spaceship?"

"Eh?"

"I mean, if it becomes necessary to sacrifice our ship in order to win the Antares system, will that be a strategically sound move?"

"I imagine so," Ramos said cautiously.

Harskin flicked a bead of sweat from his forehead. "Very well, then. Mawley, you and I and Navigator Dominic are going to take the *Peccable* on her final cruise. Klaristenfeld, I want you to get a subradio sending set inside my spacesuit, and make damned sure you don't put it where it'll bother me. Snollgren, you monitor the area and keep me posted on what the Rigelians are doing, if anything."

He pointed to the Navigator. "Come up to Control Cabin, Dominic. We're going to work out the most precise orbit you'll ever need to compute."

Antares was sinking in the sky and the blue sun was in partial eclipse. Suddenly, the *Peccable* flashed across the sky of Fafnir, trailing smoke at both jets, roaring like a wounded giant as it circled in wildly for its crash landing.

The three men aboard were huddled in their acceleration cradles, groaning in pain as the increasing grav buffeted and bruised them. Below, Fafnir sprang up to meet the ship.

Harskin was bathed in his own sweat. So many things could go wrong. . . .

They might have computed one tenth-place decimal awry—and would land square in the heart of the swampland.

The stabilizer jets might be consumed by the blaze they had set too soon, and the impact of their landing would kill them.

The airlock might refuse to open.

The gnorphs might fail to act as expected. . . .

It was, he thought, an insane venture.

The ship throbbed suddenly as the stabilizer jets went into action. The *Peccable* froze for a fraction of a second, then began to glide.

It struck the blood-red ocean nose first. Furiously, Harskin climbed from his cradle and into his spacesuit. *Now, if we only figured the buoyancy factor right* . . .

Two spacesuited figures waited for him at the airlock. He grinned at them, threw open the hatch, and stepped into the outer chamber. The door opened; a wall of water rushed at him. He squirted out of the sinking ship and popped to the surface like a cork. A moment later he saw Mawley and Dominic come bobbing above the water nearby.

He turned. All that was visible of the *Peccable* was the rear jet assembly and the tips of the once-proud wings. An oily slick was starting to cover the bright-red water. The ship was sinking rapidly as water poured into the lock.

"Look over there!" Mawley exclaimed.

Harskin looked. Something that looked like a small island with a neck was approaching him: a monstrous turtlelike thing with a thick, saurian neck and a crested unintelligent head, from which dangled seven or eight fleshy barbels.

And riding in a sort of howdah erected on the broad carapace were three gnorphs, peering curiously at the three spacesuited men bobbing in the water.

The rescue party was on time.

"Help!" cried Harskin. "Rescue us! Oh, I beg of you, rescue us, and we'll be eternally obliged to you! Rescue us!"

He hoped the converter was translating the words with a suitable inflection of piteous despair.

DOUBLEPLUS PRIORITY 03-16-2952 ABS XPF32
EXP FORCE ANTARES SYSTEM TO HIGH COMMAND TERRA:

BE ADVISED ANTARES SYSTEM IN TERRAN FOLD. RIGELIANS ON HAND HAVE VALIDATED OUR TREATY WITH INHABITANTS OF FAFNIR, ANTARES' ONE WORLD. ALL IS WELL AND NO CASUALTIES EXCEPT SHIP PECCABLE ACCIDENTALLY DESTROYED. FIF-TEEN MEMBERS OF CREW LIVING IN DOME ON COM-PANION WORLD FASOLT, THREE OF US LIVING ON FAFNIR. PLEASE SEND PICKUP SHIP DOUBLE FAST AS WE ARE CURRENTLY IN MENIAL SERVITUDE.

ALL THE BEST, LOVE AND KISSES, ETC.
HARSKIN

Solitary

Ever since the computers came to be running things pretty much their own way, handling data and forming conclusions, the only way anyone could achieve any notice in the galaxy was to do some original thinking—and by original, read *alogical*. An analog computer is a clever thing, with its countless supercooled cryotrons clicking off bits of information, but its mind is a limited sort of creature. Men, luckily, aren't limited to the flip-flop, on-off type of binary thinking that the computers specialize in.

Among those most painfully aware of this was Geourge Brauer of Crime Bureau. Because the job of keeping data on the galaxy's criminals was so complex, Crime Bureau was among the first to be completely computerized. Its employees were reduced to the level of data-predigestors, selecting information to be programmed and fed to the computers. As the centuries passed, the human members of Crime Bureau became less and less necessary to the scheme of things. They were mere adjuncts to the Totivac that did the actual work.

This irked Geourge Brauer.

At thirty-one, he felt he was at a crossroads. This was his fifth year with Crime Bureau—and in those five years he had become an increasingly more skillful computer technician, nothing more. This was not why he had joined Crime Bureau.

He had been interested, being a serious, reflective man, in the concepts of crime and punishment, the philosophical determinance of guilt, *mores* and ethos, responsibility and necessary obligation. They fascinated him.

"You ought to join Crime Bureau," his college roommate told him sourly. "Always talking about murders and things, as if you were going to commit a couple."

"It's purely a scholarly interest," Brauer said. And when he graduated, he joined Crime Bureau.

At thirty-one he was at a crossroads.

Moodily he sat at his burnished duralplast desk in the magnificent Crime Bureau Ministratory in Upper Ontario, toying with the sheets of paper before him. They listed statistics governing occurrence of voyeurism on Earth, and on the seventeen Norm Planets used as guideposts in such things. Brauer was supposed to integrate them, feed them to omnivorous Totivac, and wait while the statistics came rattling back neatly interpreted. They were to be transmitted to Lurinar IX, an Earth-type planet afflicted simultaneously with a rash of voyeurism and with a starchily puritanical ruling oligarchy, for benefit of the bemused and troubled Chief of Police there.

As he worked, Brauer found himself envying that Chief of Police. Stranded on a backwater world as he was, at least the man had a chance to deal with crime and criminals first hand, not with the ever-present Totivac peering over his shoulder. Brauer plodded gloomily through the long columns, then sent the whole tape whirring into the innards of the computer.

Pulses flitted down tantalum cryotrons; information was bandied and conclusions drawn. And Brauer ground his fist into his chin in boredom.

The computer took all the trial-and-error out of things. To be sure, Totivac operated on a trial-and-error system itself, as did any analog computer. But the interval between successive trials was often less than a micro-microsecond, and a speed of that order allowed for all the wrong guesses a machine would be likely to make in a two-minute span.

Two minutes. The data came chittering back at him. Without even looking at it, Brauer tossed it in the upper basket on his desk.

Stultification—that was the word. A man had to do a little thinking on his own. It was all right to use the computer as a tool to simplify the process of thought—but not as a substitute for it.

On a sudden impulse he stuck a requisition form in his typewriter, which was an antiquated manual model, and tapped out a brief message: *Send me data cards on current file of unsolved crimes.*

He glanced at what he had written, scowled, then added for benefit of the computer: *Time limitation: Last thirty years. Space limitation: This galaxy.*

Brauer paused, then tacked on a second postscript: *Hop to it, or I'll put ketchup in your feed lines.*

He integrated the requisition form and shot it downward into Totivac's bowels. An instant later the red light over his desk blazed, indicating a message from the computer, and the machine replied: *Coercion invalidates requisition. Please delete same or face penalty.*

Brauer could imagine the storm his whimsical threat had kicked up down in the defensive banks of the computer; probably they were busy monitoring the cooling system, the power input, and anything else that might be construed as a "feed line," on guard for a sudden influx of ketchup.

Coercion deleted, he replied. *No danger of destruction by ketchup.*

The warning-light blinked out; the computer's hackles were subsiding.

Moments later came the deluge.

He had asked for the current file of unsolved cases; he got it. It came spilling out of the computer's orifice with a rush and a roar, card after card covered with Totivac's neat typing. Brauer blinked as the cards piled up. There were a lot of people in the galaxy, and a great many crimes—and if even just a bare fraction went unsolved—

He sighed. There was no way to interrupt the machine, now that it had begun to disgorge. The computer was reaching into the depths of its files, coming up with cases that had been on the books for decades. At least five thousand cards were on his desk now, and still they came.

The communicator chimed. Brauer grabbed it and heard his superior bark, "Brauer, what are you *doing?*"

"Original research, chief," he said smoothly. "The machine's a little over-enthusiastic, that's all."

"Oh? Research on what."

"I'd prefer not to talk about it until I'm finished. I may need a short leave of absence, too."

"I suppose it can be arranged," the chief said gruffly, and broke the contact.

Brauer stared balefully at the mounting stack of cards. All right; he had announced he was working on something. Now he would have to follow through.

A second stack of five thousand cards had appeared, and it seemed as if the computer was well on its way toward delivering a third when abruptly a single card fluttered out of the orifice and the message-light flashed. Brauer snatched up the communication.

End of immediate-access open files. There will be delay of one hundred eighty seconds while secondary files are searched.

"No there won't!" Brauer half-shouted. Quickly he

pecked out a reply: *Data already delivered is sufficient for project. Terminate search without further activity.*

A pause, then the response: *Acknowledged. Terminated.*

"Thank goodness," Brauer said fervently. He stared at the heaps of data cards, feeling like the sorcerer's apprentice. But at least he had managed to shut off the flow.

He lifted the uppermost card and skimmed it. Tall thin Sirian suspected of shoplifting in Third City of Vega IV twenty-nine point nine years before, never apprehended. Further details on other side.

The second card was even less promising. Child's pet stolen by large hairy man on morning of 7 July 2561, planet Earth. Pet never recovered. Details other side.

The card had been in the files thirty years. Someone could gain more than a little prestige, Brauer thought, simply by clearing junk like this out of the memory banks. By now the stolen pet, unless it had been a Galapagos turtle, was long since dead, and the bereaved child grown to manhood. And yet the "crime" was still carried as unsolved.

He reached for a third card. Like the first two, it dated back thirty years. But it was considerably more interesting. Brauer read it once perfunctorily, then went back and examined it in detail.

Charcot, Edward Hammond. Born 21 Dec 2530, New York City, Earth (Sol III). Criminal record: petty theft, apprehended 8 Nov 2547, corrective term one month. Released for good behavior. Kidnapping, apprehended 12 Jan 2558, escaped from custody 17 Jan 2558, relocated 11 June 2559. Trial begun 18 June 2559, concluded 4 October 2559. Sentenced to cor-rectory, transshipped to Procyon IV 7 November 2559. Entered upon life term 11 Jan 2560, escaped from Procyon Correctory 12 May 2560. Still at large (see Additional Data Sheet 101 in request file).

Brauer flexed the card between two fingers and dug back in his memory—a memory not nearly as retentive as Totivac's, but unusually good as mere organic ones went. He was investigating the data stored away in his youth, in his period of greatest criminological enthusiasm, before the disillusionment of joining Crime Bureau.

Edward Charcot. Yes, he remembered Charcot, even though the case had been most notorious only a month or two after Brauer's birth. Charcot had been a cheap criminal, a petty hood of the sort that no amount of careful breeding seemed likely ever to eradicate from human genetic lines. He had committed a particularly vicious kidnapping thirty-odd years ago, and he had been caught. And, unless Brauer's memory was at fault, he was to date the only man ever to break out of the Procyon Correctory.

With nervous haste he shoved the umpteen-thousand data cards back into the computer's orifice and punched out a new requisition: *Send additional data sheet 101 on Charcot, Edward Hammond.*

Moments later the sheet arrived. To his satisfaction Brauer saw he had been right: Charcot's notoriety was based on the fact that he was the only man ever to escape from Procyon's airtight correctory.

He had stolen a one-man warpship somehow, and struck out for points unknown before anyone knew he was missing. One of the minor mysteries of the case was how Charcot had managed to escape—but since no one before or since had succeeded in getting off Procyon IV, it was considered that the experiment was nonrepeatable. The major mystery was Charcot's whereabouts.

The data sheet listed all reports, reliable and otherwise, of his location. He had been seen (or half-seen) at a dozen places radiating in a more-or-less straight line out toward the region of Bellatrix, and there the trail vanished. A sporadic search of the six planets of Bellatrix had revealed nothing.

Thoughts tumbled through Brauer's mind.

Who Edward Charcot was didn't much matter, nor the fact that Charcot had humiliated the penologists by getting out of an escape-proof correctory, nor that he was responsible for a fairly ghastly crime. No.

He had disappeared, though—and that offended Brauer's sense of order. In a galaxy so carefully regulated by computers, men didn't disappear. At least, not easily. Of course, this Charcot was a clever chap, obviously—but still, where could he have gone?

The trail led toward Bellatrix and its system. Brauer

licked his lips reflectively. A major attempt had, no doubt, been made toward finding Charcot. It had failed.

Why? Some deficiency inherent in the nature of the pursuit, no doubt. Brauer's pulse-rate started climbing. Here was a chance for original research; here was a chance for an ordinary flesh-and-blood man, with a built-in capacity for making cockeyed guesses, to show up a billion-unit cryotronic computer with its deplorably binary way of thinking.

He decided to find Edward Charcot.

The first step was to activate the communicator.

"Chief, this is Brauer. I want to request a three-month leave from duty."

"With or without pay?"

Brauer hesitated, then boldly said, "With. It's to do that special research job I was talking about."

There was a pause. "Three months with pay . . . it may be rough on our budget, Geourge. Can you tell me anything about the research?"

"I'm going to find Edward Charcot," Brauer said.

The reaction was predictable: "Who?"

"Charcot. The kidnapper who escaped from Procyon Correctory in 2560. Remember?"

"Oh—that one. Hmmm. All right. Fill out the form, integrate it yourself, and feed it to the machine. You know how to do it. I'll see to it your leave's approved."

Brauer rapidly integrated the leave-request and let Totivac have it. Then he formulated a new requisition: *Send all data available on Charcot, Edward Hammond*.

Moments later he had it, including duplicates of the data card and Additional Data Sheet 101; the machine was damnably literal about "all data" requests.

Brauer cleared his desk and proceeded to examine the information. Most of it was a repetition of what he had already learned; he skimmed through that, and also through most of Charcot's biography. He wasn't interested in that.

He was interested in the post-escape part of the data. Included in the packet were transcripts of statements by men who had allegedly seen Charcot (or thought they had) in one guise or another after his much-publicized escape. Someone—Brauer hoped it was a human being, and not just a watchful facet of Totivac—had charted a probability-pattern with each report of Charcot carefully inked in according to a weighted color-spectrum of credibility, ranging from bright cerise for *"fairly reliable"* down to dark violet for *"totally untrustworthy."*

The color-chart led undeniably toward Bellatrix. And appended to the packet was the report of the scouting-mission that had searched the area for Charcot.

Apparently Totivac had analyzed the six planets of Bellatrix and had concluded that Charcot would be on either Bellatrix II, III, or VI, all of which were inhabited by reasonably docile forms of intelligent life.

Scoutship CD102-X3 had diligently searched Bellatrix II, III, and VI. There had been no sign of Charcot. Whereupon, the trail having trickled out, the Charcot file had been dumped into *"Unsolved,"* and probably had moldered there unmolested until Brauer's requisition had released it.

Humming gently to himself, Brauer rummaged through the rest of the packet. Included was a telefax sheet, now somewhat yellowed with age, dated 12 May 2560, point of origin Procyon IV. It showed a photo of the escapee—he was a darkly handsome, almost suave-looking man, Brauer noted, with a faint mustache, deep-set eyes, a smirk rather than a smile on his lips. A shrewd man, Brauer decided, even though it was an elementary rule of criminology to place little weight upon superficialities of appearance. Yet in Charcot's case, his actions bore out the testimony of his features: it took a shrewd man to get out of Procyon Correctory.

The telefax sheet went on to mention the reward offered for information leading to Charcot's recovery, described him, gave a brief biography. Doubtless there still were some of these sheets mounted on post office walls in obscure parts of the galaxy, Brauer thought.

He put the telefax sheet back in the file packet and restored the other material as well. He dumped it all into the receiving orifice.

Send data on the Bellatrix system, he ordered the computer.

Bellatrix was a star of magnitude plus 1.7, located 215 light-years from Earth. Relative to Earth, it was located in the constellation Orion, but of course visual proximity from an external point had nothing to do with actual three-dimensional location in the universe.

According to the data Brauer had, Bellatrix had a planetary system comprising six worlds; Bellatrix I was 500,000,000 miles from its blazing primary, and the other five planets were arrayed in normally distributed orbits up to a distance of three billion miles.

Brauer quickly ran through the survey reports on the six worlds.

Bellatrix I was uninhabited and uninhabitable; it took a regular roasting from the sun, and had a mean temperature of about 300 degrees F.

Bellatrix II *was* inhabited; it was a watery world (the "water," however, in actuality being a mixture of liquefied halogens). The natives were amiable chlorine-breathers whose hide resisted etching by the lakes of hydrogen fluoride common on the planet.

Bellatrix III was likewise inhabited; this was a large, low-mass world peopled by ruminant herbivores, four-legged but intelligent; the record showed a Terran settlement in operation there.

Brauer continued to read. Bellatrix IV and V were both uninhabited: IV was a rocky unappealing world with a scant population of lichens and nothing else. Life had simply not yet gained a foothold there. Bellatrix V was a gas giant of massive gravitational attraction; its surface was unstable, and explorers had deemed it unwise to land.

As for Bellatrix VI, it was an Earth-type world, somewhat colder on the mean, inhabited by humanoid creatures just entering the food-producing stage of culture. The scouts had recommended a closed status for this world, for fear of upsetting the normal development of the expanding culture. The closure had been approved.

Brauer then studied the report of the search once again. He was not surprised to read Totivac's evaluation of Charcot's possible whereabouts.

Bellatrix VI, being a closed world, was the most likely place for a callous criminal to hide, since there was little chance of his discovery on a closed world. Therefore VI had been the prime target of the searchers.

After that came III, since it was a livable and inhabited world. Further down the scale of probability was II, the water-world, where an Earthman could manage to survive if properly protected.

The other three worlds had been rather casually dismissed: V, the gas giant, was eliminated completely, since it was impossible to survive long on a world without a solid surface; I, with its temperature of 300 degrees, was docketed for only a cursory once-over since it, too, was hardly promising as a hideout for an escaped criminal.

As for Bellatrix IV, the utterly barren world, it was likewise dealt off by the computer with a mere once-over. After all, it was illogical that a fleeing man would choose to settle even for a few days on a world devoid of all life.

Brauer chuckled happily as he read Totivac's solemn conclusion. Illogical, indeed! Sure it was illogical. But all that meant was that no self-respecting computer would ever choose to hide there.

Happily, Brauer put away his data, confirmed his leave, and arranged for transportation. He requisitioned a one-man cruiser equipped with warp-drive and plenty of charts.

He was heading for Bellatrix.

Just before he left, he requisitioned the data file on Charcot once again, to check something. Yes; the reward was fifty thousand dollars. He wondered if it still stood, after these thirty years.

Even by warp-drive, 215 light-years takes a while to traverse. Brauer spent the time pleasantly, reading his collection of classics: Radin, Fell, Staub and Alexander, Caryl Chessman, Hornsfall and Wagley. They were part of his prized collection of twentieth and twenty-first century criminology. Back then, he thought, a man had a chance to use his wits—not simply punch data in or out of a bunch of cryotrons.

Crime, after all, was an irrational manifestation. It was foolish, then, to depend wholly on an inflexible rational binary-oriented mind, or pseudo-mind, to make the top level decisions.

Take this business of Bellatrix, he thought. The silly search, over areas carefully preselected by Totivac. Had any of the searchers bothered to deviate from the prescribed pattern? Probably not—and if they had, they probably had decided it would be unsafe to report such actions to the computer.

He emerged from warp uncomfortably close to Bellatrix itself. Brauer was not an experienced spaceman by any means, but a warpship was a simple device to operate. It had a built-in safety control that saw to it that its operator could do no wrong: in the event of a materialization in an impossible place (such as within a planet) no paradox would result; the ship would simply and swiftly demolecularize itself. In the event of a crashlanding, the ship was equipped with a device that would automatically radiate a distress-pulse on a wide-band carrier that could be picked up anywhere within a radius of twenty light-years.

He popped back into normal space not far from Bellatrix I, which happened to be at aphelion: just as well, he decided. Even half a billion miles from Bellatrix was too close to suit him.

Brauer had a definite plan of action which called for a speedy survey of the six planets, more to familiarize himself with the territory than anything else, and then a fine-toothing of his two prime suspects.

He therefore brought the ship into a closed orbit around Bellatrix I, for his first look-see. And it was fairly evident that if Charcot had landed here, he had not survived. Bellatrix I was similar in general appearance to the day side of Sol I: its baked, blistered surface was airless and lifeless. Shimmering pools of metal lay on the sands, as on Mercury. Here, though, there was no dark side and no merciful twilight belt for an escaped convict to settle in: Bellatrix I rotated quite nicely on its axis, presenting each hemisphere in turn to the sun.

Brauer moved on. Bellatrix I held little promise.

He approached III next, since II was currently at the far end of its orbit. III was the low-mass world dominated by herbivores; Brauer allowed himself an amused chuckle at the thought of the ecology prof who had gravely assured him that such a situation was impossible.

He scouted low; no sign of human inhabitation. Of course, on a quick buzz like that he had little expectation of uncovering Charcot. But III had already been covered fairly thoroughly by government searchers and he trusted them to do a good job—within their limits.

Similarly II. Totivac had directed them to search II, III, and VI. He was willing to assume they had done it properly.

The other three planets were different matters.

Brauer took an interested look at Bellatrix II, moved on, buzzed barren IV, circled VI, and doubled back to V. As he had been warned, and as he expected, it was impossible—or at least certainly risky—to get too close to mighty V. A landing was out of the question.

Having been through the entire system, Brauer now drew back, locked the ship in a stable orbit, and, pacing the cabin, began to develop hypotheses.

"The computer," he said aloud somewhat self-consciously, "is primarily rational. Having made the quasi-rational deduction that Charcot was somewhere in the Bellatrix system, it then proceeded to eliminate possibilities.

"Three of the planets are so unappealing that no man in his right mind would land on them. A fourth—II—is inhabitable but scarcely satisfactory. The remaining two are possible choices for a man looking for a place to hide until the search for him died down.

"Item: Charcot stole a warship. This tells the computer a number of things. One of them is that Charcot must have landed the ship voluntarily and not crashlanded somewhere, because had he crashlanded the ship, it would automatically have sent out distress signals. Since no distress signals were sent out, the ship did not crashland. *Ergo*, he either came out of warp in an impossible place and was demolecularized, or he landed safely on one of the inhabitable worlds. Probability favors the latter. Therefore, the computer suggested that planets VI, III, and II be searched, in that order."

Brauer smiled. The computer had acted in perfect sanity—with one mistake. It hadn't allowed for the possibility that a man might be so demented as to deliberately *remove* so integral a part of his ship's equipment as the automatic distress-signal.

It was possible for Brauer to proceed computer-fashion from that one alogical postulate. Assuming Charcot either landed safely or crashlanded on one of the Bellatrix worlds, then either he landed safely on one of the three habitable worlds, and thus would have been found by Totivac's searchers—or he crashlanded on one of the other three planets.

Since Charcot had not been found by the Totivac searchers, and since he would not voluntarily have landed on worlds I, IV, or V, the conclusion had to be that Charcot had crashlanded on one of those planets.

Brauer grinned smugly. It was pure deduction—unlike the celebrations of the legendary Mr. Holmes, whose alleged "deductions" were actually more induction. The only thing that remained was the proof.

Brauer thought feelingly of the poor dupes feeding info to Totivac, back there in Upper Ontario. How they would envy him!

He readied himself for the search.

Here, too, he was able to winnow down his candidates with a little thought. Had Charcot crashlanded on either I or V, the evidence of his presence would long since have been erased by the elements. Furthermore, V was impossible for Brauer to search.

But IV, lonely, barren IV—

Had Charcot crashed there, amid the disinterested lichens, there would still be proof: the wrecked spaceship, tools, perhaps even the body. Brauer had the most to gain by Charcot's having crashed on IV, and so he chose IV to begin his search.

He expected searching to be a painstaking job. He calculated he could cover the entire land mass of the planet in broad sweeps and do the job properly in a month's time. Brauer was a patient man; he had many examples from the past as his guides to criminological technique.

No patience was needed, though. Luck, which is often scoffed at but which is a valid factor in detection, entered here—and, seventeen hours after his ship had entered the first of its search-maneuvers, Brauer's elaborate construction of guesswork and deduction was solidified when his mass-detectors recorded the presence of a spaceship crumpled on the rocks below.

A pulse thundered in his ears as he brought his ship down tenderly on Bellatrix IV's forbidding surface. It was a neat landing; atmospheric check reported the air breathable, and he rushed from his ship.

A hundred yards away lay another one-man job, identical to his own. It had struck tail-first heavily, toppled, bashed its snout against an outcrop of what looked like dark basalt. Luckily it had landed hatch-upright, so its lone occupant had been able to clamber out. The hatch was open now.

Brauer approached, looked around for some sign of the skeleton. There was none; evidently Charcot had wandered for some distance over the bare, arid world before his food ran out.

Brauer photographed the ship from several angles, then hoisted himself up and climbed inside. He blinked in surprise. The interior didn't seem to have been empty thirty years. The ship looked lived-in. *How—?*

Then he saw how. The resourceful Charcot had somehow tucked a Karster food synthesizer away in the ship before blasting off. A man could live a long time with just a food synthesizer. To one side of the machine lay a little heap of crushed rocks; evidently Charcot had been feeding rock to the synthesizer's molecular converter and thus literally living off the planet.

Otherwise, the ship was bare—no tapes, no comforts, just a cradle and the synthesizer. Brauer lurked around until he had confirmed another of his theories—the distress signal device had been crudely but efficiently ripped loose.

He took careful photos, then climbed through the hatch again.

And gasped.

A thin, ancient-looking figure, bent and angular, with a shaggy yellow-white beard, was straggling across the barren plain toward the ship.

Returning from a stroll, no doubt.

Charcot.

It had to be Charcot. Thirty years of solitude had left their mark, but behind the dried skin and unkempt beard was still the sharp-eyed face of the shrewd young criminal pictured on the telefax sheet. Half-dizzy with incredulity, Brauer scrambled down the side of the ship, jumped—felt the impact of the rock jarring his feet—and hesitantly approached the old man.

It was not until they were twenty feet apart that the ancient showed any sign of having seen Brauer. Suddenly the old man paused, wobbled unsteadily on his feet, raised one gnarled hand, pointed from Brauer's ship to Brauer.

His dry lips worked. A harsh rumbling sound came forth; after much effort, the oldster managed to shape a tremulous word. *"You—you—"*

The effort and the shock was too great. He tottered, pivoted wildly, fell forward.

Brauer was galvanized out of his numbness. He ran to the old man, knelt, slid his hand inside the ragged shirt, felt the bony chest.

Silence. The silence of death.

Brauer's finger encountered something folded beneath the old man's shirt; with trembling hands he drew it out and examined it. It was tattered, depigmented with age, but still legible. It was the telefax sheet with the photo of the escaped convict. Brauer glanced from the smirking youthful face to the old man's.

There was no doubt. This was Charcot. Somehow he had clung to life, with only the food synthesizer for a companion. He had been totally alone for thirty years, without so much as a book or a pet, on lifeless Bellatrix IV.

Brauer shuddered. No doubt, Charcot had believed he was gaining freedom when he broke out of the Correctory— but there, at least, he had been in humane hands, among men who would try to provide some sort of therapy and rehabilitation. Solitary confinement was cruel, barbarous; penal codes had outlawed it decades earlier.

He had trapped himself in a prison without walls. He had lived here thirty years alone. His "freedom" had in actuality been a punishment more terrible than any court would mete out. The shock of seeing another living being again had killed him.

Broodingly, Brauer pocketed the tattered telefax sheet and kicked away a pebble. Then he shuffled back toward the outjutting hill. There wasn't even any soil on the planet in which to bury Charcot. He began to gather rocks for the old man's cairn.

Later, he subradioed a simple message to the nearest pickup-point for Totivac's data collectors. It said: *In the matter of the escape of Charcot, Edward Hammond—the case is closed.*

Journey's End

Barchay rode into the V'Leeg village alone, on the back of a swaybacked pink running-beast that he had caught and broken himself, five years past. He had been traveling westward six days and six nights from the Earth encampment on the distant eastern shore of the continent, feeding himself en route with whatever his gun could bring down.

He sat stiffly upright in the saddle, head staring forward so solidly and so massively that it might seem his neck had calcified. He had spent the whole trip in much the same posture, as the cloven hoofs of the running-beast carried him along, westward, and in a sense backward in time as well. It was twenty years since he last had visited this particular V'Leeg village, or indeed the flat lake country here in the west at all. And he was the first Earthman to venture out of the encampment on the ocean shore since the massacre, three months since, when the sullen V'Leegs had risen suddenly to claim eight hundred Terran lives.

A cold wind whistled down from the ice-flecked jagged hills to the north, pushing up little clouds of the red infertile soil as Barchay rode on. Lorverad was a strange world, an alien world, and Earth-bred Barchay had never grown to love the red soil or the odd angular animals or the iron-gray sky with the white hard unwarm dot of light in it that was this planet's sun. He still remembered Earth, though now it was more self-deceit than memory as he thought of that warm green planet bathed by golden light, so far across the sky and so remote in his own experience.

He was fifty, and looked forty, and felt sixty. He had settled on Lorverad with the first group of Terran settlers, twenty-three years before. He had come with a wife, whom he remembered as he did Earth, in a romanticized vision that could never really have been, and she had borne him a son, and now he was alone, riding into a V'Leeg village far from the sod hut he called home.

The village was at the edge of a thin elongated lake that curved around a bend and vanished somewhere in the prairie beyond. The waters of the lake were dull gray and lusterless, not the bright blue-green of Barchay's memory-enhanced Earth lakes. Sweeping up from the shore were the V'Leeg huts, low and squat, hugging the barren ground. All V'Leeg villages looked more or less alike, just as to Earth eyes all V'Leegs were more or less twins to each other, but Barchay knew that this was the right place. He had been here before, twenty years ago, when his dark hair had been thicker and the sight of his cool blue eyes more keen. Now he was back again, searching through his own past for the one thing that would give him continued life.

He dismounted and walked his beast into the village. It was a sign of humility.

As it happened, the first V'Leeg he encountered was a boy of about eight, who sat crosslegged outside a hut, stirring in the sand with a broken twig. As Barchay approached, the boy rose, glared at him, spat, and faded quickly into the hut.

A fine welcome, Barchay thought.

He waited a moment, and two adult V'Leegs appeared from within the hut. The man was tall for his race, five-eight or so, but still a good four inches shorter than Barchay. He had intense black lidless eyes set square in the middle of his heavy-jawed face, flanked on either side by corrugated protective ridges. His apple-red skin was thick and leathery, almost hinged. He was naked; modesty among V'Leeg men was not a common trait.

The woman was much shorter than he, and unlovely: a beast of the fields more than a woman, her body thickened and stooped by toil, her pendulous breasts more udders than breasts. She wore a blue twist of cloth around her middle.

"We thought we had seen the last of your kind," said the man in the consonant-glutted V'Leeg language. "We killed enough of you, didn't we? We drove you back over the hills to your place in the east. We left hundreds of you for the sky-birds to pick the eyes of."

Barchay didn't flinch. "The war is over," he said quietly in fluent V'Leeg. "It was agreed that man and V'Leeg would fight no more."

"And that you would stay by the sea and leave us alone! Why do you come here?"

Barchay saw rage building up in the V'Leeg, and he knew what strength there was in those thick corded muscles. His hand stole to the blaster in his waist; he did not want to die just yet.

"I came searching for something," he said. "When I find it, I'll return. There won't be any trouble."

The V'Leeg clenched his fists and began to reply; suddenly from within the hut came another member of the family. She was a girl, perhaps fifteen, with long dark hair and a slim body as yet untouched by the rigors of living. Her breasts were high and firm, her hips gently curved and to Barchay's tired eyes she looked almost human. *Human enough*, he thought, comparing her with her shapeless mother.

The V'Leeg man whirled, hissing sounds without words, and angrily ordered her back into the hut.

"I only came to look—" she protested wistfully, in a pleasant high voice, and then, seeing her father's hand raised to her, she stole a glance at Barchay and went back into the hovel.

"You've come to steal women," the V'Leeg said bitterly. "As always, with you Earthmen."

"Believe me, I have no such ideas. Your daughter is safe from me." Barchay's days of cradle-robbing were long since dead. "Tell me: does V'Malku the chief still rule in this village?"

Alien eyes confronted him stonily. "Perhaps. And perhaps not."

"I'd like to know," Barchay said, feeling sweat roll down his body. He wanted to grab the obstinate alien by the throat and throttle the fact out of him, but he held back, knowing that that was the wrong way, the way that had cost eight hundred Terran lives when the V'Leeg finally rose in anger. "It's important to me."

"Do I care?"

Barchay shrugged and picked up his mount's reins. As he started to lead the beast away, the woman spoke for the first time.

"V'Malku lives."

Her husband uttered a muffled snort of rage and suppressed fury and knocked her sprawling with one fierce jolt of his elbow. She made no attempt to rise, but lay staring bitterly at the soil as if that were somehow to blame. A cloud passed over the distant sun, casting a dark shadow over the group and seeming to chill the air.

"Well?" Barchay asked. "Is this true?"

"V'Malku lives," the man confirmed sullenly. "I'll take you to him."

The man led him silently down a winding path that took him from the outskirts of the village to the place where the huts were clustered close together, and past clump after clump of dark-eyed inquisitive V'Leegs. Small children, some of whom probably had never seen an Earthman before, ran out to stare in frank curiosity at him, and then to run away in terror. Here, there, tall idle V'Leeg bucks lounged against posts and stanchions, staring at him obliquely from the corners of their eyes.

Barchay felt hate only for these idlers. These were the ones who had fomented the sudden swift uprising the autumn before. Earthmen and V'Leeg had lived together side by side in remote cordiality for more than twenty years, neither caring too greatly for the other's company, neither having much to do with each other. There had been scattered cases of violence, of Earthmen finding a stray V'Leeg warrior and ringing him like a hare ringed with hounds, or of V'Leegs killing an Earthman to whom they had taken a dislike. But over twenty years these things were to be expected of two alien though biologically similar races struggling for life on the same barren infertile world, one race native and the other imported from the stars.

Until three months ago, when a sudden notion had swept up among the bitter young V'Leeg men, and they had ridden out of their villages carrying keen swords. There had been ten thousand Earthmen on Lorverad, and eight hundred of them had died in that one furious attack, eight hundred who had been living scattered on the plains between the sea and the western lands. The attackers had not penetrated far eastward; they had contented themselves with wiping out the buffer Earthmen in the inlands, and then, in horror at their own bold act, had returned to their homes to clean the blood from their blades.

There had been no punitive action on the part of the Earthmen. They had simply withdrawn within the confines of their original settlement, until the spring came and they could make peace with the V'Leeg again, and hope to establish a lasting harmony. But Barchay could not wait until spring. After the massacre's victims had been buried, he knew he would have to make *now* the journey he had thought of for so long and so often postponed.

Now he moved past these bucks, some of whom had probably killed Earthmen in the season past, following this V'Leeg on the way to the tribe's chief.

He arrived finally at an ornate vaulted building somewhat more impressive than those surrounding it. A V'Leeg woman waited there, looking apprehensively at Barchay.

"He wants to talk to the chief," the V'Leeg told her.

Nervously she beckoned him within. He hitched his animal's reins outside, and followed her through a dark corridor, into a dark anteroom, and on into an even darker sitting chamber beyond.

"He is blind," she explained. "He doesn't like light."

Blind? Barchay thought. He remembered V'Malku tall and sturdy, in the prime of life, and tried to picture him blind. It was difficult at first, until he realized that the chieftain had been growing old even then, and twenty years now separated him from the V'Malku he had known.

He stood blinking in the darkness for a moment until his eyes cleared and he could see. He saw a terribly old, shrunken V'Leeg seated in the far corner, wearing some kind of fur wrap, his jaws sunken and toothless, his eyes open but clearly unseeing. The old one was desiccated from age; his body shook like a dry leaf in the wind.

"Chief, there is an Earthman to see you," the house-keeper said. Barchay looked back and saw his V'Leeg guide, standing behind him, one hand on the pommel of a deadly-looking machete. That showed how greatly they trusted him.

In a quavering voice that Barchay barely was able to recognize as V'Malku's, the old chief said, "An Earthman here? Why? Is there trouble?"

"No trouble," Barchay said loudly. "The trouble is over. I've come alone, and in peace."

There was a sharp instant of silence. Then V'Malku said, "Let me hear that voice again. I think I know it."

"You *do* know it, V'Malku."

"Of course. Barchay. Why have you come back, after so many years?"

It would have been startling enough had V'Malku recognized him by face and form, but to be recalled on his voice alone took Barchay thoroughly aback. Had he been found out by the dark blue birthmark on his hip, which had caused so much attention when he had bathed in the lake on his second or third day in the village twenty years ago, that might have been understandable. But his voice—!

His mind drew back over that scene. It had been the second day, he recalled now; he had ridden into the village alone and dusty, covered with sweat, and V'Malku had invited him to be his guest, since Earthman and V'Leeg were on better terms back then.

They had fed him, and he had slept alone on a hard flaxen matting against the cold ground, and in the morning he had asked where he could bathe.

"In the lake," V'Malku said. "It's the only place."

Barchay's command of the language had not been too good then, but he knew what the chief had said, and that there was little point in raising any objections.

So after he ate he went down to the edge of the dull-gray lake, and stripped and bathed away the sweat and dust of travel, trying to overlook the fact that half the village had congregated at the water's edge to see the Earthman take his bath. V'Malku had been there, and V'Malku's wife and his daughter, and many children and women and a few of the other men.

Barchay had ignored them, and finished his bath, and came from the water naked and dripping, feeling clean for the first time since he had left the settlement and ridden westward on this scouting trip. And a high voice had said, giggling, "What is that on your hip, Barchay?"

He glanced down at the blue blotch the size of a child's hand that spread over his left hip and smiled, and said, "It's a birthmark. I was born with it, and it kept growing with me as I grew." Then he looked to see who the speaker had been.

He saw her: V'Malku's daughter, a slim tall girl of seventeen, full of breast and wide of hip, who was smiling brightly at him. He had seen her before, in the house, wearing a colorless smock as she served a meal to him, but now she wore only a hip-cloth, and he saw with some amazement that she was beautiful. Alien, yes, but it was possible to overlook the leathery red skin and the lidless eyes, and the protective ridges at their sides. These were minor things, trifling differences. And Barchay had traveled alone for nearly a month, and his wife was far away at the seaside colony, tending their infant son.

Somewhat brusquely Barchay had shaken the water from

him and climbed back into his clothes, while the cluster of aliens commented happily and at length on this portion or that of his anatomy, dwelling chiefly on his birthmark. And at length V'Malku the chief had said, "I like his voice best of all. It's the voice of a man."

Barchay had spent the day with them, and when night came he went to sleep on his cold hard mat against the floor, and halfway through the night he rose and moved silently through the dark rooms, hoping his wife and son far away would forgive him for what he was about to do.

He found the girl's room as if he had lived in this house all his life. He entered. She was sleeping lightly, as a cat might, breathing gentle shallow sighs of breath. She awoke to his touch, and smiled at him without saying anything, and drew him down to her side. In the darkness he could not see the lidless eyes or the redness of the skin, and it felt not leathery but soft to the touch, and warm.

In the morning he left the village despite V'Malku's insistence that he stay on with them a while longer. He said his good-byes and left, unable to meet his host's eyes or the eyes of his daughter. He rode eastward, back to the Terran settlement to deliver his report. When he returned he found that his wife had contracted some unknown alien disease and was dying and soon would be dead, and that he would have the task of raising his son alone.

Soon she died, and Barchay grew that much older. Twenty years passed, bringing him in the course of time back to the V'Leeg village again.

And blind old V'Malku had recognized him by the sound of his voice.

He looked across the darkness and across the gulf of years at the blind chief and said, "I'm happy to find you still alive, V'Malku. After all these years."

"The years have been good, Barchay."

"For some of us."

"For some of us," agreed the chief. After a long awkward pause he added, "Though I doubt not for you. Are we alone in here?"

"No. There's a man and a woman with us. The man is making sure I don't 49you."

"I don't want them here. Go away! Away!"

The housekeeper and the man V'Leeg exchanged puzzled glances but remained where they were. Barchay said, "They're still here, V'Malku."

With more than a shred of his old commanding voice, the chief snapped, "I ordered you to get out and leave me alone with this Earthman. Do I have to repeat that order? Go!"

This time they left, edging out reluctantly with many a backward glance. When the cane door closed Barchay said softly, "They're gone, V'Malku. We're alone."

"Good," grunted the chief. "Now: tell me why you came back. There must have been a reason."

"There was." Speaking into the darkness Barchay said, "I came to see your daughter. If she still lives, that is."

"My daughter? I've had many daughters, Earthman. Which daughter is it you mean?"

He's toying with me, Barchay thought. "When I was here, only one daughter lived with you in your house. That's the one I mean. I've forgotten her name, but I'd like to see her again. To talk to her."

"Oh," V'Malku said, and the undertones of that single syllable made Barchay quiver and turn away his face from the sightless man. "You mean Gyla. Yes, that's the one you mean. Isn't it?"

"Yes," Barchay said. "Gyla."

"You came back after twenty years to see her. I like that, Barchay. Yes, I do. Tell me: did you have any trouble when our young men attacked you Earthmen not long ago?"

Barchay set his face stonily. "No. I didn't have any trouble. I was hunting alone in the hills, and didn't find out about it until it was all over. That's always been my fate. When the plague struck the colony and killed my wife, I was away . . . here."

V'Malku coughed. "Fetch that woman who let you in. Tell her I want her."

Barchay stepped outside and saw the housekeeper and the man waiting there for him, the man with machete drawn and a fierce expression on his face, as if he was ready to burst into the chief's chamber at the first hint of any sort of trouble.

"He wants to see you," Barchay said to the woman.

When they returned V'Malku said to her, "Bring me my daughter Gyla. There's someone here to talk to her."

They brought Gyla to the chief's room, and Barchay

looked at her in the darkness as she stood blinking, trying to adjust her eyes to the dimness. He wondered if the years had been as hard on him as they had been on her; he doubted it.

He remembered her as she had been that day down at the lake, her warm young body almost bare, her dark eyes flashing brightly in laughter as she pointed to the birthmark on his hip. She had been seventeen and very alive.

Now she was thirty-seven, and she was an old woman, who could have been the twin of the woman he had seen on the village's outskirts, or perhaps that woman herself. Her breasts had flattened and lost their beauty; her hair was sparse and stringy, her eyes dull, her shoulders slumped and rounded. She waited patiently to know what her father wanted of her, and Barchay saw that all spirit and all life had long since departed from her. He hoped he had not been the one who had done this to her.

He had been thirty then; now he was fifty, and knew he had not changed half as much as she.

The old chief said, "Speak to her, Earthman. She's here. This is the one you seek."

"Do you remember me, Gyla?"

She looked up, frowning dimly. Her features were thick and coarse now; she was ugly and alien, and he wondered how he could ever once have desired her. "Do you remember anything about me?" he asked. "My voice, maybe."

"Your voice—"

"Yes. Think back a long way, Gyla. Twenty years back. To the time of your maidenhood."

Thinking, remembering, required a visible effort on her part, a shifting of the heavy facial planes, a pursing of the wide lips, a drawing-back of the nostrils. She seemed to turn inward on herself and search backward.

"I remember something," she said finally. "But not well. Not at all. I forget."

"My name is Barchay. Does that help you? Do you remember a time when I came here, and bathed in the lake, and slept at your father's house?" He realized he was quivering inwardly. V'Malku was staring unseeingly at both of them.

"Maybe," she said. "Barchay. Yes. Yes, I think I remember something. You stayed with us. Yes. Yes."

Barchay caught his breath. "She remembers so little," he said to V'Malku. "Gyla, do you have children?"

"Yes. Of course."

Barchay moistened his lips. "I—I would like to see your children," he said.

"Gyla, get your children," ordered V'Malku.

It took perhaps fifteen minutes for her to round them up; fifteen minutes while Barchay stood dry-lipped and uncomfortable, trying not to look at the old man, trying not to think of the wrong he had done V'Malku two decades ago. At last, the children arrived.

"These are my children," Gyla said.

There were eleven of them. Three tall full-grown males, gazing belligerently at Barchay as if they wished to kill him right here in front of their mother and grandfather; two nearly-grown girls, one of whom looked astonishingly like her mother once had looked; a half-grown boy, digging his toes shyly into the ground; a girl perhaps a year younger than he, coltish, awkward, with half-formed breasts; two smaller boys, a very young girl, and a toddler of indeterminate sex. All were clad except the two small boys and the youngest girl.

Barchay surveyed them hopelessly, looking, looking.

"These are all your children?" he said in a dry voice, studying their flat alien faces.

"These are all that lived. Two others died."

"Do you see what you came here to see?" V'Malku asked, from his seat in the dark corner.

"No," Barchay said. "I think I came in vain." His stomach was a hollow lump of meat inside him; his shoulders sagged and he felt eighty now, not sixty. He was very tired. He might just as well not have lived at all.

"I guess I'll go back to the settlement," he said drearily. "Thanks for helping me. It's too bad I was wrong."

"You were right," V'Malku said.

"What?"

"Your trip was not wasted."

Barchay looked at the alien children again, and shook his head. "None of them . . . it would be one of the ones that died, then?"

"No. V'Rikesh is the one you seek. The oldest boy."

"Impossible!" Barchay said, looking at the tall boy in the back of the group, seeing his wide nonhuman eyes and thick leathery skin. There was nothing human about him at all. "He can't be," Barchay said.

V'Malku sighed. "V'Rikesh, come forward."

The boy shouldered his way through the knot of his brothers and sisters and stood alone in the center of the room, glaring angrily at Barchay in unvoiced hatred.

"He must be wearing clothes," the chief said.

"He is. A cloth around his waist."

"V'Rikesh, take off your clothes," ordered the old one.

The boy scowled at Barchay. His lean fingers went to the fastening of the loincloth and yanked sharply, and the cloth fell away, dropping to his feet.

Barchay eyed the boy's nakedness for an instant, then turned away, the beginning of a tear forming in the corner of his eye. He had thought he had forgotten how to cry.

"He's the one, isn't he?" V'Malku asked.

"Yes," Barchay said softly. "He's mine."

There was no doubt about it. The boy V'Rikesh bore a mark on his body—a blue birthmark on his left hip, the size of a child's hand.

Later, when Barchay saddled up and started to ride, slowly and alone, out of the V'Leeg village, a group of young V'Leegs clustered up in front of him, and brusquely ordered him off his mount.

He had expected it. Violence had been brewing ever since he had arrived here. He got down, keeping one hand on his blaster, and snapped, "What is it you want? I'm leaving in peace. I have a safe-conduct from the chief."

Someone laughed. "That blind fool? His safe-conduct's a warrant of death!"

They crowded around him. "Keep back!" he shouted. "I'm armed!"

He drew his blaster, knowing they would swarm over him before he had a chance to use it, and backed away, listening to their accusing chant: *seducer*. They knew who he was. They would punish him for it. Well, it didn't matter now, he thought wearily.

Someone's nails raked his chest and he slapped the hand away, and got his blaster up and fired, destroying an alien head. They surged around him; he kicked out, knocking another to the ground, and fired again. The blue flare of the blaster cut a swath through the crowd.

"Let him go!" someone shouted, far on the outer edge of the mob. "He has a safe-conduct! He's my fath—"

Then they roared in over him, and Barchay knew the journey had come to its end, that the alien world Lorverad would claim his life as it had twenty years ago claimed the life of his wife and as it had last autumn claimed the life of what he feared had been his only son, the boy who had died in the massacre. But Barchay had ridden to the V'Leeg village for a purpose, and that purpose had been fulfilled; he knew now, as the hands groped for his throat, that he had had *two* sons, not one, and when he died he would not just be winking out like a candle flame, leaving nothing of himself behind. A V'Leeg blade slicked his flesh, and he smiled painfully and waited for the end. He *had* left something of himself behind—even if it was only a blue birthmark on the hip of an alien boy.

The Fangs of the Trees

From the plantation house atop the gray, needle-sharp spire of Dolan's Hill, Zen Holbrook could see everything that mattered: the groves of juice-trees in the broad valley, the quick rushing stream where his niece Naomi liked to bathe, the wide, sluggish lake beyond. He could also see the zone of suspected infection in Sector C at the north end of the valley, where—or was it just his imagination?—the lustrous blue leaves of the juice-trees already seemed flecked with the orange of the rust disease.

If his world started to end, that was where the end would start.

He stood by the clear curved window of the info center at the top of the house. It was early morning; two pale moons still hung in a dawn-streaked sky, but the sun was coming up out of the hill country. Naomi was already up and out, cavorting in the stream. Before Holbrook left the house each morning, he ran a check on the whole plantation. Scanners and sensors offered him remote pickups from every key point out there. Hunching forward, Holbrook ran thick-fingered hands over the command nodes and made the relay screens flanking the window light up. He owned forty thousand acres of juice-trees—a fortune in juice, though his own equity was small and the notes he had given were immense. His kingdom. His empire. He scanned Sector C, his favorite. Yes. The screen showed long rows of trees, fifty feet high, shifting their ropy limbs restlessly. This was the endangered zone, the threatened sector. Holbrook peered intently at the leaves of the trees. Going rusty yet? The lab reports would come in a little later. He studied the trees, saw the gleam of their eyes, the sheen of their fangs. Some good trees in that sector. Alert, keen, good producers.

His pet trees. He liked to play a little game with himself, pretending the trees had personalities, names, identities. It didn't take much pretending.

Holbrook turned on the audio. "Morning, Caesar," he said. "Alcibiades. Hector. Good morning, Plato."

The trees knew their names. In response to his greeting

their limbs swayed as though a gale were sweeping through the grove. Holbrook saw the fruit, almost ripe, long and swollen and heavy with the hallucinogenic juice. The eyes of the trees—glittering scaly plates embedded in crisscrossing rows on their trunks—flickered and turned, searching for him. "I'm not in the grove, Plato," Holbrook said. "I'm still in the plantation house. I'll be down soon. It's a gorgeous morning, isn't it?"

Out of the musty darkness at ground level came the long, raw pink snout of a juice-stealer, jutting uncertainly from a heap of cast-off leaves. In distaste Holbrook watched the audacious little rodent cross the floor of the grove in four quick bounds and leap onto Caesar's massive trunk, clambering cleverly upward between the big tree's eyes. Caesar's limbs fluttered angrily, but he could not locate the little pest. The juice-stealer vanished in the leaves and reappeared thirty feet higher, moving now in the level where Caesar carried his fruit. The beast's snout twitched. The juice-stealer reared back on its four hind limbs and got ready to suck eight dollars' worth of dreams from a nearly ripe fruit.

From Alcibiades' crown emerged the thin, sinuous serpentine form of a grasping tendril. Whiplash-fast it crossed the interval between Alcibiades and Caesar and snapped into place around the juice-stealer. The animal had time only to whimper in the first realization that it had been caught before the tendril choked the life from it. On a high arc the tendril returned to Alcibiades' crown; the gaping mouth of the tree came clearly into view as the leaves parted; the fangs parted; the tendril uncoiled; and the body of the juice-stealer dropped into the tree's maw. Alcibiades gave a wriggle of pleasure: a mincing, camping quiver of his leaves, arch and coy, self-congratulations for his quick reflexes, which had brought him so tasty a morsel. He was a clever tree, and a handsome one, and very pleased with himself. Forgivable vanity, Holbrook thought. You're a good tree, Alcibiades. All the trees in Sector C are good trees. What if you have the rust, Alcibiades? What becomes of your shining leaves and sleek limbs if I have to burn you out of the grove?

"Nice going," he said. "I like to see you wide awake like that."

Alcibiades went on wriggling. Socrates, four trees diagonally down the row, pulled his limbs tightly together in what

Holbrook knew was a gesture of displeasure, a grumpy harrumph. Not all the trees cared for Alcibiades' vanity, his preening, his quickness.

Suddenly Holbrook could not bear to watch Sector C any longer. He jammed down on the command nodes and switched to Sector K, the new grove, down at the southern end of the valley. The trees here had no names and would not get any. Holbrook had decided long ago that it was a silly affectation to regard the trees as though they were friends or pets. They were income-producing property. It was a mistake to get this involved with them—as he realized more clearly now that some of his oldest friends were threatened by the rust that was sweeping from world to world to blight the juice-tree plantations.

With more detachment he scanned Sector K.

Think of them as trees, he told himself. Not animals. Not people. *Trees.* Long tap roots, going sixty feet down into the chalky soil, pulling up nutrients. They cannot move from place to place. They photosynthesize. They blossom and are pollenated and produce bulging phallic fruit loaded with weird alkaloids that cast interesting shadows in the minds of men. Trees. Trees. Trees.

But they have eyes and teeth and mouths. They have prehensile limbs. They can think. They can react. They have souls. When pushed to it, they can cry out. They are adapted for preying on small animals. They digest meat. Some of them prefer lamb to beef. Some are thoughtful and solemn; some volatile and jumpy; some placid, almost bovine. Though each tree is bisexual, some are plainly male by personality, some female, some ambivalent. Souls. Personalities.

Trees.

The nameless trees of Sector K tempted him to commit the sin of involvement. That fat one could be Buddha, and there's Abe Lincoln, and you, you're William the Conqueror, and—

Trees.

He had made the effort and succeeded. Coolly he surveyed the grove, making sure there had been no damage during the night from prowling beasts, checking on the ripening fruit, reading the info that came from the sap sensors, the monitors that watched sugar levels, fermentation stages, manganese intake, all the intricately balanced life processes on

which the output of the plantation depended. Holbrook
handled practically everything himself. He had a staff of three
human overseers and three dozen robots; the rest was done by
telemetry, and usually all went smoothly. Usually. Properly
guarded, coddled, and nourished, the trees produced their
fruit three seasons a year; Holbrook marketed the goods at the
pickup station near the coastal spaceport, where the juice was
processed and shipped to Earth. Holbrook had no part in that;
he was simply a fruit producer. He had been here ten years
and had no plans for doing anything else. It was a quiet life, a
lonely life, but it was the life he had chosen.

He swung the scanners from sector to sector, until he had
assured himself that all was well throughout the plantation. On
his final swing he cut to the stream and caught Naomi just as
she was coming out from her swim. She scrambled to a rocky
ledge overhanging the swirling water and shook out her long,
straight, silken golden hair. Her back was to the scanner. With
pleasure Holbrook watched the rippling of her slender muscles. Her spine was clearly outlined by shadow; sunlight
danced across the narrowness of her waist, the sudden flare of
her hips, the taut mounds of her buttocks. She was fifteen; she
was spending a month of her summer vacation with Uncle
Zen; she was having the time of her life among the juice-trees.
Her father was Holbrook's older brother. Holbrook had seen
Naomi only twice before, once when she was a baby, once
when she was about six. He had been a little uneasy about
having her come here, since he knew nothing about children
and in any case had no great hunger for company. But he had
not refused his brother's request. Nor was she a child. She
turned, now, and his screens gave him apple-round breasts
and flat belly and deep-socketed navel and strong, sleek
thighs. Fifteen. No child. A woman. She was unself-conscious
about her nudity, swimming like this every morning; she knew
there were scanners. Holbrook was not easy about watching
her. Should I look? Not really proper. The sight of her roiled
him suspiciously. What the hell: I'm her uncle. A muscle
twitched in his cheek. He told himself that the only emotions
he felt when he saw her this way were pleasure and pride that
his brother had created something so lovely. Only admiration;
that was all he let himself feel. She was tanned, honey-
colored, with islands of pink and gold. She seemed to give off a
radiance more brilliant than that of the early sun. Holbrook

clenched the command node. I've lived too long alone. My niece. My niece. Just a kid. Fifteen. Lovely. He closed his eyes, opened them slit-wide, chewed his lip. Come on, Naomi, cover yourself up!

When she put her shorts and halter on, it was like a solar eclipse. Holbrook cut off the info center and went down through the plantation house, grabbing a couple of breakfast capsules on his way. A gleaming little bug rolled from the garage; he jumped into it and rode out to give her her morning hello.

She was still near the stream, playing with a kitten-sized many-legged furry thing that was twined around an angular little shrub. "Look at this, Zen!" she called to him. "Is it a cat or a caterpillar?"

"Get away from it!" he yelled with such vehemence that she jumped back in shock. His needler was already out, and his finger on the firing stud. The small animal, unconcerned, continued to twist legs about branches.

Close against him, Naomi gripped his arm and said huskily, "Don't kill it, Zen. Is it dangerous?"

"I don't know."

"Please don't kill it."

"Rule of thumb on this planet," he said. "Anything with a backbone and more than a dozen legs is probably deadly."

"*Probably!*" Mockingly.

"We still don't know every animal here. That's one I've never seen before, Naomi."

"It's too cute to be deadly. Won't you put the needler away?"

He holstered it and went close to the beast. No claws, small teeth, weak body. Bad signs: a critter like that had no visible means of support, so the odds were good that it hid a venomous sting in its furry little tail. Most of the various many-leggers here did. Holbrook snatched up a yard-long twig and tentatively poked it toward the animal's mid-section.

Fast response. A hiss and a snarl and the rear end coming around, *wham!* and a wicked-looking stinger slamming into the bark of the twig. When the tail pulled back, a few drops of reddish fluid trickled down the twig. Holbrook stepped away; the animal eyed him warily and seemed to be begging him to come within striking range.

"Cuddly," Holbrook said. "Cute. Naomi, don't you want to live to be sweet sixteen?"

She was standing there looking pale, shaken, almost stunned by the ferocity of the little beast's attack. "It seemed so gentle," she said. "Almost tame."

He turned the needler aperture to fine and gave the animal a quick burn through the head. It dropped from the shrub and curled up and did not move again. Naomi stood with her head averted. Holbrook let his arm slide about her shoulders.

"I'm sorry, honey," he said. "I didn't want to kill your little friend. But another minute and he'd have killed you. Count the legs when you play with wildlife here. I told you that. Count the legs."

She nodded. It would be a useful lesson for her in not trusting to appearances. Cuddly is as cuddly does. Holbrook scuffed at the coppery-green turf and thought for a moment about what it was like to be fifteen and awakening to the dirty truths of the universe. Very gently he said, "Let's go visit Plato, eh?"

Naomi brightened at once. The other side of being fifteen: you have resilience.

They parked the bug just outside the Sector C grove and went in on foot. The trees didn't like motorized vehicles moving among them; they were connected only a few inches below the loam of the grove floor by a carpet of mazy filaments that had some neurological function for them, and though the weight of a human didn't register on them, a bug riding down a grove would wrench a chorus of screams from the trees. Naomi went barefoot. Holbrook, beside her, wore knee boots. He felt impossibly big and lumpy when he was with her; he was hulking enough as it was, but her litheness made it worse by contrast.

She played his game with the trees. He had introduced her to all of them, and now she skipped along, giving her morning greeting to Alcibiades and Hector, to Seneca, to Henry the Eighth and Thomas Jefferson and King Tut. Naomi knew all the trees as well as he did, perhaps better; and they knew her. As she moved among them they rippled and twittered and groomed themselves, every one of them holding itself tall and arraying its limbs and branches in comely fashion; even dour old Socrates, lopsided and stumpy, seemed to be trying to show off. Naomi went to the big gray storage box in midgrove where the robots left chunks of meat each night, and hauled out some snacks for her pets. Cubes of red, raw flesh; she filled her arms with the bloody gobbets and danced gaily around the grove, tossing them to her favorites. Nymph in thy orisons, Holbrook thought. She flung the meat high, hard, vigorously. As it sailed through the air tendrils whipped out from one tree or another to seize it in midflight and stuff it down the waiting gullet. The trees did not *need* meat, but they liked it, and it was common lore among the growers that well-fed trees produced the most juice. Holbrook gave his trees meat three times a week, except for Sector D, which rated a daily ration.

"Don't skip anyone," Holbrook called to her.

"You know I won't."

No piece fell uncaught to the floor of the grove. Sometimes two trees at once went for the same chunk and a little battle resulted. The trees weren't necessarily friendly to one another; there was bad blood between Caesar and Henry the Eighth, and Cato clearly despised both Socrates and Alcibiades, though for different reasons. Now and then Holbrook or his staff found lopped-off limbs lying on the ground in the morning. Usually, though, even trees of conflicting personalities managed to tolerate one another. They had to, condemned as they were to eternal proximity. Holbrook had once tried to separate two Sector F trees that were carrying on a vicious feud; but it was impossible to dig up a full-grown tree without killing it and deranging the nervous systems of its thirty closest neighbors, as he had learned the hard way.

While Naomi fed the trees and talked to them and caressed their scaly flanks, petting them the way one might pet a tame rhino, Holbrook quietly unfolded a telescoping ladder and gave the leaves a new checkout for rust. There wasn't much point to it, really. Rust didn't become visible on the leaves until it had already penetrated the root structure of the tree, and the orange spots he thought he saw were probably figments of a jumpy imagination. He'd have the lab report in an hour or two, and that would tell him all he'd need to know, one way or the other. Still, he was unable to keep from looking. He cut a bundle of leaves from one of Plato's lower branches, apologizing, and turning them over in his hands, rubbing their glossy undersurfaces. What's this here, these minute colonies of reddish particles? His mind tried to reject the possibility of rust. A plague striding across the worlds, striking him so intimately, wiping him out? He had built this plantation on leverage: a little of his money, a lot from the bank. Leverage worked the other way too. Let rust strike the plantation and kill enough trees to sink his equity below the level considered decent for collateral, and the bank would take over. They might hire him to stay on as manager. He had heard of such things happening.

Plato rustled uneasily.

"What is it, old fellow?" Holbrook murmured. "You've got it, don't you? There's something funny swimming in your guts, eh? I know. I know. I feel it in my guts too. We have to be philosophers, now. Both of us." He tossed the leaf sample to the ground and moved the ladder up the row to Alcibiades. "Now, my beauty, now. Let me look. I won't cut any leaves off you." He could picture the proud tree snorting, stamping in irritation. "A little bit speckled under there, no? You have it too. Right?" The tree's outer branches clamped tight, as though Alcibiades were huddling into himself in anguish. Holbrook rolled onward, down the row. The rust spots were far more pronounced than the day before. No imagination, then. Sector C had it. He did not need to wait for the lab report. He felt oddly calm at this confirmation, even though it announced his own ruin.

"Zen?"

He looked down. Naomi stood at the foot of the ladder, holding a nearly ripened fruit in her hand. There was something grotesque about that; the fruits were botany's joke, explicitly phallic, so that a tree in ripeness with a hundred or more jutting fruits looked like some archetype of the ultimate male, and all visitors found it hugely amusing. But the sight of a fifteen-year-old girl's hand so thoroughly filled with such an object was obscene, not funny. Naomi had never remarked on the shape of the fruits, nor did she show any embarrassment now. At first he had ascribed it to innocence or shyness, but as he came to know her better, he began to suspect that she was deliberately pretending to ignore that wildly comic biological coincidence to spare *his* feelings. Since he clearly thought of her as a child, she was tactfully behaving in a childlike way, he supposed; and the fascinating complexity of his interpretation of her attitudes had kept him occupied for days.

"Where did you find that?" he asked.

"Right here, Alcibiades dropped it."

The dirty-minded joker, Holbrook thought. He said, "What of it?"

"It's ripe. It's time to harvest the grove now, isn't it?" She squeezed the fruit; Holbrook felt his face flaring. "Take a look," she said, and tossed it up to him.

She was right: harvest time was about to begin in Sector C, five days early. He took no joy of it; it was a sign of the disease that he now knew infested these trees.

"What's wrong?" she asked.

He jumped down beside her and held out the bundle of leaves he had cut from Plato. "You see these spots? It's rust. A blight that strikes juice-trees."

"No!"

"It's been going through one system after another for the past fifty years. And now it's here despite all quarantines."

"What happens to the trees?"

"A metabolic speedup," Holbrook said. "That's why the fruit is starting to drop. They accelerate their cycles until they're going through a year in a couple of weeks. They become sterile. They defoliate. Six months after the onset, they're dead." Holbrook's shoulders sagged. "I've suspected it for two or three days. Now I know."

She looked interested but not really concerned. "What causes it, Zen?"

"Ultimately, a virus. Which passes through so many hosts that I can't tell you the sequence. It's an interchange-vector deal, where the virus occupies plants and gets into their seeds, is eaten by rodents, gets into their blood, gets picked up by stinging insects, passed along to a mammal, then—oh, hell, what do the details matter? It took eighty years just to trace the whole sequence. You can't quarantine your world against everything, either. The rust is bound to slip in, piggybacking on some kind of living thing. And here it is."

"I guess you'll be spraying the plantation, then."

"No."

"To kill the rust? What's the treatment?"

"There isn't any," Holbrook said.

"But—"

"Look, I've got to go back to the plantation house. You can keep yourself busy without me, can't you?"

"Sure." She pointed to the meat. "I haven't even finished feeding them yet. And they're especially hungry this morning."

He started to tell her that there was no point in feeding them now, that all the trees in this sector would be dead by nightfall. But an instinct warned him that it would be too complicated to start explaining that to her now. He flashed a quick sunless smile and trotted to the bug. When he looked back at her, she was hurling a huge slab of meat toward Henry the Eighth, who seized it expertly and stuffed it in his mouth.

The lab report came sliding from the wall output around two hours later, and it confirmed what Holbrook already knew: rust. At least half the planet had heard the news by then, and Holbrook had had a dozen visitors so far. On a planet with a human population of slightly under four hundred, that was plenty. The district governor, Fred Leitfried, showed up first, and so did the local agricultural commissioner, who also happened to be Fred Leitfried. A two-man delegation from the Juice-Growers' Guild arrived next. Then came Mortensen, the rubbery-faced little man who ran the processing plant, and Heemskerck of the export line, and somebody from the bank, along with a representative of the insurance company. A couple of neighboring growers dropped over a little later; they offered sympathetic smiles and comradely graspings of the shoulder, but not very far beneath their commiserations lay potential hostility. They wouldn't come right out and say it, but Holbrook didn't need to be a telepath to know what they were thinking: *Get rid of those rusty trees before they infect the whole damned planet.*

In their position he'd think the same. Even though the rust vectors had reached this world, the thing wasn't all that contagious. It could be confined; neighboring plantations could be saved, and even the unharmed groves of his own place—if he moved swiftly enough. If the man next door had rust on his trees, Holbrook would be as itchy as these fellows were about getting it taken care of quickly.

Fred Leitfried, who was tall and bland-faced and blue-eyed and depressingly somber even on a cheerful occasion, looked about ready to burst into tears now. He said, "Zen, I've ordered a planetwide rust alert. The biologicals will be out within thirty minutes to break the carrier chain. We'll begin on your property and work in a widening radius until we've isolated this entire quadrant. After that we'll trust to luck."

"Which vector are you going after?" Mortensen asked, tugging tensely at his lower lip.

"Hoppers," said Leitfried. "They're biggest and easiest to knock off, and we know that they're potential rust carriers. If the virus hasn't been transmitted to them yet, we can interrupt the sequence there and maybe we'll get out of this intact."

Holbrook said hollowly, "You know that you're talking about exterminating maybe a million animals."

"I know, Zen."

"You think you can do it?"

"We have to do it. Besides," Leitfried added, "the contingency plans were drawn a long time ago, and everything's ready to go. We'll have a fine mist of hopperlethals covering half the continent before nightfall."

"A damned shame," muttered the man from the bank. "They're such peaceful animals."

"But now they're threats," said one of the growers. "They've got to go."

Holbrook scowled. He liked hoppers himself; they were big rabbity things, almost the size of bears, that grazed on worthless scrub and did no harm to humans. But they had been identified as susceptible to infection by the rust virus, and it had been shown on other worlds that by knocking out one basic stage in the transmission sequence the spread of rust could be halted, since the viruses would die if they were unable to find an adequate host of the next stage in their life cycle. Naomi is fond of hoppers, he thought. She'll think we're bastards for wiping them out. But we have our trees to save. And if we were real bastards, we'd have wiped them out before the rust ever got here, just to make things a little safer for ourselves.

Leitfried turned to him. "You know what you have to do now, Zen?"

"Yes."

"Do you want help?"

"I'd rather do it myself."

"We can get you ten men."

"It's just one sector, isn't it?" he asked. "I can do it. I *ought* to do it. They're my trees."

"How soon will you start?" asked Borden, the grower whose plantation adjoined Holbrook's on the east. There was fifty miles of brush country between Holbrook's land and Borden's, but it wasn't hard to see why the man would be impatient about getting the protective measures under way.

Holbrook said, "Within an hour, I guess. I've got to calculate a little, first. Fred, suppose you come upstairs with me and help me check the infected area on the screens?"

"Right."

The insurance man stepped forward. "Before you go, Mr. Holbrook—"

"Eh?"

"I just want you to know, we're in complete approval. We'll back you all the way."

Damn nice of you, Holbrook thought sourly. What was insurance for, if not to back you all the way? But he managed an amiable grin and a quick murmur of thanks.

The man from the bank said nothing. Holbrook was grateful for that. There was time later to talk about refurbishing the collateral, renegotiation of notes, things like that. First it was necessary to see how much of the plantation would be left after Holbrook had taken the required protective measures.

In the info center, he and Leitfried got all the screens going at once. Holbrook indicated Sector C and tapped out a grove simulation on the computer. He fed in the data from the lab report. "There are the infected trees," he said, using a light-pen to circle them on the output screen. "Maybe fifty of them altogether." He drew a larger circle. "This is the zone of possible incubation. Another eighty or a hundred trees. What do you say, Fred?"

The district governor took the light-pen from Holbrook and touched the stylus tip to the screen. He drew a wider circle that reached almost to the periphery of the sector.

"These are the ones to go, Zen."

"That's four hundred trees."

"How many do you have altogether?"

Holbrook shrugged. "Maybe seven, eight thousand."

"You want to lose them all?"

"Okay," Holbrook said. "You want a protective moat around the infection zone, then. A sterile area."

"Yes."

"What's the use? If the virus can come down out of the sky, why bother to—"

"Don't talk that way," Leitfried said. His face grew longer and longer, the embodiment of all the sadness and frustration and despair in the universe. He looked the way Holbrook felt. But his tone was incisive as he said, "Zen, you've got just two choices here. You can get out into the groves and start burning, or you can give up and let the rust grab everything. If you do the first, you've got a chance to save most of what you own. If you give up, we'll burn you out anyway, for our own protection. And we won't stop just with four hundred trees."

"I'm going," Holbrook said. "Don't worry about me."

"I wasn't worried. Not really."

Leitfried slid behind the command nodes to monitor the entire plantation while Holbrook gave his orders to the robots and requisitioned the equipment he would need. Within ten minutes he was organized and ready to go.

"There's a girl in the infected sector," Leitfried said. "That niece of yours, huh?"

"Naomi, yes."

"Beautiful. What is she, eighteen, nineteen?"

"Fifteen."

"Quite a figure on her, Zen."

"What's she doing now?" Holbrook asked. "Still feeding the trees?"

"No, she's sprawled out underneath one of them. I think she's talking to them. Telling them a story, maybe? Should I cut in the audio?"

"Don't bother. She likes to play games with the trees. You know, give them names and imagine that they have personalities. Kid stuff."

"Sure," said Leitfried. Their eyes met briefly and evasively. Holbrook looked down. The trees *did* have personalities, and every man in the juice business knew it, and probably there weren't many growers who didn't have a much closer relationship to their groves than they'd ever admit to another man. Kid stuff. It was something you didn't talk about.

Poor Naomi, he thought.

He left Leitfried in the info center and went out the back way. The robots had set everything up just as he had programmed: the spray truck with the fusion gun mounted in place of the chemical tank. Two or three of the gleaming little mechanicals hovered around, waiting to be asked to hop aboard, but he shook them off and slipped behind the steering panel. He activated the data output and the small dashboard screen lit up; from the info center above, Leitfried greeted him and threw him the simulated pattern of the infection zone, with the three concentric circles glowing to indicate the trees with rust, those that might be incubating, and the safety-margin belt that Leitfried had insisted on his creating around the entire sector.

The truck rolled off toward the groves.

It was midday, now, of what seemed to be the longest day he had ever known. The sun, bigger and a little more deeply tinged with orange than the sun under which he had been born, lolled lazily overhead, not quite ready to begin its tumble into the distant plains. The day was hot, but as soon as he entered the groves, where the tight canopy of the adjoining trees shielded the ground from the worst of the sun's radiation, he felt a welcome coolness seeping into the cab of the truck. His lips were dry. There was an ugly throbbing just back of his left eyeball. He guided the truck manually, taking it on the access track around Sectors A, D, and G. The trees, seeing him, flapped their limbs a little. They were eager to have him get out and walk among them, slap their trunks, tell them what good fellows they were. He had no time for that now.

In fifteen minutes he was at the north end of his property, at the edge of Sector C. He parked the spray truck on the approach lip overlooking the grove; from here he could reach any tree in the area with the fusion gun. Not quite yet, though.

He walked into the doomed grove.

Naomi was nowhere in sight. He would have to find her before he could begin firing. And even before that, he had some farewells to make. Holbrook trotted down the main avenue of the sector. How cool it was here, even at noon! How sweet the loamy air smelled! The floor of the grove was littered with fruit; dozens had come down in the past couple of hours. He picked one up. Ripe: he split it with an expert snap of his wrist and touched the pulpy interior to his lips. The juice, rich and sweet, trickled into his mouth. He tasted just enough of it to know that the product was first-class. His intake was far from a hallucinogenic dose, but it would give him a mild euphoria, sufficient to see him through the ugliness ahead.

He looked up at the trees. They were tightly drawn in, suspicious, uneasy.

"We have troubles, fellows," Holbrook said. "You, Hector, you know it. There's a sickness here. You can feel it inside you. There's no way to save you. All I can hope to do is save the other trees, the ones that don't have the rust yet. Okay? Do you understand? Plato? Caesar? I've got to do this. It'll cost you only a few weeks of life, but it may save thousands of other trees."

An angry rustling in the branches. Alcibiades had pulled his limbs away disdainfully. Hector, straight and true, was ready to take his medicine. Socrates, lumpy and malformed, seemed prepared also. Hemlock or fire, what did it matter? Crito, I owe a cock to Asclepius. Caesar seemed enraged; Plato was actually cringing. They understood, all of them. He moved among them, patting them, comforting them. He had begun his plantation with this grove. He had expected these trees to outlive him.

He said, "I won't make a long speech. All I can say is good-bye. You've been good fellows, you've lived useful lives, and now your time is up, and I'm sorry as hell about it. That's all. I wish this wasn't necessary." He cast his glance up and down the grove. "End of speech. So long."

Turning away, he walked slowly back to the spray truck. He punched for contact with the info center and said to Leitfried, "Do you know where the girl is?"

"One sector over from you to the south. She's feeding the trees." He flashed the picture on Holbrook's screen.

"Give me an audio line, will you?"

Through his speakers Holbrook said, "Naomi? It's me, Zen."

She looked around, halting just as she was about to toss a chunk of meat. "Wait a second," she said. "Catherine the Great is hungry, and she won't let me forget it." The meat soared upward, was snared, disappeared into the mouth of a tree. "Okay," Naomi said. "What is it, now?"

"I think you'd better go back to the plantation house."

"I've still got lots of trees to feed."

"Do it this afternoon."

"Zen, what's going on?"

"I've got some work to do, and I'd rather not have you in the groves when I'm doing it."

"Where are you now?"

"C."

"Maybe I can help you, Zen. I'm only in the next sector down the line. I'll come right over."

"No. Go back to the house." The words came out as a cold order. He had never spoken to her like that before. She looked shaken and startled; but she got obediently into her bug and drove off. Holbrook followed her on his screen until she was out of sight.

"Where is she now?" he asked Leitfried.

"She's coming back. I can see her on the access track."

"Okay," Holbrook said. "Keep her busy until this is over. I'm going to get started."

He swung the fusion gun around, aiming its stubby barrel into the heart of the grove. In the squat core of the gun a tiny pinch of sun-stuff was hanging suspended in a magnetic pinch, available infinitely for an energy tap more than ample for his power needs today. The gun had no sight, for it was not intended as a weapon; he thought he could manage things, though. He was shooting at big targets. Sighting by eye, he picked out Socrates at the edge of the grove, fiddled with the gun-mounting for a couple of moments of deliberate hesitation, considered the best way of doing this thing that awaited him, and put his hand to the firing control. The tree's neural nexus was in its crown, back of the mouth. One quick blast there—

Yes.

An arc of white flame hissed through the air. Socrates' misshapen crown was bathed for an instant in brilliance. A quick death, a clean death, better than rotting with rust. Now Holbrook drew his line of fire down from the top of the dead tree, along the trunk. The wood was sturdy stuff; he fired again and again, and limbs and branches and leaves shriveled and dropped away, while the trunk itself remained intact, and great oily gouts of smoke rose above the grove. Against the brightness of the fusion beam Holbrook saw the darkness of the naked trunk outlined, and it surprised him how straight the old philosopher's trunk had been, under the branches. Now the trunk was nothing more than a pillar of ash; and now it collapsed and was gone.

From the other trees of the grove came a terrible low moaning.

They knew that death was among them; and they felt the pain of Socrates' absence through the network of root-nerves in the ground. They were crying out in fear and anguish and rage.

Doggedly Holbrook turned the fusion gun on Hector.

Hector was a big tree, impassive, stoic, neither a complainer nor a preener. Holbrook wanted to give him the good death he deserved, but his aim went awry; the first bolt struck at least eight feet below the tree's brain center, and the echoing shriek that went up from the surrounding trees revealed what Hector must be feeling. Holbrook saw the limbs waving frantically, the mouth opening and closing in a horrifying rictus of torment. The second bolt put an end to Hector's agony. Almost calmly, now, Holbrook finished the job of extirpating that noble tree.

He was nearly done before he became aware that a bug had pulled up beside his truck and Naomi had erupted from it, flushed, wide-eyed, close to hysteria. "Stop!" she cried. "Stop it, Uncle Zen! Don't burn them!"

As she leaped into the cab of the spraying truck she caught his wrists with surprising strength and pulled herself up against him. She was gasping, panicky, her breasts heaving, her nostrils wide.

"I told you to go to the plantation house," he snapped.

"I did. But then I saw the flames."

"Will you get out of here?"

"Why are you burning the trees?"

"Because they're infected with rust," he said. "They've got to be burned out before it spreads to the others."

"That's *murder*."

"Naomi, look, will you get back to—"

"You killed Socrates!" she muttered, looking into the grove. "And—and Caesar? No. Hector. Hector's gone too. You burned them right out!"

"They aren't people. They're trees. Sick trees that are going to die soon anyway. I want to save the others."

"But why kill them? There's got to be some kind of drug you can use, Zen. Some kind of spray. There's a drug to cure everything now."

"Not this."

"There has to be."

"Only the fire," Holbrook said. Sweat rolled coldly down his chest, and he felt a quiver in a thigh muscle. It was hard enough doing this without her around. He said as calmly as he could manage it, "Naomi, this is something that must be done, and fast. There's no choice about it. I love these trees as much as you do, but I've got to burn them out. It's like the little leggy thing with the sting in its tail: I couldn't afford to be sentimental about it, simply because it looked cute. It was a menace. And right now Plato and Caesar and the others are menaces to everything I own. They're plague-bearers. Go back to the house and lock yourself up somewhere until it's over."

"I won't let you kill them!" Tearfully. Defiantly.

Exasperated, he grabbed her shoulders, shook her two or three times, pushed her from the truck cab. She tumbled backward but landed lithely. Jumping down beside her, Holbrook said, "Dammit, don't make me hit you, Naomi. This is none of your business. I've got to burn out those trees, and if you don't stop interfering—"

"There's got to be some other way. You let those other men panic you, didn't you, Zen? They're afraid the infection will spread, so they told you to burn the trees fast, and you aren't even stopping to think, to get other opinions, you're just coming in here with your gun and killing intelligent, sensitive, lovable—"

"Trees," he said. "This is incredible, Naomi. For the last time—"

Her reply was to leap up on the truck and press herself to the snout of the fusion gun, breasts close against the metal. "If you fire, you'll have to shoot through me!"

Nothing he could say would make her come down. She was lost in some romantic fantasy, Joan of Arc of the juice-trees, defending the grove against his barbaric assault. Once more he tried to reason with her; once more she denied the need to extirpate the trees. He explained with all the force he could summon the total impossibility of saving these trees; she replied with the power of sheer irrationality that there must be some way. He cursed. He called her a stupid hysterical adolescent. He begged. He wheedled. He commanded. She clung to the gun.

"I can't waste any more time," he said finally. "This has to

be done in a matter of hours or the whole plantation will go."
Drawing his needler from its holster, he dislodged the safety
and gestured at her with the weapon. "Get down from there,"
he said icily.

She laughed. "You expect me to think you'd shoot me?"

Of course, she was right. He stood there sputtering
impotently, red-faced, baffled. The lunacy was spreading: his
threat had been completely empty, as she had seen at once.
Holbrook vaulted up beside her on the truck, seized her, tried
to pull her down.

She was strong, and his perch was precarious. He succeeded in pulling her away from the gun but had surprisingly
little luck in getting her off the truck itself. He didn't want to
hurt her, and in his solicitousness he found himself getting
second best in the struggle. A kind of hysterical strength was
at her command; she was all elbows, knees, clawing fingers.
He got a grip on her at one point, found with horror that he
was clutching her breasts, and let go in embarrassment and
confusion. She hopped away from him. He came after her,
seized her again, and this time was able to push her to the
edge of the truck. She leaped off, landed easily, turned, ran
into the grove.

So she was still outthinking him. He followed her in; it
took him a moment to discover where she was. He found her
hugging Caesar's base and staring in shock at the charred
places where Socrates and Hector had been.

"Go on," she said. "Burn up the whole grove! But you'll
burn me with it!"

Holbrook lunged at her. She stepped to one side and
began to dart past him, across to Alcibiades. He pivoted and
tried to grab her, lost his balance, and went sprawling,
clutching at the air for purchase. He started to fall.

Something wiry and tough and long slammed around his
shoulders.

"*Zen!*" Naomi yelled. "The tree—Alcibiades—"

He was off the ground now. Alcibiades had snared him
with a grasping tendril and was lifting him toward his crown.
The tree was struggling with the burden; but then a second
tendril gripped him too and Alcibiades had an easier time.
Holbrook thrashed about a dozen feet off the ground.

Cases of trees attacking humans were rare. It had happened perhaps five times altogether, in the generations that

men had been cultivating juice-trees here. In each instance
the victim had been doing something that the grove regarded
as hostile—such as removing a diseased tree.

A man was a big mouthful for a juice-tree. But not beyond
its appetite.

Naomi screamed and Alcibiades continued to lift. Holbrook could hear the clashing of fangs above; the tree's mouth
was getting ready to receive him. Alcibiades the vain, Alcibiades the mercurial, Alcibiades the unpredictable—well
named, indeed. But was it treachery to act in self-defense?
Alcibiades had a strong will to survive. He had seen the fates
of Hector and Socrates. Holbrook looked up at the ever closer
fangs. So this is how it happens, he thought. Eaten by one of
my own trees. My friends. My pets. Serves me right for
sentimentalizing them. They're carnivores. Tigers with roots.

Alcibiades screamed.

In the same instant one of the tendrils wrapped about
Holbrook's body lost its grip. He dropped about twenty feet in
a single dizzying plunge before the remaining tendril steadied
itself, leaving him dangling a few yards above the floor of the
grove. When he could breathe again, Holbrook looked down
and saw what had happened. Naomi had picked up the
needler that he had dropped when he had been seized by the
tree, and had burned away one tendril. She was taking aim
again. There was another scream from Alcibiades; Holbrook
was aware of a great commotion in the branches above him; he
tumbled the rest of the way to the ground and landed hard in a
pile of mulched leaves. After a moment he rolled over and sat
up. Nothing broken. Naomi stood above him, arms dangling,
the needler still in her hand.

"Are you all right?" she asked soberly.

"Shaken up a little, is all." He started to get up. "I owe
you a lot," he said. "Another minute and I'd have been in
Alcibiades' mouth."

"I almost let him eat you, Zen. He was just defending
himself. But I couldn't. So I shot off the tendrils."

"Yes. Yes. I owe you a lot." He stood up and took a couple
of faltering steps toward her. "Here," he said. "You better give
me that needler before you burn a hole in your foot." He
stretched out his hand.

"Wait a second," she said, glacially calm. She stepped
back as he neared her.

"What?"

"A deal, Zen. I rescued you, right? I didn't have to. Now you leave those trees alone. At least check up on whether there's a spray, okay? A deal."

"But—"

"You owe me a lot, you said. So pay me. What I want from you is a promise, Zen. If I hadn't cut you down, you'd be dead now. Let the trees live too."

He wondered if she would use the needler on him.

He was silent a long moment, weighing his options. Then said, "All right, Naomi. You saved me, and I can't refuse you what you want. I won't touch the trees. I'll find out if something can be sprayed on them to kill the rust."

"You mean that, Zen?"

"I promise. By all that's holy. You will give me that needler, now?"

"Here," she cried, tears running down her reddened face. "Here! Take it! Oh God, Zen, how awful all this is!"

He took the weapon from her and holstered it. She seemed to go limp, all resolve spent, once she surrendered it. She stumbled into his arms, and he held her tight, feeling her tremble against him. He trembled too, pulling her close to him, aware of the ripe cones of her young breasts jutting into his chest. A powerful wave of what he recognized bluntly as desire surged through him. Filthy, he thought. He winced as this morning's images danced in his brain, Naomi nude and radiant from her swim, apple-round breasts, firm thighs. My niece. Fifteen. God help me. Comforting her, he ran his hands across her shoulders, down to the small of her back. Her clothes were light; her body was all too present within them.

He threw her roughly to the ground.

She landed in a heap, rolled over, put her hand to her mouth as he fell upon her. Her screams rose, shrill and piercing, as his body pressed down on her. Her terrified eyes plainly told that she feared he would rape her, but he had other perfidies in mind. Quickly he flung her on her face, catching her right hand and jerking her arm up behind her back. Then he lifted her to a sitting position.

"Stand up," he said. He gave her arm a twist by way of persuasion. She stood up.

"Now walk. Out of the grove, back to the truck. I'll break your arm if I have to."

"What are you doing?" she asked in a barely audible whisper.

"Back to the truck," he said. He levered her arm up another notch. She hissed in pain. But she walked.

At the truck he maintained his grip on her and reached in to call Leitfried at his info center.

"What was that all about, Zen? We tracked most of it, and—"

"It's too complicated to explain. The girl's very attached to the trees, is all. Send some robots out here to get her right away, okay?"

"You *promised*," Naomi said.

The robots arrived quickly. Steely-fingered, efficient, they kept Naomi pinioned as they hustled her into a bug and took her to the plantation house. When she was gone, Holbrook sat down for a moment beside the spray truck, to rest and clean his mind. Then he climbed into the truck cab again.

He aimed the fusion gun first at Alcibiades.

It took a little over three hours. When he was finished, Sector C was a field of ashes, and a broad belt of emptiness stretched from the outer limit of the devastation to the nearest grove of healthy trees. He wouldn't know for a while whether he had succeeded in saving the plantation. But he had done his best.

As he rode back to the plantation house, his mind was less on the work of execution he had just done than on the feel of Naomi's body against his own, and on the things he had thought in that moment when he hurled her to the ground. A woman's body, yes. But a child. A child still, in love with her pets. Unable yet to see how in the real world one weighs the need against the bond, and does one's best. What had she learned in Sector C today? That the universe often offers only brutal choices? Or merely that the uncle she worshipped was capable of treachery and murder?

They had given her sedation, but she was awake in her room, and when he came in she drew the covers up to conceal her pajamas. Her eyes were cold and sullen.

"You promised," she said bitterly. "And then you tricked me."

"I had to save the other trees. You'll understand, Naomi."

"I understand that you lied to me, Zen."

"I'm sorry. Forgive me?"

"You can go to hell," she said, and those adult words coming from her not-yet-adult face were chilling.

He could not stay longer with her. He went out, upstairs, to Fred Leitfried in the info center. "It's all over," he said softly.

"You did it like a man, Zen."

"Yeah. Yeah."

In the screen he scanned the sector of ashes. He felt the warmth of Naomi against him. He saw her sullen eyes. Night would come, the moons would do their dance across the sky, the constellations to which he had never grown accustomed would blaze forth. He would talk to her again, maybe. Try to make her understand. And then he would send her away, until she was finished becoming a woman.

"Starting to rain," Leitfried said. "That'll help the ripening along, eh?"

"Most likely."

"You feel like a killer, Zen?"

"What do you think?"

"I know. I know."

Holbrook began to shut off the scanners. He had done all he meant to do today. He said quietly, "Fred, they were trees. Only trees. Trees, Fred, *trees*."

En Route to Earth

Before the flight, the chief stewardess stopped off in the women's lounge to have a few words with Milissa, who was making her first extrasolar hop as stewardess of the warpliner *King Magnus*.

Milissa was in uniform when the chief stewardess appeared. The low-cut, clinging plastic trimmed her figure nicely. Gazing in the mirror, she studied her clear blue skin for blemishes. There were none.

"All set?" the chief stewardess asked.

Milissa nodded, a little too eagerly. "Ready, I guess. Blastoff time's in half an hour, isn't it?"

"Yes. Not nervous, are you?"

"Nervous? Who, me?" Somewhat anxiously she added, "Have you seen the passenger list?"

"Yes."

"How's the breakdown? Are there—many strange aliens?" Milissa said. "I mean—"

"A few," the chief stewardess said cheerfully. "You'd better report to the ship now, dear."

The *King Magnus* was standing on its tail, glimmering proudly in the hot Vegan sun, as Milissa appeared on the arching approach-ramp. Two blueskinned Vegan spacemen lounged against the wall of the Administration Center, chatting with a pilot from Earth. All three whistled as she went by. Milissa ignored them, and proceeded to the ship.

She took the lift-plate up to the nose of the ship, smiled politely at the jetman who waited at the entrance, and went in. "I'm the new stewardess," she said.

"Captain Brilon's waiting for you in the fore cabin," the jetman said.

Milissa checked in as per instructions, adjusted her cap at just the proper angle (with Captain Brilon's too-eager assistance) and picked up the passenger list. As she had feared, there were creatures of all sorts aboard. Vega served as a funnel for travelers from all over the galaxy who were heading to Earth.

She looked down the list.

Grigori—James, Josef, Mike. Returning to Earth after extended stay on Alpheraz IV. Seats 21-22.

Brothers vacationing together, she thought. How nice. But three of them in two seats? Peculiar!

Xfooz, Nartoosh. Home world, Sirius VII, First visit to Earth. Seat 23.

Dellamon, Thogral. Home world, Procyon V. Business trip to Earth. Seat 25.

And on down the list. At the bottom, the chief stewardess had penciled a little note:

> Be courteous, cheerful, and polite. Don't let the aliens frighten you—and above all, don't look at them as if they're worms or toads, even if some of them are worms or toads. Worms or not, they're still customers.

> Watch out for any Terrans aboard. They don't have any color-prejudices against pretty Vegans with blue skin. Relax and have a good time. The return trip ought to be a snap.

I hope so, Milissa thought fervently. She took a seat in the corner of the cabin and started counting seconds till blastoff.

The stasis-generators lifted the *King Magnus* off Vega II as lightly as a feather blown by the wind, and Captain Brilon indicated that Milissa should introduce herself to the passengers. She stepped through the bulkhead doors that led to the passenger section, paused a moment to readjust her cap and tug at her uniform, and pushed open the irising sphincter that segregated crew from passengers.

The passenger hold stretched out for perhaps a hundred feet before her. It was lined with huge view windows on both sides, and the passengers—fifty of them, according to the list—turned as one to look at her when she entered.

She suppressed a little gasp. All shapes, all forms—and what was *that* halfway down the row—?

"Hello," she said, forcing it to come out cheery and bright. "My name is Milissa Kleirn, and I'll be your stewardess for this trip. This is the *King Magnus*, fourth ship of the Vegan Line, and we'll be making the trip from Vega II to Sol III in three days, seven hours, and some minutes, under the command of Captain Alib Brilon. The drive-generators have already hurled us from the surface of Vega, and we've entered warp and are well on our way to Earth. I'll be on hand to answer any of your questions—except the very technical ones; you'll have to refer those through me to the captain. And if you want magazines or anything, please press the button at the side of your seat. Thank you very much."

There, she thought. *That wasn't so bad.*

And then the indicator-panel started to flash. She picked a button out at random and pressed it. A voice said, "This is Mike Grigori, Seat 22. How about coming down here to talk to me a minute?"

She debated. The chief stewardess had warned her about rambunctious Earthmen—but yet, this was her first request as stewardess, and besides there was something agreeably pleasant about Mike Grigori's voice. She started down the aisle and reached Seat 22, still smiling.

Mike Grigori was sitting with his two brothers. As she approached, he extended an arm and beckoned to her wolfishly with a crooked forefinger. He winked.

"You're Mr. Grigori?"

"I'm Mike. Like you to meet my brothers, James and Josef. Fellows, this is Miss Kleirn. The stewardess."

"How do you do," Milissa said. The smile started to fade. With an effort, she restored it.

There was a certain family resemblance about the Grigori brothers. And she saw now why they only needed two seats.

They had only one body between them.

"This is Jim, over here," Mike was saying, indicating the head at farthest left. "He's something of a scholar. Aren't you, Jim?"

The head named Jim turned gravely to examine Milissa, doing so with the aid of a magnifying glass it held to its eye monocle-wise. Jim affected an uptilted mustache; Mike, looking much younger and more ebullient, was cleanshaven and wore his hair close-cropped.

"And this is Josef," Mike said, nodding toward the center head. "Make sure you spell that J-O-S-E-F, like so. He's fussy about that. Used to be plain Joe, but now nothing's fancy enough for him."

Josef was an aristocratic-looking type whose hair was

slicked back flat and whose nose inclined slightly upward; he maintained a fixed pose, staring forward as if in intent meditation, and confined his greetings to a muttered *hmph*.

"He's the intellectual sort," Mike confided. "Keeps us up half the night when he wants to read. But we manage. We have to put up with him because he's got the central nervous system, and half the arms."

Milissa noticed that the brothers had four arms—one at each shoulder, presumably for the use of Mike and Jim, and two more below them, whose scornful foldedness indicated they were controlled entirely by the haughty Josef.

"You're—from Earth?" Milissa asked, a little stunned.

"Mutants," said Jim.

"Genetic manipulation," explained Mike.

"Abnormalities. Excrescences on my shoulders," muttered Josef.

"He thinks he got here first," Mike said. "That Jim and I were tacked on to *his* body later."

It looked about to degenerate into a family feud. Milissa wondered what a fight among the brothers would look like. But one of her duties was to keep peace in the passenger lounge. "Is there anything specific you'd like to ask me, Mr. Grigori?" she said to Mike. "If not, I'm afraid the other passengers—"

"Specific? Sure. I'd like to make a date with you when we hit Earth. Never dated a Vegan girl—but that blue skin is really lovely."

"Vetoed," Josef said without turning his head.

Mike whirled. "*Vetoed!* Now look here, brother—you don't have absolute and final say on every—"

"The girl will only refuse," Josef said. "Don't waste our time on dalliance. I'm trying to think, and your chatter disturbs me."

Again tension grew. Quickly Milissa said, "Your brother's right, Mr. Grigori. Vegan Line personnel are not allowed to date passengers. It's an absolute rule."

Dismay registered on two of the three heads. Josef merely looked more smug. Another crisis seemed brewing among the mutant brothers when suddenly a creature several seats behind them tossed a magazine it had been reading into the aisle with a great outcry of rage.

"Excuse me," Milissa said. "I'll have to see what's upsetting him."

Grateful for the interruption, she moved up the aisle. The alien who had thrown the magazine was a small pinkish being, whose eyes, dangling on six-inch eyestalks, now quivered in what she supposed was rage.

Milissa stooped, one hand keeping her neckline from dipping (there was no telling *what* sexual habits these aliens had) and picked up the magazine. *Science Fiction Stories*, she saw, and there was a painting of an alien much like the one before her printed on the glossy cover.

"I think you dropped this, Mr.—Mr.—"

"Dellamon," the alien replied, in a cold, testy, snappish voice. "Thogral Dellamon, of Procyon V. And I *didn't* drop the magazine. I threw it down violently, as you very well saw."

She smiled apologetically. "Of course, Mr. Dellamon. Did you see something you disagreed with in the magazine?"

"Disagreed with? I saw something that was a positive *insult!*" He snatched the magazine from her, riffled through it, found a page and handed it back.

The magazine was open to page 113. The title of the story was "Slaves of the Pink Beings," bylined J. Eckman Forester. She skimmed the first few lines; it was typical science fiction, full of monsters and bloodshed, and just as dull as every other science fiction story she had tried to read.

"I hope I won't make you angry when I say I don't see anything worth getting angry over in this, Mr. Dellamon."

"That story," he said, "tells of the conquests and sadistic pleasures of a race of evil pink beings—and of their destruction by *Earthmen*. Look at that cover painting! It's an exact image of—well, you see? This is vicious propaganda aimed at my people! And none of it's true! None!"

The cover indeed bore a resemblance to the indignant little alien. But the date under the heading caught Milissa's eye. *June 2114.* Three hundred years old. "Where did you get this magazine?" she asked.

"Bought it. Wanted to read an Earth magazine, as long as I have to go there, so I had a man on my planet get one for me."

"Oh. That explains it, then. Look at the date, Mr. Dellamon! That story's a complete fantasy! It was written more than a hundred years before Earth and Procyon came into contact!"

"But—fantasy—I don't understand—"

The sputtering little alien threatened to become apoplectic. Milissa wished prodigiously that she had never transferred out of local service. These aliens could be so *touchy*, at times!

"Excuse me, please," said a furry purple creature seated across the aisle. "That magazine you have there—mind if I look at it?"

"Here," the angry alien said. He tossed it over.

The purple being examined it, smiled delightedly, said, "Why, it's an issue I need! Will you take five hundred credits for it?"

"Five hundred—" The eyestalks stopped quivering, and drooped in an expression of probable delight. "Make it five-fifty and the book is yours!"

Crisis after crisis, Milissa thought gloomily. They were two days out from Vega, with better than a day yet to go before Earth hove into sight. And if the voyage lasted much longer, she'd go out of her mind.

The three Grigori brothers had finally erupted into violence late the first day; they sprang from their seat and went rolling up the aisle, cursing fluently at each other in a dozen languages. Josef had the upper hand for a while, rearing back and pounding his brothers' heads together, but he was outnumbered and was in dire straits by the time Milissa found two crewmen to put a stop to the brawl.

Then there was the wormlike being from Albireo III who suddenly discovered she was going to sporulate, and did— casting a swarm of her encapsulated progeny all over the lounge. She was very apologetic, and assisted Milissa in finding the spores, but it caused quite a mess.

The Greklan brothers from Deneb Kaitos I caused the next crisis. Greklans, Milissa discovered, had peculiar sexual practices: they spent most of their existence as neuters, but at regular periods about a decade apart suddenly developed sex, at which time the procedure was to mate, and fast. One of the brothers abruptly became a male, the other female, to their great surprise, consternation, and delight. The squeals of a puritanical being from Fomalhaut V attracted Milissa's attention; she managed to hustle the Greklans off to a washroom just in time. They returned, an hour later, to announce they had reverted to neuter status and would name their offspring Milissa, but that scarcely helped her nerves.

Never again, Milissa told herself, surveying the array of life-forms in the lounge. *Back to local service for me. As soon as the return trip is over—*

Eleven hours to Earth. She hoped she could stay sane that long.

Frozen asparagus turned up on the menu the final night. It was a grave tactical mistake; three vegetable-creatures of Mirach IX accused the Vegan Line of fomenting cannibalism, and stalked out of the dining room. Milissa followed them and found them seriously ill of nausea and threatening to sue. She hadn't noticed until then how very much like asparagus stalks the Mirachians looked; no one in the galley had either, apparently.

A family of reptiloids from Algenib became embroiled with a lizardlike inhabitant of Altair II. It took what was left of Milissa's tattered diplomacy to separate the squabblers and persuade them all to retake their seats.

She counted hours. She counted minutes. And, finally, she counted seconds.

"Earth ahead!" came the announcement from Control Cabin.

She went before the passengers to make the traditional final speech. Calmly, almost numbly, she thanked them for their cooperation, hoped they had enjoyed the flight, wished them the best of everything on Earth.

Mike-Jim-Josef Grigori paused to say good-bye on their way out. They looked slightly bruised and battered. For the seventh time, Milissa explained to Mike how regulations prohibited her from dating, and finally they said good-bye. They walked down the ramp snarling and cursing at each other.

She watched them all go—the Greklans, the angry little man from Procyon, the asparaguslike Mirachians. She felt a perverse fondness for them all.

"That's the last," she said, turning to Captain Brilon. "And thank goodness."

"Tired, huh?"

"All you had to do was watch the instruments," she said. "*I* was playing nursemaid to umpteen different life-forms. But the return trip will be a rest. Just Earthmen and Vegans, I hope. No strange nonhumanoid forms. I can't wait!"

* * *

She returned to the ship after the brief leave allotted her, and found herself almost cheerful at the prospect of the return trip. The passengers filed aboard—pleasant, normal Vegans and Earthmen, who whistled at her predictably but who showed no strange and unforeseeable mating habits or other manifestations.

It was going to be a quiet trip, she told herself. A snap.

But then three dark furry shapes entered the lounge and huddled self-consciously in the back. Milissa bit her lip and glanced down at the passenger list.

Three spider-men from Arcturus VII. These creatures do not have names. They are extremely sensitive and will require close personal attention.

Milissa shuddered. Even without a mirror handy, she knew her face was paling to a weak ultramarine. She could get used to Greklans and sporulating worms from Albireo, she thought. She could calm petulant Procyonites and fend off wolfish three-headed Earthmen. But there was nothing in her contract about travelers from Arcturus.

She stared at the hairy, eight-legged creatures. Twenty-four arachnid eyes glinted beadily back at her.

It was asking too much. No woman should be expected to take solicitous care of *spiders*.

Sighing, she realized it was going to be a long, long voyage home.

How It Was When the Past Went Away

The day that an antisocial fiend dumped an amnesifacient drug into the city water supply was one of the finest that San Francisco had had in a long while. The damp cloud that had been hovering over everything for three weeks finally drifted across the bay into Berkeley that Wednesday, and the sun emerged, bright and warm, to give the old town its warmest day so far in 2003. The temperature climbed into the high twenties, and even those oldsters who hadn't managed to learn to convert to the centigrade thermometer knew it was hot. Airconditioners hummed from the Golden Gate to the Embarcadero. Pacific Gas & Electric recorded its highest one-hour load in history between two and three in the afternoon. The parks were crowded. People drank a lot of water, some a good deal more than others. Toward nightfall, the thirstiest ones were already beginning to forget things. By the next morning, everybody in the city was in trouble, with a few exceptions. It had really been an ideal day for committing a monstrous crime.

On the day before the past went away, Paul Mueller had been thinking seriously about leaving the state and claiming refuge in one of the debtor sanctuaries—Reno, maybe, or Caracas. It wasn't altogether his fault, but he was close to a million in the red, and his creditors were getting unruly. It had reached the point where they were sending their robot bill collectors around to harass him in person, just about every three hours.

"Mr. Mueller? I am requested to notify you that the sum of $8,005.97 is overdue in your account with Modern Age Recreators, Inc. We have applied to your financial representative and have discovered your state of insolvency, and therefore, unless a payment of $395.61 is made by the eleventh of this month, we may find it necessary to begin confiscation procedures against your person. Thus I advise you—"

"—the amount of $11,554.97, payable on the ninth of

August, 2002, has not yet been received by Luna Tours, Ltd. Under the credit laws of 1995 we have applied for injunctive relief against you and anticipate receiving a decree of personal service due, if no payment is received by—"

"—interest on the unpaid balance is accruing, as specified in your contract, at a rate of 4 percent per month—"

"—balloon payment now coming due, requiring the immediate payment of—"

Mueller was growing accustomed to the routine. The robots couldn't call him—Pacific Tel & Tel had cut him out of their data net months ago—and so they came around, polite blank-faced machines stenciled with corporate emblems, and in soft purring voices told him precisely how deep in the mire he was at the moment, how fast the penalty charges were piling up, and what they planned to do to him unless he settled his debts instantly. If he tried to duck them, they'd simply track him down in the streets like indefatigable process servers, and announce his shame to the whole city. So he didn't duck them. But fairly soon their threats would begin to materialize.

They could do awful things to him. The decree of personal service, for example, would turn him into a slave; he'd become an employee of his creditor, at a court-stipulated salary, but every cent he earned would be applied against his debt, while the creditor provided him with minimal food, shelter, and clothing. He might find himself compelled to do menial jobs that a robot would spit at, for two or three years, just to clear one debt. Personal confiscation procedures were even worse; under that deal he might well end up as the actual servant of one of the executives of a creditor company, shining shoes and folding shirts. They might also get an open-ended garnishment on him, under which he and his descendants, if any, would pay a stated percentage of their annual income down through the ages until the debt, and the compounding interest thereon, was finally satisfied. There were other techniques for dealing with delinquents, too.

He had no recourse to bankruptcy. The states and the federal government had tossed out the bankruptcy laws in 1995, after the so-called credit epidemic of the 1980s when for a while it was actually fashionable to go irretrievably into debt and throw yourself on the mercy of the courts. The haven of easy bankruptcy was no more; if you became insolvent, your creditors had you in their grip. The only way out was to jump to a debtor sanctuary, a place where local laws barred any extradition for a credit offense. There were about a dozen such sanctuaries, and you could live well there, provided you had some special skill that you could sell at a high price. You needed to make a good living, because in a debtor sanctuary everything was on a strictly cash basis—cash in advance, at that, even for a haircut. Mueller had a skill he thought would see him through: he was an artist, a maker of sonic sculptures, and his work was always in good demand. All he needed was a few thousand dollars to purchase the basic tools of his trade—his last set of sculpting equipment had been repossessed a few weeks ago—and he could set up a studio in one of the sanctuaries, beyond the reach of the robot hounds. He imagined he could still find a friend who would lend him a few thousand dollars. In the name of art, so to speak. In a good cause.

If he stayed within the sanctuary area for ten consecutive years, he would be absolved of his debts and could come forth a free man. There was only one catch, not a small one. Once a man had taken the sanctuary route, he was forever barred from all credit channels when he returned to the outside world. He couldn't even get a post office credit card, let alone a bank loan. Mueller wasn't sure he could live that way, paying cash for everything all the rest of his life. It would be terribly cumbersome and dreary. Worse: it would be barbaric.

He made a note on his memo pad: *Call Freddy Munson in morning and borrow three bigs. Buy ticket to Caracas. Buy sculpting stuff.*

The die was cast—unless he changed his mind in the morning.

He peered moodily out at the row of glistening white-washed just-post-Earthquake houses descending the steeply inclined street that ran down Telegraph Hill toward Fisherman's Wharf. They sparkled in the unfamiliar sunlight. A beautiful day, Mueller thought. A beautiful day to drown yourself in the bay. Damn. Damn. Damn. He was going to be forty years old soon. He had come into the world on the same bleak day that President John Kennedy had left it. Born in an evil hour, doomed to a dark fate. Mueller scowled. He went to the tap and got a glass of water. It was the only thing he could afford to drink, just now. He asked himself how he ever managed to get into such a mess. Nearly a million in debt!

He lay down dismally to take a nap.

When he woke, toward midnight, he felt better than he had felt for a long time. Some great cloud seemed to have lifted from him, even as it had lifted from the city that day. Mueller was actually in a cheerful mood. He couldn't imagine why.

In an elegant townhouse on Marina Boulevard, the Amazing Montini was rehearsing his act. The Amazing Montini was a professional mnemonist: a small dapper man of sixty, who never forgot a thing. Deeply tanned, his dark hair slicked back at a sharp angle, his small black eyes glistening with confidence, his thin lips fastidiously pursed. He drew a book from a shelf and let it drop open at random. It was an old one-volume edition of Shakespeare, a familiar prop in his nightclub act. He skimmed the page, nodded, looked briefly at another, then another and smiled his inward smile. Life was kind to the Amazing Montini. He earned a comfortable $30,000 a week on tour, having converted a freakish gift into a profitable enterprise. Tomorrow night he'd open for a week at Vegas; then to Manila, Tokyo, Bangkok, Cairo, on around the globe. In twelve weeks he'd earn his year's intake; then he'd relax once more.

It was all so easy. He knew so many good tricks. Let them scream out a twenty-digit number; he'd scream it right back. Let them bombard him with long strings of nonsense syllables; he'd repeat the gibberish flawlessly. Let them draw intricate mathematical formulas on the computer screen; he'd reproduce them down to the last exponent. His memory was perfect, both for visuals and auditories, and for the other registers as well.

The Shakespeare thing, which was one of the simplest routines he had, always awed the impressionable. It seemed so fantastic to most people that a man could memorize the complete works, page by page. He liked to use it as an opener.

He handed the book to Nadia, his assistant. Also his mistress; Montini liked to keep his circle of intimates close. She was twenty years old, taller than he was, with wide frost-gleamed eyes and a torrent of glowing, artificially radiant azure hair: up to the minute in every fashion. She wore a glass bodice, a nice container for the things contained. She was not very bright, but she did the things Montini expected her to do, and did them quite well. She would be replaced, he estimated, in about eighteen more months. He grew bored quickly with his women. His memory was too good.

"Let's start," he said.

She opened the book. "Page 537, left-hand column."

Instantly the page floated before Montini's eyes. "*Henry VI, Part Two*," he said. "*King Henry*: Say, man, were these thy words? *Horner*: An't shall please your majesty, I never said nor thought any such matter: God is my witness, I am falsely accused by the villain. *Peter*: By these ten bones, my lords, he did speak them to me in the garret one night, as we were scouring my Lord of York's armour. *York*: Base dunghill villain, and—"

"Page 778, right-hand column," Nadia said.

"*Romeo and Juliet*. Mercutio is speaking . . . 'an eye would spy out such a quarrel? Thy head is as full of quarrels as an egg is full of meat, and yet thy head hath been beaten as addle as an egg for quarreling. Thou hast quarreled with a man for coughing in the street, because he hath wakened thy dog that hath lain asleep in the sun. Didst thou not—'"

"Page 307, starting fourteen lines down on the right side."

Montini smiled. He liked the passage. A screen would show it to his audience at the performance.

"*Twelfth Night*," he said. "The Duke speaks: 'Too old, by heaven. Let still the woman take an elder than herself, so wears she to him, so sways she level in her husband's heart: For, boy, however we do praise ourselves, our fancies are more giddy and unfirm—'"

"Page 495, left-hand column."

"Wait a minute," Montini said. He poured himself a tall glass of water and drank it in three quick gulps. "This work always makes me thirsty."

Taylor Braskett, Lt. Comdr., Ret., U.S. Space Service, strode with springy stride into his Oak Street home, just outside Golden Gate Park. At seventy-one, Commander Braskett still managed to move in a jaunty way, and he was ready to step back into uniform at once if his country needed him. He believed his country did need him, more than ever, now that socialism was running like wildfire through half the nations of Europe. Guard the home front, at least. Protect what's left of traditional American liberty. What we ought to have, Commander Braskett believed, is a network of C-bombs in orbit, ready to rain hellish death on the enemies of democracy. No matter what the treaty says, we must be prepared to defend ourselves.

Commander Braskett's theories were not widely accepted. People respected him for having been one of the first Americans to land on Mars, of course, but he knew that they quietly regarded him as a crank, a crackpot, an antiquated minuteman still fretting about the redcoats. He had enough of a sense of humor to realize that he did cut an absurd figure to these young people. But he was sincere in his determination to help keep America free—to protect the youngsters from the lash of totalitarianism, whether they laughed at him or not. All this glorious sunny day he had been walking through the park, trying to talk to the young ones, attempting to explain his position. He was courteous, attentive, eager to find someone who would ask him questions. The trouble was that no one listened. And the young ones—stripped to the waist in the sunshine, girls as well as boys, taking drugs out in the open, using the foulest obscenities in casual speech—at times, Commander Braskett almost came to think that the battle for America had already been lost. Yet he never gave up all hope.

He had been in the park for hours. Now, at home, he walked past the trophy room, into the kitchen, opened the refrigerator, drew out a bottle of water. Commander Braskett had three bottles of mountain spring water delivered to his home every two days; it was a habit he had begun fifty years ago, when they had first started talking about putting fluorides in the water. He was not unaware of the little smiles they gave him when he admitted that he drank only bottled spring water, but he didn't mind; he had outlived many of the smilers already, and attributed his perfect health to his refusal to touch the polluted, contaminated water that most other people drank. First chlorine, then fluorides. Probably they were putting in some other things by now, Commander Braskett thought.

He drank deeply.

You have no way of telling what sort of dangerous chemicals they might be putting in the municipal water system these days, he told himself. Am I a crank? Then I'm a crank. But a sane man drinks only water he can trust.

* * *

Fetally curled, knees pressed almost to chin, trembling, sweating, Nate Haldersen closed his eyes and tried to ease himself of the pain of existence. Another day. A sweet, sunny day. Happy people playing in the park. Fathers and children. He bit his lip, hard, just short of laceration intensity. He was an expert at punishing himself.

Sensors mounted in his bed in the Psychotrauma Ward of Fletcher Memorial Hospital scanned him continuously, sending a constant flow of reports to Dr. Bryce and his team of shrinks. Nate Haldersen knew he was a man without secrets. His hormone count, enzyme ratios, respiration, circulation, even the taste of bile in his mouth—it all became instantaneously known to hospital personnel. When the sensors discovered him slipping below the depression line, ultrasonic snouts came nosing up from the recesses of the mattress, proximity nozzles that sought him out in the bed, found the proper veins, squirted him full of dynajuice to cheer him up. Modern science was wonderful. It could do everything for Haldersen except give him back his family.

The door slid open. Dr. Bryce came in. The head shrink looked his part: tall, solemn yet charming, gray at the temples, clearly a wielder of power and an initiate of mysteries. He sat down beside Haldersen's bed. As usual, he made a big point of not looking at the row of computer outputs next to the bed that gave the latest details of Haldersen's condition.

"Nate?" he said. "How goes?"

"It goes," Haldersen muttered.

"Feel like talking a while?"

"Not specially. Get me a drink of water?"

"Sure," the shrink said. He fetched it and said, "It's a gorgeous day. How about a walk in the park?"

"I haven't left this room in two and a half years, doctor. You know that."

"Always a time to break loose. There's nothing physically wrong with you, you know."

"I just don't feel like seeing people," Haldersen said. He handed back the empty glass. "More?"

"Want something stronger to drink?"

"Water's fine." Haldersen closed his eyes. Unwanted images danced behind the lids: the rocket liner blowing open over the pole, the passengers spilling out like autumn seeds erupting from a pod, Emily tumbling down, down, down, falling eighty thousand feet, her golden hair swept by the thin cold wind, her short skirt flapping at her hips, her long lovely legs clawing at the sky for a place to stand. And the children falling beside her, angels dropping from heaven, down, down, down, toward the white soothing fleece of the polar ice. They sleep in peace, Haldersen thought, and I missed the plane, and I alone remain. And Job spake, and said, Let the day perish wherein I was born, and the night in which it was said, There is a man child conceived.

"It was eleven years ago," Dr. Bryce told him. "Won't you let go of it?"

"Stupid talk coming from a shrink. Why won't it let go of *me*?"

"You don't want it to. You're too fond of playing your role."

"Today is talking-tough day, eh? Get me some more water."

"Get up and get it yourself," said the shrink.

Haldersen smiled bitterly. He left the bed, crossing the room a little unsteadily, and filled his glass. He had had all sorts of therapy—sympathy therapy, antagonism therapy, drugs, shock, orthodox freuding, the works. They did nothing for him. He was left with the image of an opening pod, and falling figures against the iron-blue sky. The Lord gave, and the Lord hath taken away; blessed be the name of the Lord. My soul is weary of my life. He put the glass to his lips. Eleven years. I missed the plane. I sinned with Marie, and Emily died, and John, and Beth. What did it feel like to fall so far? Was it like flying? Was there ecstasy in it? Haldersen filled the glass again.

"Thirsty today, eh?"

"Yes," Haldersen said.

"Sure you don't want to take a little walk?"

"You know I don't." Haldersen shivered. He turned and caught the psychiatrist by the forearm. "When does it end, Tim? How long do I have to carry this thing around?"

"Until you're willing to put it down."

"How can I make a conscious effort to forget something? Tim, Tim, isn't there some drug I can take, something to wash away a memory that's killing me?"

"Nothing effective."

"You're lying," Haldersen murmured. "I've read about the amnesifacients. The enzymes that eat memory-RNA. The experiments with di-isopropyl fluorophosphate. Puromycin. The—"

Dr. Bryce said, "We have no control over their operations. We can't simply go after a single block of traumatic memories while leaving the rest of your mind unharmed. We'd have to bash about at random, hoping we got the trouble spot, but never knowing what else we were blotting out. You'd wake up without your trauma, but maybe without remembering anything else that happened to you between, say, the age of fourteen and forty. Maybe in fifty years we'll know enough to be able to direct the dosage at a specific—"

"I can't wait fifty years."

"I'm sorry, Nate."

"Give me the drug anyway. I'll take my chances on what I lose."

"We'll talk about that some other time, all right? The drugs are experimental. There'd be months of red tape before I could get authorization to try them on a human subject. You have to realize—"

Haldersen turned him off. He saw only with his inner eye, saw the tumbling bodies, reliving his bereavement for the billionth time, slipping easily back into his self-assumed role of Job. *I am a brother to dragons, and a companion to owls. My skin is black upon me, and my bones are burned with heat. He hath destroyed me on every side, and I am gone: and mine hope hath he removed like a tree.*

The shrink continued to speak. Haldersen continued not to listen. He poured himself one more glass of water with a shaky hand.

It was close to midnight on Wednesday before Pierre Gerard, his wife, their two sons and their daughter had a chance to have dinner. They were the proprietors, chefs, and total staff of the Petit Pois restaurant on Sansome Street, and business had been extraordinary, exhaustingly good all evening. Usually they were able to eat about half past five, before the dinner rush began, but today people had begun coming in early—made more expansive by the good weather, no doubt—and there hadn't been a free moment for anybody since the cocktail hour. The Gerards were accustomed to brisk trade, for theirs was perhaps the most popular family-run bistro in the city, with a passionately devoted clientele. Still, a night like this was too much!

They dined modestly on the evening's miscalculations: an overdone rack of lamb, some faintly corky Château Beychevelle '97, a fallen soufflé, and such. They were thrifty people. Their one extravagance was the Evian water that they imported from France. Pierre Gerard had not set foot in his native Lyons for thirty years, but he preserved many of the customs of the motherland, including the traditional attitude toward water. A Frenchman does not drink much water; but what he does drink comes always from the bottle, never from the tap. To do otherwise is to risk a diseased liver. One must guard one's liver.

That night Freddy Munson picked up Helene at her flat on Geary and drove across the bridge to Sausalito for dinner, as usual, at Ondine's. Ondine's was one of only four restaurants, all of them famous old ones, at which Munson ate in fixed rotation. He was a man of firm habits. He awakened religiously at six each morning, and was at his desk in the brokerage house by seven, plugging himself into the data channels to learn what had happened in the European finance markets while he slept. At half past seven local time the New York exchanges opened and the real day's work began. By half past eleven, New York was through for the day, and Munson went around the corner for lunch, always at the Petit Pois, whose proprietor he had helped to make a millionaire by putting him into Consolidated Nucleonics' several components two and a half years before the big merger. At half past one, Munson was back in the office to transact business for his own account on the Pacific Coast exchange; three days a week he left at three, but on Tuesdays and Thursdays he stayed as late as five in order to catch some deals on the Honolulu and Tokyo exchanges. Afterwards, dinner, a play or concert, always a handsome female companion. He tried to get to sleep, or at least to bed, by midnight.

A man in Freddy Munson's position *had* to be orderly. At any given time, his thefts from his clients ranged from six to nine million dollars, and he kept all the details of his jugglings in his head. He couldn't trust putting them on paper because there were scanner eyes everywhere; and he certainly didn't dare employ the data net, since it was well known that anything you confided to one computer was bound to be accessible to some other computer somewhere, no matter how tight a privacy seal you slapped on it. So Munson had to remember the intricacies of fifty or more illicit transactions, a constantly changing chain of embezzlements, and a man who practices such necessary disciplines of memory soon gets into the habit of extending discipline to every phase of his life.

Helene snuggled close. Her faintly psychedelic perfume drifted toward his nostrils. He locked the car into the Sausalito circuit and leaned back comfortably as the traffic-control computer took over the steering. Helene said, "At the Bryce place last night I saw two sculptures by your bankrupt friend."

"Paul Mueller?"

"That's the one. They were very good sculptures. One of them buzzed at me."

"What were you doing at the Bryces'?"

"I went to college with Lisa Bryce. She invited me over with Marty."

"I didn't realize you were that old," Munson said.

Helene giggled. "Lisa's a lot younger than her husband, dear. How much does a Paul Mueller sculpture cost?"

"Fifteen, twenty thousand, generally. More for specials."

"And he's broke, even so?"

"Paul has a rare talent for self-destruction," Munson said. "He simply doesn't comprehend money. But it's his artistic salvation, in a way. The more desperately in debt he is, the finer his work becomes. He creates out of his despair, so to speak. Though he seems to have overdone the latest crisis. He's stopped working altogether. It's a sin against humanity when an artist doesn't work."

"You can be so eloquent, Freddy," Helene said softly.

When the Amazing Montini woke Thursday morning, he did not at once realize that anything had changed. His memory, like a good servant, was always there when he needed to call on it, but the array of perfectly fixed facts he carried in his mind remained submerged until required. A librarian might scan shelves and see books missing; Montini could not detect similar vacancies of his synapses. He had been up for half an hour, had stepped under the molecular bath and had punched for his breakfast and had awakened Nadia to tell her to confirm the pod reservations to Vegas, and finally, like a concert pianist running off a few arpeggios to limber his fingers for the day's chores, Montini reached into his memory bank for a little Shakespeare and no Shakespeare came.

He stood quite still, gripping the astrolabe that ornamented his picture window, and peered out at the bridge in sudden bewilderment. It had never been necessary for him to make a conscious effort to recover data. He merely looked and it was there; but where was Shakespeare? Where was the left hand column of page 136, and the right hand column of page 654, and the right hand column of page 806, sixteen lines down? Gone? He drew blanks. The screen of his mind showed him only empty pages.

Easy. This is unusual, but it isn't catastrophic. You must be tense, for some reason, and you're forcing it, that's all. Relax, pull something else out of storage—

The *New York Times*, Wednesday, October 3, 1973. Yes, there it was, the front page, beautifully clear, the story on the baseball game down in the lower right-hand corner, the headline about the jet accident big and black, even the photo credit visible. Fine. Now let's try—

The *St. Louis Post-Dispatch*, Sunday, April 19, 1987. Montini shivered. He saw the top four inches of the page, nothing else. Wiped clean.

He ran through the files of other newspapers he had memorized for his act. Some were there. Some were not. Some, like the *Post-Dispatch*, were obliterated in part. Color rose to his cheeks. Who had tampered with his memory?

He tried Shakespeare again. Nothing.

He tried the 1997 Chicago data-net directory. It was there.

He tried his third-grade geography textbook. It was there, the big red book with smeary print.

He tried last Friday's five-o'clock xerofax bulletin. Gone.

He stumbled and sank down on the divan he had purchased in Istanbul, he recalled, on the nineteenth of May, 1985, for 4,200 Turkish pounds. "Nadia!" he cried. "Nadia!" His voice was little more than a croak. She came running, her eyes only half frosted, her morning face askew.

"How do I look?" he demanded. "My mouth—is my mouth right? My eyes?"

"Your face is all flushed."

"Aside from that!"

"I don't know," she gasped. "You seem all upset, but—"

"Half my mind is gone," Montini said. "I must have had a stroke. Is there any facial paralysis? That's a symptom. Call my doctor, Nadia! A stroke, a stroke! It's the end for Montini!"

Paul Mueller, awakening at midnight on Wednesday and feeling strangely refreshed, attempted to get his bearings. Why was he fully dressed, and why had he been asleep? A nap, perhaps, that had stretched on too long? He tried to remember what he had been doing earlier in the day, but he was unable to find a clue. He was baffled but not disturbed; mainly he felt a tremendous urge to get to work. The images of five sculptures, fully planned and begging to be constructed, jostled in his mind. Might as well start right now, he thought. Work through till morning. That small twittering silvery one—that's a good one to start with. I'll block out the schematics, maybe even do some of the armature—

"Carole?" he called. "Carole, are you around?"

His voice echoed through the oddly empty apartment.

For the first time Mueller noticed how little furniture there was. A bed—a cot, really, not their double bed—and a table, and a tiny insulator unit for food, and a few dishes. No carpeting. Where were his sculptures, his private collection of his own best work? He walked into his studio and found it bare from wall to wall, all of his tools mysteriously swept away, just a few discarded sketches on the floor. And his wife? "Carole? Carole?"

He could not understand any of this. While he dozed, it seemed, someone had cleaned the place out, stolen his furniture, his sculptures, even the carpet. Mueller had heard of such thefts. They came with a van, brazenly, posing as moving men. Perhaps they had given him some sort of drug while they worked. He could not bear the thought that they had taken his sculptures; the rest didn't matter, but he had cherished those dozen pieces dearly. I'd better call the police, he decided, and rushed toward the handset of the data unit, but it wasn't there either. Would burglars take *that* too?

Searching for some answers, he scurried from wall to wall, and saw a note in his own handwriting. *Call Freddy Munson in the morning and borrow three bigs. Buy ticket to Caracas. Buy sculpting stuff.*

Caracas? A vacation, maybe? And why buy sculpting stuff? Obviously the tools had been gone before he fell asleep, then. Why? And where was his wife? What was going on? He wondered if he ought to call Freddy right now, instead of waiting until morning. Freddy might know. Freddy was always home by midnight, too. He'd have one of his damn girls with him and wouldn't want to be interrupted, but to hell with that; what good was having friends if you couldn't bother them in a time of crisis?

Heading for the nearest public communicator booth, he rushed out of his apartment and nearly collided with a sleek dunning robot in the hallway. The things show no mercy, Mueller thought. They plague you at all hours. No doubt this one was on its way to bother the deadbeat Nicholson family down the hall.

The robot said, "Mr. Paul Mueller? I am a properly qualified representative of International Fabrication Cartel, Amalgamated. I am here to serve notice that there is an unpaid balance in your account to the extent of $9,150.55, which as of 0900 hours tomorrow morning will accrue compounded penalty interest at a rate of 5 percent per month, since you have not responded to our three previous requests for payment. I must further inform you—"

"You're off your neutrinos," Mueller snapped. "I don't owe a dime to I.F.C.! For once in my life I'm in the black, and don't try to make me believe otherwise."

The robot replied patiently, "Shall I give you a printout of the transactions? On the fifth of January, 2003, you ordered the following metal products from us: three 4-meter tubes of antiqued iridium, six 10-centimeter spheres of—"

"The fifth of January, 2003, happens to be three months from now," Mueller said, "and I don't have time to listen to crazy robots. I've got an important call to make. Can I trust you to patch me into the data net without garbling things?"

"I'm not authorized to permit you to make use of my facilities."

"Emergency override," said Mueller. "Human being in trouble. Go argue with that one!"

The robot's conditioning was sound. It yielded at once to his assertion of an emergency and set up a relay to the main communications net. Mueller supplied Freddy Munson's number. "I can provide audio only," the robot said, putting the call through. Nearly a minute passed. Then Freddy

Munson's familiar deep voice snarled from the speaker grille in the robot's chest, "Who is it and what do you want?"

"It's Paul. I'm sorry to bust in on you, Freddy, but I'm in big trouble. I think I'm losing my mind, or else everybody else is."

"Maybe everybody else is. What's the problem?"

"All my furniture's gone. A dunning robot is trying to shake me down for nine bigs. I don't know where Carole is. I can't remember what I was doing earlier today. I've got a note here about getting tickets to Caracas that I wrote myself, and I don't know why. And—"

"Skip the rest," Munson said. "I can't do anything for you. I've got problems of my own."

"Can I come over, at least, and talk?"

"Absolutely not!" In a softer voice Munson said, "Listen, Paul, I didn't mean to yell, but something's come up here, something very distressing—"

"You don't need to pretend. You've got Helene with you and you wish I'd leave you alone. Okay."

"No. Honestly," Munson said. "I've got problems, suddenly. I'm in a totally ungood position to give you any help at all. I need help myself."

"What sort? Anything I can do for you?"

"I'm afraid not. And if you'll excuse me, Paul—"

"Just tell me one thing, at least. Where am I likely to find Carole? Do you have any idea?"

"At her husband's place, I'd say."

"*I'm* her husband."

There was a long pause. Munson said finally, "Paul, she divorced you last January and married Pete Castine in April."

"No," Mueller said.

"What, no?"

"No, it isn't possible."

"Have you been popping pills, Paul? Sniffing something? Smoking weed? Look, I'm sorry, but I can't take time now to—"

"At least tell me what day today is."

"Wednesday."

"Which Wednesday?"

"Wednesday the eighth of May. Thursday the ninth, actually, by this time of night."

"And the year?"

"For Christ's sake, Paul—"

"The *year?*"

"2003."

Mueller sagged. "Freddy, I've lost half a year somewhere!
For me it's last October. 2002. I've some weird kind of
amnesia. It's the only explanation."

"Amnesia," Munson said. The edge of tension left his
voice. "Is that what you've got? Amnesia? Can there be such a
thing as an epidemic of amnesia? Is it contagious? Maybe you
better come over here after all. Because amnesia's my problem too."

Thursday, May 9, promised to be as beautiful as the
previous day had been. The sun once again beamed on San
Francisco; the sky was clear, the air warm and tender.
Commander Braskett awoke early as always, punched for his
usual spartan breakfast, studied the morning xerofax news,
spent an hour dictating his memoirs, and, about nine, went
out for a walk. The streets were strangely crowded, he found,
when he got down to the shopping district along Haight
Street. People were wandering aimlessly, dazedly, as though
they were sleepwalkers. Were they drunk? Drugged? Three
times in five minutes Commander Braskett was stopped by
young men who wanted to know the date. Not the time, the
date. He told them, crisply, disdainfully; he tried to be
tolerant, but it was difficult for him not to despise people who
were so weak that they were unable to refrain from poisoning
their minds with stimulants and narcotics and psychedelics
and similar trash. At the corner of Haight and Masonic a
forlorn-looking pretty girl of about seventeen, with wide blank
blue eyes, halted him and said, "Sir, this city is San Francisco,
isn't it? I mean, I was supposed to move here from Pittsburgh
in May, and if this is May, this is San Francisco, right?"
Commander Braskett nodded brusquely and turned away,
pained.

He was relieved to see an old friend, Lou Sandler, the
manager of the Bank of America office across the way. Sandler
was standing outside the bank door. Commander Braskett
crossed to him and said, "Isn't it a disgrace, Lou, the way this
whole street is filled with addicts this morning? What is it,
some historical pageant of the 1960s?" And Sandler gave him

an empty smile and said, "Is that my name? Lou? You wouldn't happen to know the last name too, would you? Somehow it's slipped my mind." In that moment Commander Braskett realized that something terrible had happened to his city and perhaps to his country, and that the leftist takeover he had long dreaded must now be at hand, and that it was time for him to don his old uniform again and do what he could to strike back at the enemy.

In joy and in confusion, Nate Haldersen awoke that morning realizing that he had been transformed in some strange and wonderful way. His head was throbbing, but not painfully. It seemed to him that a terrible weight had been lifted from his shoulders, that the fierce dead hand about his throat had at last relinquished its grip.

He sprang from bed, full of questions.

Where am I? What kind of place is this? Why am I not at home? Where are my books? Why do I feel so happy?

This seemed to be a hospital room.

There was a veil across his mind. He pierced its filmy folds and realized that he had committed himself to—to Fletcher Memorial—last August—no, the August before last—suffering with a severe emotional disturbance brought on by—brought on by—

He had never felt happier than this moment.

He saw a mirror. In it was the reflected upper half of Nathaniel Haldersen, Ph.D. Nate Haldersen smiled at himself. Tall, stringy, long-nosed man, absurdly straw-colored hair, absurd blue eyes, thin lips, smiling. Bony body. He undid his pajama top. Pale, hairless chest; bump of bone like an epaulet on each shoulder. I have been sick a long time, Haldersen thought. Now I must get out of here, back to my classroom. End of leave of absence. Where are my clothes?

"Nurse? Doctor?" He pressed his call button three times. "Hello? Anyone here?"

No one came. Odd; they always came. Shrugging, Haldersen moved out into the hall. He saw three orderlies, heads together, buzzing at the far end. They ignored him. A robot servitor carrying breakfast trays glided past. A moment later one of the younger doctors came running through the hall, and would not stop when Haldersen called to him. Annoyed, he went back into his room and looked about for clothing. He found none, only a little stack of magazines on the closet floor. He thumbed the call button three more times. Finally one of the robots entered the room.

"I am sorry," it said, "but the human hospital personnel is busy at present. May I serve you, Dr. Haldersen?"

"I want a suit of clothing. I'm leaving the hospital."

"I am sorry, but there is no record of your discharge. Without authorization from Dr. Bryce, Dr. Reynolds, or Dr. Kamakura, I am not permitted to allow your departure."

Haldersen sighed. He knew better than to argue with a robot. "Where are those three gentlemen right now?"

"They are occupied, sir. As you may know, there is a medical emergency in the city this morning, and Dr. Bryce and Dr. Kamakura are helping to organize the committee of public safety. Dr. Reynolds did not report for duty today and we are unable to trace him. It is believed that he is a victim of the current difficulty."

"*What* current difficulty?"

"Mass loss of memory on the part of the human population," the robot said.

"An epidemic of amnesia?"

"That is one interpretation of the problem."

"How can such a thing—" Haldersen stopped. He understood now the source of his own joy this morning. Only yesterday afternoon he had discussed with Tim Bryce the application of memory-destroying drugs to his own trauma and Bryce had said—

Haldersen no longer knew the nature of his own trauma.

"Wait," he said, as the robot began to leave the room. "I need information. Why have I been under treatment here?"

"You have been suffering from social displacements and dysfunctions whose origin, Dr. Bryce feels, lies in a situation of traumatic personal loss."

"Loss of what?"

"Your family, Dr. Haldersen."

"Yes. That's right. I recall, now—I had a wife and two children. Emily. And a little girl—Margaret, Elizabeth, something like that. And a boy named John. What happened to them?"

"They were passengers aboard Intercontinental Airways Flight 103, Copenhagen to San Francisco, September 5, 1991.

The plane underwent explosive decompression over the Arctic Ocean and there were no survivors."

Haldersen absorbed the information as calmly as though he were hearing of the assassination of Julius Caesar.

"Where was I when the accident occurred?"

"In Copenhagen," the robot replied. "You had intended to return to San Francisco with your family on Flight 103; however, according to your data file here, you became involved in an emotional relationship with a woman named Marie Rasmussen, whom you had met in Copenhagen, and failed to return to your hotel in time to go to the airport. Your wife, evidently aware of the situation, chose not to wait for you. Her subsequent death, and that of your children, produced a traumatic guilt reaction in which you came to regard yourself as responsible for their terminations."

"I *would* take that attitude, wouldn't I?" Haldersen said. "Sin and retribution. Mea culpa, mea maxima culpa. I always had a harsh view of sin, even when I was sinning. I should have been an Old Testament prophet."

"Shall I provide more information, sir?"

"Is there more?"

"We have in the files Dr. Bryce's report headed, *The Job Complex: A Study in the Paralysis of Guilt.*"

"Spare me that," Haldersen said. "All right, go."

He was alone. The Job Complex, he thought. Not really appropriate, was it? Job was a man without sin, and yet he was punished grievously to satisfy a whim of the Almighty. A little presumptuous, I'd say, to identify myself with him. Cain would have been a better choice. Cain said unto the Lord, My punishment is greater than I can bear. But Cain was a sinner. I was a sinner. I sinned and Emily died for it. When, eleven, eleven-and-a-half years ago? And now I know nothing at all about it except what the machine just told me. Redemption through oblivion, I'd call it. I have expiated my sin and now I'm free. I have no business staying in this hospital any longer. Strait is the gate, and narrow is the way, which leadeth unto life, and few there be that find it. I've got to get out of here. Maybe I can be of some help to others.

He belted his bathrobe, took a drink of water, and went out of the room. No one stopped him. The elevator did not seem to be running, but he found the stairs, and walked down, a little creakily. He had not been this far from his room in more than a year. The lowest floors of the hospital were in chaos—doctors, orderlies, robots, patients, all milling around excitedly. The robots were trying to calm people and get them back to their proper places. "Excuse me," Haldersen said serenely. "Excuse me. Excuse me." He left the hospital, unmolested, by the front door. The air outside was as fresh as young wine; he felt like weeping when it hit his nostrils. He was free. Redemption through oblivion. The disaster high above the Arctic no longer dominated his thoughts. He looked upon it precisely as if it had happened to the family of some other man, long ago. Haldersen began to walk briskly down Van Ness, feeling vigor returning to his legs with every stride. A young woman, sobbing wildly, erupted from a building and collided with him. He caught her, steadied her, was surprised at his own strength as he kept her from toppling. She trembled and pressed her head against his chest. "Can I do anything for you?" he asked. "Can I be of any help?"

Panic had begun to enfold Freddy Munson during dinner at Ondine's Wednesday night. He had begun to be annoyed with Helene in the midst of the truffled chicken breasts, and so he started to think about the details of business; and to his amazement he did not seem to have the details quite right in his mind; and so he felt the early twinges of terror.

The trouble was that Helene was going on and on about the art of sonic sculpture in general and Paul Mueller in particular. Her interest was enough to arouse faint jealousies in Munson. Was she getting ready to leap from his bed to Paul's? Was she thinking of abandoning the wealthy, glamorous, but essentially prosaic stockbroker for the irresponsible, impecunious, fascinatingly gifted sculptor? Of course, Helene kept company with a number of other men, but Munson knew them and discounted them as rivals; they were nonentities, escorts to fill her idle nights when he was too busy for her. Paul Mueller, however, was another case. Munson could not bear the thought that Helene might leave him for Paul. So he shifted his concentration to the day's maneuvers. He had extracted a thousand shares of the $5.87 convertible preferred of Lunar Transit from the Schaeffer account, pledging it as collateral to cover his shortage in the matter of the Comsat debentures, and then, tapping the Howard account for five thousand Southeast Energy Corporation warrants, he had—or had those warrants come out of the Brewster account? Brewster was big on utilities. So was Howard, but that account was heavy on Mid-Atlantic Power, so would it also be loaded with Southeast Energy? In any case, had he put those warrants up against the Zurich uranium futures, or were they riding as his markers in that Antarctic oil-lease thing? He could not remember.

He could not remember.

He could not remember.

Each transaction had been in its own compartment. The partitions were down, suddenly. Numbers were spilling about in his mind as though his brain were in free fall. All of today's deals were tumbling. It frightened him. He began to gobble his food, wanting now to get out of here, to get rid of Helene, to get home and try to reconstruct his activities of the afternoon. Oddly, he could remember quite clearly all that he had done yesterday—the Xerox switch, the straddle on Steel—but today was washing away minute by minute.

"Are you all right?" Helene asked.

"No, I'm not," he said. "I'm coming down with something."

"The Venus virus. Everybody's getting it."

"Yes, that must be it. The Venus virus. You'd better keep clear of me tonight."

They skipped dessert and cleared out fast. He dropped Helene off at her flat; she hardly seemed disappointed, which bothered him, but not nearly so much as what was happening to his mind. Alone, finally, he tried to jot down an outline of his day, but even more had left him now. In the restaurant he had known which stocks he had handled, though he wasn't sure what he had done with them. Now he couldn't even recall the specific securities. He was out on the limb for millions of dollars of other people's money, and every detail was in his mind, and his mind was falling apart. By the time Paul Mueller called, a little after midnight, Munson was growing desperate. He was relieved, but not exactly cheered, to learn that whatever strange thing had affected his mind had hit Mueller a lot harder. Mueller had forgotten everything since last October.

"You went bankrupt," Munson had to explain to him. "You had this wild scheme for setting up a central clearinghouse for works of art, a kind of stock exchange—the sort of thing only an artist would try to start. You wouldn't let me discourage you. Then you began signing notes, and taking on contingent liabilities, and before the project was six weeks old you were hit with half a dozen lawsuits and it all began to go sour."

"When did this happen, precisely?"

"You conceived the idea at the beginning of November. By Christmas you were in severe trouble. You already had a bunch of personal debts that had gone unpaid from before, and your assets melted away, and you hit a terrible bind in your work and couldn't produce a thing. You really don't remember a thing of this, Paul?"

"Nothing."

"After the first of the year the fastest moving creditors started getting decrees against you. They impounded everything you owned except the furniture, and then they took the furniture. You borrowed from all of your friends, but they couldn't give you enough, because you were borrowing thousands and you owed hundreds of thousands."

"How much did I hit you for?"

"Eleven bigs," Munson said. "But don't worry about that now."

"I'm not. I'm not worrying about a thing. I was in a bind in my work, you say?" Mueller chuckled. "That's all gone. I'm itching to start making things. All I need are the tools—I mean, money to buy the tools."

"What would they cost?"

"Two-and-a-half bigs," Mueller said.

Munson coughed. "All right. I can't transfer the money to your account, because your creditors would lien it right away. I'll get some cash at the bank. You'll have three bigs tomorrow, and welcome to it."

"Bless you, Freddy," Mueller said. "This kind of amnesia is a good thing, eh? I was so worried about money that I couldn't work. Now I'm not worried at all. I guess I'm still in debt, but I'm not fretting. Tell me what happened to my marriage, now."

"Carole got fed up and turned off," said Munson. "She opposed your business venture from the start. When it began to devour you, she did what she could to untangle you from it, but you insisted on trying to patch things together with more loans and she filed for a decree. When she was free, Pete Castine moved in and grabbed her."

"That's the hardest part to believe. That she'd marry an art dealer, a totally noncreative person, a—a parasite, really—"

"They were always good friends," Munson said. "I won't say they were lovers, because I don't know, but they were close. And Pete's not that horrible. He's got taste, intelligence, everything an artist needs except the gift. I think Carole may have been weary of gifted men, anyway."

"How did I take it?" Mueller asked.

"You hardly seemed to notice, Paul. You were so busy with your financial shenanigans."

Mueller nodded. He sauntered to one of his own works, a three-meter-high arrangement of oscillating rods that ran the whole sound spectrum into high kilohertzes, and passed two fingers over the activator eye. The sculpture began to murmur. After a few moments Mueller said, "You sounded awfully upset when I called, Freddy. You say you have some kind of amnesia too?"

Trying to be casual about it, Munson said, "I find I can't remember some important financial transactions I carried out today. Unfortunately, my only record of them is in my head. But maybe the information will come back to me when I've slept on it."

"There's no way I can help you with that."

"No. There isn't."

"Freddy, where is this amnesia coming from?"

Munson shrugged. "Maybe somebody put a drug in the water supply, or spiked the food, or something. These days, you never can tell. Look, I've got to do some work, Paul. If you'd like to sleep here tonight—"

"I'm wide awake, thanks. I'll drop by again in the morning."

When the sculptor was gone, Munson struggled for a feverish hour to reconstruct his data, and failed. Shortly before two he took a four-hour sleep pill. When he awakened, he realized in dismay that he had no memories whatever for the period from April 1 to noon yesterday. During those five weeks he had engaged in countless securities transactions, using other people's property as his collateral, and counting on his ability to get each marker in his game back into its proper place before anyone was likely to go looking for it. He had always been able to remember everything. Now he could remember nothing. He reached his office at seven in the morning, as always, and out of habit plugged himself into the data channels to study the Zurich and London quotes, but the prices on the screen were strange to him, and he knew that he was undone.

At that same moment of Thursday morning Dr. Timothy Bryce's house computer triggered an impulse and the alarm voice in his pillow said quietly but firmly, "It's time to wake up, Dr. Bryce." He stirred but lay still. After the prescribed ten-second interval the voice said, a little more sharply, "It's time to wake up, Dr. Bryce." Bryce sat up, just in time; the lifting of his head from the pillow cut off the third, much sterner, repetition which would have been followed by the opening chords of the *Jupiter* Symphony. The psychiatrist opened his eyes.

He was surprised to find himself sharing his bed with a strikingly attractive girl.

She was a honey blonde, deeply tanned, with light-brown eyes, full pale lips, and a sleek, elegant body. She looked to be fairly young, a good twenty years younger than he was— perhaps twenty-five, twenty-eight. She wore nothing, and she was in a deep sleep, her lower lip sagging in a sort of involuntary pout. Neither her youth nor her beauty nor her nudity surprised him; he was puzzled simply because he had no notion who she was or how she had come to be in bed with him. He felt as though he had never seen her before. Certainly he didn't know her name. Had he picked her up at some party last night? He couldn't seem to remember where he had been last night. Gently he nudged her elbow.

She woke quickly, fluttering her eyelids, shaking her head.

"Oh," she said, as she saw him, and clutched the sheet up to her throat. Then, smiling, she dropped it again. "That's foolish. No need to be modest *now*, I guess."

"I guess. Hello."

"Hello," she said. She looked as confused as he was.

"This is going to sound stupid," he said, "but someone must have slipped me a weird weed last night, because I'm afraid I'm not sure how I happened to bring you home. Or what your name is."

"Lisa," she said. "Lisa—Falk." She stumbled over the second name. "And you're—"

"Tim Bryce."

"You don't remember where we met?"

"No," he said.

"Neither do I."

He got out of bed, feeling a little hesitant about his own nakedness, and fighting the inhibition off. "They must have given us both the same thing to smoke, then. You know"—he grinned shyly—"I can't even remember if we had a good time together last night. I hope we did."

"I think we did," she said. "I can't remember it either. But I feel good inside—the way I usually do after I've—" She paused. "We couldn't have met only just last night, Tim."

"How can you tell?"

"I've got the feeling that I've known you longer than that."

Bryce shrugged. "I don't see how. I mean, without being too coarse about it, obviously we were both high last night, really floating, and we met and came here and—"

"No. I feel at home here. As if I moved in with you weeks and weeks ago."

"A lovely idea. But I'm sure you didn't."

"Why do I feel so much at home here, then?"

"In what way?"

"In every way." She walked to the bedroom closet and let her hand rest on the touchplate. The door slid open; evidently he had keyed the house computer to her fingerprints. Had he done that last night too? She reached in. "My clothing," she said. "Look. All these dresses, coats, shoes. A whole wardrobe. There can't be any doubt. We've been living together and don't remember it!"

A chill swept through him. "What have they done to us? Listen, Lisa, let's get dressed and eat and go down to the hospital together for a checkup. We—"

"Hospital?"

"Fletcher Memorial. I'm in the neurological department. Whatever they slipped us last night has hit us both with a lacunary retrograde amnesia—a gap in our memories—and it could be serious. If it's caused brain damage, perhaps it's not irreversible yet, but we can't fool around."

She put her hands to her lips in fear. Bryce felt a sudden warm urge to protect this lovely stranger, to guard and comfort her, and he realized he must be in love with her, even though he couldn't remember who she was. He crossed the room to her and seized her in a brief, tight embrace; she responded eagerly, shivering a little. By a quarter to eight they were out of the house and heading for the hospital through unusually light traffic. Bryce led the girl quickly to the staff lounge. Ted Kamakura was there already, in uniform. The little Japanese psychiatrist nodded curtly and said, "Morning, Tim." Then he blinked. "Good morning, Lisa. How come *you're* here?"

"You know her?" Bryce asked.

"What kind of a question is that?"

"A deadly serious one."

"Of course I know her," Kamakura said, and his smile of greeting abruptly faded. "Why? Is something wrong about that?"

"You may know her, but I don't," said Bryce.

"Oh, God. Not you too!"

"Tell me who she is, Ted."

"She's your wife, Tim. You married her five years ago."

By half past eleven Thursday morning the Gerards had everything set up and going smoothly for the lunch rush at the Petit Pois. The soup caldron was bubbling, the escargot trays were ready to be popped in the oven, the sauces were taking form. Pierre Gerard was a bit surprised when most of the lunchtime regulars failed to show up. Even Mr. Munson, always punctual at half past eleven, did not arrive. Some of these men had not missed weekday lunch at the Petit Pois in fifteen years. Something terrible must have happened on the stock market, Pierre thought, to have kept all these financial men at their desks, and they were too busy to call him and cancel their usual tables. That must be the answer. It was impossible that any of the regulars would forget to call him. The stock market must be exploding. Pierre made a mental note to call his broker after lunch and find out what was going on.

About two Thursday afternoon, Paul Mueller stopped into Metchnikoff's Art Supplies in North Beach to try to get a welding pen, some raw metal, loudspeaker paint, and the rest of the things he needed for the rebirth of his sculpting career. Metchnikoff greeted him sourly with, "No credit at all, Mr. Mueller, not even a nickel!"

"It's all right. I'm a cash customer this time."

The dealer brightened. "In that case it's all right, maybe. You finished with your troubles?"

"I hope so," Mueller said.

He gave the order. It came to about $2,300; when the time came to pay, he explained that he simply had to run down to Montgomery Street to pick up the cash from his friend Freddy Munson, who was holding three bigs for him. Metchnikoff began to glower again. "Five minutes!" Mueller called. "I'll be back in five minutes!" But when he got to Munson's office, he found the place in confusion, and Munson wasn't there. "Did he leave an envelope for a Mr. Mueller?" he asked a distraught secretary. "I was supposed to pick something important up here this afternoon. Would you please check?" The girl simply ran away from him. So did the next girl. A burly broker told him to get out of the office. "We're closed, fellow," he shouted. Baffled, Mueller left.

Not daring to return to Metchnikoff's with the news that he hadn't been able to raise the cash after all, Mueller simply went home. Three dunning robots were camped outside his door, and each one began to croak its cry of doom as he approached. "Sorry," Mueller said, "I can't remember a thing about any of this stuff," and he went inside and sat down on the bare floor, angry, thinking of the brilliant pieces he could be turning out if he could only get his hands on the tools of his trade. He made sketches instead. At least the ghouls had left him with pencil and paper. Not as efficient as a computer screen and a light-pen, maybe, but Michelangelo and Benvenuto Cellini had managed to make out all right without computer screens and light-pens.

At four o'clock the door bell rang.

"Go *away*," Mueller said through the speaker. "See my accountant! I don't want to hear any more dunnings, and the next time I catch one of you idiot robots by my door I'm going to—"

"It's me, Paul," a nonmechanical voice said.

Carole.

He rushed to the door. There were seven robots out there, surrounding her, and they tried to get in; but he pushed them back so she could enter. A robot didn't dare lay a paw on a human being. He slammed the door in their metal faces and locked it.

Carole looked fine. Her hair was longer than he remembered it, and she had gained about eight pounds in all the right places, and she wore an iridescent peekaboo wrap that he had never seen before, and which was really inappropriate for afternoon wear, but which looked splendid on her. She seemed at least five years younger than she really was; evidently a month and a half of marriage to Pete Castine had done more for her than nine years of marriage to Paul Mueller. She glowed. She also looked strained and tense, but that seemed superficial, the product of some distress of the last few hours.

"I seem to have lost my key," she said.

"What are you doing here?"

"I don't understand you, Paul."

"I mean why'd you come here?"

"I *live* here."

"Do you?" He laughed harshly. "Very funny."

"You always did have a weird sense of humor, Paul." She stepped past him. "Only this isn't any joke. Where *is* everything? The furniture, Paul. My things." Suddenly she was crying. "I must be breaking up. I wake up this morning in a completely strange apartment, all alone, and I spend the whole day wandering in a sort of daze that I don't understand at all, and now I finally come home and I find that you've pawned every damn thing we own, or something and—" She bit her knuckles. "Paul?"

She's got it too, he thought. The amnesia epidemic.

He said quietly, "This is a funny thing to ask, Carole, but will you tell me what today's date is?"

"Why—the fourteenth of September—or is it the fifteenth—"

"2002?"

"What do you think? 1776?"

She's got it worse than I have, Mueller told himself. She's lost a whole extra month. She doesn't remember my business venture. She doesn't remember my losing all the money. *She doesn't remember divorcing me.* She thinks she's still my wife.

"Come in here," he said, and led her to the bedroom. He pointed to the cot that stood where their bed had been. "Sit down, Carole. I'll try to explain. It won't make much sense but I'll try to explain."

* * *

Under the circumstances, the concert by the visiting New York Philharmonic for Thursday evening was cancelled. Nevertheless the orchestra assembled for its rehearsal at half past two in the afternoon. The union required so many rehearsals—with pay—a week; therefore the orchestra rehearsed, regardless of external cataclysms. But there were problems. Maestro Alvarez, who used an electronic baton and proudly conducted without a score, thumbed the button for a downbeat and realized abruptly, with a sensation as of dropping through a trapdoor, that the Brahms Fourth was wholly gone from his mind. The orchestra responded raggedly to his faltering leadership. Some of the musicians had no difficulties, but the concertmaster stared in horror at his left hand, wondering how to finger the strings for the notes his violin was supposed to be yielding, and the second oboe could not find the proper keys, and the first bassoon had not yet even managed to remember how to put his instrument together.

By nightfall, Tim Bryce had managed to assemble enough of the story so that he understood what had happened, not only to himself and to Lisa, but to the entire city. A drug, or drugs, almost certainly distributed through the municipal water supply, had leached away nearly everyone's memory. The trouble with modern life, Bryce thought, is that technology gives us the potential for newer and more intricate disasters every year, but it doesn't seem to give us the ability to ward them off. Memory drugs were old stuff, going back thirty, forty years. He had studied several types of them himself. Memory is partly a chemical and partly an electrical process; some drugs went after the electrical end, jamming the synapses over which brain transmissions travel, and some went after the molecular substrata in which long-term memories are locked up. Bryce knew ways of destroying short-term memories by inhibiting synapse transmission, and he knew ways of destroying the deep long-term memories by washing out the complex chains of ribonucleic acid, brain-RNA, by which they are inscribed in the brain. But such drugs were experimental, tricky, unpredictable; he had hesitated to use them on human subjects; he certainly had never imagined that anyone would simply dump them into an aquaduct and give an entire city a simultaneous lobotomy.

His office at Fletcher Memorial had become an improvised center of operations for San Francisco. The mayor was there, pale and shrunken; the chief of police, exhausted and confused, periodically turned his back and popped a pill; a dazed-looking representative of the communications net hovered in a corner, nervously monitoring the hastily rigged system through which the committee of public safety that Bryce had summoned could make its orders known throughout the city.

The mayor was no use at all. He couldn't even remember having run for office. The chief of police was in even worse shape: he had been up all night because he had forgotten, among other things, his home address, and he had been afraid to query a computer about it for fear he'd lose his job for drunkenness. By now the chief of police was aware that he wasn't the only one in the city having memory problems today, and he had looked up his address in the files and even telephoned his wife, but he was close to collapse. Bryce had insisted that both men stay here as symbols of order; he wanted only their faces and their voices, not their fumble-headed official services.

A dozen or so miscellaneous citizens had accumulated in Bryce's office too. At five in the afternoon he had broadcast an all-media appeal, asking anyone whose memory of recent events was unimpaired to come to Fletcher Memorial. "If you haven't had any city water in the past twenty-four hours, you're probably all right. Come down here. We need you." He had drawn a curious assortment. There was a ramrod-straight old space hero, Taylor Braskett, a pure-foods nut who drank only mountain water. There was a family of French restauranteurs, mother, father, three grown children, who preferred mineral water flown in from their native land. There was a computer salesman named McBurney who had been in Los Angeles on business and hadn't had any of the drugged water. There was a retired cop named Adler who lived in Oakland, where there were no memory problems; he had hurried across the bay as soon as he heard that San Francisco was in trouble. That was before all access to the city had been shut off at Bryce's orders. And there were some others, of doubtful value but of definitely intact memory.

The three screens that the communications man had mounted provided a relay of key points in the city. Right now one was monitoring the Fisherman's Wharf district from a camera atop Ghirardelli Square, one was viewing the financial district from a helicopter over the old Ferry Building Museum, and one was relaying a pickup from a mobile truck in Golden Gate Park. The scenes were similar everywhere: people milling about, asking questions, getting no answers. There wasn't any sign of looting yet. There were no fires. The police, those of them able to function, were out in force, and antiriot robots were cruising the bigger streets, just in case they might be needed to squirt their stifling blankets of foam at suddenly panicked mobs.

Bryce said to the mayor, "At half past six I want you to go on all media with an appeal for calm. We'll supply you with everything you have to say."

The mayor moaned.

Bryce said, "Don't worry. I'll feed you the whole speech by bone relay. Just concentrate on speaking clearly and looking straight into the camera. If you come across as a terrified man, it can be the end for all of us. If you look cool, we may be able to pull through."

The mayor put his face in his hands.

Ted Kamakura whispered, "You can't put him on the channels, Tim! He's a wreck, and everyone will see it!"

"The city's mayor has to show himself," Bryce insisted. "Give him a double jolt of bracers. Let him make this one speech and then we can put him to pasture."

"Who'll be the spokesman, then?" Kamakura asked. "You? Me? Police Chief Dennison?"

"I don't know," Bryce muttered. "We need an authority-image to make announcements every half hour or so, and I'm damned if I'll have time. Or you. And Dennison—"

"Gentlemen, may I make a suggestion?" It was the old spaceman, Braskett. "I wish to volunteer as spokesman. You must admit I have a certain look of authority. And I'm accustomed to speaking to the public."

Bryce rejected the idea instantly. That right-wing crackpot, that author of passionate nut letters to every news medium in the state, that latter-day Paul Revere? Him, spokesman for the committee? But in the moment of rejection came acceptance. Nobody really paid attention to far-out political activities like that; probably nine people out of ten in San Francisco thought of Braskett, if at all, simply as the hero of the first Mars expedition. He was a handsome old horse, too, elegantly upright and lean. Deep voice; unwavering eyes. A man of strength and presence.

Bryce said, "Commander Braskett, if we were to make you chairman of the committee of public safety—"

Ted Kamakura gasped.

"—would I have your assurance that such public announcements as you would make would be confined entirely to statements of the policies arrived at by the entire committee?"

Commander Braskett smiled glacially. "You want me to be a figurehead, is that it?"

"To be our spokesman, with the official title of chairman."

"As I said: to be a figurehead. Very well, I accept. I'll mouth my lies like an obedient puppet, and I won't attempt to inject any of my radical, extremist ideas into my statements. Is that what you wish?"

"I think we understand each other perfectly," Bryce said, and smiled, and got a surprisingly warm smile in return.

He jabbed now at his data board. Someone in the path lab eight stories below his office answered, and Bryce said, "Is there an up-to-date analysis yet?"

"I'll switch you to Dr. Madison."

Madison appeared on the screen. He ran the hospital's radioisotope department, normally: a beefy, red-faced man who looked as though he ought to be a beer salesman. He knew his subject. "It's definitely the water supply, Tim," he said at once. "We tentatively established that an hour and a half ago, of course, but now there's no doubt. I've isolated traces of two different memory-suppressant drugs, and there's the possibility of a third. Whoever it was was taking no chances."

"What are they?" Bryce asked.

"Well, we've got a good jolt of acetylcholine terminase," Madison said, "which will louse up the synapses and interfere with short-term memory fixation. Then there's something else, perhaps a puromycin-derivative protein dissolver, which is going to work on the brain-RNA and smashing up older memories. I suspect also that we've been getting one of the newer experimental amnesifacients, something that I haven't isolated yet, capable of working its way deep and cutting out really basic motor patterns. So they've hit us high, low, and middle."

"That explains a lot. The guys who can't remember what

they did yesterday, the guys who've lost a chunk out of their adult memories, and the ones who don't even remember their names—this thing is working on people at all different levels."

"Depending on individual metabolism, age, brain structure, and how much water they had to drink yesterday, yes."

"Is the water supply still tainted?" Bryce asked.

"Tentatively, I'd say no. I've had water samples brought me from the upflow districts, and everything's okay there. The water department has been running its own check; they say the same. Evidently the stuff got into the system early yesterday, came down into the city, and is generally gone by now. Might be some residuals in the pipes; I'd be careful about drinking water even today."

"And what does the pharmacopoeia say about the effectiveness of these drugs?"

Madison shrugged. "Anybody's guess. You'd know that better than I. Do they wear off?"

"Not in the normal sense," said Bryce. "What happens is the brain cuts in a redundancy circuit and gets access to a duplicate set of the affected memories, eventually—shifts to another track, so to speak—provided a duplicate of the sector in question was there in the first place, and provided that the duplicate wasn't blotted out also. Some people are going to get chunks of their memories back, in a few days or a few weeks. Others won't."

"Wonderful," Madison said. "I'll keep you posted, Tim."

Bryce cut off the call and said to the communications man, "You have that bone relay? Get it behind His Honor's ear."

The mayor quivered. The little instrument was fastened in place.

Bryce said, "Mr. Mayor, I'm going to dictate a speech, and you're going to broadcast it on all media, and it's the last thing I'm going to ask of you until you've had a chance to pull yourself together. Okay? Listen carefully to what I'm saying, speak slowly, and pretend that tomorrow is election day and your job depends on how well you come across now. You won't be going on live. There'll be a fifteen-second delay, and we have a wipe circuit so we can correct any stumbles, and there's absolutely no reason to be tense. Are you with me? Will you give it all you've got?"

"My mind is all foggy."

"Simply listen to me and repeat what I say into the camera's eye. Let your political reflexes take over. Here's your chance to make a hero of yourself. We're living history right now, Mr. Mayor. What we do here today will be studied the way the events of the 1906 fire were studied. Let's go, now. Follow me. *People of the wonderful city of San Francisco—*"

The words rolled easily from Bryce's lips, and, wonder of wonders, the mayor caught them and spoke them in a clear, beautifully resonant voice. As he spun out his speech, Bryce felt a surging flow of power going through himself, and he imagined for the moment that he was the elected leader of the city, not merely a self-appointed emergency dictator. It was an interesting, almost ecstatic feeling. Lisa, watching him in action, gave him a loving smile.

He smiled at her. In this moment of glory he was almost able to ignore the ache of knowing that he had lost his entire memory archive of his life with her. Nothing else gone, apparently. But, neatly, with idiot selectivity, the drug in the water supply had sliced away everything pertaining to his five years of marriage. Kamakura had told him, a few hours ago, that it was the happiest marriage of any he knew. Gone. At least Lisa had suffered an identical loss, against all probabilities. Somehow that made it easier to bear; it would have been awful to have one of them remember the good times and the other know nothing. He was almost able to ignore the torment of loss while he kept busy. Almost.

"The mayor's going to be on in a minute," Nadia said. "Will you listen to him? He'll explain what's been going on."

"I don't care," said the Amazing Montini dully.

"It's some kind of epidemic of amnesia. When I was out before, I heard all about it. *Everyone's* got it. It isn't just you! And you thought it was a stroke, but it wasn't. You're all right."

"My mind is a ruin."

"It's only temporary." Her voice was shrill and unconvincing. "It's something in the air, maybe. Some drug they were testing that drifted in. We're all in this together. I can't remember last week at all."

"What do I care," Montini said. "Most of these people, they have no memories even when they are healthy. But me? Me? I am destroyed. Nadia, I should lie down in my grave now. There is no sense in continuing to walk around."

The voice from the loudspeaker said, "Ladies and gentlemen, His Honor Elliot Chase, the Mayor of San Francisco."

"Let's listen," Nadia said.

The mayor appeared on the wallscreen, wearing his solemn face, his we-face-a-grave-challenge-citizens face. Montini glanced at him, shrugged, looked away.

The mayor said, "People of the wonderful city of San Francisco, we have just come through the most difficult day in nearly a century, since the terrible catastrophe of April, 1906. The earth has not quaked today, nor have we been smitten by fire, yet we have been severely tested by sudden calamity.

"As all of you surely know, the people of San Francisco have been afflicted since last night by what can best be termed an epidemic of amnesia. There has been mass loss of memory, ranging from mild cases of forgetfulness to near-total obliteration of identity. Scientists working at Fletcher Memorial Hospital have succeeded in determining the cause of this unique and sudden disaster.

"It appears that criminal saboteurs contaminated the municipal water supply with certain restricted drugs that have the ability to dissolve memory structures. *The effect of these drugs is temporary.* There should be no cause for alarm. Even those who are most severely affected will find their memories gradually beginning to return, and there is every reason to expect full recovery in a matter of hours or days."

"He's lying," said Montini.

"The criminals responsible have not yet been apprehended, but we expect arrests momentarily. The San Francisco area is the only affected region, which means the drugs were introduced into the water system just beyond city limits. Everything is normal in Berkeley, in Oakland, in Marin County, and other outlying areas.

"In the name of public safety I have ordered the bridges to San Francisco closed, as well as the Bay Area Rapid Transit and other means of access to the city. We expect to maintain these restrictions at least until tomorrow morning. The purpose of this is to prevent disorder and to avoid a possible influx of undesirable elements into the city while the trouble persists. We San Franciscans are self-sufficient and can look after our own needs without outside interference. However, I have been in contact with the president and with the governor, and they both have assured me of all possible assistance.

"The water supply is at present free of the drug, and every precaution is being taken to prevent a recurrence of this crime against one million innocent people. However, I am told that some lingering contamination may remain in the pipes for a few hours. I recommend that you keep your consumption of water low until further notice, and that you boil any water you wish to use.

"Lastly, Police Chief Dennison, myself, and your other city officials will be devoting full time to the needs of the city so long as the crisis lasts. Probably we will not have the opportunity to go before the media for further reports. Therefore, I have taken the step of appointing a committee of public safety, consisting of distinguished laymen and scientists of San Francisco, as a coordinating body that will aid in governing the city and reporting to its citizens. The chairman of this committee is the well-known veteran of so many exploits in space, Commander Taylor Braskett. Announcements concerning the developments in the crisis will come from Commander Braskett for the remainder of the evening, and you may consider his words to be those of your city officials. Thank you."

Braskett came on the screen. Montini grunted. "Look at the man they find! A maniac patriot!"

"But the drug will wear off," Nadia said. "Your mind will be all right again."

"I know these drugs. There is no hope. I am destroyed." The Amazing Montini moved toward the door. "I need fresh air. I will go out. Good-bye, Nadia."

She tried to stop him. He pushed her aside. Entering Marina Park, he made his way to the yacht club; the doorman admitted him, and took no further notice. Montini walked out on the pier. The drug, they say, is temporary. It will wear off. My mind will clear. I doubt this very much. Montini peered at the dark, oily water, glistening with light reflected from the bridge. He explored his damaged mind, scanning for gaps. Whole sections of memory were gone. The walls had crumbled, slabs of plaster falling away to expose bare lath. He could not live this way. Carefully, grunting from the exertion, he lowered himself via a metal ladder into the water, and kicked himself away from the pier. The water was terribly cold. His shoes seemed immensely heavy. He floated toward the island of the old prison, but he doubted that he would remain afloat much longer. As he drifted, he ran through an inventory of his memory, seeing what remained to him and finding less than enough. To test whether even his gift had survived, he attempted to play back a recall of the mayor's speech, and found the words shifting and melting. It is just as well, then, he told himself, and drifted on, and went under.

Carole insisted on spending Thursday night with him.

"We aren't man and wife any more," he had to tell her. "You divorced me."

"Since when are you so conventional? We lived together before we were married, and now we can live together after we were married. Maybe we're inventing a new sin, Paul. Postmarital sex."

"That isn't the point. The point is that you came to hate me because of my financial mess, and you left me. If you try to come back to me now, you'll be going against your own rational and deliberate decision of last January."

"For me last January is still four months away," she said. "I don't hate you. I love you. I always have and always will. I can't imagine how I would ever have come to divorce you, but in any case I don't remember divorcing you, and you don't remember being divorced by me, and so why can't we just keep going from the point where our memories leave off?"

"Among other things, because you happen to be Pete Castine's wife now."

"That sounds completely unreal to me. Something you dreamed."

"Freddy Munson told me, though. It's true."

"If I went back to Pete now," Carole said, "I'd feel sinful. Simply because I supposedly married him, you want me to jump into bed with him? I don't want him. I want you. Can't I stay here?"

"If Pete—"

"If Pete, if Pete, if Pete! In my mind I'm Mrs. Paul Mueller, and in your mind I am too, and to hell with Pete, and with whatever Freddy Munson told you, and everything else. This is a silly argument, Paul. Let's quit it. If you want me to get out, tell me so right now in that many words. Otherwise let me stay."

He couldn't tell her to get out.

He had only the one small cot, but they managed to share

it. It was uncomfortable, but in an amusing way. He felt twenty years old again for a while. In the morning they took a long shower together, and then Carole went out to buy some things for breakfast, since his service had been cut off and he couldn't punch for food. A dunning robot outside the door told him, as Carole was leaving, "The decree of personal service due has been requested, Mr. Mueller, and is now pending a court hearing."

"I know you not," Mueller said. "Begone!"

Today, he told himself, he would hunt up Freddy Munson somehow and get that cash from him, and buy the tools he needed, and start working again. Let the world outside go crazy; so long as he was working, all was well. If he couldn't find Freddy, maybe he could swing the purchase on Carole's credit. She was legally divorced from him and none of his credit taint would stain her; as Mrs. Peter Castine she should surely be able to get hold of a couple of bigs to pay Metchnikoff. Possibly the banks were closed on account of the memory crisis today, Mueller considered; but Metchnikoff surely wouldn't demand cash from Carole. He closed his eyes and imagined how good it would feel to be making things once more.

Carole was gone an hour. When she came back, carrying groceries, Pete Castine was with her.

"He followed me," Carole explained. "He wouldn't let me alone."

He was a slim, poised, controlled man, quite athletic, several years older than Mueller—perhaps into his fifties already—but seemingly very young. Calmly he said, "I was sure that Carole had come here. It's perfectly understandable, Paul. She was here all night, I hope?"

"Does it matter?" Mueller asked.

"To some extent. I'd rather have had her spending the night with her former husband than with some third party entirely."

"She was here all night, yes," Mueller said wearily.

"I'd like her to come home with me now. She *is* my wife, after all."

"She has no recollection of that. Neither do I."

"I'm aware of that." Castine nodded amiably. "In my own case, I've forgotten everything that happened to me before the age of twenty-two. I couldn't tell you my father's first name.

However, as a matter of objective reality, Carole's my wife, and her parting from you was rather bitter, and I feel she shouldn't stay here any longer."

"Why are you telling all this to me?" Mueller asked. "If you want your wife to go home with you, ask her to go home with you."

"So I did. She says she won't leave unless you direct her to go."

"That's right," Carole said. "I know whose wife I *think* I am. If Paul throws me out I'll go with you. Not otherwise."

Mueller shrugged. "I'd be a fool to throw her out, Pete. I need her and I want her, and whatever breakup she and I had isn't real to us. I know it's tough on you, but I can't help that. I imagine you'll have no trouble getting an annulment once the courts work out some law to cover cases like this."

Castine was silent for a long moment.

At length he said, "How has your work been going, Paul?"

"I gather that I haven't turned out a thing all year."

"That's correct."

"I'm planning to start again. You might say that Carole has inspired me."

"Splendid," said Castine without intonation of any kind. "I trust this little mixup over our—ah—shared wife won't interfere with the harmonious artist-dealer relationship we used to enjoy?"

"Not at all," Mueller said. "You'll still get my whole output. Why the hell should I resent anything you did? Carole was a free agent when you married her. There's only one little trouble."

"Yes?"

"I'm broke. I have no tools, and I can't work without tools, and I have no way of buying tools."

"How much do you need?"

"Two and a half bigs."

Castine said, "Where's your data pickup? I'll make a credit transfer."

"The phone company disconnected it a long time ago."

"Let me give you a check, then. Say, three thousand even? An advance against future sales." Castine fumbled for a while before locating a blank check. "First one of these I've written in five years, maybe. Odd how you get accustomed to spending by telephone. Here you are, and good luck. To both of you." He made a courtly, bitter bow. "I hope you'll be happy together. And call me up when you've finished a few pieces, Paul. I'll send the van. I suppose you'll have a phone again by then." He went out.

"There's a blessing in being able to forget," Nate Haldersen said. "The redemption of oblivion, I call it. What's happened to San Francisco this week isn't necessarily a disaster. For some of us, it's the finest thing in the world."

They were listening to him—at least fifty people, clustering near his feet. He stood on the stage of the bandstand in the park, just across from the De Young Museum. Shadows were gathering. Friday, the second full day of the memory crisis, was ending. Haldersen had slept in the park last night, and he planned to sleep there again tonight; he realized after his escape from the hospital that his apartment had been shut down long ago and his possessions were in storage. It did not matter. He would live off the land and forage for food. The flame of prophecy was aglow in him.

"Let me tell you how it was with me," he cried. "Three days ago I was in a hospital for mental illness. Some of you are smiling, perhaps, telling me I ought to be back there now, but no! You don't understand. I was incapable of facing the world. Wherever I went, I saw happy families, parents and children, and it made me sick with envy and hatred, so that I couldn't function in society. Why? Why? Because my own wife and children were killed in an air disaster in 1991, that's why, and I missed the plane because I was committing sin that day, and for my sin they died, and I lived thereafter in unending torment! But now all that is flushed from my mind. I have sinned, and I have suffered, and now I am redeemed through merciful oblivion!"

A voice in the crowd called, "If you've forgotten all about it, how come you're telling the story to us?"

"A good question! An excellent question!" Haldersen felt sweat bursting from his pores, adrenaline pumping in his veins. "I know the story only because a machine in the hospital told it to me, yesterday morning. But it came to me from the outside, a secondhand tale. The experience of it within me, the scars, all that has been washed away. The pain of it is gone. Oh, yes, I'm sad that my innocent family perished, but a healthy man learns to control his grief after eleven years, he accepts his loss and goes on. I was sick, sick right *here*, and I couldn't live with my grief, but now I can, I look on it objectively, do you see! And that's why I say there's a blessing in being able to forget. What about you, out there? There must be some of you who suffered painful losses too, and now can no longer remember them, now have been redeemed and released from anguish. Are there any? Are there? Raise your hands. Who's been bathed in holy oblivion? Who out there knows that he's been cleansed, even if he can't remember what it is he's been cleansed from?"

Hands were starting to go up.

Freddy Munson had spent Thursday afternoon, Thursday night, and all of Friday holed up in his apartment with every communication link to the outside turned off. He neither took nor made calls, ignored the telescreens, and had switched on the xerofax only three times in the thirty-six hours.

He knew that he was finished, and he was trying to decide how to react to it.

His memory situation seemed to have stabilized. He was still missing only five weeks of market maneuvers. There wasn't any further decay—not that that mattered; he was in trouble enough—and, despite an optimistic statement last night by Mayor Chase, Munson hadn't seen any evidence that memory loss was reversing itself. He was unable to reconstruct any of the vanished details.

There was no immediate peril, he knew. Most of the clients whose accounts he'd been juggling were wealthy old bats who wouldn't worry about their stocks until they got next month's account statements. They had given him discretionary powers, which was how he had been able to tap their resources for his own benefit in the first place. Up to now, Munson had always been able to complete each transaction within a single month, so the account balanced for every statement. He had dealt with the problem of the securities withdrawals that the statements ought to show by gimmicking the house computer to delete all such withdrawals provided there was no net effect from month to month; that way he could borrow 10,000 shares of United Spaceways or Comsat or IBM for two weeks, use the stock as collateral for a deal of his own, and get it back into the proper account in time with no one the wiser. Three weeks from now, though, the end-of-the-month statements were going to go out showing all of his accounts peppered by inexplicable withdrawals, and he was going to catch hell.

The trouble might even start earlier, and come from a different direction. Since the San Francisco trouble had begun, the market had gone down sharply, and he would probably be getting margin calls on Monday. The San Francisco exchange was closed, of course; it hadn't been able to open Thursday morning because so many of the brokers had been hit hard by amnesia. But New York's exchanges were open, and they had reacted badly to the news from San Francisco, probably out of fear that a conspiracy was afoot and the whole country might soon be pushed into chaos. When the local exchange opened again on Monday, if it opened, it would most likely open at the last New York prices, or near them, and keep on going down. Munson would be asked to put up cash or additional securities to cover his loans. He certainly didn't have the cash, and the only way he could get additional securities would be to dip into still more of his accounts, compounding his offense; on the other hand, if he didn't meet the margin calls they'd sell him out and he'd never be able to restore the stock to the proper accounts, even if he succeeded in remembering which shares went where.

He was trapped. He could stick around for a few weeks, waiting for the ax to fall, or he could get out right now. He preferred to get out right now.

And go where?

Caracas? Reno? Sao Paulo? No, debtor sanctuaries wouldn't do him any good, because he wasn't an ordinary debtor. He was a thief, and the sanctuaries didn't protect criminals, only bankrupts. He had to go farther, all the way to Luna Dome. There wasn't any extradition from the moon. There'd be no hope of coming back, either.

Munson got on the phone, hoping to reach his travel agent. Two tickets to Luna, please. One for him, one for Helene; if she didn't feel like coming, he'd go alone. No, not round trip. But the agent didn't answer. Munson tried the number several times. Shrugging, he decided to order direct, and called United Spaceways next. He got a busy signal. "Shall we wait-list your call?" the data net asked. "It will be three days, at the present state of the backlog of calls, before we can put it through."

"Forget it," Munson said.

He had just realized that San Francisco was closed off, anyway. Unless he tried to swim for it, he couldn't get out of the city to go to the spaceport, even if he did manage to buy tickets to Luna. He was caught here until they opened the transit routes again. How long would that be? Monday, Tuesday, next Friday? They couldn't keep the city shut forever—could they?

What it came down to, Munson saw, was a contest of probabilities. Would someone discover the discrepancies in his accounts before he found a way of escaping to Luna, or would his escape access become available too late? Put in those terms, it became an interesting gamble instead of a panic situation. He would spend the weekend trying to find a way out of San Francisco, and if he failed, he would try to be a stoic about facing what was to come.

Calm, now, he remembered that he had promised to lend Paul Mueller a few thousand dollars, to help him equip his studio again. Munson was unhappy over having let that slip his mind. He liked to be helpful. And, even now, what were two or three bigs to him? He had plenty of recoverable assets. Might as well let Paul have a little of the money before the lawyers start grabbing it.

One problem. He had less than a hundred in cash on him—who bothered carrying cash?—and he couldn't telephone a transfer of funds to Mueller's account, because Paul didn't have an account with a data net any more, or even a phone. There wasn't any place to get that much cash, either, at this hour of evening, especially with the city paralyzed. And the weekend was coming. Munson had an idea, though. What if he went shopping with Mueller tomorrow, and simply charged whatever the sculptor needed to his own account? Fine. He reached for the phone to arrange the date, remembered that Mueller could not be called, and decided to tell Paul about it in person. Now. He could use some fresh air, anyway.

He half expected to find robot bailiffs outside, waiting to arrest him. But of course no one was after him yet. He walked to the garage. It was a fine night, cool, starry, with perhaps just a hint of fog in the west. Berkeley's lights glittered through the haze. The streets were quiet. In time of crisis people stay home. He drove quickly to Mueller's place. Four robots were in front of it. Munson eyed them edgily, with the wary look of the man who knows that the sheriff will be after him too, in a little while. But Mueller, when he came to the door, took no notice of the dunners.

Munson said, "I'm sorry I missed connections with you. The money I promised to lend you—"

"It's all right, Freddy. Pete Castine was here this morning and I borrowed the three bigs from him. I've got my studio set up again. Come in and look?"

Munson entered. "Pete Castine?"

"A good investment for him. He makes money if he has work of mine to sell, right? It's in his best interest to help me get started again. Carole and I have been hooking things up all day."

"Carole?" Munson said. Mueller showed him into the studio. The paraphernalia of a sonic sculptor sat on the floor—a welding pen, a vacuum bell, a big texturing vat, some ingots and strands of wire, and such things. Carole was feeding discarded packing cases into the wall disposal unit. Looking up, she smiled uncertainly and ran her hand through her long dark hair.

"Hello, Freddy."

"Everybody good friends again?" he asked, baffled.

"Nobody remembers being enemies," she said. She laughed. "Isn't it wonderful to have your memory blotted out like this?"

"Wonderful," Munson said bleakly.

Commander Braskett said, "Can I offer you people any water?"

Tim Bryce smiled. Lisa Bryce smiled. Ted Kamakura smiled. Even Mayor Chase, that poor empty husk, smiled. Commander Braskett understood those smiles. Even now, after three days of close contact under pressure, they thought he was nuts.

He had had a week's supply of bottled water brought from his home to the command post here at the hospital. Everybody kept telling him that the municipal water was safe to drink now, that the memory drugs were gone from it; but why couldn't they comprehend that his aversion to public water dated back to an era when memory drugs were unknown? There were plenty of other chemicals in the reservoir, after all.

He hoisted his glass in a jaunty toast and winked at them.

Tim Bryce said, "Commander, we'd like you to address the city again at half past ten this morning. Here's your text."

Braskett scanned the sheet. It dealt mostly with the relaxation of the order to boil water before drinking it. "You want me to go on all media," he said, "and tell the people of San Francisco that it's safe for them to drink from the taps, eh? That's a bit awkward for me. Even a figurehead spokesman is entitled to some degree of personal integrity."

Bryce looked briefly puzzled. Then he laughed and took the text back. "You're absolutely right, commander. I can't ask you to make this announcement, in view of—ah—your particular beliefs. Let's change the plan. You open the spot by introducing me, and *I'll* discuss the no-boiling thing. Will that be all right?"

Commander Braskett appreciated the tactful way they deferred to his special obsession. "I'm at your service, doctor," he said gravely.

Bryce finished speaking and the camera lights left him. He said to Lisa, "What about lunch? Or breakfast, or whatever meal it is we're up to now."

"Everything's ready, Tim. Whenever you are."

They ate together in the holograph room, which had become the kitchen of the command post. Massive cameras and tanks of etching fluid surrounded them. The others thoughtfully left them alone. These brief shared meals were the only fragments of privacy he and Lisa had had, in the fifty-two hours since he had awakened to find her sleeping beside him.

He stared across the table in wonder at this delectable blonde girl who they said was his wife. How beautiful her soft brown eyes were against that backdrop of golden hair! How perfect the line of her lips, the curve of her earlobes! Bryce knew that no one would object if he and Lisa went off and locked themselves into one of the private rooms for a few hours. He wasn't that indispensable; and there was so much he had to begin relearning about his wife. But he was unable to leave his post. He hadn't been out of the hospital or even off this floor for the duration of the crisis; he kept himself going by grabbing the sleep wire for half an hour every six hours. Perhaps it was an illusion born of too little sleep and too much data, but he had come to believe that the survival of the city depended on him. He had spent his career trying to heal individual sick minds; now he had a whole city to tend to.

"Tired?" Lisa asked.

"I'm in the tiredness beyond feeling tired. My mind is so clear that my skull wouldn't cast a shadow. I'm nearing nirvana."

"The worst is over, I think. The city's settling down."

"It's still bad, though. Have you seen the suicide figures?"

"Bad?"

"Hideous. The norm in San Francisco is 220 a year. We've had close to five hundred in the last two and a half days. And that's just the reported cases, the bodies discovered, and so on. Probably we can double the figure. Thirty suicides reported Wednesday night, about two hundred on Thursday, the same on Friday, and about fifty so far this morning. At least it seems as if the wave is past its peak."

"But *why*, Tim?"

"Some people react poorly to loss. Especially the loss of a segment of their memories. They're indignant—they're crushed—they're scared—and they reach for the exit pill. Suicide's too easy now, anyway. In the old days you reacted to frustration by smashing the crockery; now you go a deadlier route. Of course, there are special cases. A man named Montini they fished out of the bay—a professional mnemonist, who did a trick act in nightclubs, total recall. I can hardly blame him for caving in. And I suppose there were a lot of others who kept their business in their heads—gamblers, stock-market operators, oral poets, musicians—who might decide to end it all rather than try to pick up the pieces."

"But if the effects of the drug wear off—"

"Do they?" Bryce asked.

"You said so yourself."

"I was making optimistic noises for the benefit of the citizens. We don't have any experimental history for these drugs and human subjects. Hell, Lisa, we don't even know the dosage that was administered; by the time we were able to get water samples most of the system had been flushed clean, and the automatic monitoring devices at the city pumping station were rigged as part of the conspiracy so they didn't show a thing out of the ordinary. I've got no idea at all if there's going to be any measurable memory recovery."

"But there is, Tim. I've already started to get some things back."

"*What?*"

"Don't scream at me like that! You scared me."

He clung to the edge of the table. "Are you really recovering?"

"Around the edges. I remember a few things already. About us."

"Like what?"

"Applying for the marriage license. I'm standing stark naked inside a diagnostat machine and a voice on the loudspeaker is telling me to look straight into the scanners. And I remember the ceremony, a little. Just a small group of friends, a civil ceremony. Then we took the pod to Acapulco."

He stared grimly. "When did this start to come back?"

"About seven this morning, I guess."

"Is there more?"

"A bit. Our honeymoon. The robot bellhop who came blundering in on our wedding night. You don't—"

"Remember it? No. No. Nothing. Blank."

"That's all I remember, this early stuff."

"Yes, of course," he said. "The older memories are always the first to return in any form of amnesia. The last stuff in is the first to go." His hands were shaking, not entirely from fatigue. A strange desolation crept over him. Lisa remembered. He did not. Was it a function of her youth, or of the chemistry of her brain, or—?

He could not bear the thought that they no longer shared an oblivion. He didn't want the amnesia to become one-sided for them; it was humiliating not to remember his own marriage when she did. You're being irrational, he told himself. Physician, heal thyself!

"Let's go back inside," he said.

"You haven't finished your—"

"Later."

He went into the command room. Kamakura had phones in both hands and was barking data into a recorder. The screens were alive with morning scenes, Saturday in the city, crowds in Union Square. Kamakura hung up both calls and said, "I've got an interesting report from Dr. Klein at Letterman General. He says they're getting the first traces of memory recovery this morning. Women under thirty, only."

"Lisa says she's beginning to remember too," Bryce said.

"Women under thirty," said Kamakura. "Yes. Also the suicide rate is definitely tapering. We may be starting to come out of it."

"Terrific," Bryce said hollowly.

Haldersen was living in a ten-foot-high bubble that one of his disciples had blown for him in the middle of Golden Gate Park, just west of the Arboretum. Fifteen similar bubbles had gone up around his, giving the region the look of an up-to-date Eskimo village in plastic igloos. The occupants of the camp, aside from Haldersen, were men and women who had so little memory left that they did not know who they were or where they lived. He had acquired a dozen of these lost ones on Friday, and by late afternoon on Saturday he had been joined by some forty more. The news somehow was moving through the city that those without moorings were welcome to take up temporary residence with the group in the park. It had happened that way during the 1906 disaster, too.

The police had been around a few times to check on them. The first time, a portly lieutenant had tried to persuade the whole group to move to Fletcher Memorial. "That's where most of the victims are getting treatment, you see. The doctors give them something, and then we try to identify them and find their next of kin—"

"Perhaps it's best for these people to remain away from their next of kin for a while," Haldersen suggested. "Some meditation in the park—and exploration of the pleasures of having forgotten—that's all we're doing here." He would not go to Fletcher Memorial himself except under duress. As for the others, he felt he could do more for them in the park than anyone in the hospital could.

The second time the police came, Saturday afternoon when his group was much larger, they brought a mobile communications system. "Dr. Bryce of Fletcher Memorial wants to talk to you," a different lieutenant said.

Haldersen watched the screen come alive. "Hello, doctor. Worried about me?"

"I'm worried about everyone, Nate. What the hell are you doing in the park?"

"Founding a new religion, I think."

"You're a sick man. You ought to come back here."

"No, doctor. I'm not sick any more. I've had my therapy and I'm fine. It was a beautiful treatment: selective obliteration, just as I prayed for. The entire trauma is gone."

Bryce appeared fascinated by that; his frowning expression of official responsibility vanished a moment, giving place to a look of professional concern. "Interesting," he said. "We've got people who've forgotten only nouns, and people who've forgotten who they married, and people who've forgotten how to play the violin. But you're the first one who's forgotten a trauma. You still ought to come back here, though. You aren't the best judge of your fitness to face the outside environment."

"Oh, but I am," Haldersen said. "I'm doing fine. And my people need me."

"Your people?"

"Waifs. Strays. The total wipeouts."

"We want those people in the hospital, Nate. We want to get them back to their families."

"Is that necessarily a good deed? Maybe some of them can use a spell of isolation from their families. These people look happy, Dr. Bryce. I've heard there are a lot of suicides, but not here. We're practicing mutual supportive therapy. Looking for the joys to be found in oblivion. It seems to work."

Bryce stared silently out of the screen for a long moment. Then he said impatiently, "All right, have it your own way for now. But I wish you'd stop coming on like Jesus and Freud combined, and leave the park. You're still a sick man, Nate, and the people with you are in serious trouble. I'll talk to you later."

The contact broke. The police, stymied, left.

Haldersen spoke briefly to his people at five o'clock. Then he sent them out as missionaries to collect other victims. "Save as many as you can," he said. "Find those who are in complete despair and get them into the park before they can take their own lives. Explain that the loss of one's past is not the loss of all things."

The disciples went forth. And came back leading those less fortunate than themselves. The group grew to more than one hundred by nightfall. Someone found the extruder again and blew twenty more bubbles as shelters for the night. Haldersen preached his sermon of joy, looking out at the blank eyes, the slack faces of those whose identities had washed away on Wednesday. "Why give up?" he asked them. "Now is

your chance to create new lives for yourself. The slate is clean!
Chose the direction you will take, define your new selves
through the exercise of free will—you are reborn in holy
oblivion, all of you. Rest, now, those who have just come to us.
And you others, go forth again, seek out the wanderers, the
drifters, the lost ones hiding in the corners of the city—"

As he finished, he saw a knot of people bustling toward
him from the direction of the South Drive. Fearing trouble,
Haldersen went out to meet them; but as he drew close he saw
half a dozen disciples, clutching a scruffy, unshaven, terrified
little man. They hurled him at Haldersen's feet. The man
quivered. His eyes glistened; his wedge of a face, sharp-
chinned, sharp of cheekbones, was pale.

"It's the one who poisoned the water supply!" someone
called. "We found him in a rooming house on Judah Street.
With a stack of drugs in his room, and the plans of the water
system, and a bunch of computer programs. He admits it. He
admits it!"

Haldersen looked down. "Is this true?" he asked. "Are
you the one?"

The man nodded.

"What's your name?"

"Won't say. Want a lawyer."

"Kill him now!" a woman shrieked. "Pull his arms and legs
off!"

"Kill him!" came an answering cry from the other side of
the group. "Kill him!"

The congregation, Haldersen realized, might easily turn
into a mob.

He said, "Tell me your name, and I'll protect you.
Otherwise I can't be responsible."

"Skinner," the man muttered miserably.

"Skinner. And you contaminated the water supply."

Another nod.

"Why?"

"To get even."

"With whom?"

"Everyone. Everybody."

Classic paranoid. Haldersen felt pity. Not the others; they
were calling out for blood.

A tall man bellowed, "Make the bastard drink his own
drug!"

"No, kill him! Squash him!"

The voices became more menacing. The angry faces came closer.

"Listen to me," Haldersen called, and his voice cut through the murmurings. "There'll be no killing here tonight."

"What are you going to do, give him to the police?"

"No," said Haldersen. "We'll hold communion together. We'll teach this pitiful man the blessings of oblivion, and then we'll share new joys ourselves. We are human beings. We have the capacity to forgive even the worst of sinners. Where are the memory drugs? Did someone say you had found the memory drugs? Here. Here. Pass it up here. Yes. Brothers, sisters, let us show this dark and twisted soul the nature of redemption. Yes. Yes. Fetch some water, please. Thank you. Here, Skinner. Stand him up, will you? Hold his arms. Keep him from falling down. Wait a second, until I find the proper dose. Yes. Yes. Here, Skinner. Forgiveness. Sweet oblivion."

It was so good to be working again that Mueller didn't want to stop. By early afternoon on Saturday his studio was ready; he had long since worked out the sketches of the first piece; now it was just a matter of time and effort, and he'd have something to show Pete Castine. He worked on far into the evening, setting up his armature and running a few tests of the sound sequences that he proposed to build into the piece. He had some interesting new ideas about the sonic triggers, the devices that would set off the sound effects when the appreciator came within range. Carole had to tell him, finally, that dinner was ready. "I didn't want to interrupt you," she said, "but it looks like I have to, or you won't ever stop."

"Sorry. The creative ecstasy."

"Save some of that energy. There are other ecstasies. The ecstasy of dinner, first."

She had cooked everything herself. Beautiful. He went back to work again afterward, but at half past one in the morning Carole interrupted him. He was willing to stop, now. He had done an honest day's work, and he was sweaty with the noble sweat of a job well done. Two minutes under the molecular cleanser and the sweat was gone, but the good ache of virtuous fatigue remained. He hadn't felt this way in years.

He woke to Sunday thoughts of unpaid debts.

"The robots are still there," he said. "They won't go away, will they? Even though the whole city's at a standstill, nobody's told the robots to quit."

"Ignore them," Carole said.

"That's what I've been doing. But I can't ignore the debts. Untimately there'll be a reckoning."

"You're working again, though! You'll have an income coming in."

"Do you know what I owe?" he asked. "Almost a million. If I produced one piece a week for a year, and sold each piece for twenty bigs, I might pay everything off. But I can't work that fast, and the market can't possibly absorb that many Muellers, and Pete certainly can't buy them all for future sale."

He noticed the way Carole's face darkened at the mention of Pete Castine.

He said, "You know what I'll have to do? Go to Caracas, like I was planning before this memory thing started. I can work there, and ship my stuff to Pete. And maybe in two or three years I'll have paid off my debt, a hundred cents on the dollar, and I can start fresh back here. Do you know if that's possible? I mean, if you jump to a debtor sanctuary, are you blackballed for credit forever, even if you pay off what you owe?"

"I don't know," Carole said distantly.

"I'll find that out later. The important thing is that I'm working again, and I've got to go someplace where I can work without being hounded. And then I'll pay everybody off. You'll come with me to Caracas, won't you?"

"Maybe we won't have to go," Carole said.

"But how—"

"You should be working now, shouldn't you?"

He worked, and while he worked he made lists of creditors in his mind, dreaming of the day when every name on every list was crossed off. When he got hungry he emerged from the studio and found Carole sitting gloomily in the living room. Her eyes were red and puffy-lidded.

"What's wrong?" he asked. "You don't want to go to Caracas?"

"Please, Paul—let's not talk about it—"

"I've really got no alternative. I mean, unless we pick one of the other sanctuaries. Sao Paulo? Spalato?"

"It isn't that, Paul."

"What, then?"

"I'm starting to remember again."

The air went out of him. "Oh," he said.

"I remember November, December, January. The crazy things you were doing, the loans, the financial juggling. And the quarrels we had. They were terrible quarrels."

"Oh."

"The divorce. I remember, Paul. It started coming back last night, but you were so happy I didn't want to say anything. And this morning it's much clearer. You still don't remember any of it?"

"Not a thing past last October."

"I do," she said, shakily. "You hit me, do you know that? You cut my lip. You slammed me against the wall, right over there, and then you threw the Chinese vase at me and it broke."

"Oh. Oh."

She went on, "I remember how good Pete was to me, too. I think I can almost remember marrying him, being his wife. Paul, I'm scared. I feel everything fitting into place in my mind, and it's as scary as if my mind was breaking into pieces. It was so good, Paul, these last few days. It was like being a newlywed with you again. But now all the sour parts are coming back, the hate, the ugliness, it's all alive for me again. And I feel so bad about Pete. The two of us, Friday, shutting him out. He was a real gentleman about it. But the fact is that he saved me when I was going under, and I owe him something for that."

"What do you plan to do?" he asked quietly.

"I think I ought to go back to him. I'm his wife. I've got no right to stay here."

"But I'm not the same man you came to hate," Mueller protested. "I'm the old Paul; the one from last year and before. The man you loved. All the hateful stuff is gone from me."

"Not from me, though. Not now."

The were both silent.

"I think I should go back, Paul."

"Whatever you say."

"I think I should. I wish you all kinds of luck, but I can't stay here. Will it hurt your work if I leave again?"

"I won't know until you do."

She told him three or four times that she felt she ought to go back to Castine, and then, politely, he suggested that she should go back right now, if that was how she felt, and she did. He spent half an hour wandering around the apartment, which seemed so awfully empty again. He nearly invited one of the dunning robots in for company. Instead, he went back to work. To his surprise, he worked quite well, and in an hour he had ceased thinking about Carole entirely.

Sunday afternoon, Freddy Munson set up a credit transfer and managed to get most of his liquid assets fed into an old account he kept at the Bank of Luna. Toward evening, he went down to the wharf and boarded a three-man hovercraft owned by a fisherman willing to take his chances with the law. They slipped out into the bay without running lights and crossed the bay on a big diagonal, landing some time later a few miles north of Berkeley. Munson found a cab to take him to the Oakland airport, and caught the midnight shuttle to L.A., where, after a lot of fancy talking, he was able to buy his way aboard the next Luna-bound rocket, lifting off at ten o'clock Monday morning. He spent the night in the spaceport terminal. He had taken with him nothing except the clothes he wore; his fine possessions, his paintings, his suits, his Mueller sculptures, and all the rest remained in his apartment, and ultimately would be sold to satisfy the judgements against him. Too bad. He knew that he wouldn't be coming back to Earth again, either, not with a larceny warrant or worse awaiting him. Also too bad. It had been so nice for so long, here, and who needed a memory drug in the water supply? Munson had only one consolation. It was an article of his philosophy that sooner or later, no matter how neatly you organized your life, fate opened a trapdoor underneath your feet and catapulted you into something unknown and unpleasant. Now he knew that it was true even for him.

Too, too bad. He wondered what his chances were of starting over up there. Did they need stockbrokers on the moon?

Addressing the citizenry on Monday night, Commander Braskett said, "The committee of public safety is pleased to report that we have come through the worst part of the crisis. As many of you have already discovered, memories are beginning to return. The process of recovery will be more swift for some than others, but great progress has been made. Effective at six A.M. tomorrow, access routes to and from San Francisco will reopen. There will be normal mail services and many businesses will return to normal. Fellow citizens, we have demonstrated once again the real fiber of the American spirit. The founding fathers must be smiling down upon us today! How superbly we avoided chaos, and how beautifully we pulled together to help one another in what could have been an hour of turmoil and despair!

"Dr. Bryce requests me to remind you that anyone still suffering severe impairment of memory—especially those experiencing loss of identity, confusion of vital functions, or other disability—should report to the emergency ward at Fletcher Memorial Hospital. Treatment is available there, and computer analysis is at the service of those unable to find their homes and loved ones. I repeat—"

Tim Bryce wished that the good commander hadn't slipped in that plug for the real fiber of the American spirit, especially in view of the necessity to invite the remaining victims to the hospital with his next words. But it would be uncharitable to object. The old spaceman had done a beautiful job all weekend as the Voice of the Crisis, and some patriotic embellishments now were harmless.

The crisis, of course, was nowhere near as close to being over as Commander Braskett's speech had suggested, but public confidence had to be buoyed.

Bryce had the latest figures. Suicides now totaled nine hundred since the start of trouble on Wednesday; Sunday had been an unexpectedly bad day. At least forty thousand people were still unaccounted for, although they were tracing one thousand an hour and getting them back to their families or else into an intensive-care section. Probably seven hundred and fifty thousand more continued to have memory difficulties. Most children had fully recovered, and many of the women were mending; but older people, and men in general, had experienced scarcely any memory recapture. Even those who were nearly healed had no recall of events of Tuesday and Wednesday, and probably never would; for large numbers of people, though, big blocks of the past would have to be learned from the outside, like history lessons.

Lisa was teaching him their marriage that way.

The trips they had taken—the good times, the bad—the parties, the friends, the shared dreams—she described everything as vividly as she could, and he fastened on each anecdote, trying to make it a part of himself again. He knew it was hopeless, really. He'd know the outlines, never the substance. Yet it was probably the best he could hope for.

He was so horribly tired, suddenly.

He said to Kamakura, "Is there anything new from the park yet? That rumor that Haldersen's actually got a supply of the drug?"

"Seems to be true, Tim. The word is that he and his friends caught the character who spiked the water supply, and relieved him of a roomful of various amnesifacients."

"We've got to seize them," Bryce said.

Kamakura shook his head. "Not just yet. Police are afraid of any actions in the park. They say it's a volatile situation."

"But if those drugs are loose—"

"Let me worry about it, Tim. Look, why don't you and Lisa go home for a while? You've been here without a break since Thursday."

"So have—"

"No. Everybody else has had a breather. Go on, now. We're over the worst. Relax, get some real sleep, make some love. Get to know that gorgeous wife of yours again a little."

Bryce reddened. "I'd rather stay here until I feel I can afford to leave."

Scowling, Kamakura walked away from him to confer with Commander Braskett. Bryce scanned the screens, trying to figure out what was going on in the park. A moment later, Braskett walked over to him.

"Dr. Bryce?"

"What?"

"You're relieved of duty until sundown Tuesday."

"Wait a second—"

"That's an order, doctor. I'm chairman of the committee of public safety, and I'm telling you to get yourself out of this hospital. You aren't going to disobey an order, are you?"

"Listen, commander—"

"Out. No mutiny, Bryce. Out! Orders."

Bryce tried to protest, but he was too weary to put up much of a fight. By noon, he was on his way home, soupy-headed with fatigue. Lisa drove. He sat quite still, struggling to remember details of marriage. Nothing came.

She put him to bed. He wasn't sure how long he slept; but then he felt her against him; warm, satin-smooth.

"Hello," she said. "Remember me?"

"Yes," he lied gratefully. "Oh, yes, yes, yes!"

Working right through the night, Mueller finished his armature by dawn on Monday. He slept awhile, and in early afternoon began to paint the inner strips of loudspeakers on: a thousand speakers to the inch, no more than a few molecules thick, from which the sounds of his sculpture would issue in resonant fullness. When that was done, he paused to contemplate the needs of his sculpture's superstructure, and by seven that night was ready to move to the next phase. The demons of creativity possessed him; he saw no reason to eat and scarcely any to sleep.

At eight, just as he was getting up momentum for the long night's work, he heard a knock at the door. Carole's signal. He had disconnected the doorbell, and robots didn't have the sense to knock. Uneasily, he went to the door. She was there.

"So?" he said.

"So I came back. So it starts all over."

"What's going on?"

"Can I come in?" she asked.

"I suppose. I'm working, but come in."

She said, "I talked it over with Pete. We both decided I ought to go back to you."

"You aren't much for consistency, are you?"

"I have to take things as they happen. When I lost my memory, I came to you. When I remembered things again, I felt I ought to leave. I didn't *want* to leave. I felt I *ought* to leave. There's a difference."

"Really," he said.

"Really. I went to Pete, but I didn't want to be with him. I wanted to be here."

"I hit you and made your lip bleed. I threw the Ming vase at you."

"It wasn't Ming, it was K'ang-hsi."

"Pardon me. My memory still isn't so good. Anyway, I did terrible things to you, and you hated me enough to want a divorce. So why come back?"

"You were right, yesterday. You aren't the man I came to hate. You're the old Paul."

"And if my memory of the past nine months returns?"

"Even so," she said. "People change. You've been through hell and come out the other side. You're working again. You aren't sullen and nasty and confused. We'll go to Caracas, or wherever you want, and you'll do your work and pay your debts, just as you said yesterday."

"And Pete?"

"He'll arrange an annulment. He's being swell about it."

"Good old Pete," Mueller said. He shook his head. "How long will this neat happy ending last, Carole? If you think there's a chance you'll be bouncing back in the other direction by Wednesday, say so now. I'd rather not get involved again, in that case."

"No chance. None."

"Unless I throw the Chi'ien-lung vase at you."

"K'ang-hsi," she said.

"Yes. K'ang-hsi." He managed to grin. Suddenly he felt the accumulated fatigue of these days register all at once. "I've been working too hard," he said. "An orgy of creativity to make up for lost time. Let's go for a walk."

"Fine," she said.

They went out, just as a dunning robot was arriving. "Top of the evening to you, sir," Mueller said.

"Mr. Mueller, I represent the accounts receivable department of Acme Brass and—"

"See my attorney," he said.

Fog was rolling in off the sea now. There were no stars. The downtown lights were invisible. He and Carole walked west, toward the park. He felt strangely light-headed, not entirely from lack of sleep. Reality and dream had merged; these were unusual days. They entered the park from the Panhandle and strolled toward the museum area, arm in arm, saying nothing much to one another. As they passed the conservatory Mueller became aware of a crowd up ahead, thousands of people staring in the direction of the music shell. "What do you think is going on?" Carole asked. Mueller shrugged. They edged through the crowd.

Ten minutes later they were close enough to see the stage. A tall, thin, wild-looking man with unruly yellow hair was on the stage. Beside him was a small, scrawny man in ragged clothing, and there were a dozen others flanking them, carrying ceramic bowls.

"What's happening?" Mueller asked someone in the crowd.

"Religious ceremony."

"Eh?"

"New religion. Church of Oblivion. That's the head prophet up there. You haven't heard about it yet?"

"Not a thing."

"Started around Friday. You see that ratty-looking character next to the prophet?"

"Yes."

"He's the one that put the stuff in the water supply. He confessed and they made him drink his own drug. Now he doesn't remember a thing, and he's the assistant prophet. Craziest damn stuff!"

"And what are they doing up there?"

"They've got the drug in those bowls. They drink and forget some more. They drink and forget some more."

The gathering fog absorbed the sounds of those on the stage. Mueller strained to listen. He saw the bright eyes of fanaticism; the alleged contaminator of the water looked positively radiant. Words drifted out into the night.

"Brothers and sisters . . . the joy, the sweetness of forgetting . . . come up here with us, take communion with us . . . oblivion . . . redemption . . . even for the most wicked . . . forget . . . forget . . ."

They were passing the bowls around on stage, drinking, smiling. People were going up to receive the communion, taking a bowl, sipping, nodding happily. Toward the rear of the stage the bowls were being refilled by three sober-looking functionaries.

Mueller felt a chill. He suspected that what had been born in this park during this week would endure, somehow, long after the crisis of San Francisco had become part of history; and it seemed to him that something new and frightening had been loosed upon the land.

"Take . . . drink . . . forget . . ." the prophet cried.

And the worshippers cried, "*Take . . . drink . . . forget . . .*"

The bowls were passed.

"What's it all *about*?" Carole whispered.

"Take . . . drink . . . forget . . ."
"Take . . . drink . . . forget . . ."
"Blessed is the sweet oblivion."
"Blessed is the sweet oblivion."
"Sweet it is to lay down the burden of one's soul."
"Sweet it is to lay down the burden of one's soul."
"Joyous it is to begin anew."
"Joyous it is to begin anew."

The fog was deepening. Mueller could barely see the aquarium building just across the way. He clasped his hand tightly around Carole's and began to think about getting out of the park.

He had to admit, though, that these people might have hit on something true. Was he not better off for having taken a chemical into his bloodstream, and thereby shedding a portion of his past? Yes, of course. And yet—to mutilate one's mind this way, deliberately, happily, to drink deep of oblivion—

"Blessed are those who are able to forget," the prophet said.

"Blessed are those who are able to forget," the crowd roared in response.

"Blessed are those who are able to forget," Mueller heard his own voice cry. And he began to tremble. And he felt sudden fear: he sensed the power of this strange new movement, the gathering strength of the prophet's appeal to unreason. It was time for a new religion, maybe, a cult that offered emancipation from all inner burdens. They would synthesize this drug and turn it out by the ton, Mueller thought, and repeatedly dose cities with it, so that everyone could be converted, so that everyone might taste the joys of oblivion. No one will be able to stop them. After a while no one will *want* to stop them. And so we'll go on, drinking deep, until we're washed clean of all pain and all sorrow, of all sad recollection, we'll sip a cup of kindness and part with auld lang syne, we'll give up the griefs we carry around, and we'll give up everything else, identity, soul, self, mind. We will drink sweet oblivion. Mueller shivered. Turning suddenly, tugging roughly at Carole's arm, he pushed through the joyful worshipping crowd, and hunted somberly in the fog-wrapped night, trying to find some way out of the park.

ABOUT THE AUTHOR

ROBERT SILVERBERG was born in New York and makes his home in the San Francisco area. He has written several hundred science fiction stories and over seventy science fiction novels. He has won two Hugo awards and four Nebula awards. He is a past president of the Science Fiction Writers of America. Silverberg's other Bantam titles include *Lord Valentine's Castle, Majipoor Chronicles, The Book of Skulls, Born With the Dead, The World Inside, Thorns, The Masks of Time, Dying Inside, Downward to the Earth,* and *The Tower of Glass*.

A special preview of two major new novels
by

Robert Silverberg

The fall of 1984 will be an especially exciting time for the readers of Robert Silverberg's majestic fiction, as *two* important new novels will be published for the first time in paperback:

LORD OF DARKNESS—A dramatic, exotic tale of one man's horrifying journey into the darkest heart of Africa in the 16th century.

VALENTINE PONTIFEX—The triumphant conclusion to the beloved trilogy begun in LORD VALENTINE'S CASTLE and MAJIPOOR CHRONICLES.

Read the following pages for the powerful opening chapters of these extraordinary novels.

Lord
of
Darkness

*On sale August 15, 1984,
wherever Bantam paperbacks are sold*

ALMIGHTY GOD, I thank Thee for my deliverance from the dark land of Africa. Yet am I grateful for all that Thou hast shown me in that land, even for the pain Thou hast inflicted upon me for my deeper instruction. And I thank Thee also for sparing me from the wrath of the Portugals who enslaved me, and from the other foes, black of skin and blacker of soul, with whom I contended. And I give thanks too that Thou let me taste the delight of strange loves in a strange place, so that in these my latter years I may look back with pleasure upon pleasures few Englishmen have known. But most of all I thank Thee for showing me the face of evil and bringing me away whole, and joyous, and unshaken in my love of Thee.

I am Andrew Battell of Leigh in Essex, which is no inconsiderable place. My father was the master mariner Thomas James Battell, who served splendidly with such as the great Drake and Hawkins, and my mother was Mary Martha Battell, whom I never knew, for she died in giving me into this world. That was in the autumn of the year 1558, the very month when Her Protestant Majesty Elizabeth ascended our throne. I was reared by my father's second wife Cecily, of Southend, who taught me to read and write, and these other things: that I was to love God and Queen Elizabeth before all else, that I was to live honorably and treat all men as I would have myself be treated, and that we are sent into this world to suffer, as Christ Jesus Himself suffered, because it is through suffering that we learn. I think I have kept faith with my stepmother's teachings, especially in the matter of suffering, for I have had such an education of pain, in good sooth, that I could teach on the subject to the doctors of Oxford or Cambridge. And yet I am not regretful of my wounds.

I remember a visitor my father had, a great-shouldered rough-skinned man with hard blue eyes and a shaggy red beard and a stark smell of codfish about him, though not an unpleasant one. He snatched me up—I was then, oh, seven or eight years old, I suppose—and threw me high and caught me, and cried, "Here's another mariner for us, eh, Thomas?"

"Ah, I think not," said my father to him.

And this man—he was Francis Willoughby, cousin to Sir Hugh that was lost in Lapland seeking the northeast passage to China—shook his head and said to my father, "Nay, Thomas, we must all go forth. For this is our nation's time, we English, going out to be scattered upon the earth like seeds. Or thrown like coins, one might better say: a handful of coins flung from a giant's hand. And O! Thomas! We are bright glittering coins, we are, of the least base of metals!"

I do recall those words most vividly, and seeing in my mind the giant walking to and fro upon the continents and over the seas, and hurling Englishmen with a mighty arm. And thinking then, too, how frightening it must be to be hurled in such a way, but how wondrous to come to earth in some far land, where the sunlight is of another color and the trees do grow with their roots in the air, and their crowns below!

My father nodded his agreement, and said, "Aye, each race has its special destiny, and the sea now is ours, as empire-making was for Rome, and conquest was for the Normans. And I think our people will indeed go far into the world, and embrace it most exuberantly, and bring this little isle of ours into a clasp with every distant land. And the Queen's mariners will know a good many strange places, and peradventure some strange fates, too. But not my Andy, I think. I think I will have him stay closer by me, to be a comfort for my older age. I may hold one son back, may I not? May I not, Francis?"

And I thought it most unfair, that if all we English were to be flung by the giant, and exuberantly embrace distant lands, that I alone should be kept from the sport. And I told myself in private, while my father and Francis Willoughby jested and laughed and drank their ale, that I, too, would have my turn at those strange places and strange fates. That I remember. But I also remember that when Francis Willoughby had taken his leave, and the warmth of the moment had cooled, I allowed those dreams to fade in me for a time.

I was destined to be a clerk. But as I studied, I watched the coming and going of the ships and listened to the talk of my father and brothers, and a different desire arose in me. My brother Henry it was in particular, the first privateer of our family, that led me to the sea. Henry was the second son, bold and impatient. He fought greatly with my father, they tell me. (All this happened when I was small, for that I was so much younger than my brothers.) "You may happily ply between Leigh and Antwerp, between Antwerp and Leigh, if you like," declared this brazen Harry, "but I long for a broader sea." He went out from home and was not seen for a time, and then one day he was back, taller than my father now and his skin almost black from the tropical sun and a cutlass-scar across his cheek, and he jingled a purse of gold angels and threw it on the table in my father's house and said, "Here, this pays for the lodging I have had at your hands!"

He had been to sea with John Hawkins of Plymouth, to raid the Portugals in West Africa of blacks, and sell them in the New World to the Spaniards as plantation slaves. And he came back rich: more than that, he came back a man, who had gone away little more than a boy. John Hawkins went again to Africa the next year with five ships, and Henry was with him again, and also John my brother, and when they returned, sun-blackened and swaggering, they had pouches of pearls and other treasures. I was still a child then. My brother Henry walked with me along the shore and told me of fishes that flew and of trees that dripped blood, and then he gave me a pearl that looked like a blue tear, hung from a beaded chain, and put it about my throat. "With this pearl you may buy yourself a princess one day," said my brother Henry.

Again Henry and John went to sea out of Plymouth and took slaves from Guinea and carried them to Hispaniola, but this time the Spaniards were sly and the English captain, John Lovell, was a dullard, and they came home with neither gold nor pearls, but only the tint of the hot sun on their skins to show for their pains. "All the same," said Henry to my father, "the voyage was not entirely a loss, for there was a man aboard our ship who has the grace of a king, and he has plans and schemes for doing wonders, and I will follow him wherever he sails." That man was the purser aboard Lovell's vessel, and his name was Francis Drake. I lay awake upstairs listening as Henry and John told my father of this man, of how he bore himself and how he laughed and how he swore and how he meant to grow rich at King Philip's expense, and I imagined myself going off to sea with my brothers when they signed on with Francis Drake.

That was mere fantasy, for I was not yet ten. But Drake and John Hawkins sailed, and my two brothers sailed with them on Drake's *Judith*, and now my third brother Thomas, the eldest, went also with them. How my father raved and raged! For Thomas was licensed by Trinity House after his years of study, and was guiding those who traded at Channel ports, when this fit of piracy came over him. "Who will be our pilots at home," my father demanded, "if all the mariners rush to the Indies?" Yet it was like crying into the wind to ask such things. Thomas had seen the pearls. Thomas had seen the angels of gold and the gleaming doubloons. And methinks he envied our brothers their scars and their swarthy skins.

Everyone knows the fate of that voyage, where Hawkins and Drake were forced by storms to take shelter at San Juan de Ulloa on the Mexican coast, and there by Spanish treachery were foully betrayed, so that they barely escaped alive and many of their men were slain. One of those who perished was my brother Thomas. You might think that my father would draw dark vindication from such news, as people do when their warnings are ignored, but my father was not of that sort. He mourned his firstborn son properly, and then he sought out Francis Drake and said, "I have given three sons to your venture, and one of them the Spaniards slew, and now I ask if you have need of a skilled pilot who is not young when next you go to raid their coasts."

So in 1570 he was with Drake on the *Swan* to harry the Spanish Main, and again in 1571, and a year later he was one of those from Drake's *Pasha* that seized the royal treasury at Nombre de Dios on the Isthmus of Panama.

And I? I had my first taste of the water. At sixteen I was hired aboard the *George Cross*, a 400-ton carrack in the merchant trade, that hauled casks of claret from Bordeaux. She was a slow and clumsy old tub, three-masted, square-rigged on fore and main with lateen mizens, not much like your pirate brigantine or your caravel of exploration: a coarse heavy thing. But when you are at sea for the first time you find any vessel a wonder, most especially when land is out of sight and the hard waves wash at the hull.

For eleven months I served on the George Cross. I knew some seamanship before I went aboard, from what I had heard at home and seen in the Thameside docks; that is, I knew not to piss to windward, and which side was larboard and which starboard, and what was the quarterdeck and what the forecastle, and not a whole much more. I had little hope of learning a great deal waddling about between Dover and Calais, but as it happened the old carrack went wider than that, to Boulogne and Le Havre and once to Cherbourg, so I saw something of storms and concluded a few conclusions about winds and sails. That would be useful to me, though I knew not then why. There was aboard the ship a certain Portugal as the carpenter, one Manoel da Silva, very quick with his hands and with his tongue, who long ago had married an English wife and given up Papistry. He had a fondness for me and often came to the cabin where I struggled with invoices and accounts, and in his visits he spoke half in English and half in Portuguese, so that by and by I picked up the language from him: um, dois, tres, quatro, and so forth. I learned that I had a skill with language. And that would be useful to me one day also.

In those months I grew a liking for good red wine, I discovered the way of walking a deck without sprawling, I had my first real fight and gave better than I got, and, long overdue, I left my aching virginity in the belly of a dark-haired French whore. Thereafter I worried about the pox for days, without need. I found I could sleep well on hard planks and I came not to mind the drench of salt spray. My body hardened and my legs lengthened, and I told myself I was now a man, and the sound of that had a good ring in my ears. Betimes I imagined myself a thousand leagues from home, on my way to the Japans or Hispaniola or Terra Australis on a voyage that no one would ever forget. Well, and I was only plying a tub between England and France, ferrying wine.

Nor did I even then think to make the sea my trade. For all my eagerness to straddle the globe and see strange lands and marvels and fill my purse with Spanish gold, my true and deepest notion was to set by some pounds and one day buy me the freehold of a farm, and marry and prosper, and live comfortably in hard work and the bosom of a family, reading books for pleasure and attending the plays betimes in London, like a gentleman. At the end of my year's voyage I found I had set by not as much as I had expected—two shillings less than two pounds. But even that seemed a fair fortune for a lad of seventeen, and more than I could have earned ashore, for in those days a skilled workman—a thatcher, say—could hope for no more than seven and sixpence a week, out of which must come rent and clothing and food and all, and a young clerk hardly that much. So I went to sea again after two months at home.

This time it was a farther voyage, to Flanders and Norway, and the year after that all the way to Russia aboard a vessel of the Muscovy Company, and a cold time I had of it then. But these journeys were making a complete sailor of me, for each time I did less clerking and more seamanship, and I was finding my way around the maps and charts, the compasses and leads, not because it was asked of me but because my curiosity led me to know at first hand what sort of trade my father and his son Thomas the pilot had plied. So the years of my early manhood went.

In those years the Spaniards began once more to break the truce between their lands and ours, and the Queen sent Drake out to punish them with the loss of gold and silver. This was in 1577, and it was destined to become a voyage around the world, though that was not Drake's first plan. My brother Henry was with him aboard his flagship, the *Pelican*, that Drake would rename *The Golden Hind* in mid-passage. My father, too, applied for command of another ship, the pinnace *Christopher*, but he was refused with thanks, on account of his age. I also would have gone, but my father would not let it, saying, "Thomas is dead and John is fled to Ireland and Henry sails with Drake, and I want one son for England." I could have thwarted him in that, but I had no heart for it. He was suddenly old, and he did not so much forbid me as implore me, and how could I say him nay?

So Henry Battell went with Drake through Magellan's Strait and up to Valparaiso and on to loot the gold of Peru, and to unknown northern lands of horrid fog and cold, and out into the South Sea to the Spice Islands and Java and Africa, and home again in just short of three years, leaving his left arm behind, that had become inflamed by a poison dart on some tropic isle. In the meanwhile Andrew Battell sailed four times to Antwerp and thrice to Sweden and once to Genoa. Which I suppose is no small travelling, but hardly a patch on going to the Spice Islands or Java, and often I thought ruefully of Drake's prediction of how far I should journey. Who could possibly go farther than Henry, who had encompassed the globe? But there is voyage outward and there is voyage inward, as I would learn, and my twenty years inward to the heart of African deviltry took me farther indeed than Drake himself could have gone. By one step and another I set myself all unknowingly on the path that would carry me far from home for so many years, to Africa, to the torments the Portugals laid upon me, to the royal courts of Kongo and the Angola, to the jungles of coccodrillos and elephantos and the broad plains spangled with zevveras and gazelles; I began my long journey to the side of that diabolical Jaqqa cannibal, Imbe Calandola, the incarnation of the Lord of Darkness, whose lieutenant I became and whose monstrous wisdom rings to this day in my soul like terrible discordant music.

LORD OF DARKNESS is the gripping, adventure-filled tale of Andrew Battell. The young British seaman will be captured by Portuguese cutthroats in Brazil and shipped to the hot, steamy colony of Angola. He will be forced to act as a ship's pilot to the covetous, slave-trading colonists. And he will find himself increasingly drawn into the most arcane mysteries of African tribal life—into the world of the satanic Lord of Darkness himself, whose cannibalistic rites he will be compelled to endure.

Read LORD OF DARKNESS, on sale August 15, 1984, wherever Bantam paperbacks are sold.

Valentine
Pontifex

On sale October 15, 1984,
wherever Bantam paperbacks are sold

Valentine swayed, braced himself with his free hand against the table, struggled to keep himself from spilling his wine.

This is very odd, he thought, this dizziness, this confusion. Too much wine—the stale air—maybe gravity pulls harder, this far down below the surface—

"Propose the toast, lordship," Deliamber murmured. "First to the Pontifex, and then to his aides, and then—"

"Yes. Yes, I know."

Valentine peered uncertainly from side to side, like a steetmoy at bay, ringed round by the spears of hunters.

"Friends—" he began.

"To the Pontifex Tyeveras!" Deliamber whispered sharply.

Friends. Yes. Those who were most dear to him, seated close at hand. Almost everyone but Carabella and Elidath: she was on her way to meet him in the west, was she not, and Elidath was handling the chores of government on Castle Mount in Valentine's absence. But the others were here, Sleet, Deliamber, Tunigorn, Shanamir. Lisamon and Ermanar, Tisana, the Skandar Zalzan Kavol, Asenhart the Hjort—yes, all his dear ones, all the pillars of his life and reign—

"Friends," he said, "lift your wine-bowls, join me in one more toast. You know that it has not been granted me by the Divine to enjoy an easy time upon the throne. You all know the hardships that have been thrust upon me, the challenges that had to be faced, the tasks required of me, the weighty problems still unresolved."

"This is not the right speech, I think," he heard someone behind him say.

Deliamber muttered again, "His majesty the Pontifex! You must offer a toast to his majesty the Pontifex!"

Valentine ignored them. These words that came from him now seemed to come of their own accord.

"If I have borne these unparalleled difficulties with some grace," he went on, "it is only because I have had the support, the counsel, the love, of such a band of comrades and precious friends as few rulers can ever have claimed. It is with your indispensable help, good friends, that we will come at last to a resolution of the troubles that afflict Majipoor and enter into the era of true amity that we all desire. And so, as we make ready to set forth tomorrow into this realm of ours, eagerly, joyously, to undertake the grand processional, I offer this last toast of the evening, my friends, to you, to those who have sustained me and nurtured me throughout all these years, and who—"

"How strange he looks," Ermanar murmured. "Is he ill?"

A spasm of astonishing pain swept through him. There was a terrible droning buzz in his ears, and his breath was as hot as flame. He felt himself descending into night, a night so terrible that it obliterated all light and swept across his soul like a tide of black blood. The wine-bowl fell from his hand and shattered; and it was as if the entire world had shattered, flying apart into thousands of crumbling fragments that went tumbling crazily toward every corner of the universe. The dizziness was overwhelming now. And the darkness—that utter and total night, that complete eclipse—

"Lordship!" someone bellowed. Could that have been Hissune?

"He's having a sending!" another voice cried.

"A sending? How, while he is awake?"

"My lord! My lord! My lord!"

Valentine looked downward. Everything was black, a pool of night rising from the floor. That blackness seemed to be beckoning to him. Come, a quiet voice was saying, here is your path, here is your destiny: night, darkness, doom. Yield. Yield, Lord Valentine, Coronal that was, Pontifex that will never be. Yield. And Valentine yielded, for in that moment of bewilderment and paralysis of spirit there was nothing else he could do. He stared into the black pool rising about him, and he allowed himself to fall toward it. Unquestioningly, uncomprehendingly, he plunged into that all-engulfing darkness.

I am dead, he thought. I float now on the breast of the black river that returns me to the Source, and soon I must rise and go ashore and find the road that leads to the Bridge of Farewells; and then will I go across into that place where all life has its beginning and its end.

A strange kind of peace pervaded his soul then, a feeling of wondrous ease and contentment, a powerful sense that all the universe was joined in happy harmony. He felt as though he had come to rest in a cradle, where now he lay warmly swaddled, free at last of the torments of kingship. Ah, how good that was! To lie quietly, and let all turbulence sweep by him! Was this death? Why, then, death was joy!

—*You are deceived, my lord. Death is the end of joy.*

—*Who speaks to me here?*

—*You know me, my lord.*

—*Deliamber? Are you dead also? Ah, what a safe kind place death is, old friend!*

—*You are safe, yes. But not dead.*

—*It feels much like death to me.*

—*And have you such thorough experience of death, my lord, that you can speak of it so knowingly?*

—*What is this, if it is not death?*

—*Merely a spell,* said Deliamber.

—*One of yours, wizard?*

—*No, not mine. But I can bring you from it, if you will permit. Come: awaken. Awaken.*

—*No, Deliamber! Let me be.*

—*You must, my lord.*

—*Must,* Valentine said bitterly. *Must! Always must! Am I never to rest? Let me stay where I am. this is a place of peace. I have no stomach for war, Deliamber.*

—*Come, my lord.*

—*Tell me next that it is my duty to awaken.*

—*I need not tell you what you know so well. Come.*

He opened his eyes, and found himself in midair, lying limply in Lisamon Hultin's arms. The Amazon carried him as though he were a doll, nestling against the vastness of her breasts. Small wonder he had imagined himself in a cradle, he thought, or floating down the black river! Beside him was Autifon Deliamber, perched on Lisamon's left shoulder. Valentine perceived the wizardry that had called him back from his swoon: the tips of three of the Vroon's tentacles were touching him, one to his forehead, one to his cheek, one to his chest.

He said, feeling immensely foolish, "You can put me down now."

"You are very weak, lordship," Lisamon rumbled.

"Not quite that weak, I think. Put me down."

Carefully, as though Valentine were nine hundred years old, Lisamon lowered him to the ground. At once, sweeping waves of dizziness rocked him, and he reached out to lean against the giant woman, who still hovered protectively close by. His teeth were chattering. His heavy robes clung to his damp, clammy skin like shrouds. He feared that if he closed his eyes only for an instant, that pool of darkness would rise up again and engulf him. But he forced himself toward a sort of steadiness, even if it were only a pretense. Old training asserted itself: he could not allow himself to be seen looking dazed and weak, no matter what sort of irrational terrors were roaring through his head.

"Where am I?" Valentine asked.

"Another moment and we'll be at your chambers, lordship," Sleet said.

"Have I been unconscious long?"

"Two or three minutes, only. You began to fall, while making your speech. But Hissune caught you, and Lisamon."

"It was the wine," Valentine said. "I suppose I had too much, a bowl of this and a bowl of that—"

"You are quite sober now," Deliamber pointed out. "And it is only a few minutes later."

"Let me believe it was the wine," said Valentine, "for a little while longer." The corridor swung leftward and there appeared before him the great carved door of his suite, chased with gold inlays of the starburst emblem over which his own LVC monogram had been engraved. "Where is Tisana?" he called.

"Here, my lord," said the dream-speaker, from some distance.

"Good. I want you inside with me. Also Deliamber and Sleet. No one else. Is that clear?"

"May I enter also?" said a voice out of the group of Pontifical officials.

It belonged to a thin-lipped gaunt man with strangely ashen skin, whom Valentine recognized after a moment as Sepulthrove, physician to the Pontifex Tyeveras. He shook his head. "I am grateful for your concern. But I think you are not needed."

"Such a sudden collapse, my lord—it calls for diagnosis—"

"There's some wisdom in that," Tunigorn observed quietly.

Valentine shrugged. "Afterward, then. First let me speak with my advisers, good Sepulthrove. And then you can tap my kneecaps a bit, if you think that it's necessary. Come—Tisana, Deliamber—"

He swept into his suite with the last counterfeit of regal poise he could muster, feeling a vast relief as the heavy door swung shut on the bustling throng in the corridor. He let out his breath in a long slow gust and dropped down, trembling in the release of tension, on the brocaded couch.

"Come, Tisana, sit next to me," Valentine said.

She settled down beside him and slipped her arm around his shoulders. Yes, he thought. Oh, yes, good! Warmth flowed back into his chilled soul, and the darkness receded. From him rushed a great torrent of love for Tisana, sturdy and reliable and wise, who in the days of his exile had been the first openly to hail him as Lord Valentine, when he had been still content to think of himself as Valentine the juggler. How many times in the years of his restored reign had she shared the mind-opening dream-wine with him, and had taken him in her arms to draw from him the secrets of the turbulent images that came to him in sleep! How often had she given him ease from the weight of kingship!

She said, "I was frightened greatly to see you fall, Lord Valentine, and you know I am not one who frightens easily. You say it was the wine?"

"So I said, out there."

"But it was not the wine, I think."

"No. Deliamber thinks it was a spell."

"Of whose making?" Tisana asked.

Valentine looked to the Vroon. "Well?"

Deliamber displayed a tension that Valentine had only rarely seen the little creature reveal: a troubled coiling and weaving of his innumerable tentacles, a strange glitter in his great yellow eyes, grinding motions of his birdlike beak. "I am at a loss for an answer," said Deliamber finally. "Just as not all dreams are sendings, so too is it the case that not all spells have makers."

"Some spells cast themselves, is that it?" Valentine asked.

"Not precisely. But there are spells that arise spontaneously—from within, my lord, within oneself, generated out of the empty places of the soul."

"What are you saying? That I put an enchantment on myself, Deliamber?"

Tisana said gently, "Dreams—spells—it is all the same thing, Lord Valentine. Certain auguries are making themselves known through you. Omens are forcing themselves into view. Storms are gathering, and these are the early harbingers."

"You see all that so soon? I had a troubled dream, you know, just before the banquet and most certainly it was full of stormy omens and auguries and harbingers. But unless I've been talking of it in my sleep, I've told you nothing of it yet, have I?"

"I think you dreamed of chaos, my lord."

Valentine stared at her. "How could you know that?"

Shrugging, Tisana said, "Because chaos must come. We all recognize the truth of that. There is unfinished business in the world, and it cries out for finishing."

"The shapeshifters, you mean," Valentine muttered.

"I would not presume," the old woman said, "to advise you on matters of state—"

"Spare me such tact. From my advisers I expect advice, not tact."

"My realm is only the realm of dreams," said Tisana.

"I dreamed snow on Castle Mount, and a great earthquake that split the world apart."

"Shall I speak that dream for you, my lord?"

"How can you speak it, when we haven't yet had the dream-wine?"

"A speaking's not a good idea just now," said Deliamber firmly. "The Coronal's had visions enough for one night. He'd not be well served by drinking dream-wine now. I think this can easily wait until—"

"That dream needs no wine," said Tisana. "A child could speak it. Earthquakes? The shattering of the world? Why, you must prepare yourself for hard hours, my lord."

"What are you saying?"

It was Sleet who replied: "These are omens of war, lordship."

Valentine swung about and glared at the little man. "War?" he cried. "War? Must I do battle again? I was the first Coronal in eight thousand years to lead an army into the field; must I do it twice?"

"Surely you know, my lord," said Sleet, "that the war of the restoration was merely the first skirmish of the true war that must be fought, a war that has been in the making for many centuries, a war that I think you know cannot now be avoided."

"There are no unavoidable wars," Valentine said.

"Do you think so, my lord?"

The Coronal glowered bleakly at Sleet, but made no response. They were telling him what he had already concluded without their help, but did not wish to hear; and, hearing it anyway, he felt a terrible restlessness invading his soul. Unfinished business, Tisana had said. Yes. Yes. The Shapeshifters. Shapeshifters, Metamorphs, Piurivars, call them by whatever name you chose: the true natives of Majipoor, those from whom this wondrous world had been stolen by the settlers from the stars, fourteen thousand years before. For eight years, Valentine thought, I've struggled to understand the needs of those people. And I still know nothing at all.

He turned and said, "When I rose to speak, my mind was on what Hornkast the high spokesman just had said: the Coronal is the world, and the world is the Coronal. And suddenly I *became* Majipoor. Everything that was happening everywhere in the world was sweeping through my soul."

"Hornkast spoke the truth," said Tisana quietly. "You *are* the world, lordship. Dark knowledge is finding its way to you, and it comes through the air from all the world about you. It is a sending, my lord: not of the Lady, nor of the King of Dreams, but of the world entire."

Valentine glanced toward the Vroon. "What do you say to that, Deliamber?"

"I have known Tisana fifty years, I think, and I have never yet heard foolishness from her lips."

"Then there is to be war?"

"I believe the war has already begun," said Deliamber.

For all the readers who thrilled to the first two volumes of the Majipoor Trilogy, LORD VALENTINE'S CASTLE and MAJIPOOR CHRONICLES, here is the dramatic conclusion to that majestic saga. A titanic conflict is about to rock the long peace of Majipoor. And only Valentine and the people he trusts the most can prevent the unthinkable from happening.

Read the powerful novels of award-winning author

ROBERT SILVERBERG

One of the most brilliant and beloved science fiction authors of our time, Robert Silverberg has been honored with two Hugo awards and four Nebula awards. His stirring combination of vivid imagery, evocative prose, and rousing storytelling promise his audience a reading experience like no other.

- ☐ WORLD OF A THOUSAND COLORS (24059 • $2.95)
- ☐ DYING INSIDE (24018 • $2.50)
- ☐ LORD VALENTINE'S CASTLE (23063 • $3.50)
- ☐ MAJIPOOR CHRONICLES (22928 • $3.50)
- ☐ DOWNWARD TO THE EARTH (24043 • $2.50)
- ☐ MASKS OF TIME (23494 • $2.95)
- ☐ THORNS (23573 • $2.75)

Prices and availability subject to change without notice.

Read these fine works by Robert Silverberg, on sale now wherever Bantam paperbacks are sold or use the handy coupon below for ordering.

SPECIAL
MONEY SAVING
OFFER

Now you can have an up-to-date listing of Bantam's hundreds of titles plus take advantage of our unique and exciting bonus book offer. A special offer which gives you the opportunity to purchase a Bantam book for only 50¢. Here's how!

By ordering any five books at the regular price per order, you can also choose any other single book listed (up to a $4.95 value) for just 50¢. Some restrictions do apply, but for further details why not send for Bantam's listing of titles today!

Just send us your name and address plus 50¢ to defray the postage and handling costs.